MAMA ROSE

BY BERNADENE HIGH COLEMAN

Published By
MILLIGAN BOOKS
Cover Design By
JOHN ROSENKRANZ/THE DESIGN DOCTOR
Formatting By
SAM BARTELS & OREET HERBST

Published and Distributed by:
Milligan Books
An imprint of Professional Business Consultants
1425 W. Manchester Blvd., Suite B,
Los Angeles, California 90047
(323)750-3592

Second Printing, October, 1999
10 9 8 7 6 5 4 3 2 1

ISBN 1-881524-35-3

ACKNOWLEDGEMENTS

In memory of my great grandmother, MAMA ROSE.

The seed of this book was planted by my great-grandmother who remained proud of her accomplishments all the days of her life. She encouraged her children, grandchildren and great-grandchildren to set goals and to have dreams and to have the courage and strength to make them happen.

Heart and soul was given to this book by all those who shared bits of rememberences with me and encouraged me to write this story. I am especially grateful to my sister, Anne High Dailey, who had enough faith in my writing ability to prod me into actually doing it. Thanks to Georgia Lumpkin who took me to my first writing class, and to Mary Huddleston, my first writing teacher.

I do not really know how to express my thanks to my three sons, Courtney, Kevin and Craig, and their families, who prompted, guided, inspired and supported this effort every step of the way.

My gratitude to Oreet Herbst, Sam Bartels, Edie Levenson and John Rosenkranz for technical and literary assistance and to my Alpha Kappa Alpha Sorority sisters for their encouragement.

I thank God, my comforter, my strength, who continues to smile on me.

ABOUT THE AUTHOR

Bernadene Coleman was born in rural Louisiana and grew up in Los Angeles. She graduated from Los Angeles City College, received her B.A. from California State University at Los Angeles, and an M.S. from Loyola Marymount. She has studied at U.C.L.A.'s School or Writing. Bernadene has always had a passion for books and reading. her first love for writing is poetry. She has a large collection of her poems. Her poetic style is often reflected in her writing. Since her retirement, she has begun to chronicle events and stories she first heard about in her youth. This is her first published work. Bernadene is a widow, a mother of three sons and grandmother of eight. She resides in Culver City, California.

COMMENTS FROM READERS

Mama Rose is a delightful book! The underlying theme of this book is faith and trust. Your detailed description of the food made me hungry. At times, I could even smell and taste it. ***Audry Smith***

I truly enjoyed reading **Mama Rose.** there is something about the book that I want to call charming and sweet - like the story of a lost paradise. Rose was both those things. But she was also brave and determined. I loved her! I liked him a lot, too - what an unusual man. ***Jean Milgram***

MAMA ROSE

You have opened a window on the lives of our elders. I laughed and I cried and I beamed with pride as I read **Mama Rose**! *Delores Thompson*

Thank you for such a magnificant book! It is a book that should be read by everyone. I loved your beautiful descriptions. **Mama Rose** is an awesome book! *Delores Graham*

Once I picked up your book, I couldn't put it down. Thank you for a wonderful story. I truly look forward to the sequel with great anticipation. I'm sure **Mama Rose** will be a top seller! *Carolyn Welch*

Mama Rose touched me deeply! Rose was an awesome woman! Mr. Ford was the kind of man every woman should have. *Rose Waggener*

Mama Rose is an extraordinary story! Your descriptions of the south during that era are so beautiful. I felt as if I was right there communicating with the characters. *Martha Lightner*

Reading **Mama Rose** brought back marvelous memories of visits to my grandparent's farm and the wonderful stories they would tell us. *Alice Kirksey*

I loved the writing! I particularly liked the many descriptions of nature and of the food. The use of 'Spirituals' always came at such appropriate times. What a beautiful story! *Lois Williams*

More than anything else, your book showed what a real, true love story should be. From the love Zeke showed for his daughter to the unpretentiousness of Mr. Ford. It's a jewel! *Renee Bridges*

Chapter One

Rose knew that the time had come for her to move on again. This family she was living with now, was as mean and cruel to her as the previous one had been. The terror she had just gone through made up her mind for her. While she was chopping cotton one afternoon, the older boys in her adopted family had accosted her. They dragged her behind some bushes, removed her clothes and did terrible things to her. She didn't understand, nor did she clearly remember everything they did, but she knew that she had been violently misused. She felt deep shame. And she hurt all over.

They left her on the ground bruised and bloodied and walked away laughing. That very night, she hatched her plan to escape. All the next day, Rose drank as much water as her body could hold. After being made to work as much as fourteen hours a day, she was so tired by bedtime, she would always sleep the whole night through. But with so much water inside her, she knew she would wake up when everyone else in the house would be sleeping soundly.

She fled in the middle of the night, carrying only a walking stick, a hunting knife and a croker sack. She decided to travel along the river bottom, resolved to keep going until her legs gave out, wanting to get as far away as possible from that horrible family.

Rose ran the entire distance to the river, moving as swiftly as the darkness would permit. Strange noises erupted from the animals that lived in the marshes, trees and shrubbery that grew along the banks of the river. The summer night was dark and muggy, the brush, dense and eerie looking, but she was not deterred, knowing that somewhere out there was someone as kind as Papo. This thought alone gave her the needed energy and desire to move on.

"If I follow the river," she said aloud, "I won't go in circles an' end up close to that farm an' that fam'ly. So I follow the river."

She ran on and on, stopping only for short periods to rest and catch her breath. Rose realized that this attempt at running away must be successful because there might not be another chance.

The shrieking sounds of the animals did not frighten her. The churning sound of the river encouraged her to move on like the water itself moved on. Even though it was dark and gloomy, she wished that the darkness could continue on and give her more time to get farther and farther away.

During the entire night, Rose never stopped for more than a few minutes. She knew that when the family discovered her missing, they would go looking for her.

"I 'druther jump in the river than go back to that house!"

There was only a small slice of moon in the sky, but the stars shone down like brilliant diamonds welcoming Rose to a beautiful freedom, one that she had known and enjoyed when she lived with the old man she called Papo. It was his walking stick and hunting knife that she now had in her possession. She had lived with him until one night, long ago, for reasons she did not know, he left her with another family.

There was an incessant hum of mosquitoes and waves of gnats soaring above her; still, she moved on. A few times, she encountered small animals but they were less interested in her than she was in them.

The night suddenly got darker. It must be midnight, thought Rose, because she had concluded that was the darkest time of the night. She knew daybreak would come sooner than she would be ready for it, so she quickened her pace. At times, she would become entangled in the brush, but with her hunting knife, she could easily free herself. Because she could barely see, she was cut by the brush several times. She licked the wounds and tasted her salty blood. And moved on.

Rose had run away before, but she was bigger and older now. The first family Papo left her with when he went away abused her so much she escaped to another, and they were no better than the first. This was the third family she was fleeing.

"This time, I go far away," she said to herself and to the river. "This time, they never gon' catch me."

Soon, a light glinted in the sky as if it were trying to decide whether to wake up the day. Slowly, a little more light. Then a little more. Although Rose could see her path better, she wasn't sure that she was ready for the night to disappear. She felt she was not as far away as she needed to be. She felt sleep coming on but she knew there was no time for that.

"Sleep, you gots to go 'way now. You kin come back later." she mumbled.

Too soon, the birds began to make their early morning calls and shrills, others echoed back. Rose could see and hear there was more life on the river than she'd ever imagined. The calls of some animals were piercing, but the one sound that she could hear most clearly, above all the rest, was the sound of freedom.

The early sun began to cast amber rays upon the earth. The ruby-throated songbirds filled the air with music. The calls of the wild were both dissonant and melodious. Momentarily, Rose thought of the times she had spent in the woods with Papo. With him, the woods were pleasant and friendly. Now, her heavy eyes and the thick leafy bushes were slowing her progress, and she knew she would soon have to make a decision.

She knew, also, that the day was going to be hot and humid. But she would continue on until she found a suitable place to rest. She had seen a few houses and barns but they were all on the other side of the river, and she longed to be on that side. She would feel safer.

The position of the sun told her that it was mid-morning. She needed to find a spot to rest in, because the midday sun would be brutal for one who had no protection. Abruptly, the river came to a deep angle. As Rose rounded the bend, she saw buildings off in the distance, but knew that it was too early to make her move, so she went on. Somehow, she managed to stay on her feet until the sun was directly overhead.

"Sleep, I guess it's time fo' you to come a callin.'"

Ahead, Rose saw some pine trees. When she reached the clump of trees, there were needles on the ground. She tugged at the branches until she was able to get enough to make a pallet to lie on. She used her knife to cut branches from a willow tree for a makeshift canopy to protect her from the hot sun while she slept. Hurriedly, she spread out the croker sack. It was when she finally lay down that she noticed cuts and scratches all over her body, and how tattered, torn and bloody her dress had become.

In the early evening, after a long, deep sleep, she woke up. For a few brief moments she was disoriented and extremely thirsty and hungry. As her mind came back into focus, she remembered a nettle plant she had passed a few paces before reaching the pine trees. With her knife she carefully cut off one of the large leaves. She recalled that Papo had shown her how to scrape away the stingers. The nettle would supply good nourishment.

"Thank you, Papo," she said aloud. "I thanks you for the knife, too."

Rose continued walking in the direction of another small house. From afar, she saw a man and a boy chopping cotton. Two younger boys played in the yard and a woman gathered vegetables from the garden. There was a shed out back that provided shelter for some animals. The day was fast disappearing and Rose knew she needed a place to stop for the night. She was too exhausted to continue her journey away from that family.

When Rose saw a light in the house and heard noises from inside, she made her move. She picked some half-ripe tomatoes from the garden and she drew water from the well. Then she lay down on her croker sack and slept. Early the next morning, she was startled by the sound of voices.

"Ma! Come quick!" a man's voice cried out. Rose opened, then quickly closed her eyes but made no attempt to move. She fell asleep again.

"Whats' a matter?" asked a woman's voice.

"Who dis be?"

"I has no idee. Po' chile, she dead to the world."

"Ma, you ought wake her up an' find out. Po' thang, she been hurt."

Mamie gently shook the little girl until she finally sat up. Rose grabbed her sack, put it around her and asked, "Where um at?"

Rose looked at the two of them with her big round eyes.

The Turners had a gentle and kind appearance.

"Who you, chile?" Mr. Turner asked. Rose said nothing.

"Where you come from?" Mrs. Turner inquired. Still, nothing. "What yo name?"

Rose was not afraid, she was busy thinking and planning.

"Who you be? We ain't gonna hurt you, chile. You mus' be hungry! Com' on, we gi' you somethin' to eat."

Rose hesitated, then she slowly followed them into the house. They gave her a bowl of buttermilk and some cornbread. She began eating it very slowly, although, the truth was, she was quite hungry and tired. She had been on her feet for almost a whole night and most of a hot, sticky day, she could not quite remember just how long. As she ate, Rose noticed a baby lying on a pallet.

She gently smiled and she spoke again. "I name Rose, I name Rose," she whispered softly.

"Rose, where yo Mama? Where yo Papa?" asked Mr. Turner.

"I got no Mama an' I got no Papa."

"They's dead?" questioned Mrs. Turner.

"I don't know. Kin I hol' the baby?"

"Sho," said Mrs. Turner. " We have three mo' sleepin' in the house."

"If you got no Mama an' no Papa, chile, who you be living with?"

"I live in many houses with lots o' people, but they's all beat me up," she answered. "So I looking fo' a good place to go where they's don' beat me no mo. 'Um a good worker, I work the field, I work the garden, I wash an' iron the clothes, I clean the house, I cook, but I won't let them beat me no mo,' I run way again, I will, I will!" She was speaking faster now and with conviction and emotion, but she had no tears.

"Um Ezekiel Turner an' this be my wife, Mamie. Welcome to this house, chile. You kin stay here 'til we knows who yo folks is. We ain't gonna break no law, no sah!"

Mr. and Mrs. Turner could think of nothing more to say to the child. They left the room while Rose finished her food, steadily keeping her eyes on the baby.

She finished eating and got down and played with the baby. She sang her a song, patted the baby's hands and feet and in a few minutes, Rose was sound asleep with the baby crawling all over her.

The Turners needed some time to sort out the story they had heard. They knew all of the families within a seven to ten mile radius. They had never seen or heard of this young girl. They wondered where she came from. She was much too frail to be sent out into the countryside alone.

In Rose's possession, were only a few meager belongings. The dress she was wearing was dirty and ragged. They also noted her strange shoes. They were made of leather soles and were secured to her ankles with many thin straps. They had never seen anything like them before.

"Where you reckon she come from?" Mr. Turner asked his wife. "What we gonna do?"

"I declare," replied Mrs. Turner, "she gonna stay right here till we find out wha's goin' on. Po' thing, we can't send her out in the wilderness."

"Sho is the truth," agreed Mr. Turner.

They both thought of some of the horrid stories they had heard about runaway slaves. But slavery was now history, even though it would haunt them forever.

Rose slept most of the morning. She woke up, played with the baby and then slept through dinner and on into the afternoon. When she finally got up, she could smell the delicious aroma of supper on the stove. She heard the noises of happy children playing and of a mother softly humming to her baby.

She said to herself, This house sounds an' smells like a good house, I gonna like it here an' If I can stay, I gonna work real hard an' make them happy, they gonna like Rose. "Afta'noon, M'am," Rose said as she bounded through the door to the front porch. "What kin I do to hep' you?"

"Did you sleep good, chile?" asked Mamie. "You sho' been sleeping a long time. This here is baby Annie, out there is Samuel. Ova' there be Aaron an' Ephriam. They's too little to help Papa in the field but they helps me in the house an' in the garden. Samuel helps some with chopping an' picking cotton. Nex' year, maybe Ephriam starts to help. We grow some mighty fine veg'ables 'round here too, ever'body loves 'em."

Rose looked at Mrs. Turner and eagerly said, "I can hep' wit' all that, an' I can hep' wit' the field plantin,' too. Right now, I say hello an' play wit' the boys!"

Rose did just that and immediately won their attention and affection. Mrs. Turner smiled and thought to herself, "I sho' do like that gal, she special, whoever she be. I think havin' her here gonna' be fine with me!"

At that moment, the boys heard a sound that told them their Papa was coming in from the field and they took off running to join him across the way. Zeke Turner was tired and sweaty from the long hours of work and the extremely blazing sun on this day. Nevertheless, he greeted his sons eagerly and set them astride the mule for the ride to the house.

"Papa, Papa," they shouted almost in unison, "Come see Rose, come see Rose. She pretty, she nice, too."

Rose was continuously thinking and planning. With each passing hour, she could see that some luck may have finally come her way. After a few years, and she had no idea of how many, of being treated so harshly, she surmised that this just might be a good place to stay for a while. She also knew that she could only truly trust and depend upon herself. It had been that way for almost as long as she could remember.

She did, however, recollect that very early in her life, Papo had often spoken to the "Great Spirit." She recalled, also, that he had taught her how to use her eyes, her ears, her hands and even her nose, to understand the things about her. She must heed the wind, the sun, the moon and the stars. She must be wise and observe all living things and she must always respect them.

He taught her that there were lessons to be learned everywhere and if she remained sharp and quiet, she could learn the ones necessary to take her through life. The old man told her that she could be her own best friend or her own worst enemy, and he told her to look fear in the eye until it retreated. Rose never forgot the wise words or the lessons she learned from him.

At bedtime, when she lay on the pallet on the floor, she was far too happy and excited to sleep. This night, she thought about Papo more than she had ever thought of him in the past. She tried hard to recapture many of the things that had mostly disappeared from her memory. She could recall only segments of her early life. In her mind's eye, there were glimpses that quickly flashed in and out. She remembered such things as gathering fruits, nuts and berries from trees and bushes, and there was an expanse of sky and wide-open spaces.

She could see the two of them riding horses and climbing trees. She caught brief images of fishing, hunting and skinning. There were always many animals. Rose saw visions of Papo making moccasins and clothing with the hides.

There were memories of helping prepare food out-of-doors. She remembered sleeping on pallets very different from the one she was on now.

Gracious, she almost shouted aloud, in Papo's house, they was warm and furry, an' sof' to the touch.

Rose tried to think of someone else that fitted into that picture, and the view always came up empty. But she knew that Papo was someone she loved and who loved her.

At this moment, Rose was overwrought with joy that she had run away. It was already clear to her that she was in a home filled with love. She was fiercely independent and cherished the freedom she had had with Papo. She possessed extraordinary strength, intelligence and determination. She never complained about all the hard work she was asked to do. She worked in the fields and did other heavy chores from sunup until sundown. She liked being outside all the time because she felt a sense of freedom and control. Being outdoors was almost like being with Papo.

Rose loved hearing the birds and crickets sing and watching them as they flitted through the air. She loved the wide-open spaces, the tall soaring trees and the blue skies. She loved the rolling hills of the countryside. She even loved it when it rained. She loved the smell of the earth as the soft drops fell upon it, especially when the rain was gentle. She loved the noises the animals made as they moved with free abandon through the fields and pastures. She loved observing their fluid and unbridled movements.

The Turner house was small and cozy. It had only two rooms. The largest was the children's living quarters, which was also the kitchen and the dining room. It contained a big fireplace that Mamie had insisted on when Zeke and his friends did the crude building. The second room was for the parents and the baby. Each year, Zeke did little innovations to make it warm and comfortable for his family. One day, he couldn't say when, he would add other rooms.

This was the kind of home Rose had longed for. Flowers were planted along the side and front of the house. There was an oak tree in the front yard along with a beautiful, blooming crepe myrtle and a mulberry tree out in the back. Also, there was a chinaberry tree that stood between the house and the fenced-in animal sheds.

The Turners did what they could to make Rose feel content, and in turn, Rose worked harder and longer than anyone they had ever known. Every night when Rose went to bed, she gave thanks to the Great Spirit for her new home. But at the same time she worried over how long they would let her stay. Her mind was not yet at rest. She never knew if any of the families with whom she lived for short stays looked for her or not. Her beloved Papo, with whom she lived longest, had left her with a neighbor and he had never returned. Rose had some idea of what had happened to him, but she had yet to ask the questions that clouded her thoughts.

The Turners knew that Rose did not know her age. Mamie, who had no formal education, but possessed good common sense and wisdom, kept up a flow of questions in order to get some idea of a time line. As of the present, however, Rose could not even name the months of the year, nor the year, 1872. Mamie soon took care of that matter, along with the names of the days in the week.

She was also pleased to see how eager Rose was to learn anything. However, she did know how to do some counting. She knew how many days there were from full moon to new moon and she always knew when the moon would change. Mamie soon realized that she possessed an uncanny sixth sense.

There was something else Rose was good at. She sang wonderful little songs every night. Each evening, the entire family sat on the front porch and listened to her singing. Mostly, she used her lips and tongue to make strange sounds. She also used sticks, her fingers, hands and feet to create rhythm.

Afterwards, Mamie would lead them in the singing of Spirituals. They were different than Rose's songs, which contained beats and rhythms they'd never heard before. Rose loved learning and singing the Spirituals and she felt happier than she had ever imagined she could be.

Still, she wondered and worried if this happiness would last.

It was the best summer Rose ever remembered having, even though she was up early every day chopping cotton, and later on, picking it. Zeke let her take an extra long break at dinnertime, because, at that time of day, the sun was without mercy. He knew that, later on, she would be in the garden weeding until it was dark.

Twice a week Rose placed wood under the black iron pot in the yard. Later, she would make a fire in order to boil clothing and other items that needed special brightening. She would draw water from the well to fill the pot. She started the fire before going to the field in the morning. On the other mornings, she would do regular washing. Rose was fascinated with that black pot because it reminded her of Papo's place. Mamie told her the pot was a symbol of good health and prosperity.

Each morning when Mamie prepared family breakfast, Rose observed every move she made in case she was ever asked to do it. Mamie stayed home with the younger children until it was cotton-picking time. When the cotton was ready, everyone had to help in some way and she went to do her picking while Rose was eating dinner and watching the smaller children. The two older boys went to the field with their mother.

Zeke did not take a full break during cotton-picking time. He fully understood this was the time of year to be as productive as possible because the funds derived from the sale of his cotton had to see them through the long winter and spring months when there was little or no money coming in. He would do his resting and hunting in the winter months.

Rose helped in every way she could. She was learning how to cook food the way the family liked it and she was pleased with herself. She was beginning to smile and talk more with Mr. and Mrs. Turner. They praised her for all the work she did on the farm and with the children. She knew they were a good, strong family who loved and respected each other, and she longed to be one of them.

She thought about how much she loved Papo and she had lost him. She remembered hearing Papo constantly coughing. She always had to go to the stream down the hill from their little shack for water. Papo always wanted more water and more tea, which they made with leaves or with bark from the trees and plants found in the woods, the marshes and the meadow.

"The earth yields up wonderful things," Papo told Rose. "You just need to learn how to use them."

Papo had goats that provided them with milk, and on special occasions, they would cook one for food and invite neighbors. He used the skins to make containers for the meat, and in spring and summer he would put them in the cool stream to keep the meat fresh. He said the water couldn't get inside the skins. Rose recollected that they made slippers and pouches from the skins. Papo did many useful things with those goat hides.

There were a few chickens that produced eggs and occasionally, Papo would cook a chicken over hickory wood. Rose remembered a few other animals, especially Papo's horses and some that were in the nearby woods. Sometimes in the dark, Rose would hear Papo shooing off some wild animal from those woods, animals that had come to the yard looking for an easy meal.

At night, Papo told Rose some of the stories that had been told to him over the years and now, she began to reconstruct those tales as best she could. At times, she repeated them to herself just to make sure she would not forget them. Those stories made her feel warm and comfortable all inside and they fired up her imagination.

Each evening after supper, Rose helped Mamie to put the children to bed. During the night, she could hear Zeke and Mamie talking. They always began with talks about the children, what they did each day, how they were progressing in their daily routines, and about how many new words they knew. They talked about how the children loved Rose and said they didn't know if they could manage as well without her. Still, they wondered where her family was.

She also heard them discussing the money they would be receiving from this year's crop, which was better than last year's crop.

"Money mus' be very important, "Rose decided. "Uma learn how to git some."

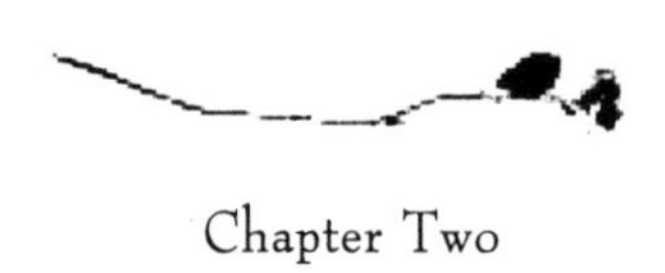

Chapter Two

About every three months or so, when the weather was favorable, the whole family went to town to purchase supplies from the stores. It was approximately eight weeks after Rose's arrival, when the time came for such a journey. This was a big and important event for them. The mule was hitched to the wagon and everyone was up early, dressed and ready for this special outing.

"Awright, ever'body. Put on yo' best manners, we headin' fo' town!" Zeke ordered.

The ride into town took almost an hour. The town was quite small but it appeared enormous to Rose because she had never been to a town. First, Zeke went to the hardware and feed stores to purchase some necessities for running the farm.

Mamie went to buy items and supplies for the house, as well as some food staples. Sometimes, she went to the dry goods store, and on this day, she went there to buy materials and other items for Rose who had no clothes of her own. She had been using garments that belonged to Mamie or Zeke, and of course, nothing fit her.

"I wants to see what Rose look like wit' somethin' decent to wear," Mamie said.

Rose could not believe her eyes when she saw shelves filled with bolts of all kinds of pretty fabrics. She saw all kinds of utensils, ready-made clothing, shoes, stockings, bonnets, purses, even furniture! Her eyes bulged when she saw pipes, tobacco and row upon row of cans of snuff. There were glass cases with assorted and colorful candies and sweets. Items Rose had never, ever seen.

They returned home with more supplies and groceries than Rose had seen in her whole life. There was flour, salt, sugar, lard, spices and a few other items. Rose had no idea that food could come like this. Papo had used mostly foods that came from the earth. Until today, she had never even been in a store.

Rose was very excited to have her first new stockings, new underwear and two new dresses. She did not want the new shoes they offered to buy for her. She preferred her own shoes because they were light like a feather and she could move swiftly with them.

Mamie made Rose a fancy nightgown to sleep in. It was the first one she ever remembered owning. She also made her a skirt and a "waist" to work in, with a bonnet to match the skirt. Rose would be wearing the two dresses, along with other bonnets Mamie had made, to worship and to other church-related activities, which almost always took place on Sundays.

Although she had attended twice, Rose still did not understand what church was, but she would soon know. The Turners would see to that, for they were devout worshipers and the church was a major influence in their lives.

Reverend Pennywell, the minister, came to their country church once a month and went to other churches on each of the other Sundays. He told his parishioner they were blessed to have their Pastor once each month 'cause some country churches only have a Pastor once every two or three months. Others, none at all.

This was conversation that went far beyond Rose's understanding at that time. She did, however, finally make a connection between Papo's talking to the Great Spirit and the Turners praying to Jesus, the Heavenly Father. In her head, there were many questions, she just didn't know how to get them out. That too, would come later.

Late fall on the farm was a very busy time. Although the cotton had long been ginned and sold, other chores were just beginning. Rose was excited when she went to a neighboring farm with Mr. Turner, where the men were turning sugar cane stalks into ribbon cane syrup.

She saw a mule walking around in circles rotating a big wheel, while the men put pieces of sugar cane in a container in the middle of the wheel. The sweet juices from the cane fell into a large bucket. There was a fire where the liquid was heated and then cooled. This was a process she had never seen.

Zeke sent Rose into the house to help the ladies prepare dinner for the men. Rose had brought along some of her own prized vegetables and she was quite happy to be in the company of these ladies.

When the food was laid out on the table, Rose felt a particular pride in her preparations. She heard one of the men say, "thes the best greens I ever ate and the 'taters good, too."

"Taste the butter beans," said another, "they shonuff good! The beets is, too. I'd give a pretty penny to have food like this on my table."

"Rose, chile, you can cook fo' me anytime," said another.

She also went with Mr.Turner when the men from a few of the farm families gathered together to slaughter hogs and pigs in order to cure and put away meat for the cold winter months. Two or three of the men would each provide shoats and hogs, and the meat would be cut up and divided between five or six families. The next time, the other families would supply the animals and the process would be repeated.

While the men were busy with their routine, the women gathered inside to prepare a sumptuous meal. The table would be laden with assorted greens, hot water corn bread, black-eyed peas, ham-hocks, squashes, corn, potatoes, chow-chow, canned fruits, jelly cakes and sweet potato pies. On rare occasions, there was home-cured ham or roast beef.

This ritual provided the ladies with the opportunity to enjoy each other's company, and share news of their neighbors and their children. Various other subjects such as church, sewing and how white people treated them would also be covered.

"Did you know Sistah Cole 'bout to have 'nother chile? This make six in six years."

"You shouda seed the way white folks treat us last time we was in town!"

"They's still blamin' us for losin' the war."

Rose was again asked to prepare her wonderful vegetable dishes. Usually, she made her favorite ones, boiled cabbage, sweet potatoes and corn pudding. By now, it was both the men and the women who praised Rose's fine vegetables and her extraordinary cooking skills. It seemed that everyone wanted something that had been grown in her garden. And she was more than pleased to accommodate them.

Fall was also the time of year when Mr. Turner was hired to do odd jobs at the slaughter house near town. Rose asked him to see if he could obtain a few of the animal hides. She wanted to see if she could still remember how to make her favorite moccasins. She preferred them to shoes, although often, she went barefoot.

On a day when Mr. Turner had finished doing some cleaning chores at the slaughterhouse, he asked the owner for a couple of the cow hides. He brought home two beautiful brown and white ones from yearlings. He placed them out on the fence to begin the drying and tanning process.

When Rose saw the hides, she was filled with the excitement of challenge because it had been such a long time since she had made sandals and moccasins. Also, she had had some help at the time. Now, she hoped she would remember.

"Um gonna try to make moccasins for everyone in the family," she announced.

When Mr. Turner told her she could make whatever she wanted, she was happy.

"Now I try to make some moccasins for ev'rybody and they be ready by Christmas."

Soon, she began measuring and cutting the tanned leather. There was lots of work to be done if she was going to finish in time for Christmas. She also wanted to make slippers for Reverend Pennywell and his wife. Rose was busy all day, every day, and on into the night. She loved every moment of it. Again, she thought about Papo as she used his knife to cut the hides.

With each passing day, she was feeling more and more like an important part of this wonderful family. They were always kind and pleasant to her. They accepted her as one of their own. Still, they had no clue as to where she came from and they never heard any talk about a runaway girl.

Mrs. Turner taught Rose how to do a variety of things. By now she had learned how to sew, to quilt, and how to make soap and candles. She also taught her how to cook other kinds of foods, such as sugar cookies and gingerbread. Rose learned how to can fruits and vegetables and how to dry them.

Mamie showed her how to comb and style her long, thick hair, and how to make bonnets. Rose was feeling very grown up and satisfied now. Sometimes she had to pinch herself in order to see if she was dreaming.

The children, too, were a special joy in Rose's life. She had been with families who had children, but she always had to wait on them and serve them. And if she didn't do it fast enough, she was yelled at and often beaten.

She had never been allowed to play and have fun with them. She watched over them and cleaned up the mess they constantly made. Here, at the Turners, she played games with the children and she ran and laughed and hugged and kissed them. She taught them how to climb trees, how to roll hoops and wheelies, how to play games and how to treat the animals with kindness and respect, just as Papo had taught her. She told them about the plants and the trees and how useful they are.

"Soon, I gonna teach you somethin' 'bout the moon an' the stars," she told them.

The kitchen was a very busy place these days. Of course, the kitchen was also the bedroom for Rose and two of the children. On this day, Mrs. Turner and Rose were up early and were busy boiling jars and tops. They were preparing to make jellies, jams and preserves.

It was a very precise operation that required a good deal of team work because an eye still had to be kept on the children who were constantly underfoot. There was always the danger of spilling something hot or of burning the fruits or even yourself. They peeled, chopped, cooked and stirred fruit the whole day long, while at the same time, caring for and feeding the children.

By nightfall, Rose and Mamie were pleased to finally have the opportunity to sit and look at the beautiful jars of fruit that sat gleaming and cooling on the table.

"It a lotta hard work but I loves it," said Rose.

"Tomorrow, I show you how to make chow-chow," promised Mamie.

Mamie used cabbage, peppers, onions, spices, vinegar and green tomatoes which she had canned in the spring. Rose was fascinated by the taste of this dish. She had tasted it before, but this chow-chow was something special.

Another food item that interested Rose were the delectable fried pies Mamie made using dried fruits, sugar, butter and aromatic spices for the filling. The cooked ingredients were placed inside the crusts and the edges were sealed with a pinch. Some of the pies were fried and others were baked in the oven. These pies were wonderful treats for the family and were only made for very special occasions.

"I loves teaching you, Rose, because you always so eager an' quick to learn."

Mamie taught her how to add and subtract, and how to tell time. She could not teach her how to read, because she herself didn't know how.

Both she and Mr. Turner could read and write their names and the names of their children, but nothing more. They had been taught how to achieve this feat by the Reverend Pennywell. He believed in taking the time to share his education with his church members. And the Turners were always anxious to learn whatever they could.

"Reverend Pennywell taught us lots'a things," Mamie told Rose. "He taught us how to tell time, an' when we learnt' he gave us a clock. This is his reward to all us who learns to write our names an' to tell time."

Rose was intrigued with all of the new concepts she was learning. She was an apt student and was especially good with numbers. She quickly learned the process of adding and subtracting. Soon she began counting, adding and subtracting everything in sight, including chickens, pigs, fence posts, and trees; she even tried to count the stars.

One night, while looking at the stars, she recalled that Papo had told her a story about stars. She remembered he had said his family used to sit around a fire and the old men told tales. He told her what a wonderful time they had sitting and listening to stories told by their wise leaders. Sometimes the stories were about brave warriors, but many times they were about animals.

Rose decided she would like to tell a story to her family but had some difficulty recollecting Papo's stories. However, when she looked at the sky that night and saw a bright star shining towards them, she knew immediately it was the Alpheratz Star, the one that had helped him and his little friends find their way back to their village one night when they became lost. Papo told her to remember that the Alpheratz Star could help her find her way home if she was lost.

I can tell that story, she thought.

Before bedtime, Rose told as much of Papo's story as she could remember. What she couldn't recall, she made up. Everyone was sitting quietly, listening intently.

> "One time a bunch o' boys decided to go huntin' for some rabbits to make some rabbit stew. Some boys had slingshots, some boys had bows an' arrows. They climbed up a big hill, they went over a gully an' thru' the big trees. They spotted a big one an' away they all run. That rabbit run so fast an' the boys wanted him 'cause he was big. So the boys run fast, too. The rabbit run over a big tree that lay 'cross a stream. The rabbit run an' run, faster an' faster the rabbit went. The boys went after it. The big 'ole rabbit outsmart the boys an' run 'round in circles. The boys do the same thing--run 'round in circles. Sudden' like, the rabbit disappear, nobody see it.
>
> Now, it be gettin' dark an' the boys, they be confused from all that running in circles. Nobody know which way to go. They don' even have no rabbit. "What we go' do now?" ax one boy, we lost! "Look," say another boy, "There is the Alphe' Star. Chief say if you gets lost from village, follow Alphe' Star, it will take you home."
>
> The boys follow the bright star and pretty soon they hear voices. The men from the village be coming to look for them. They were happy to be home again even though they don' got no rabbit. That ole rabbit is still runnin.'

Rose knew she didn't exactly tell the story like she'd heard Papo tell it But the family listened to every word she said and she enjoyed doing something that made everyone feel the way she had felt so long ago when Papo told stories to her.

"I must try hard to 'member mo' stories like that," she thought to herself, "They love my story."

After that, the children often asked Rose to tell them a story. She knew she would have to try and create some stories in her head, so she decided she would just patch together the bits and pieces she remembered from Papo's tales and simply add to them as she went along. Rose tried hard to bring to mind something else that Papo had told her about the stars. She vowed that one day she'd remember.

Chapter Three

Rose had been with the Turners for about three years now. She knew this because Mamie kept some markings on the cupboard in the kitchen. Since Rose had become good at reading numbers, she could figure out many things that she never knew before.

She still could neither read nor write. On the other hand, she could remember everything Mr. and Mrs. Turner had taught her about running the farm.

Mamie often said, "In case sump'n' happen to us, you knows how to care for yo'self an' the chil'ren."

By now, Rose could hitch up the mule and plow the fields as well as any man. She knew when and how to sow the seeds. She also knew when and how to harvest the crops. She was very adept at chopping weeds from cotton, picking it and preparing it to go to the cotton gin.

And no one in the whole area could grow a field of vegetables in quite the same manner and with the great results that Rose achieved.

The Turners had ceased asking Rose about the homes where she had lived in the past. When they had asked, Rose always told them those people were not her Ma and Pa and they all had mistreated her.

She told them, "Before then, when I was very little, I lived with Papo an' one night he took me to live with another family. He gave me his knife an' his cane an' he told me to always hold on to them. That family was so unkind to me. They beat me for no reason, so one day, I ran away. The same thing happen all over with the next family. So I run away again. Wherever Papo is, I know he don' want me to be beat up. He was kind to ev'ry living thing, he never beat me. Papo teach me to always be good an' brave."

Now that Rose was older and had learned so much from Mamie Turner, she came to understand that Papo was, perhaps, too ill to continue to care for her. So he did what he thought was best. He took her to live with a nearby family.

Rose told them that before Papo went away, he was always coughing and how she had to make special teas for him. She also said she made food for him to eat. When he left her, she thought it would only be for a short while. She didn't want to admit it, but she finally knew he would never return.

"I wish I had been older an' wiser so I could have cared for him the way he cared for me as far back as I kin remember. Maybe he could still be living."

Rose decided that surely Papo had become one with the Great Spirit, and that he was somewhere smiling down at her this very moment.

"I will do everything 'n my power to make him proud of me."

Then she silently thanked the Great Spirit once again for Papo and for her now being a part of this family.

` ` ` ` ` ` ` ` ` ` `

On a rainy afternoon, Rose and Mr. Turner had to come in early from the field. There was a familiar aroma of something special being prepared in the kitchen. Rose knew right away it was a cake. But Mr. Turner's nose caught the distinct smell of chicken and dumplings, his favorite meal.

While Mr. Turner cleaned himself up in the barn, Rose ran into the house wondering all the while, what on earth's happening?

As she entered the kitchen, she yelled out, "What be goin' on?"

"It be Mr. Turner's birthday," answered Mamie. "I made supper special; we all work so hard, we need to take a little time to have some fun. Now git yo' self cleaned up an' put the plates an' forks on the table. You don' have to clean up the chil'ren, I already don' that, but you can sweep the dirt off the porch."

Mamie always insisted on forks because, in slavery time, they never had forks to use and they had intrigued her when she saw them being used in the 'big house.' She also, always insisted on a clean floor like the one in the 'big house.'

Rose sat in the number three tin tub which was filled with water that Mamie had used to bathe the children. Without a doubt, she knew Mamie herself had also used the same water as this was the custom, unless it was raining, and then all the children made a game of catching their own bath water.

Rose always caught the water for the two younger children. But today, there had been no time to do that. Mr. Turner usually washed himself at the shed, using the well water, which was always cold. Every Saturday, though, Mamie would make a warm bath for him in the number three tub, and she would scrub his back.

When she finished her bath, Rose put on her prettiest dress. After all, it wasn't often they got to celebrate anything and she reasoned that her pretty calico dress, with the bright yellow roses and two ruffles, would soon be too small for her.

She knew that in the past few years she had done a good deal of growing since Mamie also made lines on the wall to measure each child's growth. Rose had put on a little weight, too, because the first dress Mamie made for her was now too small, even though when she made it, it was much too big.

Mamie had said, "I left you some room to grow, chile."

Rose used little time bathing and dressing because she was in a hurry to get the celebration started and she was especially anxious to eat the foods with the delicious smells. She quickly put the plates and forks on the table and gathered the children who sat on the porch patiently waiting for their father.

It was a wonderful dinner. There was chicken and dumplings, black-eyed peas, potatoes and cornbread, followed by the best jelly cake in all the world. The children said "Happy Birthday" to their father. Mrs.

Turner prayed a long prayer and thanked God for giving them such a wonderful husband and papa.

Mamie continued, "Ezekiel deserves to have a special celebration 'cause of all the nice things he do for his family an' 'cause he works long, hard hours an' never complains. Mostly, he is always thankful to God for giving him the health an' stren'th to be able to work an' take care of his family."

After finishing supper, and the singing of the Spiritual, "What Would I Do Without the Lord," the children asked Rose to tell another one of her stories. She was pleased they asked:

> "Once upon a time there was this tiny little girl. She lived near the big river with her Grandpapa. Now, he didn't know where her Mama an' Papa were. One day, they just up an' disappear. Some say maybe they drown in the river. But nobody know.
>
> Others say maybe they run away from the mean boss man. Still, they never return home to their tiny little daughter.
>
> In the morning you could hear tiny little girl singing down at the river as she looked for her Mama an' Papa. All the other little children knew where they Mama an' Papa be.
>
> The other boys an' girls grew bigger an' got older each year.
>
> But the tiny little girl stayed tiny. She didn't even get older because no one knew when it be her birthday. Her Grandpapa didn't even know 'cause her Mama an' Papa didn't tell him before they went away.
>
> Tiny little girl grew more lovely and more beautiful every day. But she did not grow older 'cause she don' have no birthday. All the other boys an' girls are now ladies an' gentlemens. Tiny little girl is very beautiful but she is still a little girl to this very day 'cause nobody knows when her birthday comes.
>
> Until they know when her birthday be, maybe she be a little girl forever an' ever an' ever!"

Mrs. Turner had tears in her eyes when Rose finished her story. She knew there was a special message in that story and she vowed to do something about this young lady who had become so much a part of their lives.

The children now referred to her as 'Big Sister.' She loved being accepted as part of the family, but she fiercely wanted everyone to call her Rose. She loved the sound of that name, she liked how pretty roses are and she loved their sweet fragrance.

"Rose. Rose. Rose Turner." That sounds real nice. I like that name! I want to be Rose Turner!" she would often say to herself.

A few days following the birthday celebration, Mrs. Turner sat in the swing on the porch and asked Rose to come and sit with her.

"See those bushes out there, Rose, the ones with the tiny buds just beginning to grow?"

"Yes' m."

"Well, in just another few weeks, it be July, an' those roses be in full bloom. You name Rose, right? Well now, come the firs' day of July, when the roses bloom, it be yo' birthday! Yes, sir, come firs' day of July, it be Rose's birthday!" she declared.

Rose sat very still for a moment, too stunned to respond. Then suddenly she jumped from the swing with a scream louder than any one had ever heard her make. She hugged and kissed Mrs. Turner over and over, again and again.

"Thank you! Thank you! Thank you! Now I have a birthday like ev'rybody."

Abruptly, she stopped her celebration and sat strangely silent on the porch, staring downward.

"Rose, what's a' matter, baby? What's wrong?" Mamie inquired.

Rose looked up at her with her big, round amber eyes and asked, "Can I be Rose Turner, please, please? Can I be Rose Turner?" she pleaded.

"You shonuff can, baby. "You be Rose Turner from now on.

In order to show her appreciation for the wonderful gift of a name, Rose got up each day even earlier than usual to begin her chores. She was so filled with joy and a newfound energy that she wanted to do everything for her new Pa and Ma. She fed the animals. She filled their water troughs. She made a fire under the big, black, fat bellied cast iron pot in the yard, the one that's supposed to bring good health and prosperity.

She swept the porch, and she washed the clothes. She put some of the laundry in the boiling pot to remove stains and to get them extra bright and clean. She went to the garden and gathered the vegetables that were heavy with early morning dew.

Her plans were to do it all before the Turners awakened, but each day, before she could finish, she would hear them stirring around and carrying on their early morning conversation and prayer. Before going inside, she hung the clothes out to dry.

Rose walked in with her bushel basket of string beans, tomatoes, squash and beets and laid them on the table.

"Good mornin'!" she said, "Did ya' sleep well? Why ya' up so early? Shall I start the fire? Uh, oh, ya' started it already!"

Mr. Turner replied, "Slow down, Rose. You don't have to do ev'rythin' 'round here. This is Sat'day mornin'. You knows the 'oman starts a little' late on Sat'day. We goin' church tomorrow an' after service, we gonna have a church dinner an' you gotta fix some food."

"We fine this mornin', thank you," Mrs. Turner responded. "Rose, these veg'ables look mighty good! You choose what you gonna cook. I gonna make fried pies. Come on now, let's make breakfast while the kids still sleep."

She gave Mr. Turner a cup of hot water with honey which he gulped down in almost a single swallow and then left the house to begin his chores. He would return for breakfast in about an hour.

"Rose," began Mrs. Turner, "you know your birthday is next week, right? Well, I done some thinkin' an' I figure you mus' be 'bout fifteen years old, course, I don' 'xactly know, but fifteen seems right to me. Is that okay with you?" she asked.

Rose smiled and said, "That be just fine! Whatever you say, it sounds good to me."

Later that afternoon, after all the chores were finished, Rose decided she needed to take a walk. She needed some time to be alone. Some thinking time. She wanted to be out in the open spaces with the wind. She wanted to see the birds floating on air. She wanted to look out at the vast blue sky. She wanted to hear the trees whistling with the wind. And she wanted to see the animals frolicking in the woods and meadow.

At times, she walked; at times, she ran and skipped along the country lane. She talked aloud to herself and she sang some of the songs she knew. She even sang and hummed some of the Spirituals she had learned from Mrs. Turner.

> I'm gonna sing when the Spirit says sing
> I'm gonna sing when the Spirit says sing
> I'm gonna sing when the Spirit says sing
> An' obey the Spirit of the Lord.

Rose was so happy, she was intoxicated. She felt that her small body could not contain all of the gladness and joy she was feeling. She needed to share it with all the living things around her, she needed to commune with the things the earth produced. She needed to tell Papo.

She stopped here and there to gather a flower or to kiss a plant. She hugged the trees and threw rocks and pebbles just to see them sail through the air. She kicked at small clods of dirt that touched the toes of her fancy moccasins with the many straps wound about her fragile ankles.

She swirled and swayed and lifted her skirt and she pranced and danced through rows of tall corn growing in the field. As she emerged from the cornfield, she was near a giant oak tree. She climbed almost to the top of that tree, whose branches seemed to beckon her.

From that vantagepoint, she could see for miles and miles. She saw things she'd never seen before.

"How lovely and how wonderful everything looks from up here!"

The Turner farm seemed much smaller than she thought. When she chopped or picked the cotton, she could have sworn that it went for miles and miles. From up here, she could even see other surrounding farms and the houses of their neighbors, which had always seemed to be so far away. Rose closed her eyes and said she would remember this view forever. She would imprint this day as a lasting memory!

She wondered if anyone in the whole wide world could feel as happy as she was at that very moment. She was now part of a family she loved and that loved her. They had given her the best presents in the whole world. They gave her a home. They gave her their love and their name. Now she had a whole name and she had a birth date. Also, she was fifteen years old!

As she sat and meditated, the spirit of Papo descended over her and tears came to her eyes. She retraced some of their times together. Again, she thought about what must have happened during the times she could no longer clearly recall. Tears continued to fill her eyes and she cried, but only for a moment.

Then she threw her head back and called out, "Papo! Papo! I promise to make you proud of me as I am proud of you! The Great Spirit has given me the best family in the whole big world and I give big thanks! Thank you! Thank you! Thank you-ooooooo."

Her voice echoed and carried on the wind.

Rose sat at the top of the oak tree for a long time, consumed in her thoughts and her new state of elation. Finally, she climbed down from the towering tree with a vow to return to that special place again.

She ran all the way home, as fast as she could go. This was, after all, a very notable and treasured time for her. She would recapture this day again. And she would forever be grateful for having her own family.

The next week, Rose busied herself again doing every chore she could think of. She did some of them over and over again thinking that by doing so, she could make the week pass faster. She was overwhelmed with excitement and anticipation!

This would be her first birthday ever! As hard as she tried, she could not remember Papo ever telling her about a birthday. Now she was going to have her own birthday and a second name. How she loved the sound of her name, "Rose Turner, Rose Turner." She would repeat it over and over again. When the children called her "Big Sister," she reminded them her name was Rose Turner.

She wanted the whole wide world to know her name was Rose Turner! She whispered it on the wind, she told it to the animals, she even shouted it to the clouds and the stars.

Sleep was an elusive visitor that night. The half moon lay limp and languid in the dark sky. Rose heard the songs of the night creatures whose sounds joined with the soft winds, settling and echoing on the gentle, rolling hills encompassing the low farm lands.

On the first day of July, in the year 1875, Rose Turner celebrated her birthday. She was fifteen years old. In honor of this occasion, Ezekiel and Mamie Turner gave their eldest child a plot of land on which to grow her very own vegetables.

One day, she might even have her very own house there. Rose did not know the dimensions of that plot of land but she did know it surpassed anything that anyone could have ever given her, except of course, her second name and a birth date.

After the celebration, when everything had been cleaned, and the children had been put to bed, Rose recited her litany of thanks to the Turners. She was grateful they had taken her into their home and treated her as if she was their own. She thanked them for being her Mama and Papa and for giving her brothers and a sister. She was very thankful for the plot of land on which she would grow her vegetables.

But most of all, she was happy and appreciative for her second name and for a birth date and an age to go with it! After reassuring Rose that she was deserving of whatever they had done for her and they were very pleased to have her as part of their family, they left her alone and went into the house.

It was a night much too hot and humid to be sitting and thinking. But Rose sat there for what must have been hours with thoughts and visions racing through her head. She saw the lights from the fireflies but she never heard the noises made by the frogs and the crickets. She saw the lightning but she never heard the thunder.

` ` ` ` ` ` ` ` ` ` `

Among her thoughts that night were those of selling vegetables to all the people who always said hers were the best in the whole area. She would work harder and grow even more vegetables than she ever had because she knew people would buy them. The rain fell from the sky that night, but she never even noticed it.

When Rose finally went to sleep, she dreamed about having the largest and most beautiful garden in the whole world! She also dreamed she had her own horse to ride. The horse was just like one that Papo had owned. Golden brown, big, fast and strong!

The next day, everything returned to normal again. The whole family went to the field to chop weeds from the cotton plants. It would not be too long now, before the cotton would be ready for picking. It was late to begin a summer garden, but in a little while, Rose would plant seeds that could be harvested late summer and early fall. There was plenty of time to make plans for a bountiful spring garden for next year.

In the fall of the same year that Rose celebrated her fifteenth birthday, she sold her very first vegetables. She sold collards, beans and corn to friends and neighbors of the family.

Rose was excited to have money of her very own. Mamie gave her an empty syrup can to put her coins in. Although she had only forty cents, she was elated just to have money and she promised herself that one-day she would have lots of money.

In the middle of October, Rose decided it was time to try out another idea which had been running around in her head for some time.

On their trips into town, they always passed by the railroad station and she noticed how large numbers of people milled around the station. Sometimes a few of them scurried to the store across the way to make purchases, and then quickly ran back to the train at the sound of the whistle.

There were some, however, who continued to hang around the platform even after the train left. They were the locals who simply enjoyed the activity that the train stop generated. Rose believed that some of those people would like her jars of food and her gingerbread.

She told Mr. and Mrs. Turner of her plan to sell some items at the train station. Mr. Turner did not like the idea at all because he thought the townspeople would make trouble for her. Mamie was skeptical but said it might just work and she persuaded her husband to let Rose give it a try. She suggested that he could take Rose to the edge of town in the wagon and she could walk to the train station from there.

Rose chose the very next Saturday for her first selling attempt because she knew many people would be in town that day. She filled two baskets with her favorite goodies. There were jars of chow-chow, plum jelly, peach jam, gingerbread and sugar cookies

Zeke and Mamie were both apprehensive about this venture, but Rose was not afraid to try because Papo had taught her not to fear anything. Still, she couldn't help feeling just a little nervous, but it was not because of the selling. It was because almost everyone at the station was white and Rose was not used to being around white folks. She only came in contact with them when the family went on their shopping trips.

To the townsfolk, Rose seemed to have appeared on the platform of the train station from out of nowhere. She always wore ankle-length skirts with matching blouse and bonnet. Her clothing looked like a patchwork quilt, with figures embroidered on various brightly colored patches. Her bonnet, blouse and skirt were always starched and ironed with an impeccable precision. On her feet, she wore crudely made Indian moccasins with leather laces wrapped around her thin ankles.

Rose knew precisely what time each train would arrive at the local station and she was always there when it pulled in. She was the color of a copper penny that had been left in the sun too long. She had long, black, coarse hair that she wore in two braids, coiled around her small head. She was short and thin, barely reaching five feet in height and weighed less than a hundred pounds. Her eyes were big, wide and the color of deep amber.

Rose held her head high when she reached the station. She set her basket down and called out, "Cookies! Jams!" "Cookies! Jams!"

One person came to look and picked up a bag which held twenty cookies and said, "How much?"

Rose held up five fingers. She was given five pennies.

Back and forth she walked along the platform calling out the same two words: "Cookies! Jams!"

Each time she was asked "how much?" she held up five fingers.

Before long, Rose had sold everything she had brought to the station. She ran home as fast as the rabbits in the meadow could run. Her baskets were empty, but carrying them still slowed her down. Finally, she arrived home, excited and breathless!

Mrs. Turner and Rose sat at the table and quickly counted the money. There was eighty-five cents. They both jumped and laughed and shouted for joy!

"This is a miracle!" exclaimed Mamie.

Even the children joined in the celebration, though they had no idea what was going on. When Zeke came home, he was also excited at the good news.

Rose wanted to know when she could go again. Mamie had to remind her that it took time to make a supply of cookies and gingerbread.

"But," she added, "next Saturday will be a good time."

"I don't know if I kin wait 'til then, tha's seven whole days away," Rose said.

Since most of the harvesting had already been done, Rose and Mamie did have more time than usual. Because of this, or so she said, Mamie helped Rose with her preparations of the items she would be selling the following Saturday. As each day passed, Mamie crossed it off on the almanac.

On Friday night, there were a number of gleaming jars of canned foods lined up on the cabinet shelf. In addition, there were sugar cookies, ginger-bread and sorghum bread, that Mamie had made. Rose counted her goods over and over again and she wiped the jars until they all shone.

"My, my," said Rose, "they do look delicious."

When she went to bed that night, she hardly slept at all. But when the sun came up, it was Mamie who had to wake her. The sun was filling the land with light.

"I'm surprised you still sleep, girl. Com' on, les' get somethin' on the table."

Rose bounded out of bed, washed up, looked at her goods one more time and began her morning chores.

To the townsfolk, Rose was an Indian lass and they presumed her family simply preferred to remain separate from the rest of them. This belief worked in Rose's favor because if they had known that she was indeed a Negro, mixed with Indian, they would probably have made trouble for her as they did for the Negroes after the war ended. Many of the whites seemed to look for opportunities to re-enslave them, doing anything in order to make their lives miserable.

The local whites blamed their loss of the War Between the States, and their subsequent suffering, on the Negroes. They became the scapegoats for all the losses the south sustained. Because they were poor and generally defenseless, the Negroes were vulnerable. The whites thought the freed coloreds were a menace to their lives, property, liberty and to the local government.

The decade of the seventies was not a time for them to make a living selling to whites. Additionally, this dreadful decade was filled with graft and corruption. Bribery and thievery ran rampant everywhere in the south. Losing the Civil War for the southerners meant the loss of their positions in world economy and the loss of their genteel way of life. Consequently, life for the Southern Negro was horrendous. And it wasn't much better for poor whites.

It was for these reasons Zeke never took Rose all the way into town. Let them continue to think she was an Indian, he reasoned.

The following Saturday, after breakfast, Ezekiel hitched up the mule to the wagon for the trip to town. The baskets were filled so he set them in the wagon in a position that Rose could hold on to them. He wasn't sure that she could walk to the station with such a heavy load. Even though they contained fewer jars this time, her baskets seemed to be just as heavy as before.

So Zeke decided he would watch Rose as she walked to the station. He tied the mule to a tree and walked along the edge of the trees being careful not to be seen, while at the same time getting a view of Rose. He could see that she was struggling with her baskets. However, he was confident she would make it because he knew how determined she was. Still, he continued to follow and to watch. It was difficult for her, but she made it to the station on time.

This time, Rose was more assertive than before. She sat her baskets down, held up a jar of jam and several bags of cookies.

"COOK-EES, JAMS!" she boldly called out.

She repeated the call only when necessary. Two or three people came up to make purchases.

Then others began to come and inspect and buy from her. She recognized a few faces as having bought from her on the previous Saturday. Some of them asked questions to which she replied with a shake of her head or with hand gestures. She smiled continuously, but rarely said anything besides "cookies," "jams," or "sweets." Even when someone inquired, "Where do you come from?" She smiled and pointed her finger.

It took a little more than two hours for Rose to sell everything she had. And it didn't take her long to figure that she could make more money selling, than working those long hot hours in the cotton field. This time, when Rose started running home, Zeke Turner was in the trees observing her movements.

After she had passed by without ever seeing him, he decided to get the wagon and go after her. When he caught up, she had run more than half the distance home. He pulled close behind her in order to slow down her pace. She climbed in and was relieved to have this ride home. The empty baskets were awkward to carry.

They counted one dollar and twenty-six cents! Rose and Mamie could hardly contain their joy. They began planning the next selling trip right then and there.

Every Saturday thereafter, Rose followed the routine of going to the train station to sell her goodies. Some of the townsfolk would be there waiting for her when she arrived. Zeke continued to drop her off before reaching the station, but he did so at various places in order for her to arrive from different directions.

The week before Christmas, Rose and Mamie put together packages of all the nuts they had gathered over the last few months. Some of them had been brought home by Zeke for his family to enjoy during the winter months. He didn't want to give them up but they brought in money he could use in the spring when he would purchase seed and equipment to get his crops ready for planting.

Mamie and Rose did a good job of dividing the money that was made from the selling. Zeke was quite proud of that money, so he gave up his stash of nuts. The family could make do with goobers, which were plentiful.

The ladies did most of their baking and preparations at night when the children were asleep. This week, they concentrated on making sweet potato and pumpkin pies sorghum and gingerbreads and sugar cookies. These were now the big-selling items because there were only a few jars of jams and jellies remaining. It was impossible to make more because the fruit-bearing season had ended.

Rose planned to continue selling until the weather was too cold.

Early in the day, on the Friday before Christmas, everything was all ready for the trip to the station the following day. Rose knew this Saturday offered the possibility of making more money than she'd ever made in a single day. She went to bed early in order to be ready for the big day.

It started during the middle of the night. First, the wind whispered, then it had a mournful wail. Next, it howled. It came roaring down the hill and through their valley. Finally, it blew so hard that it awakened everyone in the house. Afterwards, the rain came. It fell in torrents, so intense that the family knew for sure there would be all kinds of mud and water problems after the rain stopped.

Rose choked back her tears since she didn't want them to see her cry. She knew the family would be safe because she had seen this kind of storm before. But she also knew that her big day at the train station was ruined. There was no way she could go into town even if the rain stopped. The rivers of mud would make the roads impassable.

She would not have the money that she had counted on. She was deeply disappointed, but she tried hard not to show it.

"I must 'member never to count on money that's not in my hand," she said.

Rose remembered the hides that had been cured and were stored out in the shed. Since it was still pouring and there was little else to do, she figured that now would be a good time to finish the moccasins she had promised the family.

She spent the next few days cutting, tooling and lacing the patterns together. She also burned designs into parts of the leather. She made moccasins for everyone but she made sandals for herself. She burned the hair from the leather and cut thin strips in order to make her lacings. She owned store-bought shoes that Mamie had insisted on. Still, she preferred her sandals because they felt better. She conceded, however, that the 'store-bought shoes' felt good in the cold weather even though her feet felt imprisoned.

Chapter Four

That winter of 1875-76, was particularly cold and wet. The family stayed indoors most of the time. Mamie showed Rose how to write her name and how to read and recite the alphabet. Rose, however, had learned how to draw a rose and she thought that far more interesting than writing the word. Sometimes she made a rose and put an 'X' in the middle of it, and other times she drew one and put an 'R' in the center. She could not decide which way she liked it best.

During the cold winter evenings, the family often roasted goobers and sometimes they roasted yams or sweet potatoes in the hot ashes of the fireplace. They all sat around eating, talking, singing and playing games. Sometimes they asked Rose to tell them stories. By now, she was becoming quite accomplished at storytelling.

"Well, I do declare," Mamie whispered to Zeke one night, "that gal's got a fine 'magination!"

It had been two months since Rose had been to the train station to sell her goodies. She was becoming restless and she was quite anxious to return. She knew she had something special going and she didn't want to lose her customers. She wondered if they had been looking for her or if they missed her as much as she missed them. She would soon find out.

Even though the weather was still cold, it was a clear day. Rose decided it was time to get back to her business. She made gingerbread, sweet potato pies and a new recipe that she had learned at the church, "tea-cakes." Because her load was light this Saturday, she decided that she would walk to town. It was a long walk but she savored every minute of it. After her successful return to the station that day, she ran and skipped all the way home. Rose was brimming with delight. She was so pleased that the weather was good enough for her to be back selling. Her pockets were filled with money. She could hardly wait to share the events of the day with Mamie.

a new baby. . . . .

But Mamie had some good news of her own. She told Rose she was going to have a baby. Rose was so excited to hear that a baby was coming, she forgot all about her successful day. She had all kinds of questions for Mamie since she knew practically nothing pertaining to the events of motherhood. Mamie knew that now was a good time to explain to her as much as she herself knew.

So she told her about conception and the nine months of gestation when the baby would grow inside her stomach and about birth and labor pains. She added that a midwife would come to deliver the baby when the time came.

"Zeke would like 'nother boy," she told Rose, "but I would like to have 'nother girl, so Annie can have a lit'l sister."

Spring came at last on the farm, and much of Rose's time was spent in the garden. She continued, however, to do all her household chores. Zeke did most of the cotton planting, with help from Samuel. He took Rose with him only when he wanted to share with her particular aspects of soil conditions or of sowing the seeds. Ephriam was also helping his father in the field but Zeke always brought him home for the day, when they came in for dinner.

Before long, Rose was going to the train station every Tuesday and Saturday. She believed she should add another day because she always sold everything she took with her. She was growing vegetables and gathering fruits in a much larger quantity.

Rose proposed another idea to Mamie and Zeke. "I would like to buy a horse. If I had a horse like the one Papo had, I wouldn' have to use up so much time on my trips goin' back an' forth to the station. I could use that time helping out on the farm or giving Ma some extra help at the house. Then I would have mo' time with the children."

At first, she had a difficult time convincing Zeke, but Mamie agreed with her from the beginning. Mamie possessed a good sense for business. She knew right away that what Rose was doing was unusual and that it was also successful. She persuaded Zeke to promise he would check around to see where he could find a horse suitable for a young lady. After all, she had enough money to purchase a horse.

"I promise I do my best. I keep my ears an' eyes op'n."

On an extremely hot night in August, the Turners' new baby girl made a quick entrance into the world. Mr. Turner had gone in the wagon to get the midwife. Mamie was having slight contractions, about thirty minutes apart. She decided to go on the porch and sit in the swing to see if she would be more comfortable and maybe a little cooler. She walked around. She sat down. She stood up. She squatted. Then she repeated each movement. Over and over. She was miserable! The pains were now getting closer. She began praying and making strange noises. She sweated profusely. Rose constantly wiped and patted her with a towel.

Finally, Rose coerced her to lie on the bed. When she did, she let out a scream! Rose did not panic, neither did she know what to do. Mamie directed her to put some water on the stove to boil and to bring in some bed sheets. When Rose brought in the sheets and muslin cloths and towels, Mamie screamed again. This time she called for Jesus to come, and she called for her mother whom she said had gone to live with Jesus. She started singing between gasps.

My mother's in heaven an' I want to go there
to shout an' sing Hosanah
My mother's in heaven an' I want to go there
to shout an' sing Hosanah
I want to go there, I want to go there

The screaming would stop suddenly and she would sing another Spiritual, and she would talk to 'Dear Jesus' some more. The cycle of contractions was closer and closer and Rose listened desperately for sounds of the wagon returning with the midwife. There were no sounds. No one was coming.

"What could be takin' them so long?" Rose mourned pitifully.

Between contractions, Mamie told Rose what to do and Rose tried as best she could to follow her directions. She was aware of Mamie's straining and groaning and she wished Mr. Turner was there with that midwife. They'd surely know what to do.

Finally, Mamie yelled, "It's coming! It's coming! Help me, Rose! Help me, Rose!"

Rose heard the wagon coming up the path just as the baby came out in her hands.

In only a few minutes, the midwife had everything under control. Mamie was quiet and smiling. Soon, the baby girl was all cleaned up and sleeping peacefully in her mother's arms. Mr. Turner was tired but relieved.

Rose made everyone some bark tea with honey in it. That was when she noticed the sun brightening up the horizon, ready for another scorching day.

Mr. Turner engaged the midwife to stay with the family a full week because this was a critical time for harvesting the cotton. She did the cooking and she took care of Mamie and the new baby. Zeke, Rose and the three boys went to the field to pick cotton. Rose only went to the station once that week but vowed not to miss her regular rounds again.

The next few weeks were especially difficult for Rose because there was so much to do at the farm and Mamie could only help a little. Rose never thought a little baby could keep everyone in the house so occupied.

Everyday, Rose worked from before sun up until late into the night. Fourteen or fifteen hour days seemed commonplace. And she was determined to prepare and store as many jars of canned food as she thought she could sell during the fall and winter months.

Rose was quite proud of how much she was able to do without Mamie as a full partner. She did, however, let Ephriam assist her in gathering and washing the fruits and vegetables. He was really growing up and had become an important contributor around the farm. The hot summer and the gentle rains had produced big, ripe and luscious produce.

The cotton-picking season finally came to an end and the entire household was cheerful. After the cotton had been ginned and sold, Zeke went out and located what he believed was the best horse he could find for Rose. He bought a two-year-old, golden saddle horse one Saturday while Rose was at the station.

He rode the horse towards town and waited until he saw Rose leave for home. Zeke followed her for a little while and when he could wait no longer, he galloped up behind her. She was alarmed to hear someone call her name. When she looked around and saw Mr. Turner, she was relieved.

"Gracious goodness!" she shouted, "Where did this horse come from?"

"He all yours, Rose," said Mr. Turner. "T'was money you earned that bought him. Climb up behind an' let's go home."

` ` ` ` ` ` ` ` ` ` `

Rose's entire life was changed by having that horse. She called him "Spirit" because he brought to her mind memories of Papo's horse and the good times they had riding together. Zeke gave her a few lessons on riding and on commanding her horse. She was so eager to ride, she absorbed every word he spoke and every direction he gave.

It didn't take her long to be in full charge of Spirit. It seemed as if they had always been together. Rose took care of him in the same manner in which a mother carefully tends her baby.

Each morning, before anyone in the house awakened, Rose was out in the barnyard brushing and feeding him. Afterwards, she rode him along the country lanes that bordered the other farms.

Rose loved to ride as fast as Spirit would go. She loved to feel the wind on her face and in her hair. Riding Spirit gave her a complete sense of freedom and temporary escape from the many responsibilities she had. She felt as if she could ride forever and be oblivious to the rest of the world. But she knew when it was time to turn around and head for home. She fully realized there were chores that had to be done and she also knew her life was very good now. And very special.

Rose made a new schedule for selling at the train station. She went every Monday, Wednesday and Saturday. She lived for those wonderful days!

On Mondays, she mostly took jars of canned foods, sugar cookies and molasses bread. Wednesdays, she took seasonal vegetables, assorted fruits and gingerbread. Saturdays, she carried vegetables and fruits, along with her special tea-cakes and sweet potato pies. She knew this was a good program and only the dictates of the season would cause her to vary her new routine.

The business venture continued to go well for Rose. She usually sold most everything she took and she gave almost half of the money she made to Zeke and Mamie. They had no problems at all with this arrangement. In fact, they were very pleased because in spite of all the effort put into selling, Rose continued to work in the fields and around the house.

Zeke could even consider reducing his cotton production next season because she was contributing almost as much money as the cotton brought in. And unless the weather was inclement, she did it year round. Mamie once again began helping Rose with the canning duties, and often she sent along her fried pies for Rose to sell.

The train passengers bought the pies immediately and always clamored for more. Those pies quickly became a hot-selling item.

Rose's business was paying off handsomely and she continuously thought of ways to increase her sales. Now that she had Spirit, she could get to the station and back in a much shorter time.

She suggested that Mamie make aprons for her to sell. But that idea did not work as well as she had imagined. So she quickly discarded it. Rose continued to sell food items only, and by year's end, they had made a good sum of money. Zeke and Rose buried most of it in jars and cans at different places on the farm.

` ` ` ` ` ` ` ` ` ` `

One day, the following spring, Rose was returning home from the station when some white boys began throwing rocks at her. She figured they were trying to rob her, so she threw her bag of coins at them and took off on Spirit. Without realizing it, she guided him down a strange lane in her effort to get away from them.

She had Spirit galloping at top speed because she believed the boys were going to harm her. When she finally looked back to see if they were still chasing her, she missed seeing a tree that had fallen across the trail. Spirit jumped the tree but his unexpected lurch caused her to lose her balance. Her leg hit the tree trunk and she landed with one arm pinned under her body. When she tried to get up, she couldn't. And what was worse, Spirit had kept on going.

Rose could see no cuts or bruises, so she felt relieved. But there was severe pain in her arm and leg. She knew she must keep calm and not panic. She wondered if this trail was one that was often used. She figured after a while the pain would go away, so she lay very still and quiet. She wondered if Spirit would go on home, but she remembered they had never been down this path before.

Perhaps, it will take Spirit a long time to find his way home, she thought. She never let herself think for a moment he could not find the farm or that he would not soon return to her.

She was glad she had thrown her money to the white boys. She thought giving up the money was why they had not followed her.

"I must be havin' a bad dream," said Rose. "I'll wake up directly."

She lay there for a long time, unable to get up. After a while, she began to drag herself back down the trail. It was a very slow and painful process. She could not move one leg at all so she dragged it, as she inched her way down the lane.

Pain shot through the other leg as well. Still, she did not cry. The struggle to move, plus the sharp pain, caused her breathing to become quite heavy and she began to softly hum one of the Spirituals that Mamie had taught her. She used her arms, her hands and her one good leg to move her body forward.

> I want Jesus to walk with me;
> I want Jesus to walk with me;
> All along my pilgrim journey,
> Lord, I want Jesus to walk with me

"I must get home. I gotta get home. Am I home yet?" her voice trailed off.

"I can't see the bright star," she murmured, "But maybe Papo sees it. Yes, he will see it and he will come for me. Papo, Papooo...."

The very next thing Rose was aware of was lying on a blanket in a strange bed and being given water by a huge white man with long flowing hair and a beard. She tried to get up but couldn't! It was then that she became aware that her leg and arm were wrapped with muslin strips that had been soaked in liniment. She was familiar with its strong odor.

Rose felt the big white man wiping her arm, her forehead and her other leg with a cloth soaked in vinegar. She continued to lie still without uttering a sound.

Where am I? Who is this? How did I get here? she thought in silence.

She tried to sit up, but the man's strong arm kept her down.

Finally, the big man spoke, "You had a nasty fall, little lady. I saw your horse wandering around. I followed him for a while and he led me to you. You were unconscious, so I had to bring you here."

He continued, "You probably have some broken bones. You need to lie still for a few days. You feel quite warm, fever must be trying to set in. I fixed plenty broken bones during the war; don't you worry none, I'll have yours fixed in no time. Good thing I spotted your horse. I don't know how long you been out on the trail. I'll help you get better, then I'll see to it that you get home safely."

There were sharp pains shooting from Rose's head all the way down to her toes. She was afraid to cry out. She was afraid to say a word. He left her alone when he thought she had fallen asleep. But the pain was unbearable and eventually, Rose let out an uncontrollable moan. This brought the tall white man back to her side. He thought he heard her call out, "Papo, Papo."

This time, he gave her something in a cup and told her to swallow it. She was afraid but she was also desperate and suffering, therefore, she swallowed the liquid stuff. It made her cough and gag, but in the end, it all went down. In a few minutes, the man returned to the room with a bowl of peach leaves, which he placed, on her face and body to help in breaking fever and aid in relaxing her.

Whatever he did, it worked. She fell asleep and slept for several hours before she was awakened by the pale light rays of a new day. She was frightened at being in a white man's bed and thought she must be dreaming, but as she went to sit up, gripping pain went through her whole body. Then she remembered.

"Oh my God! Ma an' Pa Turner! They must think I run away agin, I got to tell them, I got to let them know!" she cried out in a weakened voice.

In a little while, the white man with the flowing hair and beard brought something for her to eat.

"Good morning, little lady," he greeted her. "I brought you some breakfast. You must be starved by now. How're you feeling? You had a rough night didn't you? Maybe you'll be better today."

He handed her a bowl of hot oatmeal and put a glass of milk on the nightstand.

Rose looked up at him with her big round eyes, the mellow sunlight adding brilliance to their amber hue.

"Where am I? I wants to go home," she said softly. "Ma an' Pa maybe out looking for me."

The man pulled up a chair and sat down.

"I have some questions too, he said. "Where did you come from and why were you riding on my property?" he asked in his deep voice. "No one ever comes on my property."

His words frightened Rose but she did not want him to know it.

"Some white boys thro'd rocks an' chased me an' my horse. We musta' took a wrong turn, then my horse, Spirit, jumped over a fallen tree, I fell to the ground an' hurt my leg," she replied softly, adding, "if you put me on my horse, I go home right now."

"You're in no shape to go anyplace, little lady," he said. "But in a day or two, I'll have you as good as new."

"No, no," Rose protested. "I have to go tell Ma an' Pa Turner. They'll think I ran away agin. You needs to unnerstan.' Where um at anyway an' who you?"

"My name is Jesse Ford, the white man said. "I own this land around here, almost three hundred acres in all. My brother, Frank, owns the land bordering mine. There are many wild stories in town about us being outlaws from the West; so no one around here has anything to do with us. Nobody sets foot on our land. Truth is, when we were here during the war, we saw this rich bottomland and bought it when the war was over 'cause the price was dirt-cheap. It should produce fine cotton along with a few other good crops."

"Please, sah," said Rose, not responding at all to what Mr. Ford had just said. Besides, she didn't understand the talk about "war" even though she had heard that word before. "I needs to let my Ma an' Pa know um all right," said Rose.

"We'll get you home, little lady, but your leg will need attention for another day or so. Your Ma and Pa will still be home waiting for you." Mr. Ford tried to reassure her.

"When I know that I can leave you alone, I'll do what I can to get word to them, but I need to get your fever to subside," he said. "If not, infection could set in."

Rose tried eating the bowl of oatmeal, but it tasted awful so she just left it on the stand. She needed some time to think about what her next move would be.

First, she was suspicious of a white man being so kind to her when she had been told to keep away from them, even told not to look at them. Her selling food to them was different; besides, she knew her customers thought she was an Indian. She heard them calling her names like "Squaw" and "Little Indian Maid."

She knew a little about slavery and about white people being mean and cruel but Papo had told her that every living thing comes from the one Great Spirit.

"Even the different animals of the forest respect each other," he had said, "therefore, we should not do less than they. The Great Spirit produces good!"

Rose kept her eyes on Mr. Ford as he left the room. She was sure something was wrong with her being in his house. She knew that Spirit was out in his barn, although she could not see the barn from where she was confined. When he goes to sleep, she thought, I'll get my horse and run away, I'm not afraid.

Later that night, when Rose heard Mr. Ford snoring, she decided it was time to go. She sat up and felt severe pain in her leg that went all the way to her back. She knew she could bear the pain, but she could not lift her leg. In her frustration, she cried out. Mr. Ford came running to her side and for the first time since the accident, tears came. She sobbed uncontrollably.

Mr. Ford, probably against his better judgment, cradled her in his arms and tried to comfort her. But all of the hurt and disappointment that was inside her began to pour from her small body. He tenderly patted her.

Later that night, when she needed to relieve herself, Mr. Ford put her on the nightjar. She was so embarrassed, she cried again. She knew then that she was helpless. Her leg was bound in splints and she couldn't even bend her knee.

When she finally settled down, Mr. Ford went to the sideboard and poured a glass of whiskey. He had the good sense to add honey and water to it, making it easier for her to swallow. He coaxed her into drinking it all and then he eased her back into bed. When she fell asleep, the last thing she remembered was seeing him sitting quietly in the chair looking at her.

On the third day of her stay in Mr. Ford's house, she asked to be carried to the kitchen to do some cooking. She had been unable to eat anything Mr. Ford made for her. To her surprise, the kitchen was separated from the house. It was connected by a breezeway. Rose thought it was about the strangest thing she had ever seen. Kitchens were always connected to the house. In places where she had lived, people always slept in kitchens. In her mind, a kitchen was part of the house!

"Why it's not in the house?" asked Rose.

"Because of the dangers of fire. With all of the fire that's necessary for cooking, you could have a fire at anytime and lose the whole house. This way, if there is a fire, you only lose the kitchen."

Rose was so preoccupied with her thoughts about this strange arrangement, she never replied to his explanation about the location of the kitchen.

She told him what items to bring to the table and how to make the fire in the wood stove just right, even though she had never seen a stove as grand as this one. In just a short time, the kitchen was smelling like Mr. Ford had never known it could.

Rose learned how difficult it was to prepare a good meal while sitting in a chair with one leg propped in another. Her arm was not broken as he had feared, only bruised and sprained. Nevertheless, she carefully prepared an interesting dinner, which included 'Hoppin John' made with ham hocks, rice, okra and corn bread. Mr. Ford brought up some canned peaches from the cellar to finish off this wonderful meal.

"That's the tastiest food I have ever eaten," declared Mr. Ford. "Maybe I can hire you as my housekeeper." His words were intended as a compliment, but Rose bristled at the very thought. She loved her business and never intended to work for anyone except herself.

She smiled and said, "I thanks you kindly, sah, but I mus' get home to my family."

"I plan to take you tomorrow. Your leg appears healed enough to make the ride. Now tell me about your family," he inquired.

Rose quietly told him about the Turners and how she had come to live with them. After hearing her story, he understood her eagerness to want them to know she was safe and had no intentions of leaving them. He hoped, for her sake, she would be up to the journey tomorrow.

That night, a terrible thunderstorm blew in from the northwest. The lightning was so fierce, it lit up the whole area. The claps of thunder were so violent, they caused Rose to shake and to worry about her family. The water came down in torrents and quenched the parched lands of the countryside. The sky opened and the rains pelted the area for two days with little let up.

There was flooding everywhere. The gulleys overflowed, water came up on the lawn and surrounded the barn. The streams that fed into the river spilled over and the nearby meadows became swamps. Mr. Ford spent a good part of the time making sure the animals were safe and dry. He checked the river. It was not at flood level.

All the roads and lanes would be impassable except by horseback and Mr. Ford knew that Rose was in no shape to travel on her horse. She had not healed enough to withstand such a rough ride on back trails, even though she tried to convince Mr. Ford she could ride on Spirit and, what's more, she could even go home alone if he just pointed her in the direction of the train station.

Mr. Ford knew she could not make it very far and he fully intended to take Rose home, himself. He was strangely curious about this beautiful, dark skinned young lady with wide amber eyes and long black hair, who was also a wonderful cook. He could not bear to let her disappear as mysteriously as she had appeared. Perhaps, he thought, she would reconsider his offer and come to work for him.

After five days and nights at Mr. Ford's home, the conditions were finally right for the trip to the Turners' place. When Mr. Ford carried Rose outside, she observed that his wagon had been made comfortable for what would be a long, rough ride.

Spirit was hitched to the back of the wagon. The roads were still an awful mess from the storm but Rose was just spunky enough to want to ride on Spirit instead of in the wagon. It took Mr. Ford a long time to convince her that his way was the best and most sensible way to go.

Rose knew that in order to have it her way, she would have to wait a few more days since her leg had not healed sufficiently. But she'd barely been able to wait until now, so she agreed to travel his way. Her heart and soul began to exult with joy at the prospect of being reunited with her family. How she had missed them!

The time she spent in Mr. Ford's home had been like a strange dream. She was thankful that he found her and took her to his home and cared for her so graciously and tenderly. Just the thought of all the attention he had given her brought a smile to her face and many questions to her thoughts. She would deal with the reality of it all later. Now she was on her way home!

She knew her family had grieved and worried about her whereabouts. She knew also they would wonder where this strange white man came from. But Rose was too happy to dwell on this now. The wagon wheels were bumping and grinding over the rough roads. She didn't care, In a short while she would be seeing her family again!

Mr. Ford had to head towards the train station because then Rose could give him clear directions for getting to her house. When they neared the station, Rose crouched down with her head covered.

Mr. Ford asked, "Is there something wrong, Rose?"

"Nosah." she responded. The truth was, she felt uncomfortable in this white man's wagon. And, above all, she did not wish to be seen

She tried to think of something else to say, then silently thought, but never said aloud, I don't wanna be seen ridin' in a wagon with no white man.

Rose did not raise her head up until they neared the gate to the Turner Farm. The children were the first to hear the wagon coming. Mr. Turner thought he recognized Spirit, but when he didn't see Rose, his heart sank!

Chapter Five

Pa! Pa!" Rose shouted! "Um home!"

Simultaneously, Zeke and the boys began running towards the wagon as Jesse Ford brought it to a rolling stop. The boys jumped in and greeted Rose with hugs and kisses.

Zeke began to shout, "Thank you, Jesus! You brot' our Rose home! We was worried to death!"

Then he guided the wagon slowly into the yard, where Mamie stood holding the baby with Annie clutching at her skirts.

"Praise God! Praise God A'mighty!" Mamie shouted over and over.

Jesse Ford sat in silence watching this family reclaim their 'lost' daughter. Zeke picked her up from the wagon and saw that she was hurt. That's when the jumping, shouting and hugging stopped. That's when they really noticed the man who was driving the wagon. Saw that he was a white man. A white man!

At that moment, Jesse Ford got out of the wagon and introduced himself to Rose's family. He quickly explained to them the events of the last few days. That was when Zeke saw the holsters with two six shooters in them. He also saw a rifle strapped on the horse.

Mamie quieted the children in order to hear and understand every word the big white man with long hair and long matching beard was trying to tell them. He told them about the accident, how he had found Rose unconscious, with a broken leg and bruised arm, and how she had run a high fever and could not be safely moved.

"We would have come two days ago, but the big storm made travel impossible. We had to wait it out."

Jesse Ford told them how he had tended many wounded soldiers during the War Between the States, and he figured that Rose's leg was going to heal nicely. He'd made a good splint so the bone should set well. But if they were worried, there was a Doctor Johnston in the next town, they could take her to have the leg checked.

The Turners had never been to a doctor and the next town was half a day's journey away. They trusted this stranger because he brought their daughter home and because he showed compassion and kindness. They had never felt this way about any white people with whom they had come in contact.

The Turners thanked Mr. Ford for saving their daughter's life and for returning her safely home. Mamie told him to wait while she fixed him a basket of goodies to express their appreciation for what he had done. Zeke offered to pay him for his troubles.

"Weren't no trouble a'tall," Jesse Ford responded.

In a few minutes Mamie appeared with a basket filled with jars of canned jams, jellies fruits and vegetables. She also added some cooked black-eyed peas and okra.

"These come from Rose's garden; we put 'em up last fall. You'll find they's mighty good eatin," she said.

"Thank you, Mam. Based on Rose's cooking, I can believe that."

Jesse Ford and his horse and wagon headed back up the road.

Mamie herded her family inside and directed them to sit around the table.

"It is now time" she stated, "to give praise an' thanks to the Almighty for sending Rose back to us an' for the stranger what took her in. Thank you, Jesus!"

They sang and praised God for the next thirty minutes. Mamie prayed a prayer that seemed to last forever. This was followed by singing the Spiritual, "Didn't My Lord Deliver Daniel!"

Didn't my Lord deliver Daniel,
deliver Daniel, deliver Daniel?
Didn't my Lord deliver Daniel,
An' why not a' every man

The celebration ended with another Spiritual, "Let Us Break Bread Together

The children became too restless for them to continue praying and singing any longer, which was surely what Mamie had intended to do.

After supper, they sat around talking and enjoying just being together again as a complete family. Eventually, Mamie and Zeke put the children down for the night, although Ephriam and Samuel resisted. They wanted Rose to tell them a story; this time it was just another excuse to stay up longer. But Mamie and Zeke sternly "shooed" them off to bed.

As soon as they thought all of the children were asleep, a barrage of questions started coming.

"Have you ever seen the boys who throwed rocks at you?"

"Did this ever happen befo'?"

"Where was you when this took place?"

"How did you end up on Mr. Ford's property?"

"What did he do to you?"

"What did he say to you?"

"Where did you sleep?"

"Where did he sleep?"

"What did he do to your leg?"

"What did he tell you about hisself?"

"Where is his house?"

"How come he so kind?"

Rose took her time and answered each question carefully and she reconstructed the events on the day of the accident. Mamie and Zeke appeared to be satisfied with her answers and the information she gave them.

After she had told them all that she could remember, Zeke said he had overheard stories about the two white brothers from out west settling in the area. He had also heard the brothers always wore their holsters with six shooters and carried rifles on their horses.

Some of the gossip making the rounds said they were outlaws running away from lawmen. Still another rumor said maybe they were deserters from the Union Army or maybe heaven forbid! the Confederate Army. All of those rumors kept the locals from having any association with the Ford Brothers.

Another week went by before Rose could put any weight on her foot. She stayed home with the children while Mamie went to the field to help Zeke with chopping cotton.

This time alone with the children gave Rose some understanding of how to deal with and solve the multitude of problems that, heretofore, she had not especially taken note of. She learned that Susie, the baby, was the easiest one to care for.

Rose was delighted when she was finally able to hobble out to her garden. She was surprised to see how much it had grown. What she had not known was that Zeke and the boys had carefully weeded it and even transplanted some of the vegetables.

Again, she was reminded of how blessed she was to have such a loving and good family. Tears came to her eyes when she thought about all of the miraculous events that had taken place during these last five years of her life. She knew that it had been an adventurous journey and that somehow, this interesting passage had made her a special person.

The day finally came for Rose to go back to her selling at the train station. She was up as soon as the sun's warm rays caressed her face. Rose moved about as quietly and as deftly as a church mouse so she would not awaken anyone at this early hour. She dressed quickly and hurried out to her garden to gather vegetables while they were at their peak.

Afterwards, she laid out everything she would be taking to the station. Then she started a fire in the stove to get it ready for cooking breakfast.

About mid-morning, Rose went to the shed to place the saddle blanket on Spirit. Mamie had designed the blanket with special pockets for holding the canned goods. Rose thought Mamie was surely the smartest woman around because she could always come up with ideas for solving most of their problems.

Once everything was in place, Rose was off. She was a little cautious because she was thinking about the last time she was on this same road. What she didn't know this time, was that Zeke was on his mule trailing her at a safe distance.

It seemed odd to her that some of her customers told her they were glad to have her back, but no one questioned where she had been. People seemed to take things in stride in this quiet, rural southern town.

By mid afternoon, Rose had sold everything she had. She was always pleased when that happened because it meant she could travel home at a fast pace. She loved it when she could take Spirit at top galloping speed. And she had the distinct feeling that the horse liked it, too.

Unexpectedly, Rose saw an imposing, yet familiar looking, figure on horseback riding as fast as she was, going through the woods. At first, she thought it might be trouble. Her heart began to beat faster and just for an instant, she was afraid. But like always, she remembered Papo's advice, "Never be afraid!"

Rose began to go slower. The strange horseman slowed his pace. She increased Spirit's gallop. The galloping horseman quickened his pace. Abruptly, Rose brought Spirit to a complete halt. Then out of the thicket rode the immense horseman. She was both speechless and relieved. It was Mr. Ford!

He rode up beside Rose's horse. "Hi ya, Rose. I thought I saw you at the station today. I have seen you there before, but I didn't recognize you under that pretty bonnet that covers too much of your face."

"Yessah," answered Rose, "I sells my food at the station but I don' make trouble fo' nobody."

"You're no trouble, Rose. Maybe I can buy some of your food if you have any left. I want to talk to your Pa and Ma. In the meantime, I'll be happy to ride 'shotgun' for you," he smiled.

That statement went right over Rose's head. Even though she saw his guns, she didn't understand the words "ride shotgun."

Mr. Ford followed Rose to the Turner farm. By the time they arrived, the family was outside waiting because they had both heard and seen them coming.

Zeke had a worried look on his face and wondered what trouble Rose was in this time. He could think of no other reason for Mr. Ford to be arriving with Rose unless something bad had happened.

Jesse Ford quickly dismounted and greeted them, "Afternoon, Mr. and Mrs. Turner, I trust everyone is well."

Zeke and Mamie were puzzled by his politeness. They had never been addressed as Mr. and Mrs. by a white person. Mr. Ford was the kindest and most polite white person they had ever met.

"It seems as if Rose was plumb out of food to sell, so I followed her home to see if I'd be able to purchase some fresh vegetables and to see if you have any of those sweets that you both make so well. I can still taste that wonderful food you gave me when I brought Rose home after her accident," he added. "And if it's all the same with you folks, I'd like to come here and place my orders 'cause I don't like going to town and I know the folks in town like it that way."

"It be all right wit' us," Zeke said. "You a mighty friendly white man. Better be careful, though, it could cause you trouble in these parts."

"Now don't you worry 'bout that," replied Mr. Ford, "I reckon I can handle any problems that come my way. I know that people 'round here already have their own misguided opinions and thoughts about both me and my brother. Maybe one day they'll understand and know the whole truth."

They completed the transaction. Mr. Ford ordered molasses bread and teacakes and said he'd be back the following week to pick up his order.

"While you're at it," he continued, "I'd like a pot of chicken and dumplins' and also some mustard greens."

Just as he had promised, Mr. Ford returned to the Turner Farm a week later to pick up the items he had ordered. First, though, he asked Zeke to show him around the farm. Zeke obliged, and the two of them rode off on horseback discussing how best to grow certain crops, especially cotton, in this region.

Mamie turned to Rose and said, "There's somethin' real odd 'bout that Mr. Ford, ya mark my words."

"What you reckon it is?" questioned Rose. "He seems normal like to me. Course, I don' quite know how white men 'spose to act."

"Well, they sho' don't visit with colored folks," responded Mamie. "I jus' can't figure it out."

After a while, the men returned to the house. Mr. Ford paid for his food and reminded them of his order for the coming week. He said good-by to the family and went down the lane whistling a tune.

"Now, that is 'bout the strangest thing I seen lately. Why do that white man want to order food from us all of a sudden like?" Mamie questioned. "I don' know if I like this a'tall."

Rose looked at Mamie and said, "Well, I don't see nothin' unusual 'bout it. I sells most ev'rythin I take to the station to white folks n' you never question 'bout that."

"Tha's different," answered Mamie. "They don' come to the house n' they don' even know yo' name. Now, get this through yo' head, white folks don' have nothin' to do with Negroes less'n they buyin', sellin' or workin'."

"Befo' us got our freedom," she continued. "White folks say we chil'ren of the devil, an' then, they teached us to be Christins.' Now, they wants to kill us. Tell me, who can understan' they strange habits?"

Late spring was always a busy time on the farm. Mamie wanted this year's crop to be the best yet because she had heard there were some plans being made to open up a school in the fall of the year. She wanted her children, who were old enough, to attend, and she wanted to be available to do whatever she could to help out. Even when she was a child, her papa told her how important it was to learn to read and write.

Rose was doing exceptionally well with her business and the money it earned, plus the money from the cotton gave them a decent living. For the Turners, life was moving along smoothly.

They were able to accomplish this by working as a family unit. They all had a job to do. Zeke, Mamie and Rose did the heavy work. The children helped according to their age and size. They chopped cotton. They helped with the picking. They fed and watered the animals. They gathered fruits and vegetables, both on the farm and those that grew wild. They collected fresh eggs and kept the hen house clean and safe from predators.

Mamie was the backbone of the family. She could always make a way out of no way. It was obvious that she had a good head on her shoulders. She knew how to barter instead of using money for needed items. She made clothing for everyone and she made sure they grew all of the food they ate.

Zeke provided a quiet strength and dedication for his family because his mother had instilled in him teachings from her African heritage, especially the importance of family and children.

There was a sense of balance on the Turner Farm. Above everything else, there was a sense of respect both from the parents and the children. In the midst of it all, they loved one another. Rose knew she was finally in a safe place.

Mr. Ford continued to drop by, sometimes twice each month to place his order and to pick up his food. He seemed thoroughly pleased with this arrangement. On one of his visits, his brother, Frank, came along with him and placed his own order. Frank would be unable to come on a regular basis but would make it every now and then. At other times, he could pick up items from his brother's home which was closer to his own place.

Mamie asked them if they would arrange to come after sunset. She was beginning to like the two men and thought they were quite friendly and honest but she did not trust the other white people in the town or on the near-by farms. With a nod of understanding, the brothers agreed to always arrive after sunset. With that decision, Mamie breathed a sigh of relief.

The whole family stood watching the Ford Brothers ride off until they seemed to be swallowed up by the rolling hills in the distance.

"Do you think they was once slave hunters?" Mamie asked her husband. "I've never seed men wit' so many guns befo'!"

"Now, calm yo'self, woman. Mr. Ford tol' us once, an' he tol' me again, that him an' his brother was Union Soldiers an' they come south to buy farmland. He has ax' me a lot of questions 'bout clearing virgin land an' 'bout growing cotton. I guess he jus' one good white man. After all, we was tol' there was some white people that helped slaves 'scape to freedom, so there mus' be some good white peoples."

The Ford Brothers continued to drop by the farm on a regular basis to pick up food items and to discuss farming. Of course, Jesse came more often than Frank, and he always purchased a few items for his brother. Rose and the Turners considered them their very best customers. Mamie, however, still thought the Fords were strange men.

That year was a very good year for Rose's business. Mamie and Zeke were more than pleased with the money she was giving them. Most of it was put in cans and jars.

For a rainy day," Mamie said.

Chapter Six

The next few weeks Mamie was busy making clothes for the children because they would be attending school right after crop gathering. The whole household was excited about the new school which would open at their very own church in the fall.

"We can all learn to read an' write!" announced Mamie, proudly.

Only Rose was indifferent about the whole thing. She remained silent.

Mamie continued, "Um 'so happy I could shout!"

Rose was working extra hard these days at her selling, because she had decided she never wanted to pick cotton again. If need be, she would use her own money to pay someone to help Zeke in the field. Besides, she loved tending her garden, cooking, her work at the station and riding her horse.

On days when she finished early at the train station, she found herself guiding Spirit in the direction of the oak tree over in the meadow. She would tie Spirit to a small tree and then scamper up the big oak, using the same climbing techniques that Papo had taught her so long ago. She always felt such exhilaration and freedom when she sat high up in that tree. An euphoric feeling came over her that she never experienced at any other place. This was her private hideaway! From this place, she could connect with nature. Here, she could commune with Papo and the Great Spirit. She could talk with Jesus, the Heavenly Father. She could have beautiful visions about what her future might be.

It was in this tree, too, that Rose thought about Mr. Ford. She recollected how he tended to her injuries and cooled her fevers. She remembered how he brought in a night jar, sat her on it and left the room so she could eliminate in private.

She thought about all the food he bought from her. It always seemed that he purchased more than one person could ever eat. And he also paid her a few cents more than was asked. He really is a strange man, she thought, just like Mamie had said. More than a few times, he rode "shotgun" as she made her way home from the train station. Yet, he always remained some distance behind her. There were times when she knew he was there and there were times when she never knew.

a school opens. . . . .

Near the end of October, 1878, the new school opened just as it had been announced. They had to wait until the crops were gathered. Mamie was the most excited member in the household on that first day of school. She was up long before daybreak, making breakfast and lunches at the same time. When she was finished with the food, she got everyone out of bed.

"Get up, get up ever'body, we' goin' to school today! Ain't that jus' wonderful? We' going to learn how to read an' write. This is the second most 'portant day in our life," she proclaimed!

"Um not going!" yelled Rose. "Um too old to go to school! Besides I got my business to take care of. I knows how to sell my goods n' count my money, tha's all I need to know."

Mamie waited for Rose to finish her protesting, then she spoke softly, "Rose, when I was held in slavery, I heard whites say that if slaves learn to read, they know what we know, then they think they jus' as smart as we are. Ever' since," she added, "I wanted to learn how to read n' write. We ain' gonna miss this chance. It may never come again. An' Rose, we is jus' as smart as they is. Remember that, ya hear!"

A few minutes later, the whole Turner Family, except Rose, was in the wagon and on their way to the Sunrise Colored Methodist Church. Rose had insisted on riding Spirit, and Mamie reluctantly agreed.

The Turners arrived thirty minutes ahead of the scheduled time and found several families already inside talking with the teacher. Rose, however, remained outside. More families continued arriving, all eager for some kind of schooling. Some children walked for miles, some came on mules, and some came in wagons.

At precisely nine o'clock, there was the clanging of metal on a suspended horseshoe. Boys and girls, both large and small, moved inside the church and joined the others. Some parents followed after them, anxious to learn about the new school The Rev. Pennywell opened with a prayer of thanksgiving and praise and asked everyone to join in singing his favorite Spiritual:

> Oh, freedom! Oh, freedom!
> Oh, freedom over me!
> And before I'd be a slave,
> I'll be buried in my grave,
> And go home to my Lord and be free!

Afterwards, Rev Pennywell introduced Mr. Bowen, the new teacher, who was from Georgia. Mr. Bowen greeted everyone, thanked them for coming and told about his background. He had been assigned by the church to come to this location and teach for one school year. He informed them that a white Methodist Church in Pennsylvania would pay his salary. They had also sent some books and other learning materials. He would need some help from a few of the adults and they too, were welcome to come study and learn, whenever possible.

After considerable discussion, wrangling and compromise, Mamie finally persuaded Rose that she should attend school at least an hour or two each day for a month. At the end of that time, they could make a final decision about her continued attendance. Rose would keep her promise. Mamie hoped she would change her mind, and continue school after the month was up.

"I go for a little while," agreed Rose. "But I can't be neglectin' my business. I already learnt' what I needs to know, how to make m'self enough money."

At the end of the four week period, Rose went to her favorite place to think about what she was going to tell Mamie concerning her decision not to continue school. She was dreaming about her future selling plans. By now, she understood well the necessity of having your own money. And she certainly knew how to make money.

Rose was happy when she was at this place. As she climbed up the big oak, her head was completely filled with possibilities for expanding her business. She would sit in this massive tree and talk to the wind which always made her feel better. Then the spirits would help her to make suitable decisions.

She was so preoccupied in her thoughts she never heard the rider who stopped just a little way from the tree. The sun was beginning to set as she started to climb from her perch. She was feeling comfortable with the decisions she had made.

"Rose." She heard someone softly whisper her name.

"Don't be frightened, I just want to talk to you. I've seen you go up the tree before and I guessed it was your secret place. But you were up there so long this time, is something wrong?" The voice belonged to Jesse Ford.

She was almost in tears because she'd never done anything to make Mamie unhappy. And this was the first time she would rebel against Mamie's wishes. Rose knew Mamie was probably right, as she usually was, but she also knew that school simply wasn't for her. She was already good at growing and selling and that was what she wanted most to do.

"Mr. Ford," she said in an unsteady voice, "Ma said I should go to the new school so I can learn to read an' write but I don't have time to do that. I got my business to run."

"Now you just take your time, Rose, and tell me the whole story, maybe I can help you," replied Mr. Ford.

"I always do ever'thing Ma an' Pa ask me to do. They took me in an' raise' me just like I was they own, but now I'm all grown up an' I can take care of m'self. I like what I do an' there just ain't 'nough time in the day to do ev'rythin' that's required plus all the time that it takes goin' back an' forth to sell at the station."

Rose was speaking so rapidly, her words were beginning to run together.

"Whoa! Slow down, Rose. You're talking faster then I can hear," proclaimed Mr. Ford, interrupting her flow. "Here, let me put my blanket down and we can sit and try to sort out this whole school predicament."

Rose sat quite still on the blanket for a moment, silent in her thoughts. Then she jumped up. Her voice was still quivering as she pronounced, "I will not go to school an' that's that!"

"My offer is still open for you to come live in my house and be my housekeeper," Mr. Ford said in an appealing voice.

"I thanks you just the same, Mr. Ford, but as I said befo,' an' I say agin', I will only work fo' m'self!"

"Sit down, Rose," said Mr. Ford, gently. "You said that you were no longer a child, so let's talk about this and come up with some answers to help satisfy everyone."

"But you a white man. My Ma an' Pa says white folks don't like Negro folks an' they can never be your friends."

Mr. Ford thought for a minute and replied in a soft voice.

"You know that isn't exactly true, don't you? You and your family are my friends, in fact, you're my only friends in these parts. And, Rose, you have become a very special little lady to me. You are so sweet, innocent and lovely. Just looking at the cute expression on your face right now, causes fish to swim around in my stomach."

"It' gettin' dark, I better be gettin' home," Rose said as she got to her feet again.

The truth was that she didn't know how to respond to Mr. Ford's words. She knew he liked and even respected her family, but that was an unacceptable liaison around here. She had heard Mamie and Zeke talk about Mr. Ford many times. Their conversations left her with more questions than answers. And she had emphatically been told to keep away from white men.

"We haven't solved the school problem and we need to do that before you go home," said Jesse Ford. "I have something to propose that may help you in making your decision.

"On my last trip to Houston, I bought a carriage. I never use it, it just sits there. I'll loan it to you and you can use it to take the children to school and then use it to transport your goods to the station. Try it for a while, if it doesn't work out, then you can make another decision."

This proposition sounded exciting to Rose. She had seen buggies only on rare occasions and thought how grand they were! But never, even in a wild dream, would she think she could actually drive one. She promised to give the idea a try.

As she was about to mount Spirit for the ride home, Mr. Ford said to her, "Rose, you look like you could use a hug. I know I could sure use one. It's been a long time since I had someone give me a hug, may I?"

Rose started backing up, her mouth open in a frozen expression.

"Rose, it's all right. I would never do anything to hurt you. Remember, you spent five days alone with me in my home. I washed you and tended you. I saw your nakedness and I helped to dress you. Did I offend you in any way?"

Rose opened wide her arms and he embraced her tenderly and the hug became warm and strong with a good feeling. Rose experienced a tingling sensation in her whole body, one that she had never felt before and it was wonderful and good as she stood there with her head buried in his chest.

She uttered, "Thank-you, thank-you, Mr. Ford. You' a good an' kind friend. I guess we both needed a hug."

Jesse Ford slowly released his hold on her and tilted her chin upward so their eyes could meet.

"Rose," he said, "I promise never to do anything that would offend you. You are so beautiful, pure and precious. I just know it's providence that brought us together. Someday you'll see, Rose. We can be friends. We will be friends," he reassured her.

Jesse followed Rose to the gate that opened to the lane leading to the Turner place. He stood at a distance and watched as Rose slowly rode to the house. It was unusual for her to arrive this late and to come in at such a pace.

Mamie was the first one out the door, "What's a' matter, Rose, what's wrong? Why you so late? You sick? Anyone bother you? You okay?" she questioned, all without taking a breath.

"Everything's fine, Ma," answered Rose. But Mamie knew better.

After supper and after the children were put to bed, Mamie and Rose were finishing up their usual night chores when suddenly Mamie asked a question.

"Care to tell me what' on your mind?"

Rose gave a faint smile and responded.

"You don't miss much, do you, Ma? Mr. Ford came to the station today."

"I knew it! I knew it! I knew all 'long that white man was up to no good! Did he insult you, did he try to rape you? Pretending to be our friend"

"No, Ma. Mr. Ford didn't do any of them things. He truly is our friend. In fact, he say that we the only friends he have. Ma, he wants to let us use his buggy."

Rose told Mamie about their conversation concerning school and the use of the buggy. But she did not tell her about the tree and the hug nor the strange but wonderful feelings that went through her body when he hugged her and how good she felt in his strong arms.

` ` ` ` ` ` ` ` ` ` `

That night, after finally getting to sleep, Rose kept dreaming the same dream over and over again. She kept going to sleep and waking up. And when she'd get back to sleep, the dream would continue in the same manner.

She dreamed that she was living with Mr. Ford as his housekeeper. And in each dream vignette, he was good and kind to her but she did not like being a housekeeper and she pointedly told him so! His answer each time was that she was so beautiful and so wonderful and he was so lucky to have her in his home. And he begged her to stay with him forever.

As dawn peeped over the horizon to welcome the day, Rose awakened to the sound of voices coming from outside. Of course, she knew Pa's voice and she thought the other was... she raced to the window to make sure. It was! She almost said his name aloud, Mr. Ford. At the mere sight of him, her heart began to pound so loud and fast, she thought for sure she was going to yell out.

Rose sat very still beside the window, peeping and listening. She heard Mr. Ford and Pa talking about clearing the land and getting it ready for plantin' cotton come next spring.

"Oh, my God!" she exclaimed aloud, when she realized that the two men were standing next to a buggy.

"Lookit that! It's beautiful."

"What's a matter?" Mamie yelled, as she jumped out of bed, "we late for school?"

This time, Rose's stay in school lasted almost two weeks. She learned to recognize the letters of the alphabet and how to read and write numerals. Best of all, she learned how to compute. Arithmetic was her favorite subject. She had little or no interest in anything else. On her ninth day of attendance, she boldly announced that she would not return. She added that she had more important things to do.

The following day, she used all of her time preserving fruits, canning vegetables and making breads and teacakes. Mamie had taken the children to school in the buggy. By the time the entire family was home, Rose was finished with her chores and had supper waiting on the stove.

Mamie took one look around the kitchen, and after surveying everything, she knew that Rose had made a decision which was best for her. In fact, Rose looked happier than Mamie had seen her look in a long time.

A few people at school and at church inquired about the buggy. But most of them knew how long and hard Rose worked so they probably concluded that she had saved enough money to buy most anything she wanted.

On Saturday, when she went to the station in her buggy, she arranged to leave Spirit and the buggy next to the home of one of the church members. By now, it seemed that no one cared who Rose was or where she came from. They were more interested in her wonderful foods and the low prices she charged. Indeed, she had a loyal and grateful following.

When Rose started home that afternoon, she was sure she was being followed. Her keen eyes and ears told her that it was Mr. Ford who was keeping his distance behind her. She could feel her heart pounding and also feel the sense of joy leaping around inside of her. She wasn't sure why, but his presence made her feel awfully good. After a while, she knew that he was no longer there, but she never knew when or how he disappeared.

Rose realized that she had come to the exact spot she had been when the white boys began throwing rocks at her. That was the time she met Mr. Ford. She never thought she would ever see him again after he took her home. She never dreamed a white man could be friends with Negro people.

"I really do like him," she murmured to herself. "He' a real gentleman, a good man."

As she slowed to negotiate a turn in the road, she was suddenly aware that he was standing there, gently calling out her name, "Rose, follow me," he directed her. "I need to talk to you. I know a spot where no one will see us."

Rose hesitated. Should she dare to follow him? In her head she wasn't sure it would be all right, but in her heart, she wanted to go. So she followed her heart.

They went down the road she had taken to escape from the boys. It led to the same lane where she had fallen and been rescued by Mr. Ford. This time, she was aware of where she was going but she silently questioned why.

In a short while, he guided her away from the lane to a spot under an old magnolia tree whose large white blossoms were languishing but were still fragrant, even under a cooling autumn sky.

"May I sit beside you in the carriage, Rose?"

She nervously uttered her permission. "I guess it's all right."

"Of course it's all right, I've given you my word that I'll never do or say anything to upset you." he answered, climbing into the buggy beside her. He carefully placed his rifle under the buggy seat but his holster was still around his hips. He noticed how Rose always looked at his guns but never said a word. He decided to put her at ease.

"Where I come from, a man always carries his guns with him 'cause he never knows when or where trouble will find him. Sometimes, a gun can be your best friend."

"Rose," he continued, "I've been doing an awful lot of thinking about you, about how lovely you are and how marvelous you are with everything you do. Well now, I'm a lonely man and I need some companionship." He paused. Then he looked into her eyes. " My heart and my soul have been telling me to ask you to be my wife."

He was nervous and he could feel his blood painting his skin bright red, but he continued. "We can't legally get married in this state, but nobody can keep us from living together just like a husband and wife. What I'm saying, Rose, is that I love you and I need you in my life, not just as a friend, I want you there with me all the time."

Rose sat with a blank expression on her face. There was a long, empty silence. Occasionally, you could hear the swish of bronze leaves falling to the ground. Or the call of a bird off in the distance. Then silence again.

"You're almost eighteen and a half years old, Rose, and that's plenty old enough to live as a wife. If you say yes, I'll talk to Zeke. I think I can convince him that I love you and this is the right thing to do. But you'll have to talk to Mamie; I'm not so sure that I can handle her."

"But, Mr. Ford," protested Rose, "we can't do that, white folks an' Negro folks can't even be together 'round here. Ma an' Pa says terrible things would happen to them."

"I don't worry none about what other people think," he quickly responded, and patted his gun saying, "One thing I learned well is how to take care of myself and my family." They sat in silence for a while.

"Do you have an answer, Rose? Or do you need some time to think about it?"

He put his strong arms around her and whispered softly in her ear.

"I love you! I want you to be with me. That's all that matters. You're a woman now and you need to express yourself as a woman. You need to love and be loved by a man and I want to be the one who teaches you the meaning of that."

Rose nestled her head into his chest and suddenly it occurred to her how small she seemed beside this man who was so different from everything she knew. She began to sob softly because she was unable to express the mixed up feelings she had. Jesse Ford leaned over and gently tried to kiss away her tears.

But it was her tears that told him she had warm feelings for him.

They sat embracing each other for a long time. Finally, she looked up at him and smiled. He began spontaneously kissing her fingers, her hands, arms, shoulders and neck. He held her at arm's length, looked deep into her amber eyes and she noticed tears welling up in his eyes.

He kissed her chin, her cheeks, her ears, her nose, her forehead, and then, he gently kissed her lips. He could feel the soft, sensuous movements of her body, but outwardly, she was not responding. He sensed that she was very afraid.

"Rose," he whispered, "I am sure, beyond a reasonable doubt, that we are meant to be together. Whenever I see you, I have this strong stirring in my body and I sense that you have it, too. Desire is a gift from God and so is our friendship. You needn't be afraid."

He abruptly released his hold on her and quietly asked her a question.

"Did Mamie and Zeke ever talk to you about love between a man and a woman?"

"No," she replied. "They don't talk like that."

"Just what I thought" he said to himself. But to Rose he said, "When I have your answer about sharing life with me, then we can discuss a warm, passionate, loving relationship between a man and a woman. We have to talk to Zeke and Mamie right away. I don't want them thinking I'm trying to take advantage of you. I need their friendship. Let's meet here four weeks from today and I'll ask you for your answer."

He accompanied her back to the main road and watched her as she headed off in the direction of home. When at last she was out of sight, he turned on his steed and galloped back in the opposite direction, toward his own home.

For the next few weeks, Rose tried to lose herself in her work. She picked and canned the autumn fruits. She dried peas and beans. She gathered nuts. She washed and ironed everyone's clothes. She cleaned the house until it was spotless. She provided food for the men when they slaughtered the hogs.

Rose simply did not know how to deal with Mr. Ford's proposition. On several occasions, she wanted to discuss it with Mamie but she knew her opinions about whites and Negroes mixing.

Mamie was even afraid to have Mr. Ford visit there during daylight hours. Rose had trouble sleeping at night because she would dream again and again of being with Mr. Ford. One night she dreamed that the two of them climbed up the old oak tree and as they climbed, the tree grew taller and taller until it reached into the clouds and no one would ever know they were there.

"I could stay here forever and ever," she said.

"Only time goes forever and ever," he responded.

When Rose went to the station the next day, she made more money than she had ever made in a single day. She knew that was because she had worked such long hours and produced so many items. She had long since learned that persistence and hard work paid off and she was no stranger to hard work.

On her way home, she kept looking over her shoulder for Mr. Ford. She had a weird feeling that he was somewhere nearby, but she never saw him. Rose took Spirit as fast as he could safely go while pulling the buggy. When the weather was good, the buggy would glide over the red, clay covered, dirt roads. Today, it seemed to sail!

Rose continued to give Mamie and Zeke part of the money she earned and she put some in a jar for the children, a pattern she had developed of late. She truly wanted to tell Mamie about Mr. Ford, but each time she attempted to do so, she panicked. She knew that in a few days, she was expected to give him her answer.

Chapter Seven

As was their custom, the Turner Family went to church the following first Sunday. After almost two hours of the usual long prayers, the testifying, Scripture reading and the singing of several Spirituals, the Rev. Pennywell finally got up to preach. His sermons were always messages of hope, deliverance and justice. This one started out differently and in a different cadence. He was telling a story. An oral history.

His sermon got Rose's attention immediately. She sat there with her eyes and mouth opened as if she was hypnotized. Part of the story the Reverend Pennywell included in his sermon would change her life forever.

He told about his father, who was born a slave in South Carolina, but had been sold to someone who lived in Georgia. His father was a member of a Baptist church which had both colored and white members. They were served by the same minister. The whites went to service at eleven o'clock on Sundays and the coloreds went at three o'clock in the afternoon. At night services, both colored and white went at the same time. The whites sat up front and the coloreds in the rear. His father was a deacon in the church and his job was to look after the affairs of the colored members. He would report to the minister and a few of the white deacons, but the white deacons never reported to any colored deacon... Occasionally, however, a white deacon would visit with his father to discuss.

That part of the story kept ringing over and over in Rose's head. "So Negroes and whites do get together," she said to herself, "It really can happen, it really does happen."

By the time the good Reverend got to the part where his father had learned the trade of blacksmithing and finally was able to buy his freedom, Rose was fixated. His father returned to South Carolina, where he went to school and learned to read and write. He built his own business with the help of a white sponsor. He bought land, and together with a few relatives, became a successful farmer. When the war ended, he returned to Georgia.

Rose never heard the rest of that sermon. By now her imagination was working overtime and she began to wonder what life might really be like living with Mr. Ford.

"He is such a kind an' gentleman," she mused. "Maybe we can live together."

Rose already knew she liked Mr. Ford. Now she knew she could be with him and that she wanted to be with him. No one else had attracted her interest the way he had. She felt safe with him and when she was in his presence, her body filled up with butterflies and all kinds of beautiful dancing flowers and rainbows. He made her feel like racing in the wind, like picking lovely flowers and like galloping away on puffy clouds. Rose could hardly wait for the next few days to arrive. She had made her decision!

The night before she was to give her answer to Mr. Ford, she sat in the swing on the porch, with the children. They were swinging and singing one song after another, Spirituals, gospels, folk songs and silly songs. Everyone was feeling good and after a while, Rose decided to tell a story:

"There was once this little deer. She was the fastest and the faires' deer in the forest. She was always the firs' to know when there was trouble and she warned the other animals of the forest. Some of the animals were jealous of her because they thought that she got too much attention from the other animals. Faires' Deer played games with the other animals. They played hide-and-seek. They played follow-the-leader and other games, like race-across-the-meadow. Faires' Deer always won the races and the other animals always let her be the leader.

One day when they were playing hide-and-seek, Faires' Deer was caught in a trap and she could not escape. A few of the animals who saw her get caught were envious of her and pretended not to see her. They went to their forest homes without her an' reported that she ran away an' would never return. The older animals was very sad an' said they would miss Faires' Deer because she was the best an' kindes' animal in the whole forest.

But deep in the woods, an old Indian hunter had come upon this little deer in the trap. He decided that she was not quite big enough to take back to the tribe. Besides, he needs more than just one deer what with winter coming. Maybe she could lead him to other larger animals, so he sets her free. She ran an' the hunter tried to follow her, but she was too fast an' too smart for him. As she ran toward her home in the forest, she was also lookin' for her friends. When she stopped at a stream for a drink, she saw her reflection in the water an' suddenly, she realized that she had growed up. She was not such a little deer anymore. While she was drinkin,' she saw 'nother reflection in the water. It was a beautiful stag but its color was red, not brown like she was. He wanted her to go away with him but she wasn't sure that she should because his color was different than hers.

However, he was beautiful, bold, playful an' strong. " Maybe I go with him for a little while," Faires' Deer thought. "But I mustn't go too far from my family an' friends 'cause we'll miss each other too much."

Red Deer an" Faires' Deer are now the most beautiful deers in the entire forest an' all of the animals enjoy watchin' them run and play together. To this day, they're still tellin' the other animals when danger is near an' now they have the most beautiful fawn in the whole forest."

Mamie sang a soft lullaby, which told the children that it was time for bed.

"They enjoyed my story," said Rose as she prepared for bed. But it was neither her story nor going to sleep she was thinking about. She knew that Mr. Ford would be meeting her tomorrow.

Rose tossed and turned all night. She kept going over and over what she thought she would say when she saw him. She thought she would never fall asleep. As the new day dawned, however, she had to be awakened from a deep sleep.

Just as her previous day at the station had been her best, this day turned out to be one of her slowest. It was the first time in a long while that she did not sell everything she brought to the station. She had some teacakes and a few jars of preserves left. She packed up her belongings and began the journey of her life.

When she arrived at the fork in the road, her whole body was shaking. Jesse Ford was waiting there as she knew he would be. He had always kept his word. He guided Spirit and the carriage through the trees and into the clearing where they could be alone.

After settling the horses down, he climbed into the carriage and took Rose into his arms and gave her a kiss which she responded to with surprising feeling. Somehow, he knew that the key to his future was about to be revealed.

"How did Mamie take the news?" he asked.

"I didn't tell her," she answered, "I' just gon' run away like I useto."

"No, no, that won't do," he almost shouted, but knew that would upset her.

"Rose, I told you that we need them! We have to do this the right way. We have no other friends in this parish, or in this world, and you have to have friends to get by. We have to tell them, there's no other way."

Rose knew Mr. Ford was right, so she promised she would tell Mamie everything. She remembered the decision she had made in church last Sunday.

Jesse felt relieved with her promise to tell Mamie and he settled back to try and retrieve the happy feelings that had suddenly drained from him. He sat so still and quiet that Rose figured she had made a big mistake in not having told Mamie. She saw his disappointment. She had a feeling right then and there, that you did not want to make Mr. Ford angry. Even though he always appeared to be soft and gentle, he was also serious and determined.

She carefully observed him. He was so large in stature, so secure in his ability to be protective. So agile, strong and physical in appearance. Yet she saw a man who said he loved her and wanted her for his wife. At that moment, she felt she could love him and be happy with him even in this place which did not openly accept Negro and white relationships.

"Mr. Ford," she whispered at last, "I go an' live with you, but I want to go now."

"Whoa!" he bellowed, "That is not what we just said and that is not the way we're going to do it. You're going to tell Mamie and I'm going to have a man-to-man talk with Zeke about our plans. It is the right and proper thing to do."

Jesse gave Rose a big kiss and he held on to her for a long time. Divine exuberance filled both their hearts as they clung to one another, feeling their love.

"Mr. Ford," she whispered, "the earth just moved."

"That was my heart,' he said, as he gathered her in his arms once more.

"My lovely and beautiful Rose, everything will work out! From now on, you'll be my sweetheart, my wife, my bride and my mate. I will always love you and whatever we do, we'll do together."

He looked into her deep amber eyes and whispered, "Darling Rose, the good Lord meant us to be together, and together we shall be, until death!"

Jesse Ford sent her home to tell Mamie about their decision. He would be there first thing the next morning to have his talk with Zeke.

Rose gave Jesse the left over jars of preserves and tea-cakes and headed for home feeling both exhilaration and condemnation.

She traveled at a snail's pace trying to compose the words she would use to tell Mamie about her relationship with Mr. Ford.

"This is not going to be easy," she said aloud as she entered the gate to the farm.

She decided that the best time to talk with Mamie was when the two of them were cleaning up after supper. But the children asked Rose to tell them a story. When she said she was too tired from the day's activities, Ephriam asked if Mamie and Ezekiel would tell them some more about the times when they were slaves.

"Now, you get this here straight, Ephriam. I don't wanna hav' to tell you this no mo'. Your Pa n' me wasn't no slaves! White people don' stole our ancestors an' brought them to this land in captivity. In our minds, hearts an' spirits, we was always free. My Ma don' told that to me, her Ma told it to her an' she told me to tell my young uns' that they ain't never no slaves. They be captives in a strange land an' just 'cause you captive, don't make you no slave. Yo' mind an' yo' spirit be free an' one day your body be free, too.

"I 'member when my Papa ran away. Said he was headed for a place called Hamburg, South Ca'lina, where he last saw his Papa when the two of them were sold. He heard his Papa went to work on the railroad in Georgia. My Papa said that his papers showed that he belonged to a man in Newman, Georgia.

"He knew that it would be a treach'rous journey but he wanted to go farther north 'cause he had heard 'bout some of the 'scape routes to Canada. He left Ma an' the children to look for his Papa an' to look for freedom. Papa returned only once that I know of. He come an' took my two brothers an' said he' come back fo' us when they found a safe place up no'th. We never heard from him again. I think po' Ma died from a broken heart. Papa was a free man, but he wanted his body an' his fam'ly be free."

Mamie talked in this manner for a long time and afterwards, everyone joined her in singing some of her favorite Spirituals and she shouted out, "Free At Last."

Rose knew this was a terrible time to tell Mamie she was going to live with a white man. But at the same time, she knew she could not wait until morning when Mr. Ford would arrive.

` ` ` ` ` ` ` ` ` ` `

After the children were put down for the night, Rose softly called to Mamie.

"Ma, I needs to talk to you."

"Is you havin' a problem at the station, child?" asked Mamie.

"No, Ma," answered Rose. "Ma, Mr. Ford wants me to come live with him."

"I knew it, I knew it! I knew there was somethin' wrong with that white man from the beginning!" she yelled. "You just go tell your Mr. Ford, slavery is over! You gon' stay righthere."

"Ma, he ax me to marry him, but he said the State of Louisiana won't permit it, nor would any other state in the south." Replied Rose in a pitiful voice.

"Rose, Rose, my beautiful child, you don' know what you' saying. You can't do this! Has this Mr. Ford completely lost his mind? He's older than you. He must know he can't live with no Negro woman 'round here. Rose, you don' have to do this just 'cause he asked." she said.

"Ma, I know it seems strange, but Mr. Ford says he loves me, an' Ma, I think I loves him, too."

Rose spoke in a voice that was sounding stronger even though she was still afraid.

"No, no, Rose, you don' know what you' saying. You can't love no white man. A white man can't love you. White fo'ks, especially white men, is the enemy," Mamie tearfully responded. She even pleaded.

"What about that Price boy who's been tryin' to get your 'tention? You can really marry him, he make you a fine husban'. What I tryin' to say is, Rose, you needs a Negro husband. My God, Rose! Child, you don' know what you is saying!"

"Good night, Rose." Mamie abruptly ended the conversation. "I can't talk about this no mo' tonight, I gotta sleep onit."

Mamie continued. "The minute I laid eyes on that Mr. Ford, I knew there was something strange about him," she said under her breath as she went into her room.

Rose went out and sat in the swing for a long time. First, she thought about the feeling that came over her when Mr. Ford touched her. It was such a wonderful feeling. It caused delightful stirrings all inside her body. Feelings that she had never known before. Next, she thought about what Mamie had said and she knew there were some truths in her words. Especially about Negroes and whites. She knew that Mamie loved her and only wanted what would make her happy. What if Mamie was right?

She quickly dismissed the fears from her head and settled her thoughts on the magnificence and wonder of their love. They were just two people who desired to be together. This love between them had been planned by the Great Spirit, she thought.

"Maybe Jesus had a part in it, too."

Rose looked up at the stars and saw them twinkling and dancing and smiling at her. As she prepared for bed, she heard Mamie softly singing, "Over My Head, I See Trouble In The Air."

> Over my head, I see trouble in the air
> Over my head,I see trouble in the air
> There must be a God somewhere

Rose barely slept that night. Mamie's words of warning had affected her more than she thought they would. Although, she had not personally been exposed to any race atrocities, she had heard some horrible stories of what white folks did to some Negroes. Rose also knew that Negro people in this area did not go near whites unless they worked for them or had goods to buy or sell. She knew that Negro people were so threatened by whites, they almost never left their homes after dark. The post slavery era was a very unsettling time for many people, both white and Negro. But the Negroes were also victims of violent, physical atrocities.

In between scary dreams that night, Rose peered out the window at the moon. Earlier, it had seemed so friendly, but now it took on a grisly appearance. Rose pulled the sheet over her head and waited for a new dawn, one she knew she was not quite prepared to meet.

Except for the morning greeting, there were no words spoken between Mamie and Rose. By the time Mamie left for school with the children, Rose was already at work in her garden. And she had no idea if Mamie had discussed their conversation with Zeke who was busy working out in the cotton field. She wondered what his reaction would be. She didn't have long to wonder before she saw Mr. Ford coming down the lane as he had said he would. He guided his horse down the long rows arriving where Zeke was busy carving with his hoe. He dismounted, shook Zeke's hand, and the two men began to talk. Ezekiel leaned on his hoe, listening intently to the white visitor. Then the white visitor listened to Ezekial.

Rose could see the two men standing there engaging in heavy conversation. But of course, she couldn't hear any of it; she could only guess what was being said. She hoped their talk would go better than her talk with Mamie had gone.

The conversation between the two men seemed to last an eternity. Rose saw Zeke scratch his head. She saw him shake his head. She saw him wildly gesturing with his arms and then she saw his arms reach up towards heaven. Finally, Rose saw Mr. Ford come riding toward the house. She left the garden and walked in that direction. Jesse Ford practically leaped from his horse, gathering her in his arms, alternately kissing and hugging her. His body and his clothing were dripping wet from perspiration.

"Rose Turner, I love you," he said, "I've loved you all of my life because God made me to love you and I know He made us for each other, there is no other answer."

"What did Pa say?" Rose asked impatiently. "Tell me, tell me!"

"In the end, your Pa simply wanted to know if I loved you and if I could manage all the problems that we would face. Finally, he gave his blessings, Rose, and in late spring, if you agree, I want to take you as my wife."

"You knows we can't do that," responded Rose. "Ma says, an' you said it too, they won't let white an' Negro folks marry."

He looked her squarely in the eyes and tersely said, "We will marry under God's law, not theirs."

"The time will be here before you know it," Jesse said. "I'd better get going. Now that we have this settled, I've got a thousand things to do."

Rose went about her usual chores of gathering her produce, cooking her goodies and selling at the station. During the next few months, she worked harder than usual because she didn't know if she would be able to continue selling from Mr. Ford's home and she wanted to save some extra money. They had not discussed this part of their union at all. Rose's wish was to go on as usual and Mr. Ford probably assumed that, as his wife, she would remain at home.

Mamie, although she did not approve of the marriage at all, soon found herself unhappily making a dress for the wedding. Zeke told her the two would go off and live together if they did not give their blessings. He convinced Mamie the two of them truly loved each other. Mr. Ford wanted the ceremony to be held at his home but Mamie let it be known that her family would not go to a white man's house.

Mr. Ford agreed to Mamie's plan. The ceremony would be held right after sunset at the Turner home. He wanted to keep peace in the family. Mamie felt that she had no real choice in this 'marriage', especially since Zeke had given them his blessings.

Jesse Ford told Rose he would be going by train to Houston in order to buy items for the house as well as supplies for clearing some more land. He was away on the business and shopping trip for almost three weeks. He returned just a few weeks prior to the planned ceremony and saw her just once during that time. He came to the house early one evening to go over details of the ceremony and to tell the Turners that his brother, Frank, would be coming with him to the wedding.

He brought some gifts for the family that he had purchased in Houston. He had pearl necklaces for Mamie and Rose, and some special slippers for Rose to be married in. He gave a pocket watch to Zeke and he had assorted toys for the children. These were their first store-bought toys. The Turner home was filled with wonder and excitement. Mamie, however, remained stoic. She was convinced that Rose was making a big mistake, one she would forever regret.

Later that evening, Mamie said, "Mr. Ford a very kind man, I 'spect he make you a good mate, Rose, but still I know there's gonna be some kind o' trouble on down the road. I don't know if you ready for that, chile, but we gonna pray about it."

"Now, Ma," said Zeke, "maybe the good Lord is puttin' them together like Jesse said, maybe He's doing it for a mighty fine reason, we just don' know."

"Let us pray about this," said Mamie, and she proceeded to pray for nearly a quarter of an hour by Zeke's new watch. This was followed by the singing of the Spiritual, "Standin' In the Need of Prayer."

> It's me, it's me, it's me, oh Lord
> Standing in the need of prayer.
> Not my mother, not my sister, not my brother
> It's me, oh Lord, standing in the need of prayer.

The Turners never told anyone what was about to happen in their family, even though some of their good friends and church members knew about Mr. Ford and his brother buying food from them. But they didn't know about his love for Rose.

The Turners told their friends about the brothers being ex-Union soldiers who decided to make themselves a new life in the south. They were interested in growing cotton on some land they had purchased at the end of the Civil War. It was no secret that the land in this northwest corner of Louisiana was broad and fertile. The Ford Brothers suspected there was an easier, better future for them in cotton than in ranching. All the Negro people knew that the whites did not like the Ford Brothers being in their area. Of course, the Fords knew this but figured that the area belonged to anyone who owned it. They had bought their land legally and had built their homes. And there they would remain and raise their families.

` ` ` ` ` ` ` ` ` ` `

On the last Sunday in May, in Eighteen Hundred Seventy Nine, at about six-thirty in the evening, Jesse Ford and Rose Turner became one before God, before Jesse's brother, Frank, and the Turner Family. Jesse took out a new Bible he had purchased and read I Corinthians, chapter 13, verses one through eight.

> Though I speak with the tongues of men and of angels, but have not love, I have become as sounding brass or a clanging cymbal.
> And though I have the gift of prophecy, and understand all mysteries and all knowledge, and though I have all faith, so that I could remove mountains, but have not love, I am nothing.
> And though I bestow all my goods to feed the poor, and though I give my body to be burned, but have not love, it profits me nothing.
> Love suffers long and is kind; love does not envy; love does not parade itself, is not puffed up; does not behave rudely, does not seek its own, is not provoked, thinks no evil; does not rejoice in iniquity, but rejoices in the truth; bears all things, believes all things, hopes all things, endures all things.
> Love never fails.
> But whether there are prophecies, they will fail; whether there are tongues, they will cease; whether there is knowledge, it will vanish away.

Then Frank read the following Bible verses:

> "Beloved, let us love one another, for love is of God; and everyone who loves is born of God and knows God. He who does not love does not know God, for God is love. He who loves his brother abides in the light, and there is no cause for stumbling in him. These verses are from I John," he announced.

Jesse Ford took Rose Turner's hand, placed a band of gold on her ring finger and said, "Rose, I take you for my wife, for you are virtuous and good and we will obtain favor from the Lord. He will bless our house and our children. We will love each other and we will be faithful to one another until death parts us."

With tears in her eyes, she looked up at Mr. Ford and softly said, "Mr. Ford, I will be yo' wife an' we will dwell together joyfully an' happily all the days of our lives. We shall be surrounded by the sun, the stars, the moon, an' other living things of the earth."

Mamie sang one of her Spirituals, "Walk Together Children," and that seemed to signal an end to the ceremony.

"Wait jus' a minute!" she yelled. "We forget somethin' very important."

She whispered to Ezekiel. He quickly produced a broom from the front porch and instructed Jesse and Rose to jump over it.

Mamie had the last word, as she usually did. Quoting from the Bible, she pronounced, "No evil shall befall you, nor shall any plague come near your dwelling. I wish you a long, happy life together an' I hopes you have many chil'ren."

Jesse busied himself putting Rose's belongings, which had been neatly placed in colorful sacks that Mamie had made, into the buggy they would be riding to his home. Rose ran to her cherished garden to take one last look because she knew it might be some time before she would see it again. This wonderful garden had given her her life. She would truly miss it.

With the darkness of the evening deepening and being overcome with the sadness of separation, Rose clung to a fence post as sobs and trembling began to possess her body. Thankfully, no one came to her nor called out to her. She just stood there for a while.

Finally, she threw her head high, ceased her sobs, raised her hands to the sky and called aloud, "Thank you, Great Spirit! Thank you, Holy Jesus! Thank you, Papo! Thank you for everything!"

Picking up her long white skirts, she ran back to the house and smothered everyone with kisses, saying "I loves you! I loves you! I come back to see you as soon as I can, I promise!"

Then, Jesse Ford helped her into the carriage. He went and spoke some final words with Mamie and Zeke. The children cried as the carriage disappeared over the hill.

Chapter Eight

Even though no problems were expected on the ride home because no one knew about the wedding vows except the Turners and the Fords, Frank rode shotgun just to make sure there were no surprises. Mamie had earlier suggested that Rose remain close to her new house and to Jesse, until she knew it would be safe to move about.

Traveling by night was slower and more uncomfortable than daytime travel. Still the three of them arrived at the Ford place sooner than expected, weary, tired and sleepy. They sat at the table eating from the basket of food which Mamie, in her wisdom, had prepared. They talked long into the night because each of them by now understood that this union was not going to go unnoticed by neither the whites nor the Negroes.

After a while, Rose was excused to go and make herself comfortable and to prepare the beds. But what the two gentlemen really wanted to do was make some plans for security, with the probability that there would be trouble in the future. The two men talked and planned until almost daybreak when Jesse finally said, "I must go to my beautiful, sleeping bride and express my love for her."

Jesse found Rose asleep in the same bed he had placed her in when he had found her unconscious in the lane near his home a few years prior. He carefully picked up her sleeping body and took her to his bedroom with the large oak bed that he had special-ordered when he finished building the house. The set was so massive that when the train delivered it to the station, it took several wagon trips to get it to the house.

He gingerly laid her down, quickly undressed and slid in bed beside her.

He enfolded her in his arms and whispered in her ear, "Thank you, for becoming my bride, I love you! I love you!" And he added, "My heart is filled with joy and passion and I want us to partake of this precious gift of love."

"Mr. Ford," she responded, "You've been so good an' kind to me and my family, I don't know if I can ever repay you."

"Rose, my beloved, we're just two people sharing in this love and this life together and that's payment enough for the both of us. Now, I think it is way past time that we celebrate this union and our pledge to love and honor each other."

Jesse Ford knew how to bring his virgin bride into her fullness and knowledge. There was a sweetness and a goodness about their love making that made him feel like they were pure pleasure givers, and that no one else in the world could possibly indulge in this beautiful ritual with the same results. No one could match the depths of their sweet passion.

They both flourished with excitement and desire by just looking at and touching one another. Rose knew that she was awkward and unknowing but she followed Jesse's smooth guidance and directions.

"Mr. Ford," Rose sighed, "I think the whole house is moving."

They slept in each other's arms, having both exhausted themselves from being so deliciously satisfied.

By mid-afternoon, Jesse was giving Rose a complete orientation of everything on and around the farm. Rose remembered the kitchen because she had already prepared some meals there. She was still amazed at the fact that it was separated by a breezeway from the main house.

After the walk-through, Jesse took Rose outside and presented her with a puppy. He said he had gotten the little terrier as a wedding gift, when he was in Houston.

"She is yours, I want you to give her a name and I want her trained to take care of you and to be at your side every minute of the day; I'll take care of the nights."

"She's so beautiful," Rose said, "Thank you! And she's so big, are you sure she's only a puppy?"

As Rose went about her chores, she noticed many items she had not seen before. There were several lovely pieces in each room, including some paintings and vases. She was curious about them and when asked, Mr. Ford said that he had also purchased them in Houston.

"When a woman lives in a house, it needs to have more feminine and frilly things, I'm glad they please you. Since we're talking about my purchases, I also bought a gun for you. Everyone needs to have a gun and to know how to use it," he added.

"Frank is the better marksman and he has promised to return and give you some lessons on how to handle guns. In the meantime, I'll show you where the guns are kept and what to do in case a problem should arise.

"Frank and I learned all about guns growing up on the ranch and all we didn't learn there, we learned during the war. I'm not a gunman, that's another reason I left the west and came south where it's said to be more genteel. But I am not sure anymore that that statement is true."

He apologized to her. "This isn't exactly the kind of conversation I would have wished to have with you at this juncture of our lives, but Mamie and Zeke reminded me to make sure that I provided proper protection for you because the whites around here are meaner than rattlesnakes looking for shade in a burning desert. I gave them my word to do that and I aim to keep it."

The following week, Frank arrived with three wagonloads of lumber, supplies, building materials, and a crew of workmen. The men immediately began building a fence around the place, enclosing the house, yard, barn and Rose's future garden.

Frank went into the house and presented Rose with his wedding present for her, a Winchester Rifle. He convinced her that it would some day come in handy. He informed Rose that he would be a houseguest until the fence was completed. With all of them working from sun up til sun down, it was estimated to take about two days. Jesse decided that Rose should remain indoors during this time.

Knowing how much Rose loved the outdoors and sensing that she was unhappy about having to stay inside all day, when evening came, Jesse took her for a walk. He said they would check on the progress the men had made on the fence. They walked hand in hand under a pale, silvery stream of moonlight, amidst the strong refreshing scent of the pinewood lumber the men were using to build the fence.

The sounds of some of the night creatures, frogs, cicadas, and crickets reverberated through the still night air and the fireflies darted here and there lighting up the night skies, as if in celebration of the two lovers. The blossoming magnolia, peach and crepe myrtle trees also added their delightfully sweet and pungent fragrance to a most delicious, balmy night.

"Rose," Jesse began, "this is my little piece of heaven and you have made it complete. You are my angel on earth and I love you completely.

That's why I want to take every precaution for your safety, you do understand, don't you?"

"Yes, Mr. Ford," she responded softly, "but you need to know that I am a brave an' strong woman. Papo taught me never to be afraid of anything. I have taken care of myself since I was a little girl."

"Rose," he replied, "I even love you for that, but some situations could arise where you may not be in a position to defend yourself. My job is to make sure that you have every possible advantage. Remember, I have fought in a war where I learned that being prepared is the best defense."

Jesse knew that gardening was one of the pleasures in Rose's life, so he took her to the spot that he had set aside for just that. It was located off to the side but between the house and the barn.

"This plot of land where we're standing is for your garden," he announced. She was filled with delight and a deep sense of satisfaction and thanks.

"You think of everything an' you make me mo' than happy!" she squealed with joy. "I'll make this garden be even better than my other one."

The work on the fence took almost three days. Rose thought she would go mad staying indoors for so long even though she talked and played much of the time with her new puppy. She also prepared wonderful meals for Jesse and Frank. And the two men praised her cooking incessantly.

She decided to name her puppy Kula and she was anxious to take her to the barn and introduce her to Spirit. "That fence is taking such a long time," she said.

The next afternoon, Frank came running to the house to announce that the work was completed, the men had been paid and were gone. Rose burst through the door with Kula following; she shouted, "Hallelujah!" The sun was still dazzlingly hot but she ran to the stable to see Spirit and to show Kula to him.

The two animals spent some time sniffing at each other. Rose recalled what Jesse had said, "This is my heaven." She smiled in agreement.

Frank had set up a target practice behind the stable and he let Rose know that he would be departing soon but wanted to give her a lesson on using the rifle. Although there were other things she'd rather do, she gave her attention to Frank. As usual, she was an energetic and exemplary student who learned quickly. Still, he made her promise to do target shooting everyday. It didn't take long. Soon, she was so good with that rifle, she was bagging rabbits, quail and squirrels for the dinner table.

Rose was up before sunrise every morning preparing breakfast and supper at the same time in order to get a jump on the searingly hot days that made cooking so uncomfortable. Jesse was also up feeding and watering the animals. The land still had not been sufficiently cleared for planting cotton. They were behind schedule.

After breakfast, Rose went to her garden and Jesse busied himself building little two-room houses for the expected sharecroppers to use the following year when the land would be ready for planting.

Rose set out some of the seedlings she brought along with her. By mid-morning each day, she always checked to see which ones survived the transplanting. Only a few rows had been cultivated, but she knew that her yield would be enough for their needs throughout this summer and into early fall. If the production was good, then there would be enough to can for the coming winter.

Jesse loved to observe her as she deftly worked among the rows, scratching and digging with her hoe to remove unwanted vines and wild grasses. At times, she knelt among the plants to thin the abundant growths, then proceeded to discard or plant them in another carefully chosen spot.

Kula was always near by, running back and forth, sniffing at the ground and barking at anything that moved. This was a rewarding sight for Jesse to behold and it brought smiles of comfort to his face. There was an incredible connection between Rose and that puppy. He knew his decision to get the dog had proven to be a wise one.

Jesse had, on many occasions, told Rose there was an earthy magnetism that existed between her and plants. He was continuously amazed at her big, ripe and luscious fruits along with the rich harvest of magnificent vegetables. He had also been overwhelmed by her business acumen. And each day he was equally amazed at the dishes she put on the table. He thought himself to be the luckiest and happiest man on earth, and he often told her so. She glowed in his frequent compliments.

Both Rose and Jesse worked hard all summer long. She spent endless hours in her garden and kitchen, he kept busy with his house building. During mid-day, when the sun baked everything it touched, he was in the shed tinkering and experimenting with inventions, that for some reason, he never discussed with her.

It was coming up to the middle of September, and summer was quickly drawing to a close. But the waning summer heat seemed reluctant to give in. Only once during these months since the wedding, had there been any contact between Rose and her family. The people at church began to ask why Rose no longer attended church services. At first, their queries were met with silence. Finally, the Turners knew sooner or later they would have to provide an answer, so they quietly told a few of the members that Rose had married and moved away.

The first contact with Rose's family came near the end of August. It had happened just about sunset. The descending sun was shooting golden streams of orange and red through the trees. The mockingbirds and crows were having one of their noisy conversations. The spreading hills touched the valleys. This beautiful scenery and the lushness of the southern landscape made Jesse grateful that he had decided to settle there. It seemed like what he imagined paradise to be.

Jesse was returning from one of his rare trips to town to make a few purchases. On impulse, he made a detour and visited the Turners. He knew they would want to hear some word from Rose and she would love hearing about them.

When Mamie saw him riding up the trail, her heartbeat quickened for fear he would be bringing some bad news about Rose. But when she considered the horse's unhurried gait, she reckoned that everything must be all right. Still, she couldn't contain her anxiety. She ran to meet him before he dismounted.

"Jesse," she shouted, "ever'things all right, ain't it?"

"Of course it is Mamie, Rose just wanted me to drop by and check on the family. Where's Zeke?" he inquired.

"Yonder in the field, still workin,' I 'spect when he sees you, he be here directly. Come on in, have a seat, I git you some cool water; now tell me 'bout Rose," she said, without stopping to take a breath.

"Rose is just fine. She keeps busy every day doing a hundred things around the house and her garden is growing magnificently, even though it is small." She handed him a canning jar filled with cool water which he almost drank in one big gulp.

"No, thank you, I can't stay, I need to get home as soon as I can; I don't like Rose being alone after dark. I did promise her that in a couple of months, it would be all right with me if she'd come and stay a few days with you. She misses you terribly."

Jesse picked up Annie and Susie, who were hiding behind their mother's skirt. He swung them about in the air a few times and gave them some peppermint candy. He answered a few more of Mamie's questions and took off before Zeke and the boys came from the cotton field. He headed for home which was almost two hours of steady riding. The summer sun was quickly disappearing beyond the hills.

Rose was excited and full of questions when Jesse told her about his visit with her family. Since the day of the wedding, this was the only news Rose had had of the family who had done so much to make her life as wonderful as it was. She felt she could barely last until the end of next month when she would visit with them.

"I thank you, Mr. Ford, for all your goodness an' for making me a happy woman. Now, I'll make you a nice hot bath and scrub your back."

That night, they lay in bed holding on to and loving each other for a long time. They were caught up in a sort of intoxicated aura provided by the quiet, smoky darkness and the divine endearment that filled their hearts. It was clear to Jesse that Rose was incredibly content and serene and he was pleased he had brought her news of her beloved family.

Life was progressing well on their farm in the deep back woods. Jesse Ford and his precious Rose were a loving and adoring couple. They worked long and hard every day and spent their evenings in amorous pursuit. Jesse's biggest dream was to become a successful farmer. With Rose beside him, he had no doubt that it would happen. He was proud of his beautiful home and his rich land that was dark and soft to the touch. He loved Rose dearly and he prayed they would some day have children. Lots and lots of children.

` ` ` ` ` ` ` ` ` ` `

It happened the following Sunday morning. It was not quite daybreak. The sun was hiding behind a bank of cumulus clouds, casting shrouds of fog through the dense woods. Rose saw the shadowy figure beneath the glimmering cottonwood leaves. She quickly called Jesse, and by the tone of her voice, he knew that something awful must have happened. Jesse grabbed his rifle and bounded out to the garden patch where Rose was gathering fresh berries and melons for breakfast.

"There is someone on horseback out in the woods, just standing there, not moving at all. What do you think he's up to?"

"Rose," he said, " take Kula and quickly go inside. Stay there until I signal you; I'll check out what's happening."

Jesse went across the yard and down a short trail that led to a gully. He traveled along the gully until it reached a spot near the woods. He climbed up the embankment, emerging into a thicket of trees directly behind the rider. From there, he could see that the stranger was on a mule, not a horse, as Rose had said. He stepped lightly so the fallen leaves beneath his feet barely made a sound; when he got closer, he cocked the trigger and yelled, "Who goes there?"

"Don't shoot! It's me, Ezekiel!" he screamed, throwing his arms up in the air.

"Zeke, you scared us to death, what on earth are you doing out here at this hour of the morning?" asked Jesse.

"I jus' wanted to see my little girl," Zeke sighed, "I didn't even git to see you when you was by the house. Why didn't you ride out 'n the field to see me like you always use to?" Zeke responded as he lowered his arms.

"Ma said she was okay, but I got to thinkin' 'bout her last night an' I couldn't sleep, jus' needed to see fo' myself that she all right. I beg yo' pardon, I didn't mean to scare ya'll. God knows, that's the las' thing I want to do. I was tryin' to make sho' I had the right place. The mist is thick this mornin.'"

The two men came out of the woods just as the sun began casting frail yellow rays across the farm. It was going to be another scorcher.

When Rose saw her Pa, she ran to him, screaming and clapping her hands.

"Pa! Pa!" she cried. "Is ev'rythin okay? Is Ma a'right?"

Zeke held his daughter in his arms for some time, then he held her at arm's length to get a good look at her and said, "Everthin's fine, Rose.

You looks pretty as ever an' yo' smile is bigger than I 'member. I can see he treatin' you right."

"Come on in an' rest yo'self while I get breakfast on the table," Rose offered. "You mus' be worn out from ridin' that ole' mule."

"That's something I aim to take care of," interrupted Jesse, "by this time next year, I'll see to it that you have a horse. A man needs a horse!"

After a hearty breakfast of fresh berries, melon, biscuits with butter and syrup, scrambled eggs, smoke-house bacon and tea, Jesse and Rose took Zeke for a walk around the place. Zeke was quite proud to have a daughter who owned a farm like some of the ones he worked on during slavery. It was not a plantation, he knew, but still, it was better and prettier than many of the places around the parish.

When they finished their walk, Jesse and Zeke took off on horseback. Zeke rode Spirit at Rose's insistence she said the mule needed to rest up for the return trip home. Rose was filled with happiness as she watched the two men she loved most ride off in the distance, together.

Before leaving for home, Zeke hugged Rose and whispered to her, "Rose, I never tho't I'd see the day when a Negro lady lives with a white man 'cept as a slave. Yo' Mr. Ford is sho' some gentl'man an' ya'll shonuff got a fine place. I feels good! The long ride out here was worth ever' minute. Um happy fo' you!"

Chapter Nine

When the time came for Rose's first visit back home with her family, she was brimming with delight. She spent hours in the kitchen making molasses bread, gingerbread and teacakes. She wanted the whole family to be happy about her visit. She knew this visit would be a big celebration. Rose filled her buggy with all the goodies she had prepared, told Jesse how to care for her fall crop of vegetables and then she and Kula were off.

They traveled for almost three hours before arriving at an empty house. Rose's disappointment was immense! Nevertheless, after tending to the animals and putting Spirit in the barn, she went inside with Kula to wait and to wonder where everyone could be. Everything inside seemed to be in order so she wondered if they had gone to town on a shopping trip.

"No!" she decided, they never went into town except on Saturday an' today was Monday. " Maybe someone died an' they went to a funeral," she thought. "Or maybe something terrible has happened!"

"Oh, Great Spirit, Oh, Heavenly Father," she prayed aloud, "please take care of Ma, Pa and the children, let no harm befall them, please, Sir! Amen!"

Rose sat in the swing with Kula beside her and decided she would replace her worry by recalling the many special occasions the family had celebrated during her stay with them.

She thought of the very first day she arrived at the Turner home and how kind they were to her. The children were so little then. Annie was a baby. Susie wasn't born.

"Theys' grown so much," she mused.

"Ephriam an' Samuel are almost as tall as Pa, an' Aaron, so polite, so neat, an Annie an' Susie, almost like twins, so giggly and wiggly and always hiding behind Ma. I remember when Susie was born, right in my hands. That was wonderful!"

She was speaking so loud now, that Kula began to bark as if in response.

Then Rose remembered Pa's birthday celebration and how she learned what a birthday was and how badly she wanted one of her own. Mamie, wise beyond her years, decided on the date that would be Rose's birthday. They even let Rose have their family name. Turner. That was the best gift Rose ever had in her whole life.

Rose reflected on the big oak tree over in the meadow. She felt she needed to be there right now, but knew that she must not leave the house. She could even hear the wind near the tree calling her name, still, she would not move from the swing. That big tree had been her favorite place to go whenever she needed to sit and think, or to talk with Papo. It was where Mr. Ford first asked her to be his wife.

Finally, she recalled her accident and being rescued by Mr. Ford near his farm, which was now her home, or at least it was where she was living. Mr. Ford referred to the house as hers but she didn't know how that could be. She loved Mr. Ford and knew that he loved her. Still, hadn't Mamie said she could not be a white man's wife?

"Why is the world like that?" she asked aloud. "If it's all right with him an' it's all right with me, why do white folks say we can't be husband an' wife?" Kula barked as if answering her.

Rose sat buried in her thoughts with tears welling in her eyes, when she suddenly recollected Papo and his teaching her to be strong, brave and never afraid. But most of all, he had taught her to love and respect all living things.

She was still daydreaming when she heard a noise far off in the distance. Thinking it to be thunder, she looked up at the sky which was blue and clear with only a few scattered clouds way up high. Although the sun had descended rapidly since her arrival, there was no hint of rain. She heard the sound again. Kula barked; he had heard it, too. Rose strained her eyes and finally saw the cloud of dust kicked up by the wagon as it neared the turn-off to their lane.

Rose began running and shouting with Kula going ahead of her, still barking. When the family saw Rose, they began their own noisy celebration.

When all of the noise quieted down, Mamie told Rose, "Today was the first day of school an' what a grand an' glorious opening it was! More boys an' girls than ever befo' showed up for this first day, even though there was still farming chores to be completed. An' now, mo' parents are beginning to understand the importance of learning to read an' write."

The children were kissing and hugging Rose and each was trying to tell her stories of their school experiences. Rose could tell they were happy to be back at school. And she was happy for them. There was even a tinge of regret that she had not learned to read and write. But she could no longer think of that. She was pleased at the direction in which her life was going.

Mamie had lots more to talk about, but said they would talk during and after supper. They all got busy with chores, including Rose, who was delighted to be with her family again. The celebration was in full swing.

Rose would be with her family for three wonderful days and nights. The next day, she even went to school with them and listened attentively to the teaching. She was fascinated with the multiplication table he was introducing and with the sounds of the reading lesson.

Rose and Mamie did some housekeeping chores in the church which still served as the school. Mr. Benson told them there was some talk of the Methodist Church sending money to build a separate building for the school.

"I sho' hope you heard right," declared Mamie. "We needs a school bad, the church jus' can't meet the needs of all our chil'ren."

At the end of the school day, Mr. Benson gave Rose a multiplication chart to keep and he thanked her for assisting in setting up the teaching zones.

After three days of homecoming celebration and togetherness, it was time for Rose to return home. She promised her family, "I won't stay 'way for so long a time again. I truly enjoyed m'self an' I love ya'll so much! Maybe I make it back 'fore Christmas."

They had had a glorious time together. Each evening after supper, Rose cleaned the kitchen while Mamie supervised the homework. Zeke took that time to talk with Rose about how things were progressing in her life with Mr. Ford. He felt reassured when Rose told him, "Pa, he loves me an' he treats me real good. He's kind an' gentle in ev'ry way. The Lord done really blessed me!"

"I thanks God for yo' happiness, Rose, an' I pray that you both continue to live in love an' peace," Zeke responded.

On this last night with her family, they prayed long prayers, sang Spirituals and Rose told one of her stories.

"Once upon a time there was a Shy Little Kitten that stayed under the house all day an' all night. The little kitten's brothers an' sisters went everywhere on the farm. They went into the fields to chase the field mice. They went to the barn to tease the other animals. They even drank their water an' ate some of their food. They climbed up in the rafters an' slid down the poles.

The kittens snapped at the grasshoppers an' other bugs. They chased the chickens 'cross the yard, but Shy Little Kitten stayed under the house an' just looked at his brothers an' sisters.

Shy Little Kitten wanted to have fun too, but he was 'fraid of all the big people who were always walking 'round the house. He was 'specially frightened of the horses an' the dogs. They were so big an' made such strange noises.

Mama cat often brought goodies for her Shy Little Kitten. But when she took the other kittens out in the field to teach them to hunt for they own food, Shy Little Kitten stayed under the house. One day, Mama Cat picked him up with her teeth an' took him out to the field. But as soon as she dropped him to the ground, he scampered back under the house.

One day, when Mama Cat an' her kittens were out huntin' in the field, a little girl was left in the yard by herself. Shy Little Kitten saw her an' he was not afraid 'cause she was so small.

Suddenly, a lizard crawled on the little girl's leg an' frightened her. She cried out in her wee small voice. Shy Kitten pounced on the lizard just as little girl's Mama came running outside.

The Mama picked up the little girl an' then she picked up Shy Little Kitten. She petted his soft fuzzy neck an' she gave him a bowl of food.

From that day on, Shy Little Kitten stayed in the house an' played with the little girl an' the two o' them became best friends. Now Shy Little Kitten is the happiest kitten in the whole world.

On the long ride home, Rose thought of how much her life had changed since the day Papo took her to live with that strange family, whose name she no longer remembered. But she did remember the cruel treatments from the people in each house she lived. Their mistreatment of her would be etched in her mind forever. But she would not let it interfere with her happiness.

That was the past and she vowed to let go of it. Now, she was the lady of her own fine home and she had a wonderful husband who was loving and kind to her. She smiled as she thought of Mr. Ford and she put the switch to Spirit making him go at a faster pace. She was anxious to get home and see her husband. Kula yipped as if in agreement.

The following year, 1880, was a disappointing year for Jesse and Rose. The winter had been unusually harsh and the clearing of the land was behind schedule. There was neither enough manpower nor an ample supply of the proper tools. It was beginning to look as if no cotton crops would be coming in because they simply underestimated the amount of work necessary for the clearance of the virgin land.

Jesse applied for a loan at the town bank in order to hire more help and buy more supplies. He was turned down. He did not want to tell Rose about the rejection because he knew it would worry her and there was nothing she could do about it. However, she had overheard his conversation with his brother. Frank's land had been cleared and he was all set to purchase his provisions and get his planting under way. He would be short of cash until harvest time, but he could manage to advance them a small sum.

Rose knew what she needed to do and she went about her days displaying unparalleled energy and discipline. She was up and in the garden each day before the sun came over the horizon. She carved the rows, cut weeds away, tilled the soil and mixed it with manure from the pasture and planted her seeds with care and love. Intentionally, she did not share her plan with Mr. Ford.

> Great day! great day!
> Great day, the Righteous marching.
> Great day! Great day!
> God's gonna build up Zion's walls.

She sang and hummed as she worked. She sang the Spirituals that she had learned from Mamie. Kula was always there in the garden with her, chasing lizards and frogs, snapping at grasshoppers, bugs, and anything else that came near. Rose loved having Kula around because he was so alert and was such good company. Kula always let her know if anybody or anything was near.

Rose did not give Jesse an explanation of why she asked for so many canning jars when he made a trip into town. She also ordered an extra large amount of sugar, flour, lard and spices. She simply went about doing what she knew she had to do. Her vegetables would soon be ready for the journey to the station.

A few weeks later, Rose filled her buggy with fresh vegetables, breads, cookies and teacakes and announced to her husband that she was going to the station.

They had their first quarrel, but in the end, Rose was the winner. "Tell me why you insist on doing this!" Jesse demanded!

"We need the money," she answered tersely.

"We are making out okay!" he countered.

"Come next spring," she responded, "we won't hav' 'nough money to get the crops goin' jes' right. Things went bad this winter."

"We need the money!" she was almost shouting. "I knows how to make money an' I 'tend to do it!"

back at the station. . . . .

She set up at the station about an hour before time for the train to pull in. As usual, people were milling about. Some to catch the train or meet passengers but most just passing time and watching the goings on. A few townsfolk saw her and slowly began to make their way to the platform. They asked her questions, complimented her and bought her goods; she just smiled and said, "Thank you."

Her customers were happy to have her back selling at the station. Each time she was there, she sold everything she had in her buggy. Mr. Ford was not in agreement with Rose's ventures but he knew how stubborn she could be once she had made a decision that she was doing the right thing. He also knew that she was excellent at selling her goods.

He did not continue his objections because he recognized that was determined. He also knew they could use the money. But deep down inside, he was afraid word would spread about their living together and trouble might start. He figured the trouble would begin with Rose because she was the one who was exposed to the public. She was the one who was vulnerable and he recognized that. And that is why he always trailed her on her trips to and from the station.

Rose clearly understood the need for money to get the cotton crops started. Jess had some money but they both knew it was a limited amount. And without enough money, running such a large farm was going to present problems that could become insurmountable. Their future together in the south would be jeopardized.

Rose put in long hours with her vegetables. She knew that raising vegetables and fruit in large quantities took lots of work and dedication. She didn't worry so much about the fruit. She knew the fruit trees would produce because she thought of them as God's gifts to His people. She felt they were nurtured by the Great Spirit of earth.

She also spent countless hours over a hot stove canning and making breads and cookies. She was more than happy that spring had decided to linger a little longer and keep the hot summer days at bay.

On the days she wasn't selling at the station, Rose and Jesse went to Frank's farm to help wherever they could. Frank's cotton had been planted and it was beginning to grow. He had also planted fields of corn, beans, potatoes, peanuts and alfalfa.

Rose set the work pace, both in chopping and in picking cotton. When the sharecroppers saw how much work she could do, they increased their pace. She went about her tasks with such zeal and enthusiasm that soon all the workers were increasing their output. Frank's crops would certainly produce a fine harvest!

Frank's sharecroppers didn't understand Rose's connection to the Ford Brothers. They whispered among themselves, but they asked no questions. They were overjoyed to be working for someone who treated them with fairness and kindness.

Rose was comfortable and committed in her work at Frank's farm, because she knew that when the crops were sold, she and Mr. Ford would be getting a share of the income. This was an agreement that had been worked out between the brothers. Frank was pleased with the deal because he knew what impact Rose and Jesse had on the workers.

At the same time, on her days at the station, Rose went about her selling more aggressively than ever because she knew they probably would never be able to depend on the bank for money. She also did not want to depend too heavily on Frank Ford. She was determined to make as much money as she could. She didn't want to be beholden to anyone, not even Mr. Frank Ford. She figured that by next spring, there would be more than enough money for them to get started on their crops. And they would have earned it themselves.

One day at the station, Rose was moving about the platform at an unusually slow pace. The heat was stifling! It was suffocating. It was hotter than hot! The earth itself, seemed to roast under a blazing, blistering sun.

Rose thought to herself, "Only a few weeks left of summer, I can hardly wait. This is the hottest weather I ever 'member us havin'."

She sat at the edge of the platform for a few minutes praying and hoping for a breeze to come her way. One of the regulars stopped to ask if she was okay because he'd never seen her sit down when she was selling.

"I mus' hurry an' finish so I can git home, something don't feel right," she said.

"Can I give you a hand with anything?" he asked. "This heat is depressing."

"No, thank you," she politely declined.

She sold her remaining items and slowly trudged to her horse and buggy and started the ride home. It would be a long, tiresome ride.

She felt better when, farther up the road, she caught sight of Mr. Ford arriving to follow her home. Several times, she wanted to cry out to him because of the discomfort she was suffering. But she managed to hold on until they arrived home.

When Jesse realized something was wrong with Rose, he tried to make her comfortable. He laid her in bed and cooled her body down with wet towels. He rushed to the kitchen to make alfalfa tea which she had told him was good for most every ailment.

As he prepared the tea, he was angry with himself for letting her go sell at the station. He began praying softly; "God, I know I don't pray often enough, but please don't let anything be wrong with Rose. I love her so much! Now, I beg you to touch and comfort her. Thank you, God! Amen! Oh! And remember, God, it was you who put us together."

Jesse finished making the tea and took it to her. He was a nervous wreck because he felt he didn't know exactly what it was that he needed to do or say. Then he realized he took care of things outside very well and left everything on the inside to Rose. But, indeed, she also knew how to handle most anything outside or inside.

She could ride a horse as well as most men. And she could certainly chop and pick cotton better than any man Jesse had seen, except Ezekiel. Now, she had learned to shoot a rifle and a pistol about as good as most men. As he thought on these things, he thanked God all over again for bringing her into his life.

As the evening wore on, Rose seemed to be resting comfortably and Jesse heaved a big sigh of relief. She slept peacefully through the night while he was waking up every few minutes to make sure she was all right.

When dawn crept over the horizon the next morning, Rose was up busying herself with her usual chores. Jesse tried in vain to coax her back to bed, but she would hear none of that. She had work that had to be done.

"Rose, Honey, you've been over-working yourself lately," Jesse said. " And I've noticed that you look tired and drained. I think the time has come for you to quit the business for good and stay home."

"Now you listen to me, Mr. Ford. I've never not finished a job I started. An' I means to finish this one, I means to reach my goal. I don't got too long to go. I make it jus' fine, thank-you. Yesterday, I just got overheated. I keep out of that hot sun today."

As Jesse Ford drank his tea, he muttered under his breath, "I guess this is another argument I'm not going to win."

Aloud, he said, "You win this battle, but remember, I'm a soldier and I aim to win the war. This is your last season to sell at the station, Rose. I'm the man of this house, from now on, I make the money and I make the important decisions."

Rose knew there was a good deal of work to be done as the sizzling hot sun was exacting a toll on some of her prized vegetables. She looked to the cloudless sky and prayed for rain. They had gone several days without any trace of rain, and the tomatoes, the squashes, the cucumbers and the greens were becoming pretty limp while the cabbage and okra were faring well. She knew if it didn't rain soon, many of her vegetables would burn up right on the vines.

A few days later, after only one light passing shower, she gathered her baskets full of the sun-ripened vegetables and headed toward the house to prepare them for canning. Kula came running and jumped up on her causing her to fall. She fell on one of the baskets and, for a few moments, lay motionless. It was Kula's incessant barking that got Jesse's attention; he ran from the barn and found her struggling to get to her feet.

Chapter Ten

It was while Jesse was helping to remove her soiled clothing, that he noticed. The rays of bright sunlight that invaded the room fell across her body. He saw a slight swelling in her breasts and stomach. He remained silent until she was quietly resting on the big oak bed. He got down on his knees and buried his head in her midsection.

"Rose," he asked softly, "are we going to have a baby?"

"I don' fo' sure know, but I be thinkin' maybe so." Jesse remained on his knees for a while, deep in thought.

"Are you upset 'bout that?" she asked.

"God, no! I'm so happy I'm speechless."

Jesse lay beside Rose asking her questions about any reactions she had been experiencing in recent weeks. He was carefully trying to help her to construct a basis to verify that she was, indeed, having a child.

When he finished his querying, he stated, "In a few weeks, we'll know beyond a doubt that we're going to have a baby. If so, it will be the best thing to ever happen to me, next to having you as my wife."

Jessie loved Rose more in that moment than he ever thought possible. They lay entwined in each other's arms for a long while, chatting and laughing about their wonderful life together. They capped off this rare mid-day time together by holding and loving each other tenderly and passionately. Each time they made love, they told each other, it was always so much better than the last time. Jesse would forever be convinced that God put them on earth to love each other. For him, there simply was no other explanation.

After a week of being spoiled by Jesse, Rose began to look prettier and happier. She was more animated than ever. Even Jesse was more productive and in good spirits. He was working everyday with his brother, and the cotton and corn yield from Frank's fields far exceeded their expectations. Jesse knew his money worries would soon come to an end. He knew Rose would no longer need to go to the station.

Rose did, however, continue to go to the station through the end of cotton-picking time because that had been her long-range plan. Even though she would do it if it was necessary, she hated picking cotton.

When Jesse suggested that she close out her selling, Rose agreed, but added, 'I needs to go just one mo' time to try an' sell the rest of my stuff an' to make some needed purchases in town."

The final day of selling went unusually smooth and easy for her. She now knew for certain she was expecting a child, although she was not visibly showing. She wound up her day early and went to make a few purchases.

She began her ride home from the station feeling very pleased with all that she had accomplished. She knew that she had made enough money to take them through the coming winter and to purchase seed and equipment for the summer crops.

When she reached the fork in the road where Jesse usually would meet her, she saw a figure on horseback. Thinking it was Jesse and that he must have finished working earlier than usual, she prodded Spirit into galloping a little faster. But as her buggy got closer, she knew the rider was not Jesse. She slowed the pace.

The white man quickly pulled in front of Spirit, and pointed his rifle at Rose. She had her gun but never had a chance to get to it. She was completely caught off guard. There had been no trouble for her since the time she was chased by the white boys, even though the Turners had told her to expect problems.

Mamie had warned her that when word spread about her living with Jesse, some where, some time, trouble would come and find her. Now, she was looking down the barrel of one of those times, thought Rose. Nevertheless, she tried to maintain her composure.

"You the Nigra what lives with that damn Yankee carpet bagger? I know you's only part In'jun and that makes you a Nigra."

Rose looked at the scraggly, filthy, fat man holding the gun, and never said a word. She just sat straight and tall in her buggy, tightly holding Spirit's rein.

"Get outta that fancy buggy an' let me see what that carpetbagger see n' a Nigra!" He shouted.

Rose never moved. The dirty, ugly, snarly white man came closer and suddenly pulled her from the buggy. She landed in a heap on the ground.

Before she could get to her feet, he dragged her across the road, almost to the same spot where she used to meet with Mr. Ford. Rose never said a word or uttered a sound.

"What's-a-matter wid you, cat got your tongue?" the man asked. " Take yo' clothes off, gal."

Rose made no effort to remove her clothing. She remained silent.

"First, that bastard helps to destroy our lives and our properties, then he has the nerve to buy land in our back yard. Now, he's sleepin' wid ex-slaves. Well, now it's my turn, I aim to see what he finds so goddamn good about you."

The man grabbed Rose's blouse and tore it off, then he pulled off her skirt, knocking her to the ground again. When he laid his rifle down, Rose tried to get it but she was not quick enough. He slapped her hard across her face and she screamed for the first time.

"Well, at least I know you ain't deaf and dumb and don't try that trick agin' or I'll shoot yo' brains out!" he yelled at her.

This nasty devil from hell, with his belly hanging, took off his pants and stood over her, saying, "It gots to be mighty special for a white man to want you so much he gotta live' wid you. He don't got enough sense to know that he can take it when he want to? Well, I'm gonna take it. I'm gonna sample it fo' myself," he said as he ~~dropped his pants and~~ straddled Rose.

"I don't think so," said a voice from behind the tree. "You will never sample any woman again, especially not my woman."

The Winchester went off and found its mark. For an instant, the man's feet were in the air. Then his body fell limp, to the earth.

Rose ran to Jesse who took only a minute to comfort her. "Quick," he ordered, "give me a hand to get him on his horse. Now you get back in the buggy and go to the house as fast as you can. I'll be there as soon as I finish with this."

Rose watched Jesse ride off through the woods, holding the reins of the horse carrying that mad man. She scrambled back into the buggy with her clothes still hanging off her body. She knew she must not panic. She knew she should get away before someone came down the road.

She went as fast as she could safely travel, praying all the while to the Great Spirit and to Jesus, the Heavenly Father.

Rose didn't remember the ride home, but she knew it was, without a doubt, the fastest one she'd ever made.

As soon as she entered the gate, Kula was all over her. Rose kissed him and patted him as if it was the last time she would ever see him. She put out fresh water and hay for Spirit, then rushed into the breezeway and filled up the big wooden tub Jesse had designed and made.

She went back outside with matches and coal oil. She stripped off her clothing and set them on fire. She choked back her tears, knowing that something terrible had happened. She glanced skyward as if seeking some spiritual intervention. But all she saw was a solemn quarter moon lurking at the edge of a puffy cloud.

The water in the tub was cold, but she didn't care; she sank down into the tub as if she had never before had a bath. She scrubbed her body until her skin became sensitive and irritable.

Then Rose consciously emptied her head of all thought. She sat in this trance-like state until sometime later, when she heard the howl of Jesse's two hunting dogs and figured they were probably after some animal out on a nocturnal prowl. Although she prayed that it would be Mr. Ford, she knew the dogs never howled upon his return home.

She continued to sit still and quiet in the bathtub while Kula slept on his mat. She heard all kinds of sounds as they pierced the darkness of the night. Kula growled, sat up, went back to sleep and repeated the process several times

Finally, they heard Mr. Ford riding in amidst the barking of the dogs. When he entered the house, he found Rose still in the tub, soaping and scrubbing her body. He picked her up, wrapped a sheet around her and laid her on the bed.

"Rose," he began, "my precious, delicate flower...I really don't have the words to express my sorrow and my anger. This won't happen again because I am never letting you out of my sight."

"Please don't say somethin' that's not possible. I be all right after while. What did you do wit' that dead man?"

"Don't you worry none about that," he answered. "No one will ever see him again. His horse is on the other side of the river and I went back to the fork and burned his clothes. His rifle is in the river."

He kissed her gently on her lips and eyes and said, "Now, you get some sleep and try never to think of this day again. We must completely erase it from our memories. It simply never happened."

They lay still and close in the quiet darkness, each with their silent thoughts. Jess was the first to break the quiet. "Honey," he said, rubbing his hand in round circles over her stomach, "we really are going to have a baby and it's growing in here."

"Shush!" she replied.

They lay awake for most of the night, alternately crying and reassuring each other of their love and devotion for one another and that everything would be all right.

Jesse made her promise never to mention the incident at the fork of the road again. "It would be best if we treat it as a forgotten nightmare," he reassured her.

That very night, Jesse made the decision that they would no longer be secretive about their relationship. As far as he was concerned, they were husband and wife, and damn anyone who wouldn't accept it He wanted the world to know, he thought. He just didn't think beyond that. He should have known that the south, especially their rural community, didn't plan to tolerate their declaration of marriage, nor their living together.

They both knew that Rose's selling days at the station were over. That was something Rose would have to clear from her mind. She was ready. Becoming a mother would be fulfillment enough for her.

For the next two months, Jesse and Rose worked at Frank's place overseeing the gathering of the last cotton crop. Together, they watched as the final few bales were loaded onto the wagons for the trip to the cotton gin. They experienced a deep sense of satisfaction and accomplishment knowing that those wagons surely held some of the down payment on their future together in the south.

As expected, Frank made a handsome sum of money. After paying them for their work, he also extended a sizable loan to Jesse in order for him to make preparations for next season's crop. It would be his first year as a southern farmer.

Jesse made another decision that was sure to make Rose unhappy. He insisted that in her condition, her work chores be confined to the kitchen. She prepared breakfast, dinner and supper all at the same time each morning, and with little else to do, she started taking long walks around the farm.

Each afternoon, she walked to the edge of the woods. She enjoyed listening to the soft swish of falling leaves and seeing their brilliant colors of red, gold, orange and brown as they nestled on the earth, heralding that fall had boldly settled in their rolling hill country.

Rose would sit under a chinaberry tree; from there, she enjoyed watching rabbits, squirrels and deer. Often, she saw an elusive fox or skunk at play. She heard the call of the resident owl and the warbled songs of the robins and blue jays. To Rose, this was the sweetest place on earth; she wondered if heaven was like this. Time stood still. The earth stood still. The sounds mellowed. The colors of the forest deepened.

In the midst of one such quiet moment, Jesse came and sat beside her. They enjoyed the exquisite pageantry nature provided. He cradled her in his arms and declared, "This is what life should be like everywhere, peaceful, beautiful and spiritual. There is a quiet, serene beauty here that surpasses anything I've ever seen. The mountains of the west are breathtaking and awesome, but the loveliness of these rolling hills are mesmerizing and are full of promise. I have chosen this place to live for the rest of my life and I have chosen you to be here with me until my life on earth ceases to be."

"Rose," he added, "I love you more than life itself. More than you can ever imagine." He shouted out his proclamation of love and it echoed back from the hills.

Rose had trouble articulating her feelings, so she sat in silence. One o' these days, she thought, I'll be able to get these thoughts out of my head an' talk real nice, like Mr. Ford.

He rubbed her tummy gently and asked, "Can you feel the baby moving yet?"

"Yes, its beginning to have movement an' I likes the feeling, it tells me everything okay."

They sat there for a while, fully transcending time and space. These precious moments would be forever engraved in their memories.

Rose finally broke the silence with a request, "I would like to visit with Mamie befo' the baby comes."

"I'll make arrangements to take you. I can't let you travel alone, it's too risky."

Harvest time was over. The molasses were made and stored. The corn meal had been ground. Hog killing time had passed. The meat had been salted, washed and smoked. The smokehouse was full. Now there was time to visit the Turner Place.

It was a cool autumn day when Rose and Jesse took the long buggy ride to the Turner farm. The trees were now mostly barren. Autumn was grudgingly giving up her last golden hues of the year. Indescribably gnarled and twisted branches and twigs were visible along the path that was strewn with oaks. Leaves and pine needles covered the ground. The crops had all been harvested. The wildlife had retreated to a part of the woods that ran along the riverbank.

As the buggy rolled and rumbled through the back roads, the buff-colored rays from the sun made splotchy patterns along the path. Rose and Jesse enjoyed the grandeur of the hill country, including the scarred and ridged fields that remained after the harvest. They had great faith in the promise of the soil in this country landscape. They knew their livelihood would be coming from this land.

Jesse had already decided to leave Rose with her family for the day. He would go into town to make a few purchases. He did not like going into town and avoided it whenever he could, but he knew the women would want to have some time alone to do their talking. Mamie would share information and bits of wisdom that would help Rose to get through her pregnancy smoothly.

The family was overjoyed to have Rose come and spend a day with them. Their time together was becoming less frequent. The Turners never visited the Ford Farm.

Of course, the Turners were brimming with happiness over the news of the coming baby. Rose wished she could stay a night or two, but Jesse didn't want her away from him at this time. Only Zeke appreciated and understood his position.

One of Rose's requests was to have Mamie make arrangements for a midwife to come and stay with her when her time was near. This probably would not be for another two months or so as they weren't quite sure when the baby was due.

After Rose answered a few of Mamie's probing questions, it was determined that the baby would probably arrive in mid-December. Mamie volunteered, "If its comin' in the middle of December, school be out an' I can come stay wit' ya, but I have to brang the two girls."

"That be jus' wonderful, won't it, Mr. Ford?" sang Rose, seeking and getting agreement.

Mamie gave Rose all of the maternal information she knew and she also told her what necessary items to have available for the birthing. Although Rose had witnessed and assisted with the birth of her baby sister, Susie, she still needed this talk and some reassurance.

It was late afternoon when they began their ride home. Jesse told Rose about an unpleasant encounter he had had at the feed store. He had overheard one of the customers calling him a "Nigra" lover. He chose to ignore the remark. But as he walked the town's boardwalk, he observed the silence and sneers of some people as he passed.

"I'm only telling you this so you understand the necessity of having your gun ready at all times. I don't like the hostility I felt today. The attitudes were noticeably different than any I've encountered before. The south is still at war and the Negro is their new enemy. By the way, I haven't seen you do target practice lately, better get back to it tomorrow. Don't want to frighten you, Rose, but being prepared is security."

The next day, a fried rabbit was on the supper table. A smile curled itself around Jesse's lips when he saw that rabbit. There were also two quails ready for the table the next day.

"My little lady is certainly no procrastinator," he said quietly. Then, he gave thanks for the meal.

Fall was fast disappearing and winter lay in wait. Ready to pounce. The once dense forest opened up and reached her bare arms towards heaven. Many of the animals had retreated to their lairs. Their sounds, which had reverberated across the farm for months, were now mostly silent except for occasional mournful cries heralding the changes. The hoots of the owls opened and closed the days. The shrieks and shrills of the remaining birds periodically pierced the silence of the back woods. The ever-present raucous crows made their presence known and heard. The mockingbirds joined in the fray with their chattering as if they were afraid of being left out of the pageantry.

Rose knew that the baby would come soon because it had dropped low in her belly. After supper, she sat by the fireplace rubbing her stomach and petting Kula intermittently. She alternately sang and hummed her Spirituals. On this night, she filled the air with, "Walk Together Children."

Walk together children, walk together children
Don't you get weary, don't you get weary,
There's a great camp meeting
In the promised land.

Jesse reviewed his plans over and over again for hiring help and beginning the planting season. Afterwards, he sat and read for a long time. He loved reading those books and papers he ordered by mail. It was times like these when Rose secretly wished she had learned how to read. One night, she asked Mr. Ford to read something from the Bible to her. From that night on, his reading the Bible to her became a nightly ritual.

In mid-December, Mamie and the two little girls, Annie and Susie came to the Ford Farm to await the birth of the baby. She brought with her a sack full of essentials she had made for the baby. She even brought two gowns she had made for Rose and a nightshirt for Jesse.

Of course, Mamie was impressed with such a fine house. She never even dreamed that Rose lived in such a sumptuous dwelling. Even during slavery, she had never seen a bed as large and as fine as the one in the Ford bedroom.

"My whole fam'ly could sleep in that bed," she gulped.

By now, they were expecting the baby any day. So far, there were no signs of an impending arrival. Three days before Christmas, Mamie sent Jesse to get the mid-wife that delivered many of the babies on the local farms. Mamie wanted and needed to be home with her family to celebrate Christmas. She had been with Rose almost two weeks without any word of her family.

Rose gave them some warm caps she had made of rabbit's fur. She added a squirrel's tail to the ones for the boys. Jesse went for Mrs. Broome. The next day, he took Mamie and the girl's home. Rose was unusually quiet and sad. Even Jesse's reading to her that night did not cheer her up.

Mrs. Broome ordered Rose to bed. Rose protested. Rose sulked and cried. She refused to leave her room. All to no avail. The midwife prevailed. She knew what was good for Rose. Nor did she allow her to get out of bed the following morning. She gave the orders. She did the cooking. She ran the household. Mrs. Broome did no˜even permit Kula in the bedroom. Rose fell more silent.

By now, Rose was certain that she did not want that woman in her house and she told Mr. Ford just that. "She has to be here, Rose," he said firmly. "We can't send her away. It's time for the baby to come. I won't take chances with that."

The following evening, December 24, 1881, Rose gave birth to Justine Eve Ford.

"Look at her, she's beautiful!" cooed a happy Mr. Ford.

"I knows you wanted a boy. You sho' you happy?" Rose quietly asked.

"Of course I'm happy! Don't even think like that, Mama Rose. We'll have more children, the boys will come. You just get your rest," he added.

"I don't need no rest," she stammered, "I ain't did nothing."

"You just delivered a baby girl and made me a proud Papa on Christmas Eve. "Merry Christmas!" Jesse said, with grandeur, "This is our merriest and best Christmas yet! Oh, how I love you, Rose! And I love our beautiful daughter! Look at her eyes! "Look at her hair! Look at her hands! Look at her feet!"

With that, Mrs. Broome took Justine, bathed her and wrapped her up like they did baby Jesus who was outside in a stable. Then she shooed Mr. Ford from the room.

It was clear that Mrs. Broome was a woman who was used to taking charge and giving orders. Rose wondered if she'd ever done anything else in life. She controlled every move Rose attempted to make. Not only didn't she allow Rose to get out of bed, she only let Rose have the baby when it was time to nurse her. And she became upset when Rose took a long time feeding Justine.

To top it all, two days later, she asked Rose, "Why in heav'n's name do you live wit' a white man? You knows you gonna be nothin' but his slave! You kin' never go anywheres wit' him. You livin' in sin an' shame! You just ax'ing fo' trouble."

Rose got out of bed, put on one of Jesse's overcoats and went out to the barn to find him. Mrs. Broome ran after her, trying to get her back inside the house.

"Mr. Ford!" she screamed. "Take her home, now! I want her out of this house, right now!"

"Rose, honey, you'll catch your death of cold, get back inside."

"Not until you promise to take her away from here!"

"If it means that much to you, I'll get ready and do it now," Jesse replied as he picked her up and took her back inside.

Chapter Eleven

Holding the baby to her bosom and with a smile on her face, Rose stood at the window and watched as Jesse hitched up the buggy and the two of them rode out into the afternoon's fading sun.

She hoped that he would be home before darkness fell. Rose felt a certain sadness that Mamie had not been there to enjoy the birth of the baby with them. At the same time, she felt a particular triumph over Mrs. Broome and her unbelievable bad attitude.

"She had no cause to say such ugly and mean things to me," thought Rose.

Sunset came early on this late December afternoon. Rose was particularly pleased to be sitting in the rocking chair in the parlor with her baby, looking out at the crisp winter day as it came to a close. She went to the kitchen to look for Kula when she suddenly remembered that Kula had not seen the baby. She quickly gave him one of Justine's blankets to play with and she smiled with a deep satisfaction as Kula tussled and played with the blanket.

Kula erupted with energy and inquisitiveness, but Rose did not let him touch or see the baby. Not yet. That would come later. She rocked and sang lullabies and all three slept in the solemn stillness before the glowing fireplace.

The sounds of the hunting dogs greeting their master awakened Rose and told her that Mr. Ford had returned from his unscheduled journey. She sleepily smiled and said, "I'm glad to have my fam'ly all to m'self!"

Rose felt useful and needed again. "I love being a Mama," she said to Jesse one day, " I loves being your wife, an' I feels like telling the whole world."

"I want to thank you, little Mama, I was thinking the exact same thing," he answered. "Why, just last night I had to pinch myself to see if I was dreaming."

Rose enjoyed sitting and observing Mr. Ford hold and play with Justine. His physical presence and his state of mind showed such naturalness. She could tell by the unpretentious look on his face, how much he adored his daughter.

"This fam'ly is gon' do real nice," said Rose. "We have had a Blessed Christmas. I think we better do what we would do if Mamie was here. Let's pray!"

The winter days were short and the nights were long and cold. There was always had a great fire constantly going in the massive fireplace. Rose often put sweet potatoes in the hot coals to bake. She learned from Mamie what a great snack they were on a cold winter's night.

Jesse was always a big coffee drinker, but Rose finally convinced him that her teas not only tasted better, but were good for so many ailments; so she served hot tea on those cold nights. And Jesse continued his nightly ritual of reading scripture to her.

Winter departed that region quickly. Jesse was pleased with the early departure because he was anxious to get started with spring planting. Rose and Jesse had gone without much contact with the outside world that winter. Occasionally, Frank would come by to pass some time with them, to share whatever news he had and to bring Jesse a few newspapers and periodicals. The two brothers shared ideas about the crops they would soon be planting.

The Turners finally came for a visit to see the baby. The roads were usually so bad this time of year, they were generally unsuitable for wagons. But as soon as there was a break in the weather, the Turners took off immediately because they knew the good weather probably would not last.

Rose and Jesse were overjoyed to have the whole family visit them. Grandma and Grandpa Turner and the children were excited over little Justine. They thought she was the prettiest baby they had ever seen. She looked like Rose but she was the color of her daddy. Rose served them dinner and asked them to stay overnight. Mamie said they needed to get home because they didn't trust the pleasant weather to hold.

"Did you see that look o' pride on Jesse's face?" asked Mamie on the way home.

"He 'bout the happiest daddy I see'd in a long time," responded Zeke.

"Sho' is a fine baby. She beautiful, too."

"She purty all right," answered Zeke. "But she look mighty white to me."

"She is a white baby," Samuel added to the conversation.

"You shet yo' mouth," Mamie said. "Nobody ax'ed you nothin.'

"Ma, is that really Rose's baby?" asked Annie, with wonder in her voice.

"It sho' nuff is." answered Mamie. "And Jesse Ford be the daddy, too."

Winter finally withdrew its blustery winds, recalled its frosty mornings and melted down its icicles. The sun began to influence the air and the budding and blossoming trees filled the land with beauty. Filled the country with a sweet and pleasant aroma. Filled the hills with freshness and wonder. The birds were returning to their summer homes. Their chattering made sweet music and their soaring and fluttering made pretty patterns in the sky.

The rabbits, squirrels, deer, even the foxes and skunks could be seen darting in and out among the forest trees. Green carpet soon began to cover the land, spilling over the hills and valleys. Spring had come forth in all its intriguing splendor to reclaim its revolving cycle in the rolling hill country.

On Easter Sunday, in the year 1882, Rose Turner and Jesse Ford, along with Frank Ford, took Justine Eve to Sunflower Methodist Church to be baptized. The Baptismal Certificate with Justine's name, her birth date, and her parent's names written on it, was a special source of joy and pride for Rose. She couldn't read it but she knew what it was. Mr. Ford would read it to her later.

The two parents beamed with pride and delight. The congregation had never before seen racial mixed parents at a baby christening. They had, more often than they cared to remember, seen children whose fathers were white. But those fathers never publicly acknowledged their children. This was something to tell your children and grandchildren about. This was a celebration of love that knew no boundaries.

On that Easter Sunday, there was also another special event. Jesse brought along a young colt and gave it to Zeke in appreciation for everything he had done for him. The colt was the son of Spirit and one of Jesse's mare. It was a promise fulfilled.

"I don' know what to say, I don' hav' words,"stammered Zeke.

"Thank you, will do just fine," said Jesse.

Mamie wanted to offer one of her prayers of thanksgiving, but Zeke persuaded her to wait until they returned to the house.

"The preacher done enough prayin' fo' now," Zeke said.

a visitor. . . . .

Justine was little more than four months old when Rose had an unexpected visitor to the farm that left her terribly shaken and frightened. She was working in her garden with the baby tethered to her back. She had just finished planting mustard, turnip, onion and squash seeds. She was beginning to space the string bean seeds when Kula sounded the warning that something or someone was approaching. She put her hand under the sack beneath the baby's sling and felt reassured by the pistol. The man rode up to the gate and called out. "I'm Sheriff Bogard. This here the Ford Farm, ain't it?"

"Yassah." Rose answered, her mind quickly going to the incident at the fork of the road that had happened almost a year ago. She tried hard not to show her panic.

"Dis be da Ford Farm. Mr. Ford, he be workin' da west end t'day, jus' ova' da hill, a piece in dat d'rection," she stammered, pointing her shaking finger.

"I hear tell there's a colored gal livin' with Mr. Ford, would you happen to know anythin' 'bout that?"

"Ya' has to ax' Mr. Ford." She was so nervous and scared she could feel her urine running down her legs.

"He ova' yonder." She pointed again in the direction where Jesse was working along with some of the newly acquired field hands. Somehow she managed to continue workin, punching holes in the soft soil with the handle of her hoe.

"That yo' baby?" the sheriff asked.

"Yassah, dis ma baby," she said in a trembling, scared voice.

"Sho' is a yaller baby," said the sheriff as he took off towards the hill.

Rose's body went limp but she summoned forth enough strength to walk to the house with Kula yapping at her feet. She was greatly relieved that the incident at the fork had not been mentioned but she still did not know the purpose of the sheriff's visit. All she could remember was his piercing eyes boring into her as he asked her questions. She would have to wait until Mr. Ford returned home before she would know why the sheriff paid him a visit.

Rose suspected she was pregnant again but she had not told Jesse. He was occupied with the business of getting their first major crops going and she didn't want him to have to use his energy on anything except just that. She would be fine. And that was that!

"Dear Lord," she prayed aloud, "Wha's this sheriff visit all about? Don' let it be bad news. Please protect us. 'Specially, protect Mr. Ford. Amen!"

When Jesse returned from the fields, there was such a stately and proud look about him, it made Rose uneasy. She thought he would be eager to tell her about the sheriff visit, but he didn't even mention it. During supper, silence splintered the air.

Finally, when Rose could take it no more, she blurted out, "What the sheriff want?"

"Oh," said Jesse," seemingly unperturbed, "He wanted to tell me that it's agin' the law to live with a colored person."

"That be it, nothing mo?" questioned Rose, feeling somewhat puzzled.

"I told him that if I saw such a couple, I would pass the word along."

"I declare, Mr. Jesse Ford," said Rose, "you is somethin' else!"

"Rose," Jesse said on a serious note. "They'll be back. And I'll shoot anyone who tries to arrest you. I am a soldier and I'll defend my family and home to the death!"

Rose didn't respond but she knew what he was thinking was no answer to the problem that Mamie had so wisely foreseen. She began to formulate a plan in her own head since she could not reach Mamie to ask for her advice.

When Jesse left for the field the next day, Rose quickly secured the baby on her back, hitched Spirit to the wagon and rode to the sharecropper's house that was occupied by Jack, his wife Molly, and their children. She went there because she knew Molly, who was heavy with child, would not be working in the field.

"Molly, I needs yo' help!" she shouted as Molly ran out to the wagon.

Molly picked up her youngest child and they left in the wagon with Rose. They went straight to the main house, gathered up a few objects and placed them in the wagon. They repeated this a few times until the wagon was filled. They made several trips taking household items to the empty sharecropper house, number three.

When Jesse returned from the field that evening, he noticed some small pieces missing from the house, including Justine's cradle.

"What's going on, Rose? What happened to some of the furniture?"

"I worked out a plan fo' us livin' together an' not breakin' the law," Rose answered.

Jesse looked at Rose with question marks all over his face. She was silent.

"Is this plan your own secret, or are you going to share it with me?" he asked.

"I moved 'nough things to number three house so's Justine an' me can live there," she began...

Jesse interrupted, "No! We will not live separated! We must be together. I want my daughter in the same house as her father. I'll return to Kansas, before I let them separate us!" he bellowed.

" Mr. Ford," she said softly, "you haven' heard all my plan."

"I'm sorry, Rose," Jesse said. "But first, tell me how you moved the furniture out to number three.

"That was easy," she smiled. "Molly n' me moved it in the wagon."

"Mr. Ford," Rose began, "me an' the baby will go to number three ev'ry day when you goes to the field. At evenin' when you comes home, then we come home."

"Do you really think this plan can work, Rose?" asked Jesse. "Can you really do this?"

"Its' got to work. Right now, we can't 'ford no trouble. The most 'mportant thing in our lives is to git the crops goin' an' ev'rythin workin'. This gotta be our year! We can't let nothin' or nobody git in the way!"

After supper, Jesse sat and thought about what Rose had said. He knew she was right and that her plans did make sense. He knew that in order to survive, this first crop must be successful. "God, what a smart and wonderful woman you gave me," he said.

That night, Jesse read the following scripture to Rose:

> Who can find a virtuous wife? For her worth is far above rubies.
> The heart of her husband safely trusts her; so he will have no lack of gain.
> She does him good and not evil all the days of her life.
> She seeks wool and flax, and willingly works with her hands.
> She is like the merchant ships, she brings her food from afar.
> She also rises while it is yet night, and provides food for her household, and a portion for her maidservants.
> She considers a field and buys it; from her profits she plants a vineyard.
> She girds herself with strength, and strengthens her arms.
> She perceives that her merchandise is good, and her lamp does not go out by night.
> She stretches out her hands to the distaff, and her hand holds the spindle.
> She extends her hand to the poor, yes, she reaches out her hands to the needy.
> She is not afraid of snow for her household; for all her household is clothed with scarlet.
> She makes tapestry for herself; her clothing is fine linen and purple.
> Her husband is known in the gates, when he sits among the elders of the land.
> She makes linen garments and sells them, and supplies sashes for the merchants.

> Strength and honor are her clothing; she shall rejoice in time to come.
> She opens her mouth with wisdom, and on her tongue is the law of kindness.
> She watches over the ways of her household, and does not eat the bread of idleness.
> Her children rise up and call her blessed; her husband also, and he praises her;
> "Many daughters have done well, but you excel them all."
> Charm is deceitful and beauty is vain, but a woman who fears the Lord, she shall be praised.
> Give her of the fruit of her hands, and let her own works praise her in the gates.
> Proverbs 31:10-31

After listening to this beautiful passage, and with tears in her eyes, Rose knew that this was the time to tell Jesse about the new baby. She deeply loved and respected him and she knew he felt the same way about her.

This union surely is a gift from God, she thought. I must tell Mr. Ford, now.

"Are you sure?" Jesse asked when she told him about the baby. "That's wonderful!"

"I waited to be sure befo' I tol' you," she replied. "I 'spect he be here 'bout Thanksgiving."

"Did God also tell you it's a boy?" Jesse teasingly inquired.

"No," Rose answered, "I jus' know it be a boy this time."

"Don't count the chick before the egg hatches," Jesse cautioned her.

"I loved your Bible reading tonight, Mr. Ford. It was beautiful an' it made me seem so special. Will you read it to me again?"

"Of course I will, and you are special, very, very special and so is our daughter."

They slept that night feeling and enjoying all the love they were capable of, and yet, dreading the move Rose knew they must make.

Sheriff Bogard made two more trips to the Ford Farm during the following month. Each time, no one was at the house. Jesse was in the field with the workers. Rose was safely inside sharecropper house number three. The sheriff had no reason to visit the houses of the sharecroppers.

On the sheriff's third visit, he was accompanied by three deputies and they arrived just at dusk when it was darker than it was light. The dogs announced their surprise arrival. Jesse circled the yard with his Winchester and his shotgun. He sent out a warning shot.

"Don't shoot! It's the sheriff!" a voice boomed out. "We here to make sure you ain't breaking no laws. It's agin' the law in this state for whites to live in the same house with coloreds."

"Ain't no coloreds in this house." Jesse was sure by now that Rose had taken off down the gully and across the field.

"Well, I'll just have my deputy check the house out, these coloreds are pretty slippery. They subject to be anywhere."

"Didn't see a soul no wheres," said the deputy, emerging from the house. "Did see 'nough food on the table fer three o' four, though."

"You wouldn't play no tricks on us, now would you, Mr. Ford?" asked the sheriff. "You know, my boys can visit 'most any time. And don't you f'get, we got guns, too, and we out number you."

"This is my home, I can invite whomever I please to my home; you have no right to threaten me," retorted Jesse.

"Now, that you can, Mr. Ford, but if they colored, they jes' can't live wit' you." The sheriff responded.

"Ya'll have a good evening, ya hear," he said, as he led his deputies away.

After that visit, Rose made the decision to spend full days at number three, not only days, but nights also. It was easy for her to get away that night, but as her belly got bigger, it would be more difficult, especially carrying Justine.

Jesse Ford was absolutely livid about the whole situation. But he was a sensible man. He knew that he wasn't bigger than the law. He knew that he badly needed to get this first year of crops completed. He would go along with Rose's plan for the present, but deep inside his thoughts, his own plan began to form.

Rose set up full housekeeping in the little two-room house. It was a lot nicer than the shanty shacks that were generally built for sharecroppers. It was better because Jesse took advice from Zeke, who told him, "If you make good provisions, you' get good workers who will stay wit' ya year in an' year out. Good workers know the earth an' they know cotton," he said. "They' give you good production an' they' be loyal. You prosper ova' the long haul. An' for Heav'n sakes, don't ever git those hand-to-mouth fo'ks. They know they be gon' come the nex' year," Zeke added.

Jesse had been happy that he followed Zeke's advice and now it was paying off in other ways. The sharecropper houses he built were the best ones in these parts.

Rose knew how to nurture the friendship she had developed with Molly, who kept Justine while she went to her garden each morning. Without Justine, she was able to do twice as much work. After dinner, she would often join the workers in the field.

The gentle spring rain, the warm sun, plus the rich soil, were producing bountiful results, both for the garden and for the crops in the fields. Rose could see fantastic possibilities, so she went to the fields more and more to demonstrate to the workers how to be more productive. Mamie had told her how during slavery, the workers sang both Spirituals and work-songs to help pass the time and to get everybody working in rhythm, and how they sneaked and alternated rest periods with each other.

Each evening, Rose gathered from her garden, fresh greens, onions, new potatoes, and pole beans and shared them with the sharecroppers. She also gave them flour and meal sacks to be used for clothing or decorations for their houses. She knew that these little acts of kindness earned their friendship, their loyalty and their good hard work in the field. She also asked Mr. Ford to pick up certain items they needed from town.

Rose made herself and her family comfortable for the time being, but she knew that once summer arrived, the little house would be nearly unbearable in the heat. There was at least one tree to provide shade at each of the sharecropper houses. But the big house was surrounded by trees which provided lots of shade and cool breezes. And, best of all, there was a screened-in porch that wrapped around the house where they could sit and talk into the night without mosquitoes eating them up.

Chapter Twelve

It was the time between cotton chopping and cotton picking that Jesse decided to use to put his own plan into action. He knew this new project would interfere with his work schedule, but his mind was made up. Each time he went to the big empty house after supper, there was a gnawing pain that tore and wrenched at his heart. The separation from Rose and his daughter was devastating, he lay awake for hours thinking about them. The little time he spent with them each evening was more painful that it was satisfying.

He knew that he could not survive for long without Rose and Justine there in the house with him. Everyone would probably think his idea was insane and that he was crazy. But he knew he would be the one who would lose his sanity if he didn't do it.

As soon as the cotton chopping was finished, several wagonloads of lumber were deposited in the yard next to the main house. Within one week, the frame went up. The next week, the roof was completed. The staccato sounds of hammer on nails echoed throughout the back woods. The work went from sun up until sun down.

The house continued to form and take shape. Rose looked on in utter astonishment and disbelief when she finally realized the magnitude of what was taking place without her having been apprised.

"I knew you would say no if I told you." Explained Jesse when she confronted him "This is my answer to a law which says a man can't live in his own home with whom he chooses."

"But, Mr. Ford," protested Rose, "we don't got 'nough money to build 'nother big house. We need what money we got to get our crops to market."

"Rose, I didn't stop you from selling at the station. That was your decision. This is my decision. No one, not even you, is going to stop me. Having my family with me is more important than anything else in the world. This house will be completed before the new baby arrives."

Rose stood looking at this man whom she loved and respected so much. He had such a look of determination on his face. She dared not try to undermine his decision nor make him agree to anything less than what he so deeply desired.

She gathered up Justine and Kula, got in the buggy and returned to number three where she could still hear the echoing sounds of the tools. She was consumed with mixed emotions. Her heart was crammed with splendid thoughts of a devoted husband and father. But her head erupted and churned with the realities of pitfalls that were sure to come. It would take too much energy and money to run two houses.

Mr. Ford had told her that a tax had now been levied on each bale of ginned cotton. Also there was talk of collecting taxes to pay for schools. There was mass illiteracy among all the people. Schools were desperately needed.

Mr. Ford means well, thought Rose, but his action is foolish.

Jesse had also told Rose that economic and social problems were getting out of hand. The post-war problems for colored and white were enormous. The effects of the war had left too much land desolate. Left too many people with little or no income. The main need, he said, was survival, and this would require hard work and dedication from everyone.

For the first time since the sheriff's last visit, number three seemed small and cramped to Rose. She had made it as comfortable as she knew how. She knew that Mamie could have made it more comfortable, even made it attractive. The little house, like the other two, sat in the middle of a barren yard at the edge of the field. Each one had a large chinaberry tree with some smaller ones beginning to grow. Rose and Molly had planted vegetables and flowers but they were still puny. Even the honeysuckle was not faring well. It had been planted late and the rain had not cooperated.

The sultry evening told her that summer was now teasing the last days of spring. Soon the hot summer days and nights and the longing for the comforts of the big house would make the little house more and more uncomfortable. Rose knew that she would have to endure this difficulty because any other choice would be counter-productive. They had to live with this plan for the time being. She vowed to make the most of it. No matter what happened, she would not let it get the best of them.

She already knew that Mr. Ford did not like the idea of the three of them having to sleep and eat there. And soon, there would be four of them....

" I guess Mr. Ford know what he' doing," she mused. Still she worried.

He no longer read to her at night. He was too tired to spend time playing and cuddling with Justine. The happy sounds that she enjoyed so much were missing. The sound she missed most was his voice as he read scripture to her, and of course she missed their indescribable nights together, especially those on the porch swing, when passion flowed unbridled between them.

Construction on the new house, which started out at such a fast pace, had now slowed to a turtle's crawl. When the cotton was ready to be picked, the house was only half finished. For the time being, harvesting the cotton came first. Building on the house had to be suspended.

The bolls had opened wide and picking was in high gear. The unprocessed cotton had to be taken to the gin. The soft fibers would be pulled off the hard seeds and the cotton ginned. The bales would be sold and sent to mills and cloth factories up North. Life in the South followed a rhythm of planting, weeding and harvesting. During this time, the field hands rose at the first light and toiled till sunset.

Rose suspected there was another reason for the slow down of the construction of the new house. She tried to unravel the mystery of the work reduction. It had trickled to near zero. Her queries met with little success. Mr. Ford was coming to number three on tenant's row each night later than usual. This change brought about some annoyance and aggravation. Eventually, she asked why the work on the house had practically stopped.

"It's taking me more time to go over the books and make plans on how to balance everything out," he answered. "I have also been spending time working on fancy little details for the house."

"Why you have to do that?" Rose asked. "Can't the workers do that?"

"Not the fine details, I know just how I want those done."

jars of money. . . . .

Rose heard some words that Jesse clearly had avoided saying. That night, she lay awake thinking of ways she could once again come through, when help was clearly needed. She knew that being pregnant, she could not go to the station again. And even if she weren't expecting a baby, Mr. Ford would never consent to her going. She realized her selling days were now history.

When morning finally came after a restless night, Rose remembered something she had forgotten or at least not thought about for some time. It was something she had, no doubt, stored in her head to bring forward at some future time. That time had come! Instinctively she knew they needed some of the buried money! The money she and Zeke had buried in the yard for bad times.

In the Turners' back yard, she and Zeke had buried many cans and jars of money. Money that she had earned selling at the to station. She knew that what Mr. Ford needed to finish the house was money. And she had some. It was just waiting to be dug up.

Rose told Jesse that she would be attending church the following Sunday. "Maybe you'd like to go," she invited him, knowing he was too busy with the crops.

"You go on with Justine. I've got too many chores that need to be finished. Frank's coming by to give me a hand with the ceiling on Sunday."

Rose was tempted to invite Molly to go with her but she wasn't ready just yet to share that part of her life. She thought of leaving Justine with her Molly but she knew that her family would be too disappointed if she came without her. Still, she was tempted to do just that because she knew how much time it would save if she rode Spirit instead of going by buggy. She also knew that Jesse might become suspicious. But, most important of all, she should not ride that far on a horse at this stage of her pregnancy. Too much bouncing around on bumpy roads.

So early on Sunday morning, she left to go to church worship service and to visit with her family. But neither church service nor family was her real objective.

It was a splendid summer morning. The glistening sun had barely made contact with the red earth. The red earth. Now that was something else that she had meant to check out. She made a mental note to some day check out that vein of red clay that lay en route to the low lands. They rode past the tall pine trees rising from the hearty and healthy soil, past the splendid, flowing wisps of willows and the cat o' nine tails that announced the small ponds and streams in the thickets. They passed the live oaks with feathery gray moss hanging from their branches. The moss swayed back and forth in the gentle morning breeze. They heard the warbled notes of songbirds singing praise to the sky and trees.

There was the floating, fragrant scent from the stately magnolias, the dogwoods and the honeysuckles. The dragonflies and the katydids darted in and out of the path. The shrill call of some jays and crows flying overhead added to the passing parade of this early Sunday morning ride.

After church service, everyone took time to pay their respects to each other. The Turners were anxious to return home and pass some time with Rose and the grandbaby. All of the Turner children, especially the girls, wanted turns to hold Justine, now that she was bigger.

They were elated at hearing about the expected baby and of course, Mamie took the opportunity to offer up a long prayer of thanks and praise. She sent the children outside because having a baby was not a topic to be discussed in their presence.

Mamie served a wonderful dinner of cabbage, tomatoes, black eyed-peas with cured ham chunks, buttermilk and corn bread. Everything was cold since it had been prepared on Saturday, and Mamie did not believe in doing any work on the Lord's day. No fire was allowed in the stove. Nothing would be heated.

When dinner was finished, Rose said to Zeke, "Pa, remember the cans and jars of money we once buried? I sure need some of it now."

"Is this somethin' you can talk 'bout? Zeke asked, with concern etched on his finely chiseled face.

"Sho' I can," Rose said as the two of them walked out to the yard. "Mr. Ford is buildin' a house jus' like the other one jus' cause the sheriff come out and say it agin' the law for whites an' coloreds to live in the same house."

"We tol' you that 'fore you gots married, didn' need no sheriff to tell you."

"But, Pa, Sheriff Bogard say he gon' arrest me and put me in jail if he catch us livin' in the same house. Then Mr. Ford say he have one house for him and one for me."

"So, now you needs money to build' the house?"

"The house almost built, Pa. Mr. Ford jes' can't finish it cause he needs what money he got left, to bring in the crops. And now, he worried sick 'cause he sleep one place, and me an' Justine, we sleep 'nother place. I'm scared, Pa. Mr. Ford don't hardly eat, he workin' long hours, he don't got time fo' me an' the baby no mo.' He say mebbe we go live in Kansas. Pa, I don't even know where that is."

"I reckon we better find that money. Now don' tell yo' Ma, but I come out there nex' Sunday to give him a hand wit' the work."

Zeke and Rose dug up a number of cans they had buried near the mulberry tree. They went inside and counted nearly three hundred dollars. Rose wanted to leave part of it but Zeke reminded her there were a few more cans still buried.

Mamie pulled out an old quilt and Zeke secured the cans under the seat of the buggy. They told Rose to leave right away and not take chances on being on the road after sunset. Zeke would ride part of the way with her. They were sure that Jesse would be riding out to look for his family before long.

"S'long, Rose. Keep well. I see you nex' Sunday," Zeke said, as he turned back and headed for home.

"Thank you, Pa. You be careful, now. See ya!"

Rose was pleased with herself and she was pleased that something she did so long ago could now help keep her family together. She hoped Mr. Ford would be as happy as she was.

As they neared home, Rose saw Mr. Ford off in the distance. He was riding against a background of a sky filled with fluid reds that came from the setting sun. The glow drenched the rolling hills in shimmering shades of gold, orange and purple.

Rose thought she was witnessing the most beautiful sight in all the world. She recalled God's promise of the meek inheriting the earth. And in that moment, she knew that she truly owned a piece of this incredible earth.

Jesse was happy to see his family. He gave Rose a kiss and took Justine in his arms for the balance of the ride to the house. Rose insisted on going to number three.

Jesse was especially irritated at the thought of not sleeping with Rose on a night when he needed to be comforted and loved. He had put in long hours of non-stop work under a sun so hot it gave off wet heat. And he was worried about not completing the house for Rose before the new baby arrived.

But this night, Jesse balked at going to number three and insisted they would all sleep in the comfort of the main house. If trouble came, then he would quickly go and sleep on the bare floor of the unfinished house.

Rose put a cold supper on the table. It was the leftovers from Mamie's dinner that she had insisted on sending home with Rose. Once again, Rose saw how wise and knowing Mamie was.

When supper was finished, Jesse and Rose sat on the porch clinging to each other. They sat in a knowing and understanding silence broken only by the sounds of the frogs and crickets, amidst the glow from the clusters of fireflies giving up their shimmering light against the night sky. They saw the gnats and mosquitoes in the streams of pale moonlight. They each knew that it would have been impossible to sit like this at number three. Here, they were safe and comfortable behind the screens. Here they comforted and loved each other in the cool of the evening.

"Mr. Ford," Rose said afterwards in a voice filled with sleepy fulfillment. "There's some tin cans and jars in the buggy, inside quilt. They filled with money."

"What on earth are you talking about, Rose? Did you borrow money from Zeke?" he asked in a raised voice. "You'll just have to return it. I will not take money from him."

"Rose, I have told you I am the man of this house. I will not accept Zeke's money. I will earn my own money for my family! Now, the subject is closed and that's final!"

The moon became frail in the sky. The delight on Rose's face faded. The noise of the crickets and frogs was louder and more intense. Louder! Louder! Louder!

After a long pause, Rose began to speak her mind, "You never gimme a chance to finish what I gots to say. That be my money. MY money! I earn' it! I put it away in tin cans and I forget all 'bout it 'til now, when I figure we need it, we got to use it! I know you don't have 'nough money to finish that house. And that's all I got to say!"

"Rose, Rose. I'm sorry. I'm sorry. Forgive me! Please forgive me! Once again, you are a precious jewel. Lord knows I could never have a life without you. This hot day and warm evening has suddenly turned into a splendid night! Are there any more surprises and miracles left in you that have not been revealed? Lord, God, you have blessed me with an angel! A Mama Rose angel!

"I feel like shouting angelic praises to the heavens." Jesse declared, "But I read the Bible better than I shout. So he took out his Bible and read:

> "And the Lord will grant you plenty of goods, in the fruit of your body, in the increase of your livestock, and in the produce of your ground, in the land of which the Lord swore to your fathers to give you.
>
> "The Lord will open to you His good treasure, the heavens, to give the rain to your land in its season, and to bless all the work of your hand. You shall lend to many nations, but you shall not borrow.
>
> "And the Lord will make you the head and not the tail; you shall be above only, and not be beneath, if you heed the commandments of the Lord your God, which I command you today, and are careful to observe them."

Deuteronomy 28:11-13

"I jes' love it when you read the Bible to me. Seems like it brangs such comfort an' peace."

Two days later, Rose again heard the staccato sounds of the hammer and nails. Construction on the house was back in full swing. The cracking sound of steel against steel and steel cutting and sawing wood echoed throughout the area.

Once again, Jesse Ford had a smile on his face and he displayed a new exuberance and joy as he went about his daily chores. He was now animated and energetic, both in mind and body. His dreams and his plans were going forth. Once more, he continued reading to Rose each night. Again, he was spending more time with her and Justine. Their world suddenly seemed right once more and it was filled with a new sweetness.

At the end of summer, Molly went into labor. Her labor began so quickly there had been no time to get a midwife, so Rose helped with the delivery of the baby. It was a grueling night because she was having a difficult labor. Jack was a complete disaster and proved to be no help at all. When Rose told him to put the bowl of hot water on the wash stand, he put it on the kitchen table. He screamed at the children. He couldn't find another lamp. He put the clean sheets on the floor and finally, he started sweating and groaning. He was more of a distraction than a help, so Rose ordered him out of the house.

"Out! Out!" she yelled. "Don't come back till I calls you"

Molly's pains and her labor came in spurts but her moaning never ceased. The water bag erupted and Rose could see that the baby's head was not quite in the right position. She directed Molly into various maneuvers hoping this would help the baby's head to turn. She put her in a squat position and told her to pant as hard as she could when the contractions began.

"Suck up! Suck up! Suck hard!" she ordered.

After several repetitions of this procedure, mercifully, and miraculously, the head finally turned. Rose knew that she was simply guessing because she had attended only one other birth. A few minutes later, the baby boy was delivered from the squatting position. Her intuition had paid off.

Jesse came out to number three and stayed with Justine for the night. His demeanor and attitude had taken an incredible upswing since the construction on the house was proceeding at a good pace. He always seemed willing to help Rose in whatever way he could and he knew that she needed him tonight.

Rose stayed with Molly until the next morning when she felt comfortable enough to let Jack take over. He was excused from working in the field that day and he promised to make up for the lost time. Jack thanked Rose for her overwhelming display of nerve, patience and determination.

"Some day, I hope to pay fo' yo' kindness. I sho' 'preciate what you done fo' us."

"You welcome," said Rose as she disappeared inside number three to try and get some much-needed rest. She even forgot that Justine was still there with her daddy.

Although Rose was heavy with child, she continued to go to the field to help in gathering the last of the cotton crops. She often had to battle with Jesse in order to convince him that she was needed at this crucial time and that it didn't in any way interfere with her having a baby.

She kept it to herself, but she knew that the field hands were more productive when she was out among them. The workers seemed to have an unspoken joy in the unusual scenario of this white boss man and his Negro 'woman' and child. If the sharecroppers talked about Miz Rose and Mr. Ford among themselves, and they did, neither Rose nor Jesse were aware of it. They were beyond happy knowing that their field hands were contented to be working at Ford Farm. And that they were excellent workers who did more than was expected of them.

If Jesse didn't know and understand their value in the beginning, he certainly did understand and know it now, as Zeke had predicted.

By the end of October, the harvesting was completed. The cotton had been ginned and sold. The corn had been husked and shelled. Some was kept for the livestock and some turned into meal. Jesse even sold some of the corn crop to a local gristmill. Molasses and syrup were made and stored. They cleared more money than they had expected to. The barn and the storehouses were filled with enough food and supplies to take them through the cold winter.

They settled with the sharecroppers and assigned them jobs to do during the remaining fall and winter months. They must clear the land and plow the fields under. There was still cane to be cut and there were a few winter crops to plant. The sharecroppers were pleased with Mr. Ford's fairness and were happy to be retained on a farm with such good working conditions.

Jesse was busy putting finishing touches on their second house. It was almost a duplicate of the first one, except it had no kitchen and no dining room. It did, however, have a breakfast room and a nursery room. The breezeway from the kitchen that served the first house was extended to connect with the breakfast room of the second house. The breakfast room had an octagonal shape with windows all around. It was Rose's favorite room. It had a warm, sunny and inviting look. In the hot summers, the open windows would allow cross breezes to cool the room. It had a view of her garden and from those windows she could see the grove of trees which led to the river.

In mid-November, Jesse took the train to Houston to make some major purchases for the new house. He ordered supplies and grain and he also ordered tools, machinery and seed for spring planting. He bought clothing for Rose and Justine and a supply of items for the baby they were expecting. He also took time to select and purchase Christmas presents for the Turners and for his sharecroppers.

Rose and Justine stayed in number three while he was away. He asked Jack and Molly to look after them during his absence. Jack told him not to worry about his family and he promised to keep an eye on them day and night. Besides that, he knew Rose always had her pistol and her Winchester nearby. By now, everyone knew what a good shot she was. She still hunted and often bagged a bevy of small game which she shared with the sharecroppers.

The grandeur of the colors of fall were diminishing quickly. Each day, the sun began to give the sky up to night at a hurried pace. The earth was looking more barren and brown. The wind blew harder and stripped the remaining leaves from the trees. The rain was more frequent and once again, most of the wild animals had retreated from sight. It seemed clear that was nature's way of providing protection from the hunters that stalked the woods during the fall and winter months.

A peaceful calm settled in the hill country. The families had more time for each other. They had more time to enjoy the results of their hard labor. The meadows were resplendent in golden hues of yellow and brown. The sky was filled with the flutter of wings as many species of fowl scrambled to get to their winter homes. The majestic call of the geese and ducks reverberated through the hills and valleys as they flew in angled shaped patterns.

Rose's stomach grew larger and she stayed indoors more and more. She was glad that Mr. Ford had completed his trip and was once again spending more relaxed evenings with her and Justine. They were happy to be enjoying the simple pleasures of life.

She was pleased with the dresses and the winter coat that he bought for her. It was the first real winter coat she had ever owned. One of the dresses reminded her of the one Mamie had made for her when she first went to live with the Turners. Like that one, this dress had lovely yellow roses on it. The shoes were too large for her tiny feet but she would put on extra stockings, stuff the toes and wear them anyway.

There were dresses for Justine, a stuffed animal, and a hand carved rocking chair that would have to wait a while before she could use it by herself.

Rose expressed her thanks to Mr. Ford for his kindness and thoughtfulness. She always wanted to be sure that he knew how much she appreciated what a good and decent man he was. He understood that she had some difficulty verbally expressing herself in some areas. Still, she knew how to communicate what she wished to say.

"I know that you haven't had much time to make presents for everyone this year," he allowed, "so I bought some extra things."

Rose nodded in agreement and said, "You sho' nuff' right. I plumb run out o' time."

The furniture for the new house was scheduled to arrive by train in a few weeks. By then, all the work on the house would be complete. In addition to furniture, Mr. Ford had ordered curtains for all the windows. Rose was anxious for everything to arrive but she told him that she would not cover the windows in the breakfast room.

More than anything, though, she was ready for the new baby to come. She was impatient with her restricted movement because of her size and because Mr. Ford always insisted on her taking it easy. He never, however, objected to her cooking their meals.

Rose knew that her time to deliver was getting near. She hinted to Mr. Ford that Molly could help in the birthing.

"Absolutely not!" shouted Jesse. "You will have an experienced midwife even if I have to go and beg Mrs. Broome to come."

After asking a few questions, Rose learned from one of the sharecroppers that there was a midwife who lived across the river. Rose wanted to make contact with her because she would never allow Mrs. Broome back in her house.

Chapter Thirteen

Cecilia Metoyer. . . . .

Towards the end of November, Rose asked Mr. Ford if he would send Jack across the river to bring the midwife because she figured the baby would be coming soon.

"That's acceptable, Rose, but I'll accompany Jack to make the arrangements myself. I need to know that she has had enough experience to make me comfortable."

Rose was relieved from the thought of Mr. Ford having to bring Mrs. Broome back. She could only hope and pray that this new midwife would be nothing like Mrs. Broome. She wanted to take no chances so she warned Molly to be ready just in case. Molly's own baby was barely four months old, and Rose didn't know how much she knew about birthing. Still, she felt better when Molly reassured her that she would be with her when she delivered.

Mrs. Metoyer was a heavy-set woman of average height, her skin was the color of caramel with too much cream. She had curly black hair which she wore piled on the top of her head. She had a big smile which exposed her yellowish teeth with one of them missing. She was warm and cheerful and Rose liked her almost immediately.

Rose liked the soft and kind way she handled Justine and that she did not ask her any personal questions. Especially, the fact that after two days, she had not mentioned Mr. Ford. She smiled often, seemed eager to please and never tried to order Rose around.

Rose figured she was Creole because of her strange-sounding talk, the way she prepared food and the coloring of her skin. But she most certainly would not ask. Rose gave her instructions and she followed them meticulously.

One evening, a few days after Mrs. Metoyer's arrival, Rose told her to light the lantern in the breakfast room. This was Rose's prearranged signal to let Molly know that she was in labor. If asked, Rose would not have been able to put in words why she wanted Molly with her at this time, but for some reason, she felt her presence would be reassuring.

Mrs. Metoyer was not in the least intimidated by Molly's presence. As a matter of fact, she could see right off that Molly could be useful to her. For one thing, she had a calming effect on Rose which Mrs. Metoyer knew was a good sign for going into labor. The two women assembled all of the utensils, muslins, towels, herbs, water and equipment they would be needing for the labor and delivery.

The midwife made a big pot of herbal tea using Chamomile, Chickweed and Tree Tea Oil. She gave Molly some red clay and asked her to spread a thin layer over Rose's stomach, back and legs. Molly thought this was a strange procedure but when Rose did not protest, she followed directions.

While Molly was spreading a thin layer of clay over Rose, Mrs. Metoyer was placing a heavy towel in the herbal mixture, wringing it and gently pressing and wiping Rose's forehead. She repeated this over and over. Rose breathed easily and seemed relaxed. Only occasionally, did a small whimper come from her lips. Mrs. Metoyer would wipe her face and her arms and give her sips of Mullein tea with honey.

Jesse had made sure the house was comfortable on this cold December night. He had a big fire going in the fireplace and he had water boiling in the kitchen. He fed Justine and put her down for the night. He sat in the big chair by the fireplace to read the almanac and the Bible. However, he got up every few minutes to see what was going on in the bedroom. He had already been admonished by Mrs. Metoyer to make himself scarce during the delivery.

"My work with the mother go' smoother if the father not in the room or even at the door," she said. "If I feels it necessary, I' keep you informed." She added in her strange accent. "I know what I be doing."

Jesse retreated to his chair by the fireplace to wait for some signal but he wasn't sure what he was waiting for so he opened his Bible and read the following:

> Behold, children are a heritage from the Lord, the fruit of the womb is His reward.
> Like arrows in the hand of a warrior, so are the children of one's youth.

> Happy is the man who has his quiver full of them; they shall not be ashamed, but shall speak with their enemies in the gate.

Psalm 127: 3-5

He tried to relax but his ears were at full attention, listening for some sound that would tell him the birth was going smoothly.

"One would think I'd know that having a baby is a normal and natural thing, especially since this isn't the first time. But I'm just as nervous as I was with Justine," he was thinking. And he paced the floor some more.

Meanwhile, Rose was being expertly cared for by an able midwife. She not only knew how to gain her patient's confidence, she knew how to ease the pain and suffering of giving birth.

Mrs. Metoyer expertly draped the heavy towel over Rose's body and wiped away the thin layer of clay. All the while, she talked to Rose in a gentle, soothing voice. She told her that the clay and tea cleaned out her pores and moisturized her skin, killed any poisons present and let in the healing and also the cleansing and pain-relieving elements.

A few minutes after mid-night, December 5, 1882, Jesse Sherman Ford was born. He made a quiet, simple and uncomplicated entry. Rose and Jesse's happiness was indescribable. It was as if the gates of heaven opened and flooded their lives with all the treasures that were within its pearly gates. Their joy was unspeakable! They would never ever forget the magic that Mrs. Metoyer performed that night. Nor would they forget how God had blessed them! They had a son! Another gift from heaven!

Mrs. Metoyer remained with Rose and the new baby for another week. She cheered the whole household with her bubbly personality, coupled with her sense of duty. She understood clearly what Mr. Ford and Miz Rose expected of her and she did her job superbly. She handled Justine with kindness and firmness. She was a delight to have in the household. Her cooking also pleased Mr. Ford.

Rose wished Mrs. Metoyer could remain with them forever. Her wish brought back memories of the time when Mr. Ford had asked her to come and work for him. Now, she understood his motive. Now, she was actually here. Not working for him, but his wife. The mother of his children! It was like living in a glorious dream!

When it was time for the midwife to return home, Rose extended an invitation for her to return and have Christmas dinner with them. Mrs. Metoyer said that she would be happy to come if she could bring her daughter with her. She would not leave her to spend Christmas alone. Rose quickly agreed with this arrangement, thinking what fun it would be for her, Mr. Ford and the children to have their first guests for a Christmas dinner.

Jack took Mrs. Metoyer home from her engagement as a midwife and early on Christmas morning, he returned for her and her daughter. It was a crisp, cold morning. The sky was clear. The scent of pine and cedar burning in fireplaces filled the air. Jack traveled as fast as he could go. He was in a hurry to get back to his family and do a little celebration of their own. This was the best Christmas they had ever had. His family was delighted with the presents from Mr. Ford and Miz Rose. He considered it a blessing as well as a stroke of luck to be working for Mr. Ford.

Mrs. Metoyer and her daughter, Lena, were ready when Jack arrived. They did, however, need some assistance in taking some heavily laden pots to the buggy and making sure they were secured. A big, black, round-bellied cast iron pot was filled with gumbo. Jack's nose caught a whiff of it and he knew, without being told, what it was. Room also had to be made for two large pecan pies and some squaw bread. Mrs. Metoyer had to hold the gumbo on her lap and Lena held onto the collard greens.

Christmas, 1882, was one that would long be remembered in the Ford household. Lena set the dinning room table. It was the first time the linen, silver and china, which Jesse had purchased in Houston the year he married Rose, would be used.

Holly and cedar garlands, heavy with berries, had already been hung on doors and walls in the sitting room by Mrs. Metoyer. Now, she put more decorations in the dining room to add cheeriness to this festive occasion. Lena put up strings of popcorn to everyone's delight. Rose brought out some candles she had made.

In the middle of preparations, everything suddenly stopped because they heard the jingle of bells coming up the road. It was Frank, who had placed a bevy of bells on his horse to herald Christmas and to bring pleasant and cheerful sounds to all who could hear. Besides gifts for the family, Frank brought along a sack full of fruits and nuts and a jug of blackberry wine and one of elderberry. He also had a hickory-smoked ham.

Finally, a bell rang announcing that it was time to gather at the dinner table. Rose came in with baby Jesse followed by Mr. Ford with a cradle in one hand and Justine in the other. After blessing the food, Mr. Ford read from the Bible:

> "He will be great, and will be called the Son of the Most High; and the Lord will give him the throne of his father David, and he will reign over the house of Jacob for ever; and of his kingdom there will be no end."

Luke 1:32-33

> And suddenly there was with the angel a multitude of the heavenly host praising God and saying,
> "Glory to God in the highest, and on earth peace among men with whom he is pleased!"

Luke 2: 13-14

"We are pleased that you and your daughter, Lena, could share this Christmas dinner with us, Mrs. Metoyer," said Jesse. "Yes, sir, it's a real pleasure."

"Thank you, Mr. Ford. We' happy to be here."

"And thank you, Mr. Frank Ford, fo' coming," added Rose. "An' thank you fo' the Christmas presents."

"The pleasure's all mine, folks. It's especially nice to meet the Metoyer family. Mam, you got yourself one pretty daughter."

Lena smiled, but said nothing. She was a truly beautiful young lady. She was Mrs. Metoyer's youngest child and her only daughter. Her two sons were married and living on different farms as sharecroppers. Their father had disappeared when the children were small. There were many stories circulating about his disappearance, but none of them were ever verified. One such story was that he had 'smarted some white man and was strung up in a tree. Others thought maybe he was killed trying to escape from slave hunters.

Mrs. Metoyer and Lena eked out a living on the small plot of land they owned. It was not large enough to support the sons and their families. The two women grew their produce and livestock which gave them plenty of food. Frequently, they were hired to chop and pick cotton for some of the local farmers. And Mrs. Metoyer did her midwife duties when called upon.

Lena's presence and her beauty did not go unnoticed by Frank. He eagerly volunteered his services to return the ladies to their home.

"They's stayin' the night," said Rose.

"Uh huh, oh, I'm staying the night also. I need to have some time with my brother and his family," Frank said awkwardly.

That first Christmas dinner with company at the Ford Farm was a delightful success. The table was beautiful, thanks to the Metoyers. The food was plentiful, lovely to look at and marvelous to eat. Rose's only regret was that her family was not there to share in this festive occasion.

Jesse and Frank surveyed the bountiful spread set before them. The honey-smoked ham and the baked hens were at the center of the table surrounded by the corn pudding, Lena's greens, wild apple sauce, corn muffins, egg bread, beets, stuffing, gravy, jams and jellies, candied yams, butter cake, pecan pies and a jar of Rose's chow-chow.

Mrs. Metoyer insisted that everyone must have a bowl of her special gumbo before any of the dinner was served. She said this had long been a custom in her family. Everyone except Rose had two bowls of gumbo before dinner.

After feasting until everyone simply could hold no more, Frank served his wine to Jesse, himself and the Metoyers and announced that the nursing Mama was not to be given anything that contained alcohol.

He lifted up his glass and made a toast.

"To my brother, Jesse, and his beautiful family, may your family and your farm increase. May God continue to bless you and keep you safe. May your love and happiness grow along with your children and may you know health and peace in the New Year!

"To Mrs. Cecilia and Lena, two beautiful ladies, I wish you much joy and happiness and that you have your wishes fulfilled in the coming year.

"And, now to us all, that the miseries that have plagued the south and its people since the end of the Civil War continue to wane and we can all know peace and prosperity."

"Good speech," Jesse said. I'll drink to that."

And they all raised their glasses and drank.

Rose went to put the sleeping baby to bed. She was followed by Jesse who carried a yawning Justine. The Metoyers began clearing the table and to their surprise, they were assisted by Frank.

While she was washing the dishes, Mrs. Metoyer's deep rich voice burst out singing, "Go Tell it on the Mountain." Lena joined in and when Rose entered the kitchen, the three women could be heard throughout the house.

Go, tell it on the mountain
Over the hills and ev'rywhare
Go, tell it on the mountain
That Jesus Christ is born

When the left-over food was put away and the dishes finished, they all sat before the fireplace sharing stories about their past Christmases. Frank told one about the time it was so cold in Kansas, that a gigantic blizzard blew in just a week before Christmas. The snow was so deep, everyone had to remain indoors. Even Santa could not finish his rounds until New Year's Eve. He remembered there were no oranges and apples. Every Christmas since then, except during the war, he's always had oranges and apples.

Mrs. Metoyer told about her family Christmases in the town of Opelousas. At the end of slavery, most of her family was able to reunite because of the secret communication that went on among the slaves. The Creoles tended to seek out one another because of their common language, their mixed blood and the special type of cooking they did.

"I thinks the year was 1866," she said. "There were 'bout fifteen o' twenty of us. Talk 'bout a celebration! We had the bigges' celebration I ever see. Ever'body bring somethin' to put in the gumbo pot. The soup cook a' long tim' 'fore we add the craw'dads and fish. Some brang corn pones, some brang poke sallet, sweet potato, egg bread, souse, pralines, fruitcakes, fried chicken, rice and red beans. I made marmalade, using lemons, oranges and black walnuts. I got ever'thin' I use from the old plantation which was abandoned. I later heard that the chickens for the stock pot done come from the same place.

"Ever'body be speaking patois. We ate an' sang an' dance' all night long. Ever'body be so happy to fin' one 'nother. We think we never gwyne be separated again. But times got so hard an' work was difficult to fin.' Some o' us has become sharecroppers. Some few was lucky, they become craftsmen. Some have drifted from place to place lookin' for a decent living. Many has left the state. But I always remember that one Christmas, the one afta' freedom come!"

Rose told about her first Christmas with the Turners. She repeated again what a loving and kind family they are and that she wished they were with them all for this special celebration of Christmas in their home.

"My Papo taught me how to make slippers, so I made a pair of slippers for each of them to show my 'preciation. The gifts we had were all homemade, mostly by Ma. But the thing that stans' out most was what was on the table. The only meat left in the smokehouse, besides some dried meat, was salt pork. Pa set out traps and brung back a possum and two coons. Pa skinned them and Ma soaked them in salt-water overnight. The next day, we boiled them twice. First, in plain water, then with hot peppers, vinegar and mo' salt. Ma cooked them in the stove fo' mo' than half the day. It was a wonderful meal! We had sweet potatoes, collards, hot water bread, fried pies, and jelly cake. What a glorious Christmas! Our possessions were few, but we was happy! We sang and prayed and sang some mo.'

"Speaking of singing," interrupted Frank, "you ladies sing so beautifully. I think it's time for another song."

> Mary had a baby, my Lord. Mary had a baby.
> Oh, Mary had a baby, My Lord, My Lord.
> What did she name him? What did she name hi m, My Lord?
> She named Him King Jesus, My Lord.
> She named Him King Jesus, My Lord.

Rose was the first to say goodnight. She had to see about her babies. Mrs. Metoyer soon retired for the evening saying she was tired and sleepy and needed to get up early the next morning.

Jesse excused himself and went off to join Rose and the children. Frank used this opportunity to see if he could get a little conversation from Lena.

Mostly, she just smiled or answered his questions with yes or no. He decided to fill their wineglasses again. He wanted to get her to loosen up just a bit. He was captivated by her beauty and wanted to know more about her.

After a while, she felt comfortable being in his presence without the others and she began to talk to him. They talked for some time before the wine and the glow and heat from the fireplace made her too sleepy to continue. She excused herself and joined her mother.

Frank sat there for some time with an interesting, quizzical little smile creasing the corners of his mouth. When the fire burned down to a bed of coals, he went to his room.

The next morning, Mrs. Metoyer and Lena were the first ones up, moving through the house. The stove was going, the fire in the fireplace was building. It was a cold, gray morning with some fog, but the house was warm and cozy.

Noise soon began to fill the house. Jesse was playing with Justine and she was squealing and laughing with delight as he rode her on his back. Baby Jesse was alarming the household making everyone aware of his need for food or his need to exercise his lungs.

When breakfast was put on the table, everyone came in. Jesse and Frank eyed the mouth-watering beaten biscuits at the same time. There were thick slices of the honey-smoked ham, grits, syrup, jam and fried apples.

Because the sky was bleak and the weather so cold and threatening, Rose persuaded her guests to remain another day. By the looks on their faces, it seemed her decision to extend the invitation was welcomed by all.

It did not go unnoticed that Frank found a way to be alone with Lena. Since there were two houses to roam through, they decided to do just that. Lena's mother already had told her that Frank 'had the eye' for her.

Frank told her funny little stories and anecdotes which had her giggling and laughing. Rose was glad to see her enjoying herself because she had been so somber, rarely talking at all. One of the details about her life that Frank uncovered was that her father's father was a white plantation owner. Lena said she was often teased about her pale color and her light eyes. Whenever she ventured into town, she was mistaken for a white woman.

When the whites across the river where they lived became aware that she was Negro, they ridiculed her. Even the Negro people did not treat her too kindly. Pretty soon, she just stayed away from people as much as possible.

The following day, Frank rigged up a cover for the wagon. He hitched his horse to the wagon and took Lena and her mother home. When he returned to Ford Farm, he told Rose and Jesse that he liked Lena and planned to see her again.

a sudden death. . . . .

Winter left a harsh calling card in the hill country. At night, the lusty winds came howling and blowing across the hills and through the valleys. Intermittent snow fell and formed soft white carpets which did not last long enough to completely blanket the ground. Sleet was blown everywhere and Jesse began to worry about the safety of the livestock. The ground was icy and slippery. Icicles hung heavy from the eaves and upon the tree limbs and branches. A few of them came crashing to the ground under their own weight.

The countryside was cold and peaceful. The curling gray smoke from the chimneys was heavy with the scent of pine and cedar and stretched to the heavens through an azure sky that was minus clouds. Very few creatures could be seen, almost no people. It was if time and life stood still. Rose and her family closed and abandoned the new house in favor of putting all their heat and energies in one place. They knew they would not be getting a surprise visit from the sheriff.

Jesse welcomed this time to spend precious time with his family. He sat on the floor with Justine who was now learning how to take her first steps. He jostled and tickled her and threw her in the air, an act which made Rose flinch. He played finger games with her and clapping hands games. Justine adored her father and he adored his first born. He passed quiet time with Baby Jesse just sitting in the rocker holding him and humming lullabies to him. When the baby went to sleep, he would place him in his cradle and continue rocking him.

Rose had regained most of her strength since the birth of Baby Jesse. But she remembered that Mamie had cautioned her to delay many "wifely" activities until the baby was at least two months old; three months would be better.

Around the last week in February, winter finally relaxed its hold on that northwest corner of Louisiana. The sunshine dappled through the clouds and softly kissed the cold earth. Intermittently, light rains fell to remind all that winter was not yet ready to give up her rotation. The sun began to hang around a little longer each day giving up enough light and warmth to summon up the stirrings of both man and animal.

About two weeks after the thaw began, a stranger rode up to the gate of the Ford Farm. His arrival had already been announced by the dogs. Jesse Ford was working in the barn. He mounted his horse and trotted to the gate. It was a Negro man that Jesse remembered having seen before.

"I come wit a message for Miz Rose, Zeke Turner sent me."

Jesse dismounted and opened the gate for the man. "Is something wrong?" he asked.

"Yessah, 'tis. They's all down sick. They's all got fever and they's all coughing somethin' awful. My wife went to take care o' them, but now she done come home sick. Zeke asked me to git word to Miz Rose. I got here as fas' as I could. The roads are bad ever'where from the winter storms."

"We sure appreciate your coming. "What's your name?"

"Eli, sah. Eli Smith.

"Come on to the house, Eli. Rest yourself and have a bite to eat."

"Nosah, I best be gettin' back befo' too late. These roads be hard and dangerous fo' my horse. Las' thing I need is to lose old Sally."

"Thank you for coming and ride safely!"

Jesse returned the horse to the barn and headed for the house. He dreaded telling Rose, but he knew he had to.

"Saddle up Spirit, I be leavin' directly," she told Jesse when she got the news.

"No, Rose. You can't go. I'll go cross the river and get Mrs. Metoyer and take her to care for the family."

"That take too long. An' we don' even know if she home or not. Can't wait another day, it might be too late. It might a'ready be too late. All I know is I got to go now!"

"Okay. Okay. Molly can keep the children, but what will little Jesse do without you for a day or so?"

"I'm taking my baby with me. He'll ride on my stomach. Us two. We be jes' fine."

Jesse said he'd take care of Justine himself. It was still too cold to do much work outside. Besides, he enjoyed spending time with her. He delighted in his daughter.

"Stay only one night and then come home," he urged her.

Less than an hour after Eli left the Ford Farm, Rose had little Jesse strapped to her chest and she was on her way to see about her family.

She could see that the sun would be slipping beyond the horizon in about an hour. It would take her almost two hours to reach the farm. She had Spirit racing at a fast clip. She needed to put distance behind her because the road, which was strewn with twigs and branches and had deep wagon wheel ruts, would be dangerous if its path was not visible to her. Then she would have to slow Spirit down to a safe walk and she would arrive way after dark.

She could feel little Jesse jostling around but there was no time to stop and adjust his wrapping. Besides, the cold air posed more of a problem than his loose blanket. The wind and cold lashed out at her causing her eyes to water and her nose to run but she kept on going. Getting there as soon as she could was her utmost priority.

Darkness began to slowly fill the land and her heart started to pound faster and faster. Terror began to gnaw at her.

"What if I don't make it in time?"

"What if som'thin already happen?"

"What if I gets lost in the dark?"

Wisps of gray fog begin to rise and float in the path, stalking the plains like a cat. She paced Spirit even faster.

Rose suddenly cried out, "Papo, I'm comin.' Papo, I'm comin.'"

At the mention of Papo's name, she began to feel a calmness moving in her and her strength and courage seemed to rise again. Her spirit was renewed. She felt the presence of Papo's spirit and she knew she would make it!

In the darkness, Rose saw the light. It was far away but she knew it was coming from the Turner house. She looked up at the sky. It was crowded with stars. For the first time on this night, she slowed down.

She briefly closed her eyes and offered up a prayer of thanksgiving.

Rose was at the family home again!

The first thing Rose did when she went inside was to make garlic and parsley soup. After she gave each one a cup to drink, she finally sat down and fed her own baby. He was tired and hungry after such a long and rough ride. She felt lucky that little Jesse went to sleep immediately because she saw there was suffering in the house.

Rose added extra wood to the fire to make sure that everyone was warm on that cold, blustery night. Winter's claim on the season was still in evidence. It had served notice that it would stay around until its time was officially up.

In the middle of the night, after she had tried to reassure and quiet everyone, Rose took boiling water, and soap, made from lye and potash, and cleaned everything in the house. After living in Mr. Ford's house, she had forgotten how small the Turner house was. She changed and stacked all of the used bedding, towels and family clothing. She would make a fire under the old black pot early in the morning and boil everything.

Before going to bed, she went into her parents. She tenderly touched them and said, "Let's pray." Always it was Mamie who prayed, but this time it was Rose, with tears falling down her cheeks, who offered up prayer and praise.

"Dear Heavenly Father, I thanks you for a safe journey for my baby an' me. I thanks you for my Ma an' Pa an' they childrens. I praise your Heavenly name. You said ax' an' you will be given. Now Lord, I ax' for your help in healing the peoples in this house. They needs you, Lord. They needs you right now. They yo' good an' faithful servants. Please, Sah, come right now an' touch they bodies. Heal them! Ma an' Pa is so good. They took me in when I had no place to go. They teach me 'bout you, Lord. Please, Sah. Right now, give them help an' strength. Thank you, Lord Jesus. Thank you, Lord!"

Its' me, its' me, its' me, Oh Lord
Standin' in the need of prayer

Its' my Ma, its' my Ma, its' my Ma, Oh Lord
Standin' in the need of prayer
Its' my Pa, its' my Pa, its' my Pa, Oh Lord
Standin' in the need of prayer
Its' my sisters, its' my brothers, its' us, Oh Lord
Standin' in the need of prayer.

Rose could hear them coughing through the night. But she was so exhausted and tired from the ride and all the work. She finally fell asleep and was awakened only when little Jesse began to cry. She nursed him, changed him and went back to sleep.

By the time daylight leaked through the cracks the next morning, Rose was up and the wood cookstove was blazing. She was preparing a pot of rice and mullein tea. She had brought a supply of herbs with her but after she saw how ill everyone was, she knew she needed to go out in the meadow for herbs that she hadn't brought. She especially wanted to gather some dandelion and lobelia. She hoped the frost hadn't killed them. She knew that everyone needed to be flushed out and she knew their bodies needed to be strengthened.

The trip to the meadow would have to be put on hold for the time being. She first had to get some nourishment in each of them. First, she used some of the tea to bathe Mamie who appeared dull and listless. She fed her a bowl of rice, followed by a cup of mullein tea, laced with boneset.

She repeated the same routine with Zeke. Rose was disturbed by the vacant look in his eyes as she swathed his body with the tea. She could hear his stomach churning so she quickly fed him his rice with parsley added.

She removed the dirty muslin bedding from the bed and replaced it with clean sheets. Mamie and Zeke offered her their feeble thanks. And to Rose's amazement, Mamie began to pray, her prayer almost inaudible.

One by one, Rose bathed and fed the entire family. Annie and Susie seemed less sick than the others. They asked for and got additional food. They wanted to play with Little Jesse. Rose left them watching him when she went outside to boil the bedding and towels.

Winter's chill still hung heavy in the air and the winds came blowing in a loud rush. Rose was thankful for the soft mid-day sun that took the sting out of the wind and dried the washing she hung on the line. There was more washing to do and she was anxious to get over to the meadow. She finished the rest of the clothes in the number three tub inside the warm kitchen

That night, after a supper of barley soup, corn pone and more mullein tea, the household slept much quieter. More and more soft conversation could be heard coming from the bedroom. Again, Rose was exhausted from the day's activities so she drifted off to sleep. Only the restlessness of Little Jesse caused her to stir and respond during the night.

The next morning, Zeke was ambling about the house and ventured into the yard.

I sho' feels better, daught,' I owes it all to you. You's such a good daughter to come an' nurse us back to health an' I wants you to know how thankful I am."

"Pa, I do anything fo' my family. I never will fo'get how you took me in an' treated me with such kindness. You give'd me yo' name. You give'd me a birthday. You give'd me love. You is my family!"

With everyone, except Mamie, up and stirring around a little, Rose could finally relax with the feeling that her family was on the road to recovery. She took Spirit from the barn and rode him straight to the meadow. It was a beautiful, sunshiny day. The wind was still blowing but the sun was warmer than the previous days, sending out notice that spring might soon be arriving.

Rose walked through the thickly growing grasses and plants. She was looking for just the right weeds and flowers. After gathering a sackfull, she started home. But then, she saw the old oak tree. She saw its branches beckon to her. She heard the breezes blowing through the shimmering leaves.

"Just one mo' time," she said. "I'll only climb up fo' a minute. Then I leave."

Rose was surprised to find that she could no longer climb as easily as she had in prior years. It took much longer to reach her favorite limb, and when she did she was all out of breath.

Looking out on the hill country, she found it to be just as magnificent as she had remembered. In fact, it was even more breathtaking on the eve of this springtime.

"How I love this place," she said. "This place represents the beginning of my real life. An' this is where Mr. Ford first tol' me that he loved me. This is the wind that echoed my name, Rose Turner, to the fields an' meadows."

"Spirit of God," she prayed. "Thank you fo' my family. Thank you fo' Mr. Ford an' fo' our little girl an' boy. Thank you fo' health an' stren'th fo' us all. An' Dear God, thank you fo' Papo."

Spirit trotted across the meadow while Rose looked back lovingly and knowingly at the tree. She had the feeling that it might be a long time before she would return to the meadow and her secret place in that tree.

When she arrived back at the house, she was pleased to see Zeke moving slowly around the barnyard. His movements were sluggish and deliberate, nevertheless, he was there. Mamie had directed Samuel to fire up the stove to begin preparing supper. Rose knew these were good signs and that she would be returning to her own home early the next morning. Her family was on the mend. God had heard and answered their prayers.

Chapter Fourteen

On the ride home, little Jesse seemed exceptionally irritable and restless. Rose had to stop twice during what was usually a two-hour ride to nurse him. She thought she should even stop a third time because he cried constantly during the next hour. And this uneasiness stretched the trip to an additional half-hour.

During the second feeding, Rose noticed that little Jesse was warmer than he should be. She prodded Spirit faster.

"He's catching a cold," she thought. "I'll bathe him in oatstraw and black walnut oil soon as we git to the house."

Mr. Ford was not at home when Rose arrived. She started immediately preparing the oatstraw and black walnut oil bath for the baby. He came home just as she finished the bathing. Jesse told her he had left Justine with Molly while he rode over to Frank's place to pick up some seed and supplies Frank had bought for him.

"Things must have been pretty bad, you stayed so long. You can't imagine how much I missed you and the baby and how happy I was when I saw that you were home. I'll get Justine after I've cleaned up a bit."

He gathered little Jesse from his mother's arms and the baby erupted in crying.

"Look at him, Rose, something is wrong! What's the matter?" he yelled.

"I don't 'xactly know. I couldn't get him quiet on the way home, so I rode faster to get here quicker. I 'spect he must be comin' down with a cold."

"You haven't told me what was ailing your folks. Maybe he caught something from them."

"It seems they all come down with the grip and the children had the croup. They was coughing something awful. I made plenty roots an' herb remedies. They's all better now."

"I don't like the way little Jesse looks. I think it's best to leave Justine with Molly a while longer."

"But I miss her so an' I wants to see her. Please bring her home! Lil' Jesse gonna be fine, jes' like my family. I make them all well."

Jesse did not go for Justine that evening. He wanted to wait until morning to see if little Jesse was going to be all right. He did not want to see both of his children sick.

During the night, little Jesse's breathing became more and more labored. Jesse and Rose got little or no sleep despite their urging each other to get some rest. They both were plenty tired from the previous day's activities and the long rides. Occasionally, one or the other would drift into sleep only to be awakened by the baby's cry or coughing. Rose bathed him again in the warm oil, hoping it would ease his breathing.

They spent four days and nights caring for and watching him. His little body was racked with fever and his chest was so congested. The coughing was agonizing for all of them. It was plain to see that the baby was having a difficult time. And despite Rose and Jesse's gigantic efforts, on the morning of the fifth day, he passed away.

Rose's body sagged with aching. Her baby's death was a burden both her spirit and her body could not bear. Jesse's eyes were vacant with tears that he could not shed. Beads of perspiration engulfed his body. His skin became a sallow yellow. His voice was silent. Rose was worried that maybe he was coming down with the grip. She, herself, had no feelings at all. They both moved about in a bewildered and detached manner. They suffered in haunting silence. Rose suffered even more deeply because she was sure that Mr. Ford blamed her for little Jesse's death.

Molly and Jack took over and ran the household. They sent messengers to inform Mr. Frank Ford, the Turner Family and the Metoyers about the death of the baby. They assigned the other sharecropper family to carry on with daily routines.

Frank Ford, along with the Metoyer ladies, was the first to arrive. He stopped by their place on his way. The Metoyers were pleased that he had stopped and invited them to ride with him. He had visited with them several times since meeting them at Christmas.

Ezekiel and Mamie arrived looking wan and weary but their children appeared robust and full of strength. Rose sat by the baby's cradle, rocking its still form. She could not be budged. Jesse was carving wood out in the barn. They found Frank busy drawing plans for a family cemetery on one of the hills overlooking the river. Frank Ford asked Samuel and Ephriam to help him with laying it out. The next day, they completed their work and announced that everything was ready for the burial.

Early the following morning, the family and a few of their friends prepared to bury Jesse Sherman Ford, Jr. in a small plot at the top of the hill.

There was a light chill in the air and the somber group stood in silence over the tiny box which had been lovingly hewn and carved by Jesse. Frank invaded the silence with his reading of Solomon's observation of God's plan for all people:

> There is a right time for everything:
> A time to be born; a time to die;

A time to plant; a time to harvest;
A time to kill; a time to heal
A time to destroy; a time to rebuild;
A time to cry; a time to laugh;
A time to grieve; a time to dance;
A time for scattering stones; a time for gathering stones;
A time to hug; a time not to hug;
A time to find; a time to lose;
A time for keeping; a time for throwing away;
A time to tear; a time to repair;
A time to be quiet; a time to speak up;
A time for loving; a time for hating;
A time for war; a time for peace.

Usually, it was Mamie who spoke for the family, but this time it was Ezekiel who commanded everyone's attention.

"To my dear daughter, Rose, an' to Jesse Ford, we here to share your grief, great tho' 'tis, you mus' let us share. You can't go on cryin' in silence. You not grievin' alone; we's all hurtin,' we all feels yo' pain. Maybe my family bears the blame, but it's the good Lord who giveth an' who done taketh. He knows we's all suffering, but he also promises us He'll stan' with us. He won't put upon us more than we can bear. We won't grieve fo'ever, though we continue to mourn. He'll give us joy in the mornin."

Mamie offered a short prayer, but no one heard it. Mrs. Metoyer, in her melodious voice, started singing "Steal Away," and everyone joined in.

Steal away, Steal away, Steal away to Jesus
Steal away, Steal away home
I ain't got long to stay here.

There was a silent procession back to the house. Even the children respected the mourning ritual and remained quiet and subdued.

Finally, Jesse spoke, "Folks, give me and Rose a few minutes, then we'll join you at the house and we'll celebrate the birth and death of our beloved son."

Jesse took Rose's hand and led her in the direction of the forest, at the end of the field. When they reached the willow tree, he spread his jacket on the ground and they sat there consoling each other for a while. No words were spoken. Their eyes and their hearts knew their innermost thoughts. There would be no blaming, only understanding, sorrow and hope. There would always be love.

The forest was alive with animals, budding plants, unfolding leaves and the promises of spring approaching. The promise of renewal! The forest always recycled itself. A few baby birds just learning to fly were flitting from bough to bough. Saplings were trying to find their place in the sun among the tall trees that crowded them out and reached heavenward. Mother animals were busy scolding while gathering food for their babies. A few deer were visible as were some rabbits and squirrels. They seemed to take time to curiously eye one another and then continue their vigorous pursuit of food and play. The woods, at least, were alive.

Rose and Jesse watched this spectacle for a long time without speaking. They each were immersed in the silence of their thoughts. Thoughts that would be unspoken for the moment. Eventually, Jesse broke the silence.

"Rose, I love you! Together we will make it through this. We must! Now, I think it's time for us to go home to our little girl and to the people who care about us."

They walked home briskly, hand in hand. When they entered the house, everyone was relieved to see faint smiles on their faces and hope in their eyes.

Jesse was first to speak, "Dear friends and family, Rose and I thank you for every thing you have done to comfort us. We graciously accept all of your expressions of sympathy and your kind acts. We are profoundly saddened and we will never forget our son, Jesse Jr., and his short life, but life for us and our precious Justine, must and will, continue. Grief will be our companion for a while, but our lives will go on.

"Mrs. Metoyer has prepared dinner for everyone. Let's all sit and eat. When tomorrow comes, we will begin a new chapter. Rose and I have lived like the pioneers of the west. We have worked long and hard and made many sacrifices. We cannot let this setback deter us from the happiness and goals we seek."

Jesse blessed the table and offered prayer.

"Lord, I am most thankful for Rose. She is the best thing that ever happened to me. She is my angel; she is my reason for life. I am grateful for our daughter Justine, whom I love with all my heart. I thank you for the short life of our dearly departed son. Please look after him in heaven and treat him special. Now, I thank you for family and friends who share both joy and sorrow with us. I am thankful for these two houses enabling Rose and me to enjoy each other's company in a measure of peace and safety. Bless my brother, Frank, who has always stood by my side.

"Bless this food we're about to receive. Let it nourish us and give us the strength to continue this journey of life. Amen."

Mrs. Metoyer, her daughter Lena, and Molly had prepared a sumptuous meal for everyone. They were glad Mr. Ford had told them to put their sorrow behind and move forward to the business of living and seeking comfort and joy.

Molly and Jack took the children to the sunroom to eat their supper. The ladies served fried chicken, sweet potatoes, black-eyed peas, beets, squash, corn bread, buttermilk and jelly cake. Of course, some of Rose's chow-chow was passed around.

The conversation at the supper table was centered around spring planting and speculating what the weather would be like this year. Jesse brought out an almanac and shared its crop and weather predictions. Although he could not read it, Ezekiel was fascinated by what Jesse read to them.

Frank talked about the amazing growth of his cotton crops in the rich soil of the river valley. Said he expected this year's crop would exceed last year's. His acreage was broad, fertile land which stretched from the valley to the hills and beyond. He didn't have the same rapport with his field hands as Jesse; consequently, he was forced to pay higher wages in order to get the production results he desired.

Frank had built his house the same year Jesse built his. But his location was more isolated than his brother's. He was still single and had indicated that he was looking for a wife but had not been as lucky as his brother.

Mamie smiled at his remarks and her ears stood at attention to catch any other message that he was sending forth. She had not missed how his eyes followed Lena everywhere she went. Nor had she missed the coy smile that seemed to be a permanent part of Lena's face.

There was still a good bit of sunlight left after the dishes had been cleared away, Molly offered to take Justine for the night but this time Jesse politely said, "No, thank you!"

Mamie and Zeke went to check on their children and to make preparations for an early morning departure. Then Mamie and Rose engaged in conversation about letting the church people know of their loss. Rev. Pennywell would be shocked by the death of the baby. There had already been talk of another christening on Easter Sunday for little Jesse Jr.

Frank asked Lena to come for a walk with him to watch the sunset. She accepted and put on her shawl to ward off the chill that came with the evening breeze. They walked along beneath the hillside where they had buried the baby. They heard the scarlet cardinals and blue jays whistling, chattering and screeching. They heard a robin singing a lilting melody.

Suddenly Frank put his arms around her, stopped and pointed.

"Isn't that just about the most beautiful sight you've ever seen?"

Off in the distance was an expanse of orange surrounded by gold and yellow, as the setting sun filled the tenuous line where the sky touched the earth. Color was spilling throughout the whole area as if someone was painting the sky and the strokes of color were being swept by the wind.

"You right," said Lena. "That' the most lovely sunset I ever saw."

"It's not as lovely as you are, Lena."

"You teasin' me, Frank."

"It's true, Lena. You're the most beautiful woman I've ever seen. Please don't be shy or afraid with me.

"Lena, I want to ask you to be my wife. I want you to know, if we get married, we won't have the same problems Jesse and Rose have. They have been openly targeted from all sides. They have suffered as a result of the post war problems which affect both coloreds and whites. We are all surviving, but the problems have been enormous and survival is tough.

It is my best guess that it will continue for some time. Folks in my area won't even notice that you're not white, so life for us will be easier."

With the setting of the sun, the shadows began to lengthen and the animals seemed to vanish into the forest. The peace and quiet of night was descending as the two began their slow walk back to the house.

Off in the distance, they could hear the cows lowing and the owls hooting as if they were leading or conducting the droning night symphony. The countryside was tranquil and calm.

Frank knew that Lena would need time to think about his sudden proposal. He guessed that Lena liked him but he worried that she would be swayed by the attitudes that were pervasive, especially there in the south.

` ` ` ` ` ` ` ` ` ` `

The next few weeks on the Ford Farm were the busiest that anyone could remember. The fields were plowed, the rows turned and the seeds planted. A new foal was born and two new calves were added to the stable.

Rose was back working in her garden. Justine, who was now walking, kept her mother company, along with Kula, who ran back and forth and in and out. Jesse had made a wagon for Justine to sit and ride in when she got tired or when she would fall down. Rose did not want her crawling on the damp ground; she might come down with a cold. She knew she was overly protective of her since the loss of little Jesse, but she couldn't help herself.

Rose and Jesse were determined not to dwell on their tragic loss. They had decided little Jesse's death was an act of God and concluded they must not question God. Ezekiel had reminded them that it was written in the Bible, "The Lord giveth and the Lord taketh.... Blessed be the name of the Lord." Inward the hurt was real deep, but outward they had each other and they had Justine and their life must persist.

"Rose," Jesse said one evening after supper when he saw a despondent look on her face and tears welling up in her eyes, "we must strive to push away sorrow. No matter how hard we wish for it, we can never have him back. We had no control of his illness nor his death. You must accept that our son is in God's hands. I would gladly have exchanged my life for his but that was not in God's plan.

"From now on, we must let our life flourish like your beautiful garden out there. It is full of goodness that helps to sustain life. It reflects the tender loving care you give to it.

"We have been abundantly blessed with love, with Justine, with homes to live in in peace and enough land to afford us a decent living. And thanks to your dad and his wise advice, we have the best field hands in the area.

"Rose, I love you so much! Just the sight of you excites my whole being."

"Mr. Ford, your kind words jus' makes my heart sing with gladness. I thanks God ev'ry day fo' havin' you as my companion. Even when I'm feelin' low, you always know how to make me feel good. You done stole my heart a long time ago."

"There's a full moon tonight, Rose. When Justine goes to sleep, let's sit on the porch like we used to."

"Thank you fo' askin,' I gonna hurry an' put her to bed early. I loves sittin' in the swing with you."

` ` ` ` ` ` ` ` ` ` `

Frank visited with Jesse and Rose on the last Sunday in August. During the prior two months, they were both so occupied with their farming chores, there had been little time for visiting. They had, in fact, not seen Frank since shortly after they buried little Jesse.

Besides discussing their cotton production and the new tax that had been levied on cotton, Frank wanted to tell Rose and Jesse that he had asked Lena Metoyer to marry him. He figured this news would please them even though she had not yet given him her answer.

"She is the most beautiful creature I've ever seen and I think she'll make me a good wife," Frank volunteered.

"You need to be sure that marriage is what you both want. And you must understand there could be some deep-rooted, racial repercussions," Jesse advised.

"I ain't fer sure what to say," Rose finally said. "I jus' know, if you love each other like me an' Mr. Ford, then there's nothin' that can keep you apart."

"You have my blessing and my good wishes. Just let us know when and where, we'll be there."

"We sho will," added Rose. "This the best news I heard in a long time. I declare, I'm plain tickled pink."

The summer heat, coupled with soft rains, nourished the rich soil and hastened the harvest which was resplendent in color and abundance. When he surveyed what the land had yielded, Jesse Ford was pleased with his decision to become a southern farmer. And he was more than pleased with the woman who had become his wife. He didn't give the swish of a horse's tail what society thought or what the law said.

At Jesse's insistence, Rose did not help with the cotton picking nor did she help in the gathering of any of their crops. It had been a difficult winter and spring for them. She had always worked hard, especially during the two previous years. This summer, he wanted her to enjoy the new house and their daughter. The sharecroppers, along with a few hired hands, dutifully pulled their workload and the harvesting proceeded smoothly.

Rose and Justine went to the garden every day. Often, Rose even looked after Molly and Jack's son Virgil, during the day, while they worked in the field. Justine liked to play with Virgil who was a few months older than she. They rode in the wagon together and Justine always scrambled after Virgil as he darted in and out among the rows of vegetables.

Rose was as successful with her gardening as she'd ever been. She grew just about any vegetable any one knew of or had heard about. Occasionally, an old friend or some church member would come by seeking a jar of her chow-chow and a mess of fresh vegetables. They would ask her the secrets of her success and pass on any news they had heard, then go on their way.

Rose continued to do her canning and she shared generously with friends, sharecroppers and hired hands. Her constant kindness and generosity inspired the workers to be diligent and to continue their loyalty to their boss.

Summer finally took its leave from the hill country but not before firmly leaving its signature as a reminder that it had called this year and would definitely return. During the first two weeks of September, the heat was relentless and stifling. Even the forest animals took note.

During the day, they were neither seen nor heard, but at sunset they ventured to the forest's edge. Their sounds send forth an eerie cacophony, piercing the stillness of a welcoming and cooling end to the hot days.

"I'se happy to see the summer go," commented Rose. "It was good fo' the crops, but then it overstayed its welcome and began to burn evry'thing. My garden done practically burnt' up."

"I loved the heat!" said Jesse. "It gave me feelings that matched the sizzle and those wonderful nights in the swing with you are unforgettable."

"There you go agin' talkin' like that...

"It's all right, Rose. Desire is a gift from God. And His gifts to me are abundant.

"When two people deeply love each other, there is a depth of passion between them that is sanctioned by God. I feel good that the stirrings in our bodies manifest the love God has blessed us to have. I am not ashamed of the pleasures we find in each other." He concluded.

"Look, Mr. Ford! Look up yonder! There's our 'wishing' star. I wish the beauty of this night an' the beauty of our love and life together goes on fo'ever an' fo'ever."

"It will, Rose. It will! That was so beautiful! I'll love you forever and then some. Even when I die, you will continue to have my love."

Chapter Fifteen

Summer completely gave way to fall. Fall's grandeur commenced to manifest itself in a thousand ways. The days and nights were cooler. The gentle breezes blew across the meadow. The golden sun kissed the trees and grasses and they were responding with bright and glorious hues of gold, red and yellow.

On a perfectly beautiful, fall Sunday afternoon, Rose and Jesse had unexpected guests. They were alerted by the barking dogs. They didn't suspect the sheriff because it had been over a year since he had dropped in for one of his surprise visits. Rose had had enough time to take Justine into the other house and they never reappeared during his visit. Rose never asked Mr. Ford about his conversation with the sheriff. She had long since learned if it was something important, Mr. Ford would tell her about it.

Jesse Ford simply had remarked, "I don't think he'll be coming here again."

As it neared the gate, Jesse spotted the fancy buggy and said, "I'll go and check it out. But my guess is that someone must be lost."

The unexpected guests were his brother Frank, with Lena Metoyer.

Neither Jesse nor Rose could believe the news that Frank and Lena had come to share with them. The news struck like a bolt of lightning! The two of them announced they had gotten married!

"But that can't be!"

"They don't 'low whites an' Negroes to marry," interrupted Rose.

"When and where did this marriage take place?" asked Jesse.

"We marriaged yestiddy," answered Lena with a cocky edge in her voice that signaled Jesse to proceed cautiously with his questions.

"Why you didn't invite us to this wedding?" Rose queried. 'Ya'll sure you's married? Seems mighty strange you didn't ax us to come, us bein' kin an' all."

Seeing the hurt and disappointment on Jesse's and Rose's faces, Frank quickly told them that on the spur of the moment, they suddenly decided to cross over the state line and get married in Texas.

"Doesn't Texas have the same law as Louisiana prohibiting marriage between the races?" asked Jesse.

"I have to be honest with you, Jesse. I'm sure they do but we didn't even ask. Look at Lena, she looks as white as I do. So it was not an issue; the question of race never came up."

"There is a principle here, little brother, and it doesn't bode too well. Some day, this whole thing may blow up in your face."

"Lena, you be denyin' who you is!" Rose said in an accusing voice.

"You mixin' beans an' corn," responded Lena. "If it don't make us no never mind, then it shouldn' make nobody else no never mind, neither."

"We've traveled a long way and now we're very tired and hungry after such a hard journey. We wanted to share the news with you first because we thought you'd be happy for us. And also we'd like to stay here for the night," interrupted Frank, who was thoroughly unprepared for the response they were receiving.

He had assumed their marriage would be no big deal and that Jesse and Rose would be happy and pleased about it. He and Lena simply had just put one over on the people at the license bureau. It was a decision that Lena had made and he thought it was a very astute one. He was actually proud of her for suggesting it. He figured Jesse and Rose would understand what they had done and even think they had made a wise decision.

Rose began to put the Sunday supper on the table. As she did so, she remembered the cold food they always ate at Mamie's house every Sunday. Even on a cold, winter Sunday, food was never cooked or heated in her house on a Sabbath. "It was the Lord's day," she had said, "and He said we should rest on His day and keep it holy."

Rose had prepared her dinner on this Sunday and the leftovers were in the warmer of the massive cook stove. It wasn't cold like Mamie's food would be because her stove had no warmer. Rose put stewed rabbit, candied yams, snap beans, rice, chow-chow, corn bread and buttermilk on the table.

Rose was now enjoying a feeling of contentment and today it was coupled with pride in being able to set such a beautiful table in such a lovely house.

"Mr. Ford an' me are not married in the eyes of the state," she said, "but we are truly married in the sight of God."

"Supper ready!" she called. "I put out the linen and china 'cause we ought to properly celebrate this marriage. I happy for you but I still thinks Lena got no right to deny who she is. I be plenty proud of my Afi'can blood."

"I don' know nothin' 'bout no Afi'can blood and you don' either, Rose. I'm born in Amer'ca and so was you."

"Now, now, ladies!" counseled Jesse, "We are all one big family. We have each other and happily so. This day is too important to engage in scrapping. I hear the baby crying, so while you get Justine, Rose, I'll go to the cellar and get some wine and we can drink a toast to the newlyweds.

"To my brother, Frank Bartholomew Ford and his lovely bride, Lena Metoyer, Congratulations on choosing each other! I wish you a long, healthy and happy life together. I truly hope you enjoy the kind of love Rose and I have for each other. I pray that God will bless your union with children and that you daily walk in His presence. I also pray that you suffer none of the hate and prejudice we have known. I end this toast with words from the disciple John, 'Beloved, if God so loved us, we also ought to love one another. If we love one another, God abides in us, and His love has been perfected in us.'

"Rose and I rejoice in your marriage and your happiness!"

Later that night, as Jesse took Rose in his arms and held her close, he reminded her of how precious and miraculous their love was. He caressed her tenderly and kissed her gently, over and over again. Ecstatic shivers flowed through her body, he buried himself in her flesh and they became one. The honey sweetness of his love went streaming inside her. The harmonious blending of their flesh transcended the stars. Transcended the heavens. Transcended the moon. Transcended time and place. Transcended spirit and drifted to a place where it could gather more riches...

The moon hung low in the azure heavens. The stars filled the sky and sent out glittering light. The grass glistened in the moonlight. The night air was fragrant with pungent smells. The scent of honeysuckle, the scent of hyacinth, the scent of roses, the scent of magnolias, the scent of love... Dew drops shone upon the trees. The frogs and the crickets sang in sweet harmony. The haunting calls of the owls only punctuated the exhilaration of a night that would be remembered for a long time.

The hot blood of desire was in abundance on this night in the Ford household. The new and blossoming love of the newlyweds, Mr. and Mr. Frank Ford. The seasoned, splendid, magnanimous love of Rose Turner and Jesse Ford.

Chapter Sixteen

Early the following morning, Rose was up preparing and arranging to serve breakfast in the sunroom. The sun had barely kissed the day hello when Jesse came in with Justine following after him and Kula scampering behind her. Kula's place was now in the breezeway between the two houses.

"Thanks for having breakfast ready so early; I know Frank will be pleased to get an early start. Anything I can do to give you a hand?"

"Umm, yes, thank-you. I could use some peach preserves from the cellar."

Rose went to the back porch and clanged on the horseshoe to signal Frank and Lena that breakfast would be on the table shortly. She knew they needed time to get dressed and washed up.

Rose was busy putting cured bacon, corn meal mush, scrambled eggs, milk, spiced apples, tea and coffee on the table when the newlyweds walked in. She would wait for everyone to be seated before she brought out the hot beaten biscuits.

Even before saying good morning, Lena asked, "Did you have to make sich a racket with that horseshoe?"

Frank, sensing an unpleasant moment coming, interrupted. "That was the best night's sleep I've had in a long time. Grooms tend to be nervous, too, you know, both before and after weddings."

"Rose, you've done it again," chimed in Jesse. "Even in the cellar, I could smell the wonderful aroma of your cooking, especially the hot biscuits. Let's eat! Uh, uh! Just a minute.

"Dear Lord! Bless this food; bless the cook. Bless the newlyweds. Bless this house-- these houses. Make us thankful for what we're about to receive, Amen!"

After taking a sip of coffee, Lena remarked, "Good Lord, Rose! Ain't you learnt how to make coffee, yet?"

"Well! If you don't likes my coffee, you kin' make some yo'self. We don't even drink the stuff! It ain't good for a body."

"Jus' cause you don't drink it don't mean you can't make it right." Lena said in a disturbing voice.

"Now, what's got into you 'Miss High n' Mighty?' I 'member when you didn't hardly talk at all. You jus' sit an' grin like a chess' cat," Rose responded.

"Rose, no one can make biscuits better than this. I'll have two more and please pass the syrup."

Frank was trying to change the heated banter between the two ladies. He could see no reason for Lena to be attacking Rose. He was astonished and surprised at her actions and concluded that the last minute marriage, together with the long trip, had left her in an agitated state.

"Can you heat the biscuits? Theys' got too cold," asked Lena.

"You heat the biscuits yo' self, Lena, an' while you at it, make mo' coffee."

"I'll do it," offered Jesse. "Let the honeymooners enjoy themselves a while longer."

Rose was getting angry at Lena's attitude but she didn't want to create an ugly scene with her guests. After all, Frank was Mr. Ford's brother and he had always been there for them when they needed him. One year, he had actually saved their farm for them. Frank and Mr. Ford had a strong bond between them and Rose wanted it to always stay that way.

She was happy that Frank had married Lena. Rose dearly wanted to have a friendly, even a sisterly, relationship with Lena. But she was completely bewildered by Lena's peculiar behavior. Perhaps, she was just nervous about being married, especially the curious circumstances surrounding it.

Rose decided that for the sake of family unity, she would overlook Lena's inexcusable attitude. Probably, Lena had not liked Rose's remark about her denying her race. Or, maybe, she needed more time to get used to married life and being part of the Ford family. Rose offered to pack some foods from the cellar for them to take home. Frank was delighted with the offer but Lena seemed indifferent.

The brothers went out to get the horse and buggy ready for the last leg of the journey home for the newlyweds. Lena went to the bedroom to gather their belongings and Rose went to the cellar to select items from her choice collection of canned foods. She was eager to send them on their way with good and kind feelings. And she sincerely wanted to maintain the relationship on good terms.

Rose got busy tidying up the sunroom but she couldn't put the visit of Frank and Lena to rest. She thought Lena's attitude was very strange and somewhat hostile. She was thankful when Jesse decided to take Justine for a ride in the wagon. She would have more time alone to sort through her feelings about what actually had taken place over the past two days.

Kula followed alongside Jesse as he pulled the wagon down the lane and to the edge of the meadow. To the delight of Justine, some loud hissing geese chased Kula across the meadow where he hid in the hollow of a tree. When he could no longer hear their hissing, he tucked his tail and high tailed it back to the house where he remained quiet, dozing in the safety of the breezeway.

` ` ` ` ` ` ` ` ` ` `

Late fall on the farm was an absolutely splendid time. The hurrying and scurrying was reduced to a pace that made everyone comfortable. It was not the breakneck speed that prevailed in spring and summer as the farmers and workers tried to make their deadlines. Nor was it the slow moving, dragging or hibernating kind of speed that accompanied the cold winter days and nights. Somehow, fall's speed seemed just right. People were more pleasant and more open for friendly conversations and benevolent exchanges.

There was assurance and satisfaction in knowing that harvest time was ended and everything had gone as planned. Autumn was spinning the last gold of the year as the leaves came softly twirling and tumbling to the ground.

When Mr. Ford returned from a shopping trip into town one day, Rose was saddened and perplexed by the news he read and shared. "The post war problems for the whites and Negroes were still at an all time high. The economic situation continued to be unstable and the Union currency was highly inflated. Technology was replacing the agrarian system. The Democrats had lost their political power, even in the south. Incompetent people were making political and economic reconstruction very difficult and the cotton tax for the schools was angering everyone. It seems as if it had come at a time when most farmers, Negro and white, were just trying to survive."

He went on, "There were complaints about the few teachers who had been sent from the north to staff the schools. The townspeople think their ideals are too Puritan and too liberal. Their teaching methods and philosophies are repugnant to the white south. There is a movement afoot to get rid of them by any means possible. They are ill treated and, sometimes, even physically assaulted. Many of the teachers had been sent by various denominations and rumor has it that those churches were more interested in swelling their own ranks than in providing proper education for the Negroes in the south."

It was hearing this report that set in motion Rose's desire to go for a visit with her family. Mamie could better help her to understand the ugly, prevailing mood throughout the south. She was anxious to see her family again since she had not seen them for several months. She wondered how the children were progressing in school. She wondered if the Negro attitude towards their teacher was the same as the attitude of the whites. Mamie would surely know what was happening among the Negro students.

Jesse agreed it was a good time for Rose and Justine to visit with her family. However, he insisted they only stay overnight. He was still uncomfortable with the idea of his family being away from the safety of their home. Rose was not happy with his demands but she agreed to that arrangement.

The first day of November arrived cool and crisp. The golden orange glow of the rising sun streaked through the trees and made interesting elongated patterns on the damp ground. Jesse helped in packing supplies and assorted items for the journey to Turner Place. They should arrive there by mid-morning, he thought. Spirit was in his prime now and was a well-trained, well-disciplined and dependable horse.

The golden-brown harvested fields along the trails and roads were breathtaking to behold. Rose had seen the fields hundreds of times, but each time she viewed them, no matter what the season, they took her breath away. The tied and stacked bales of hay and alfalfa that dotted the fields gave assurance that even the livestock would have sufficient food to last them through the harshest winter.

Traveling the roads and lanes in the fall always seemed to be easier and smoother than any other time. In summer, the earth was baked hard and dry by the hot summer sun. In autumn, the constant trips to the cotton gins and markets, along with the dampness, the fallen leaves and grasses helped to fill in the trenches and flatten out the roads to provide more comfortable riding. Soon, they were approaching the half way mark, the meandering stream where the animals stopped to quench their thirst and to rest in cool shady spots.

"I love the outdoors," Rose said to Justine.

"Look at the red birds and bluebirds bobbin' and soarin' over the brook. Let's us stop to rest and enjoy some of life's simple pleasures. I wants you to love nature and outdoors like I do. And like Papo, too. I gonna teach you like Papo teached me. We don' get to visit these beautiful places very much, but I make you a promise now, Justine; I gonna take you to them lots o' times."

Rose was in the midst of enjoying this exquisite vista when suddenly her heart started thumping wildly. Thoughts of the last time she was on this very road splintered her head and her heart. It was almost eight months ago. She was returning home from taking care of Ma and Pa and the children who were all sick during the wild flu epidemic. She was alone with Baby Jesse and he was sick unto death. Only she didn't realize it then. She only knew that something was terribly wrong. She quickly gathered up Justine and they were on their way again. She left behind the sounds of the gurgling brook, the singing of the velvet throated songbirds and the croaking of the frogs. She let go the grief that suddenly wrenched at her heart. The fallen leaves, whose colors had changed from green to yellow to gold to red, then brown, now carpeted the soft, damp earth around the brook.

The fields of the hill country appeared somewhat barren following harvesting. But there would still be an abundance of late growths to be reaped. People were just waiting for the fullness of time to collect the late fall and early winter gleanings.

Soon the cold northern winds would send the wild turkeys, pheasants, ducks, geese and other wild life seeking warmer climate along the meandering river that flowed through the hill country and on through the bottom land. A few days later, the hunters would be on their trail.

The whites with their guns. The boom of their guns would sound throughout. The Negroes with their traps. The traps were silent.

At mid-morning, Rose entered the gate to the Turner Place. She could see no movement nor could she hear any sounds. She considered the empty silence unusual. Almost always, when someone approached the farm, there was some kind of acknowledgement or response. Rose prodded Spirit into a faster trot.

losing the freedom. . . . .

She was not prepared for what she saw when she entered the little house. Zeke was sitting with his head resting on the table beside the rifle that Jesse had given him. The children were tending to Mamie who was lying on the bed. Her face was swollen and her eyes puffy and sunk back in her head. She had black and blue welts and bruises all over her body. The children were busy tending her wounds.

Ezekiel began sobbing and wailing; his lamentations were interspersed with praying for God's wrath to befall those who were responsible for the whipping and beating of his wife. The children all began trying to tell Rose what had happened. Rose signaled them to be quiet and to take care of Justine for her. She quickly went out to the buggy and brought in some golden salve she always kept there.

She told Samuel to put a pot of water on the stove. She saw that liniment had already been used to ease the pain. Now, Rose cleaned the wounds with mullein water. She also put mullein in the pot on the stove and she began to rub the salve all over Mamie's body.

Mamie managed to whisper in a strained, almost inaudible voice, "I knowed God would send me an' angel."

Rose worked on Mamie, dressing and soothing her wounds until late in the afternoon when Ezekiel finally persuaded her to 'sit for a spell.'

Rose asked Ephriam to make alfalfa tea for everyone. She knew it would help to soothe and calm the family.

"I knowed she didn have no business tryin' to vote. I don' know what got into her.

The preacher done tol' us we could vote if we could read. But I tol' her not to go," explained Zeke. "You know Mamie, she smart. She done learnt how to read an' with that pride she has, she figger' she owe it to our dead parents an' to all former slaves, who never knowed freedom, an' to our chil'ren, to go an' vote.

"Lord knows I didn want her to go, but she got a hard head. Sez we free now an' she gon' vote an' she gon' vote 'publican 'cause o' Mr. Lincoln. So she went to vote. An' she voted! But she nearly got kilt' doin' it. I wanted to go to town an' kill anybody I could, but she begged me not to. Sez they would beat an' kill all o' us if I showed up in town wit' a gun. Rose, what we gon' do?"

"First thing we gon' do is get Ma well an' back on her feet. Then we go' talk 'bout this votin.' I hears Mr. Ford talk 'bout votin' but I don' know nothin' 'bout it. Course, I still can't read."

Once again, Rose found herself in that kitchen which was so familiar to her. It was here that Mamie taught her how to cook. It was in this kitchen that her business was born. It was here that she did her canning and baked her goodies. It was here, too, that Baby Jesse became fatally ill.

Rose suddenly walked out of the kitchen. She walked out to the field and around her old garden. She had a good cry. She stood there for a long time, her body heaving for the pain that Mamie suffered. She felt the pain of the loss of a child, her only son, who for a short while had brought such joy. She continued to heave and to sob even though her tears had run dry. Then she composed herself, held her head high and returned to the house where she gave Justine a big hug and squeeze, kissed her several times and whispered, "Thank you, God, for all that you do an' all that you will continue to do."

She kissed and hugged her brothers and sisters and reassured them that Ma was going to be just fine. They each felt a huge sense of relief hearing those words from Rose, whom they adored and trusted. They remembered how she had nursed and cared for them that past winter, especially Ma and Pa, who were near death's door.

"The Lord is blessin' us all," she said. "He ain't gonna put burdens on us we can't bear. He done already blessed us mightily. He give'd us each other to love an' care for. He ain't gonna leave us alone. Ma's gonna be fine. Jus' fine!"

The next day, Mamie's fever began to subside but she was still too sore and stiff to get out of bed. Rose bathed her again with the mullein and rubbed the salve over her body. Mamie did something she had not done the day before. She cried out in agony each time a cut or bruise was touched. Rose knew that the day and night before, Mamie had been insulated from severe pain because she was still in a complete state of shock.

Now her pain was excruciating. Rose was faced with another decision. She knew she could not leave Mamie while she suffered so severely. Although she had given her word to Mr. Ford, she knew she had to stay at least one more night with her Ma. And that was her decision.

Rose had difficulty getting to sleep. She checked on Mamie every few minutes to see if she was all right. She was pleased with how soundly Justine slept. After a day filled with energetic activities with the big children, Rose was not surprised to see her in such a deep sleep.

"Havin' a problem settlin' down?" asked Zeke.

"Pa, I worried about Mr. Ford. I done tol' him I be back today. But I couldn' leave Ma. She needs me. I knows that Mr. Ford be thinkin' bout the last time I stay here. Baby Jesse got sick unto death. I know he worried 'bout us and now, I worried 'bout him."

"Then you git some sleep an' go home come sunrise. I have the hoss an' buggy ready for you."

"Thanks, Pa. G'night."

Zeke gave her a cup of tea, which was cold. Still she appreciated his effort. She drank the tea, settled down and tried to lull herself to sleep.

The entire family overslept the next morning, except for Zeke. When he heard the crowing of the rooster, he rolled out of bed. He was so happy to see the family still sleeping, he didn't have the heart to awaken anyone. He headed straight to the barn to prepare Spirit and the buggy for Rose and Justine.

In a little while, Ephriam was up making a fire in the stove. He was careful to move around quietly lest he wake up the rest of them, but one by one, the sleepy family began to stir. Even Mamie somehow managed to work her way to the kitchen and sit on a pillow. Black and blue marks covered her body.

Without warning, the tranquil morning was splintered by the pounding hooves of a horse and a shouting voice, then the howling and barking of the two hunting dogs the rider had brought with him.

Zeke was the first to arrive at the gate, followed by everyone else, except Mamie.

"My God, Rose! What happened? I expected you home last night. You gave me your word.

"I was up all night waiting for you. I couldn't sleep. I couldn't even think. I was worried out of my mind. I rode out looking for signs of you and Justine.

"For Chrissake, why didn't you come home like you promised?" he continued.

"Jesse, you best come out to the barn wit' me," said Zeke before Rose could even speak. He had noticed the looks of bewilderment on both Rose's and Jesse's faces.

The two men, one black, one white, trudged to the barn. One still testy, the other thankful.

Ephriam disappeared and got busy with other chores. Samuel and Aaron helped Rose to get breakfast ready. Mamie silently expressed her gratitude for still being alive and having a loving family to take care of her.

After his talk with Ezekiel, Jesse Ford went in to see and to have a talk with Mamie. At that moment, he would rather have been on the front line back at Appomattox than looking at Mamie's body and face and seeing her pain. Especially, now that he knew the reason why she had been so savagely assaulted and beaten.

He spent only a few minutes with her. When he emerged, there were tears streaming from his eyes and his skin was beet red. He headed for the barn. Moments later, his voice erupted in an impulsive scream which seemed to shake the earth. He took his rifle from his horse and fired a volley off towards the heavens. He slumped to the ground, on his knees, his head buried in his hands and he remained in that position until Zeke finally went to him and they walked arm in arm around the barn and back to the house.

"Before you take yo' leave, Ma wants us to have prayer an' sing a song," Zeke requested. "I give the prayer, Rose--you lead the singing.

"God in heav'n, we grateful you spared Ma from death. She suffered mightily, but she alive. Praise yo' Holy name! We thankful fo' our family an' that you give us a reasonable po'tion of health an' stren'th. Guide an' be wit our children as they go home. Continue to be wit us all. Thank you! In Jesus' name... in Jesus' name! Amen."

Were you there when they crucified my Lord?
Oh, sometimes it causes me to tremble, tremble, tremble
Were you there when they nailed Him to the cross?
Oh, sometimes it causes me to tremble, tremble, tremble
Were you there when the sun refused to shine/
Oh, sometimes it causes me to tremble, tremble, tremble.

On their way home, Jesse rode just ahead of his family, with his rifle at the ready. At times, he would lag behind them, surveying everything. Both anger and sadness pulsated through his body. Jesse left one of the hunting dogs with the Turners, who protested. But in the end, Zeke accepted the gift and expressed his thanks for being given such a fine animal. He would come in handy for the hunting season and he would make a good watchdog for the farm.

"His name is Lucky," Jesse had called as he rode out the gate.

It was an uneventful ride home. Somehow the countryside which had been so alive and beautiful on the ride to the Turner Place now seemed bleak and dull. Wildlife which seemed so lively and abundant on the ride out now seemed to have vanished. Even the ever-present crows, with their shrill calls, were nowhere to be seen or heard.

Mercifully, they arrived home safe and sound, without incident, as Zeke had petitioned in his prayer. They arrived amidst a cold, churning wind and just in time to see the scarlet sun vanish beyond the hills. Jesse made a fire in the fireplace to bring some warmth to a chilly evening.

"Mr. Ford, will you please read to me tonight?" asked Rose.

"Of course, my love. It'll be my good pleasure."

He read a Psalm of David.

> Bless the Lord, O my soul; and all that is within me, bless his holy name! Bless the Lord, O my soul, and forget not all his benefits, who forgives all your iniquity, who heals all your diseases, who redeems your life from the Pit, who crowns you with steadfast love and mercy, who satisfies you with good as long as you live so that your youth is renewed like the eagle's.
> The Lord works vindication and justice for all who are oppressed. He made known his ways to Moses, his acts to the people of Israel. The Lord is merciful and gracious, slow to

> anger and abounding in steadfast love. He will not always chide, nor will he keep his anger forever. He does not deal with us according to our sins, nor requite us according to our iniquities. For as the heavens are far above the earth, so great is his steadfast love for those who fear him; as far as the east is from the west, so far does he remove our transgressions from us. As a father pities his children, so the Lord pities those who fear him. For he knows our frame; he remembers that we are dust. As for man, his days are like grass; he flourishes like a flower in the field; for the wind passes over it, and it is gone, and its place knows it no more. But the steadfast love of the Lord is from everlasting to everlasting upon those who fear him, and his righteousness to children's children, to those who keep his covenant and remember to do his commandments.
>
> The Lord has established his throne in the heavens, and his kingdom rules over all. Bless the Lord, O you angels, you mighty ones who do his word! Bless the Lord, all his hosts, his ministers that do his will! Bless the Lord, all his works, in all places of his dominion. Bless the Lord, O my soul!

Psalms: 103

Listening to Mr. Ford read was such an exquisite and spiritually satisfying experience for Rose. He had read in such a rich and resonant tone. And at this moment of reflection and silence, she felt that her own soul was soaring somewhere in the heavens and that she was singing with angels. She nestled her head on his chest and began to softly hum.

And there in the cozy warmth from the fireplace and the soft glow from the lamps, Rose decided it was a perfect time to announce her news.

"Mr. Ford," she began, "I think we gon' have us another baby and....

"Rose! Are you guessing or have you known all along?" he interrupted. "You always wait so long to tell me."

"I always wants to make sho' that's really what it is. Sometimes I think it is, then a few days later, I finds out I was wrong. You git so excited when I tells you, I just don't want to disappoint you, so I waits."

"Well! My prayers are answered. I praise God and I thank you! It's been a long day and night. Let's go celebrate our blessing."

Chapter Seventeen

The chilling winter winds descended upon the hill country. The frost and sleet had become almost a daily ritual. The animals could sometimes be seen at the edge of the forest foraging for food. Often, some of them ended up being food for the hunters and sharecroppers. Occasionally, Rose would go out and bag squirrels and rabbits for their table. Even Jesse, who hated killing, would bring one or two deer home during the winter because he knew they constantly reproduced at too rapid a pace. The farmers complained of the destruction they caused to some of the crops, especially during the planting season. They both trampled and ate the tender young shoots.

Jesse busied himself designing and making furniture and toys for Justine. They would pass her baby furniture on to the unborn child. Much of the time, he worked in the barn. If the weather was too rainy or too cold, he brought small pieces into the house to sand, groove or polish.

It had been several years since Rose had made slippers for anyone, so she decided now was a good time to try it again. She would make her first pair of moccasins for Justine. The week before Christmas, she worked long hours in the kitchen baking cakes, pies, assorted breads and candies. She would share these delicacies with her family and with the sharecroppers. In her heart, she hoped that Frank and Lena would visit during the holiday or even have Christmas dinner with them.

Her hopes and desires faded miserably. They neither saw nor heard from Frank and Lena. So early on Christmas Day when Jesse saw the sadness on her face, he hitched up Spirit and Major to the carriage, added some bells to herald the season and off they went to spend Christmas Day with the Turners.

It was a cold, crisp day but they felt blessed to have clear blue skies and a warm sun shining down upon them.

"This wonderful day offers us a season of peace," said Jesse. "I just wish we could put it in a jar and hold on to it forever."

They arrived at the Turner Place at mid-day. Their visit was an unexpected and wonderful surprise for the family. Of course, Mamie cried with joy and delight when she saw them. They were pleased to see how well she had recovered from her attack. They had not seen her since that horrible time.

Later, they all sat down at a table that was filled with an assortment of wonderful and delicious foods. Mamie led the singing of "Go Tell It On The Mountain," followed by one of her prayers of praise and thanksgiving. Everyone waited patiently and when at last, she finished, they enjoyed the bountiful repast and just being together as family on Christmas day.

In early March, after relentless pressure to obtain his consent for her to take a trip into town, Mr. Ford finally agreed that Rose could go shopping. A condition was added to the agreement. Molly would make the trip with her. She was six months along and her big dress did not conceal the fact that she was with child.

The two women were ecstatic about being out without children or husbands. They passed the train station where Rose stopped for a moment to take a long nostalgic look. What fun and excitement she had on that platform during her selling days! She had taken such pride in her success. The women hitched the horse and buggy to a post and took off for their round of shopping.

After making a few purchases, the two of them headed for the door. Rose spotted Lena entering and rushed up to say hello. Lena nervously bumped into Molly, stared past Rose, and coldly said to Molly, "Why 'ont you watch wheres you walk?"

"I'se mighty sorry," replied Molly. "S'cuse me, mam."

A store clerk came running up to Lena to make sure that she was okay. But no one inquired about how Molly and Rose were. Lena immediately went towards the rear of the store. Rose and Molly quickly left and went to the dry goods store and finished their shopping.

When they got in the buggy, Rose drove away faster than Molly had ever seen her go. And she never said a word.

"Is somethin' the matter, Rose?" asked Molly, puzzled by her demeanor.

"Didn' you know who that was who bumped you back in the store?"

"I reckon I don't. Do you know who she is?"

"That was Frank Ford's wife!"

"Do she know who you is?"

"Course she do! She Cecilia Metoyer's daughter."

"Then why she act so uppity?"

"Cause she think she white, tha's why."

Rose did not have a clue as to how to tell Mr. Ford about the encounter with Lena in town. But more than that, what would happen to the relationship between the two brothers is what bothered her most. She knew that Mr. Ford loved his brother but she was also secure in the knowledge that Mr. Ford dearly loved her. He even loved her family. On Christmas Day, he promised he would help Ezekiel add two rooms to his small house to make rooms for the boys and girls who were growing up.

Rose could not understand how Lena could give up her race. Lena's mother was fair skinned but she never thought of herself as white. Her two very fair-skinned brothers were married to Negro women.

Rose wondered if Mrs. Metoyer knew about Lena passing herself off as a white person.

"What would make someone do such a horrible thing?" she wondered aloud.

"You knows I don't know nothin' 'bout that," responded Molly.

When they arrived home, Molly said, "I sho' thanks you for 'vitin' me on the trip to town, Rose. I only been to town a few times in my whole life."

"We do it again sometime, Molly," Rose answered as she headed for home.

` ` ` ` ` ` ` ` ` `

When Rose entered the house, Jess could see that something was wrong.

"Rose, you look as if you've seen a ghost!" Jesse observed.

"I think I did," she replied.

"Anyone we know?"

"Someone we useta' know."

"Is there any more to this story or was it just your imagination?"

Rose began to shake. She began to cry softly. Jesse gave her a tight squeeze and a hug. He went to check on Justine. She was occupied with the toys made from cedar that Jesse had constructed in his workshop.

Rose went out on the porch and sat in the swing. That swing had become a place that she would retreat to whenever she needed solace or just to get away by herself.

"It can't be that bad, or is it?" Jesse raised his brow.

"I just need some thinkin' time."

"It's going to be better when you get it off your chest but if you need...."

"Lena is passin' herself off as white! I jus' knowed something bad was goin' to happen when she don' tol those marriage people she was white!"

"Now, slow down, Rose. Start at the beginning, please. There must be more to this because you already knew about the marriage and you knew she didn't tell the justice she was white."

"Well, I saw 'Miss High and Mighty' in town today. She looked right at me, then right thru me. And she never said nary a word. Why, she bumps right into Molly and had the nerve to say, 'Whyon't you look where you's goin,' girl?"

"Who do she thinks she is?" Rose asked, standing with her hands on her hips.

"Calm down, Rose. No sense in getting your feathers ruffled. Maybe we should just forget the whole thing as if it never happened," suggested Jesse.

"Forgit! Did you say forgit? Never! Not for as long as I knows who I is, and not as long as I knows who she is. Never!"

"Rose, please! Won't you think about the baby? Being this upset might affect our child, and is it worth that?"

Jesse took Rose in his arms and comforted her. "Believe me, Rose, when I say I understand how you feel. I just don't want anything to upset you and cause any harm to the baby.

"Come to think of it, you've had quite a long day. I want you to lie down and get some rest. Justine and I will bring you tea in just a few minutes."

Pinkie. . . . .

"No, Rose. For the last time, I will not consent for you to go. You are in your seventh month and we both know this can be a crucial time in pregnancy," said Jesse as he made preparations to visit Mrs. Metoyer.

"I jus' need to see for myself how she thinks and feels 'bout this whole sit'ation with Lena passing for white and havin' nothin' to do with her own kind. I needs to know if she think she white, too. Cause if she do, I don't want her in my house deliverin' no baby of mines."

"Rose, I'm capable of having a discussion with Mrs. Metoyer, inquiring about her availability and whether or not she wants the job. This should have nothing to do with Lena. Mrs. Metoyer is the best midwife around these parts, unless, of course, you want Mrs. Broome." He knew Rose would bristle at the mere mention of that name.

"You win again, Mr. Ford. But willya let Mrs. Metoyer know how I feels 'bout folks who disown they own race and fam'ly?"

"I'll do that, Rose, but not before I get her to agree to come and stay with you before and after the baby comes."

Jesse kissed Rose and Justine good-by and rode off on Major headed across the river for the Metoyer home.

"I'll return as quickly as I can," he shouted.

Jesse had already made arrangements for Molly and Jack to look in on Rose and Justine even though he'd only be gone for a few hours.

When Rose was in her ninth month, Jack went to bring Mrs. Metoyer to the Ford home. Cecilia Metoyer said that she was pleased to be back with Rose, Justine and Mr. Ford.

"You is my favorite family in the whole parish for my birthing service. I feels real good that you axed me to come back. Um happy you so pleased with my work.

"Justine, just look at you! You a big girl now. Baby, you growed so much since I last seen you," she observed as she reached down to pick up Justine and give her a big hug.

It took only a little while for Rose to see that Mrs. Metoyer was the same genuine person that had attended her when Jesse Jr. was born. Rose decided not to ask her any questions about Lena's marriage and if she was living as a white woman. She was most curious, however, to know if Lena visited with her mother or if Mrs. Metoyer had visited with her daughter and her son-in-law. But Cecilia Metoyer brought with her her own kind of special joy. Just her presence made a house sing.

She was up early every morning making an assortment of delectable dishes. She served Rose breakfast in bed. Rose enjoyed the pampering but couldn't endure too much of it after a while. Besides, she didn't like being in bed when the sun was shining. So she requested to have dinner and supper served in the sunroom.

It was early summer and daylight lingered longer. The view from the sunroom was delightful and tranquil. Rose was glad that she never allowed curtains at the windows. At suppertime, the sun would glow with glints of orange and red and gold. The animals from the woods would amble up closer to the fence as if they were watching her watching them.

Each day, Cecilia made a wonderful hodgepodge of Creole and Cajun dishes. She made Rose's food separate because she didn't wish to disturb her fragile condition and take a chance on inducing early labor, even though Rose had said she was ready to get this baby out of her belly.

Justine loved Mrs. Metoyer, too. She called her 'MeMe.' They went for long walks and watched the animals in the meadow near the forest. Justine enjoyed watching the busy sparrows flying back and forth. Mrs. Metoyer even took Justine to visit and play with Molly and Jack's children. They put her in a wheelbarrow and rolled her around and around, all under Mrs. Metoyer's watchful eyes. The children also did cartwheels which made Justine laugh and laugh. She tried to imitate them.

Mrs. Metoyer had been there almost three weeks when Rose went into labor. She delivered, without any problems, a healthy baby girl on June 1, 1884.

Rose was relieved that the baby was healthy and they both came through delivery without hurt or harm. But she was visibly disappointed that it was a not a boy.

After Mrs. Metoyer went through her ritual of cleaning the baby and washing her in warm tallow, she wrapped her and put her in Mr. Ford's arms. He looked her over from head to toe checking to make sure that everything was there and was where it was supposed to be.

He placed the baby on the bed beside her mother and remarked, "She's so pink!"

Right then and there, she was named Pinkie. Rose hadn't even thought of a girl's name because she was so sure it was going to be a boy. She wanted to cry out in disappointment, but she wouldn't dare do so in Mr. Ford's presence.

Justine loved her new baby sister and wanted to hold her. But Mrs. Metoyer was adamant about not letting Justine hold her. She thought it was not a good idea to let Justine even touch her at such an early age.

"We must protec' her from catchin' anythin' at sich an early stage," she said.

But Jesse insisted on letting Justine touch her and even play with her little toes.

"Justine needs to know that she has some ownership in this baby and that her baby sister is not replacing her in this family."

If Jesse was disappointed in not getting the boy that Rose thought he so desperately wanted, he never let Rose see it on his face or in his reactions. He never even spoke about a son.

"I am so blessed and lucky," he said to Rose. "I have two of the most beautiful girls the world has ever seen. In fact, I doubt that the world will ever see any girls anywhere as beautiful as these two. Even the queen of England is jealous of their beauty. My God, I am surrounded by beautiful women!""

"Mr. Ford," smiled Rose. "You always was good with words. Now, you done out did yo'self."

"Well, it's true. And why not? After all, they have the most beautiful mother in the whole wide world. Rose, there is no one as lovely as you and I love you! My love will always be with you to surround and protect you."

"Mr. Ford, I loves you back!"

On the day before Mrs. Metoyer's last day with Rose and the family, she finally mentioned Lena's name. She told Rose that her two sons had gone to Frank Ford looking for work. Word had gotten around that he was a good white man to work for. Lena had seen her brothers when they arrived at the farm, but she never went outside when they were talking with Mr. Ford.

Frank Ford told them that he had a place for one family on tenant's row, but not for two. The brothers did not want to be separated so they told him they would come and work for him when he had space for both families. When her sons told her they had been to Frank Ford's looking for work, Cecilia decided she would go to the farm and have a talk with Lena and Frank Ford. She had no idea that Lena was passing herself off for white.

As it turned out, she didn't have to make the trip. It was Lena who came for a visit with her mama. She knew that the time had come to tell her something. She said that when she and Frank were married, she only meant to be white for the sake of getting legally married. Lena said that no one in Texas knew them and it was much simpler that way. The two of them were never asked any questions about race.

None of the farmers who live near them knew her and they never spoke to Frank anyway, so she never thought any more about it until she went shopping in town and the storekeepers treated her just like she was a white woman. With so much respect and gentleness. She liked her new treatment and the politeness and kindness they showered on her.

Now things were closing in on her just as Jesse had predicted they would. When she saw Rose and Molly in town that day, she panicked. She tried to reassure her mother that she loves her family but she feels like she dug herself deep down in a well and now she doesn't know how to get out. She never went anywhere or had any friends anyway, so she concluded no one would ever become aware of what she did in town. But when she didn't even go out and speak to her own brothers, she hated herself. Now she's suffering the agony of how to solve this unholy predicament.

"'Maybe, I just never leave the house agin,'" she tol' me.

"Lordamercy, I doesn't know what's gonna happen to my child. I guess we gon' have to pray for her." So she prayed a long prayer which reminded Rose of Mamie.

"Rose," said Cecilia, " I done got this off my chest, now I feels like shoutin', I feels like singin. I feels like clapping my hands. I feels like stomping my feet!"

There's no hidin' place down here
O' I went to the rock to hide my face
The rock cried out, "No hidin' place.
There's no hidin' place down here."

"Mrs. Metoyer," Rose said after the singing, clapping and shouting was over. "I love these Spirituals. My Ma sez we gotta pass these songs on to our chil'ren. Why it's so 'portant to do that?" What can you tell me 'bout Spirituals?

"Because, Rose, these songs come from the invisible church. Theys come from the heart an' soul of the Negro slave. These songs tells of the conditions under which the slaves live. They speak of life, births, deaths, marriages, sufferins.' sorrows, even workin,' an' things like that. These songs are ageless, timeless!

"They is messages of 'pressed people but they brings hope and faith. These songs tells 'bout love, freedom, justice an' mercy. There is a spiritual, a shoutin' or mournin' song or a jubilee song for evry' kind of sit'ation you can think of. Tha's why it important to pass these songs along.

"Yo' Ma done tol' you right. We got to pass these songs to our chil'ren. Theys got to pass them to their chil'ren and they chil'ren's chil'ren. These songs mus' always be kept alive. They are part of us. They are our history!"

"I do truly thanks you, Mrs. Metoyer, for sharing that with me. You sich a smart woman, like my Ma is. And you talks nice, too, like Mr. Ford."

"That Mr. Ford a fine gentleman! You got yo' self one good man."

" I sho' nuff knows he a good man."

"I see Jack comin' up the road. I 'spect it almost time to leave fo' home."

"I keep in touch with you and if we have 'nother baby, Mr. Ford come fo' you agin. You welcome to visit any time though, 'specially, 'round Christmas time. We be mighty proud to have you. You hear."

Exactly fifteen months later, Mrs. Metoyer was back in the Ford household with Rose awaiting the birth of another child. This birthing process was different than the previous three had been. Rose's pain was far more intense and her labor lasted much longer than was expected. Mrs. Metoyer became worried after more than eight hours passed without the baby coming. By now she could tell it was not going to be a breech birth, but in the beginning she had not discounted that possibility. She still didn't like the position the baby was maintaining.

Rose asked Mr. Ford to go and bring Molly to the house. She felt that Molly could serve as another pair of hands for Mrs. Metoyer. And Molly's presence always had a comforting effect on Rose. As the long, hot and humid September night dragged on and on, Rose grew more and more exhausted and the pain more severe. Mrs. Metoyer decided to give Rose some blue cohosh, an herb good for relieving childbirth pain and calming the nerves. Though generally, Rose was one who never needed her nerves calmed, she accepted the herb without protest.

Just when it seemed that Rose could not manage another push, the baby boy finally emerged into the world at sunrise, on a bright sunny morning, September 20, 1885. Mr. Ford, whose pride showed like a strutting peacock, said the baby would be named William.

Rose, who was completely exhausted, managed a big smile and said, "Tha's just wonderful, ev'rythin gonna be fine now!"

Jesse Ford wanted Cecilia Metoyer to stay on a few more weeks because he felt that Rose would need extra help with the girls and additional time to fully recover from the arduous labor she had gone through. Mrs. Metoyer agreed to stay providing Mr. Ford would send word to her sons. She needed them to look after her chickens and cows. Also they needed to gather her goobers from the patch and harvest her garden. She no longer planted cotton.

Jesse Ford made the trip himself to explain Mrs. Metoyer's extended stay to her sons, Thomas and Thad. He also wanted to discuss the possibility of their coming to the farm to work for him. He had acquired some additional acres and wanted to get them ready in time for spring planting. He desperately needed workers and he had heard that her sons were excellent field hands.

The brothers were pleased with Jesse's offer and said they would be ready to move in with their families before Christmas. But it was possible to begin work for him as soon as the present harvesting season was completely ended.

Another house had to be built on tenant's row because there was only one unoccupied place. Number three. The little house that Rose and Justine once lived in during the time when the sheriff continually threatened to arrest her. Jesse knew it well. Too well!

` ` ` ` ` ` ` ` ` ` `

When William was one month old, Jesse decided it was time to make his yearly trip to Houston while Mrs. Metoyer was still with the family. Along with his all-important supply of seed, he purchased farming equipment and other supplies in anticipation of next year's needs for the new land. He also bought Christmas presents for family members as well as for the sharecroppers and their families. He ordered wearing apparel for Rose and the two girls from a catalog. He hoped they would arrive in plenty of time for the holidays. Then Jesse selected from the counter, precious little gowns for William, including a special one for christening. He also purchased a grand surprise for Rose.

When Jesse arrived at the train station and claimed his large number of boxes, Jack was there with the wagon team waiting for him. Before leaving the station, Jesse and Jack covered the load with tarpaulin because they could see the rainstorm off in the distance. The clouds had been gathering all day and Jack came prepared.

It took more than five hours before they finally arrived at the house. The ravages of the wind and rain had caused the load to shift, requiring Jesse and Jack to stop more than once to right the load and to reinforce the coverings. At one point, the wagon wheels became stuck in the mud. They used two by fours and tree branches, and after what seemed like hours of struggling, they were finally able to free the wheels. The clouds opened and the rain seemed to come down in torrents. They could only see a few feet ahead of them. As they moved slowly up the road, a small river of water came rushing down upon them, stopping them in their tracks. The flow of water almost reached the top of the wagon wheels.

Jack wanted to stop and wait for the rainstorm to pass over. But Jesse was sure they could make it home. By now, they were both soaking wet and Jesse was more afraid of exposure than he was of losing his cargo.

The wind began to sweep down the hills with a mighty roar. Although it was a cold wind, Jesse was sure that it was strong enough to blow the rain clouds off their course and through the area.

"We're almost there now," said a shivering Jesse Ford. "I just hope we didn't lose any seed. That is what's most important! The other items can be replaced in due time."

At home, Rose had noticed that the force of the storm was strongest at the time Mr. Ford was due to arrive. She stood by the window watching and waiting. Mrs. Metoyer stood with her, while the little girls played about their mother's dress tail. It was as if the girls could sense something wasn't quite right.

Rose knew that Jack was dependable and reliable in almost any situation. Still, she worried. He was skilled at handling the team and the wagon. Yet, she worried. She also knew that Mr. Ford was an excellent horseman. She worried. And she began to pace the floor. The girls toddled back and forth, behind her.

She waited. She paced. And she worried some more.

Rose prayed a silent prayer that the dark clouds would disappear and a clear sky would return. In desperation, she turned to Mrs. Metoyer and said, "One o' yo' Spirituals would come in handy right now. Maybe it take away my worries."

Jordan's water is chilly and cold
God's gonna trouble the water
It chills the body but lifts the soul
God's gonna trouble the water
Wade in the water, wade in the water
If you gets there afore I do
Tell all my friend's I'm comin' too
God's gonna trouble the water

"Now, please, you gotta pray for the storm to end. All that thunderin' n' lightnin' an' rain sometime brings so much danger. I jus' wants them to make it home safe."

Cecilia Metoyer began to pray. "Lord who sen's the rain, who sen's the lightnin,' who sen's the thunder, we knows You also calms the water, an' the lightnin', an' the thunder. Right now, we's axing fo' You to calm this storm an' make it possible fo' our love ones to 'rive home safely. Father, we ax that You let no hurt nor harm come to them on they journey home. Please, sah, Father, God, hear the prayer of this po' sinner....

Rose didn't hear the end of Cecilia's prayer because, at that moment. She saw a little clearing in a parting of the sky. She saw a patch of blue and a tiny ray of light. She did notice, however, that rain was still falling. But things were getting better.

"God hear'd yo' prayer, Mrs. Metoyer! It be a real mir'cle!" Rose screamed.

Cecilia ended her prayer, got up off her knees and shouted, "Hallelujah! Praise the Lord! The Lord be praised!"

"Mrs. Metoyer, you truly is one o' God's angels. You prayed a mir'cle!"

Mrs. Metoyer went home assuring Rose that she would be back for the Christmas holidays. After all, her sons and their families would be there. She still did not feel comfortable visiting with her daughter and the other Mr. Ford.

It continued to rain on and off for the next week delaying the building of house number four. In mid-November, however, Thad Metoyer and his family moved into number three. He could now help in finishing the construction of the new house and the addition of another out house for tenant's row.

At mid-December, the house was finished and Tom and his family moved in. It was a joyous occasion for the brothers. They were all happy to be together and they were happy to be working for Jesse Ford. Because of their sister, Lena, and her attitude, they concluded they were better off working here than at the other farm.

Another notable event happened in December. The piano that Jesse bought for Rose on his trip to Houston arrived. Rose could not believe her eyes and when she sat down to play and Jesse could not believe his ears. She was able to pick out little melodies and even parts of some of the Spirituals she knew. The piano was just one more super addition to an incredible household which they both enjoyed immensely!

Since the weather was wintry and blustery and it was much too cold to be outdoors with the children, Rose mostly stayed indoors. She entertained the children during the day, playing the piano. She entertained Mr. Ford at night after the children were put to bed. She loved that piano and Jesse enjoyed her playing as much as she did. He knew he had made a very wise and good investment.

Christmas, 1885, was one glorious time at the Ford Home. Rose's Ma and Pa, along with their children, came to celebrate. Mrs. Metoyer came and brought enough food to feed everyone. Molly and Jack and their children came. Shug and his family, the sharecroppers who were there from the beginning, came. The latest sharecroppers, Thad and Tom Metoyer and their families, all came to celebrate Christmas.

The ladies all pitched in and put the food on the tables. It seemed as if tables were everywhere. During the afternoon when Rose wasn't busy with William, she was playing the piano. All the children were very excited to see and hear the piano. There was even more excitement when Mr. Ford passed around the Christmas presents. As usual, there was something for everyone.

Another surprise was when Frank passed out fruits and nuts to everyone.

After dinner and after clean up, everyone returned to their homes except the Turner Family and Mrs. Metoyer. They all retired to the new house for the evening.

Later that night, Rose asked Mr. Ford, "What give'd you the idea to buy a piano?"

"Through the years, my dear, I have heard you sing with the birds, echo the calls of most every animal in the woods and heard you make beautiful sounds on most every pot, piece of china and just about anything else you got your hands on, I knew you could play a piano once your lovely fingers touched one. And I was right, you know."

"Merry Christmas, Mr. Ford!

"Merry Christmas, my love!

"Uh, oh!"

"What is it now?"

"I forgot to say thanks again for the piano."

"You get under this quilt."

And he smothered her with kisses.

She returned them and then some.

Chapter Eighteen

After the planting was done, the spring rains came and the warm sun shone. The budding crops began to push clods of soil into mounds with little crooked slits. At first, the rain fell gently, like the farmers always wanted it to. The farmers and their workers were delighted to see the soothing rain. It meant that the ground would get soaked and the sun would come, and together they would germinate the seed and the crops would begin to grow and sprout and later emerge from their ground cover.

But this time, the rain didn't stop. It continued to fall. Moderate. Steady. And then the rain fell harder and harder. And harder. And harder. The rain continued. After a few days, the farmers and the workers began to look to the sky for some sign telling them the rain would soon cease.

People in the bottomlands began to look at the river, checking to see if they were safe or if they needed to leave their homes and go to the hill country. Some decided to stay. Others decided to take their families and move up to higher ground. When the water came up to his steps, Zeke, too, decided to put his family in the wagon and head for the hills. He boxed up the chickens, put the sow in the wagon and tied the cow, the dog and mule to it.

He figured this year's crops would be washed away. He could only wait and see what would be left. He at least hoped the house would remain standing. He saw some of his neighbors headed for the hill country in search of high ground.

Mamie sang and prayed along the way. She convinced Zeke that God had told her they should go to Mr. Ford's. Zeke was glad to hear her pronouncement because he had no idea where to go. The last time there was a big flood, it was slavery time and the massa knew where to take everyone. Zeke had no idea where it was that they went. It had been such a long time ago.

With such a heavy and awkward load, the going was slow and treacherous. It was after dark when they arrived at the gate of the Ford

Farm. Zeke approached it carefully. He called out, " Mr. Jesse Ford! Miss Rose Turner!" several times.

"You ought say 'Rose Ford'," suggested Samuel.

"No!" said Aaron. "She wants to be Rose Turner, so she be Rose Turner!"

"Stop this fussin,' boys," shouted Zeke.

"I seen a light come on. I thinks they hear us."

"Jesse, tis me, Ezekiel. Um with my family," he yelled.

"We flooded out in the bottom land."

"Just a minute, Zeke. I'll come and open the gate."

Once inside, Jesse made a roaring fire in the great fireplace so they could all get dry and warm. Rose was up in a flash bringing in dry clothing. She went in the kitchen to fix some late supper.

The hard driving rain continued throughout the night. The snapping and cracking of the trees could be heard along with the wailing and howling of the animals. Heaven's artillery was making itself both felt, seen and heard. All the family could do now was wait while the big episode played out.

The rain finally began to ease up over the next two days. Jesse, Zeke and Jack went riding out to check the fields for damage. There was some plant loss but the damage to the land in the hill country seemed to be minimal. However, the run-off would present serious problems at the foot of the hills. The high ground had escaped any significant damage.

Later that afternoon, the Fords again had surprise visitors at the gate. This time it was Frank and Lena Ford. Frank whistled his signal to announce his presence. He knew how to open the gate, so he opened it and they entered. He told them that some of his crop was under water. The house was safe sitting at the crest of the hill. If the water receded quickly, he was sure he would be able to salvage most of his crop since he was late with his planting. He wanted to discuss with his brother what steps had to be taken to rebound following the disastrous storm.

Frank was pleased to see Zeke present because he knew Zeke had had some experience with flooded fields. At the same time, he expressed sorrow that Zeke had suffered unknown flood damages. Frank greeted Mamie and all the children affectionately. Lena just stood aloof with very little to say. Rose decided she would ignore her foolishness until the two of them could be alone.

Both Jesse and Rose were pleased they could offer shelter and food to the people they loved so much. Rose felt a certain pride in the fact that Jesse had chosen his land in the hill country which was farther away and uphill from the river. When Jesse saw that river, he knew there could be the possibility of flooding. He had witnessed rivers spill over their banks, both in the mid-west and during the war.

Frank inquired whether anyone knew how Mrs. Metoyer had survived the storm. He seemed even more thoughtful and concerned than her own daughter, who had not inquired about Cecilia's safety. Jesse told him that Thad had ridden over this morning to check on his mother. She was fine and even though her place was covered with water and mud, she was in no immediate danger. She wanted to remain at home to look after her animals. She had gone through flooding before and could read the danger signs and predicted she'd be all right.

At sunrise the next morning, the rainfall was lighter. The men left to go and gauge the level of water at the river. They told the women they had no idea what time they would be returning since they wanted to check on several parcels of land. If the weather would allow it, they would even ride out and take a look at Ezekiel's farm.

Samuel's grin stretched from ear to ear when the men invited him to ride along with them. Rose said he could ride Spirit. She knew that the horse could use a good workout since it had been in the barn for a few weeks.

Rose heard Mamie preparing breakfast out in the kitchen. She had neither seen nor heard Lena all morning. She figured Lena was too embarrassed to leave her room. After all, when a crisis arose, to whom did she and Frank turn? To whom could they turn? If she wanted to be a white woman so bad and the white people treated her with such dignity and respect, why didn't she go to the white people?

Because she knew as well as Rose, that no white people cared dirt about her or either of the Ford brothers. She also knew that no white person would come to help either of them, even in time of trouble. They would help a Negro person first. Why, even Ezekiel could have gone to his white neighbors for help. He and Mamie had probably come to Jesse and Rose's only because they knew the extra house was there. And, of course, they loved every chance they got to visit with the grandchildren.

There was something about a disaster that brought people together, even in this terrible decade. Although the whites generally thought the Negroes were a menace to their lives and property, they, in fact, knew they were a gentle and helpful people. The two groups were both victimized by the war's aftermath. It kept them apart when they could have been assisting one another. If they had been working together, both groups would have been improving their 'dirt poor' status in life. And the south would have come back together far sooner than it did.

On this morning, Rose decided to stay in her room with her children as long as she could, just to see what move Lena would make. She saw Mamie outside looking up at the sky, checking out signs to make her predictions of what the weather would do. Rose heard no sound at all coming from the room where Lena and Frank had slept. She decided to take the two girls out to Mamie. She knew the older children would be delighted to look after and entertain Justine and Pinkie. Mamie had trained her children so well that Rose was pleased whenever the girls could be in their company. And, in turn, the little girls were crazy about their aunts and uncles.

There was only a misty rain falling when Mamie and the girls disappeared into the house next door. The tantalizing aroma of breakfast cooking on the stove wafted through the dampness and found its way throughout the house and boldly announced that a delicious meal could be had if one presented oneself in the sun room.

Rose began to carry on a loud and distinct conversation with little William about all the delectable goodies that awaited them. She even added that soon the room would be filled with rays of sweet warm sun that would come filtering through the clouds any minute now.

"Just you wait and see, William, God's gonna sen' that ol' sun and we gonna shout with joy when it come shinin' thru' the clouds. Maybe we ought to get ourselves ready and go join the rest of the family and have some of Ma's delicious breakfast. Now what you think o' that, lil' William?

"I think that if we goin,' we ought to get a move on.

"Do you thinks that maybe there be somebody else around here who might just' be dyin' to get theyself some o' that good food?

"Uh, huh, Ma makes the best biscuits of all, even better'n Ms. Metoyer. Now you got to go some to be that good!

"I 'spect we ready to get goin' now. Say bye-bye to anyone who's listenin'."

Rose took William and went out the breezeway, through the kitchen and into the sunroom where Mamie and the children were busy enjoying themselves and eating their breakfast.

"I think the rain finally gon' stop. I prayed hard and long fo' it to stop. The good Lord done heard my cry," said Mamie. "Ready fo' some breakfast, Rose?"

"Yes'm. I have some yo' good hot biscuits and jam with a cup o' tea."

"Where's that Lena gal, ain't she up yet?"

"Ma, Lena got some problems, there's somethin' 'bout her you needs to know."

"Right now, I don't need to hear no sad story. Ever'one who lives in the hill country got problems. Us who live in the bottomland got worser ones. We losing our crops, some of the land is plum' washed away. Some of us losing our homes. Do she got problems worse than us?"

"Nome."

"If she wants to eat, you best tell her to come now. I be cleaning up in a minute."

Rose didn't move nor did she say anything. She knew if she told Mamie that Lena was passing for white, Mamie would come down on her pretty hard and now wasn't the time for that.

The sun was fighting its way through the clouds. When it did break through, the rain still fell softly to the ground, the children sang and shouted:

"The devil's beating his wife! The devil's beating his wife!"

Finally, strong winds began to push the clouds off to the east and the sun began to shine brighter. The children went outside to run about, leaving the two mothers alone for a little while. Mamie knew it was still too wet and muddy for them to be outside but she also knew the children needed to get out of the house and into the fresh air, even if it was for only a few minutes.

Rose and Mamie watched from the windows of the sunroom as the children ran and skipped around puddles, rivers and mini-lakes the rain had created. Delight was registered on their faces as they ran and twirled about playing their simple games of catch me if you can.

The two women were pleased to see the water swiftly running off the lawn to pour into the gully down below. They knew the children would not venture outside the gate. Therefore, the swift flowing water beyond the gate would pose no problem for them as they turned their faces up towards the warming sun.

The gully was a natural drainage system which carried excess rain water all the way to the river, some few miles away. Farmers knew that eons ago, it was the water itself which had formed the gullies. Now they filled with water only when heavy rains came, and the water flowed to the river except when it flooded. When Zeke first saw the gully, he told Jesse how blessed he was to have that gully running across his land. He had also told him it was a good place to travel during a lightning storm.

"One day, you gonna see how it carry the waters," he prophesied. "I wish one run through my place. My land so flat. Its' rich, but its' flat. When that river overflows, its' gon' flood my farm."

Rose caught sight of Lena going outside. She nudged Mamie and pointed.

"Look at her. She thinks she better'n us 'cause she look like white folks. She forget who she is."

Now, Mamie was getting a clear picture of this tension between the two sisters-in-law. Her own daughter, must be thinking Lena and Frank Ford looked like a white couple, giving them extra advantage, while there was no mistaking that Rose and her Mr. Ford certainly did not.

Lena was on her way to the outhouse carrying the nightjar with her. Rose pretended she did not see her. She wanted to see what other moves Lena was going to make. She wondered what Lena must be thinking.

Mamie summoned the children to come back inside because they were getting too muddy. It didn't take them long to clean themselves of the mud. They used one of Jesse's inventions, a board with nails driven into it to clean mud from shoes and boots. It had been placed in the breezeway along with a tub of water.

"Mr. Ford always be creatin' something in the barn to help with makin' my housekeeping easy." Rose told Mamie. "I always looks forward to seein' what he gonna create next."

Rose went to the parlor in the main house and began to play the piano. One by one, the children came and gathered around the piano to listen to and enjoy the music. Some were keeping time to the music with their feet and some were clapping to the music. They were having a joyous time singing and laughing and dancing when suddenly the joy seemed to stop cold. Rose came to a halt in her playing when she looked around and saw Mamie standing there in the room holding Lena's hand.

"Is the baby crying?" Rose asked, jumping up.

"The baby still sleeping," replied Mamie.

"Why you in here?" asked Rose, looking at Lena.

"She in here 'cause I brung her," said Mamie. "Keep playing, Rose, we here to sing and enjoy your music."

Gonna lay down my sword and shield
Down by the riverside
Down by the riverside
Down by the riverside
Ain't gonna study war no mo

Mamie put her arms around Lena and the two began to sing in strong lusty voices. Lena had tears in her eyes and the children concluded she was just touched by the jubilant singing and the rousing piano playing.

It was after dark when the men returned to the house to make their weather and flood report. The river had been still rising in the morning, but it was thought that by day's end, it would reach its peak. The rain had stopped and moved off to the east, away from the river basin. Some of Frank's crops would be lost but a good deal could be salvaged. Besides, there was still time to plant again.

A few houses had been lost in the bottomland and some had been seen floating down the river. There didn't seem to be any homes lost in the hill country. Houses in the bottomland had sustained more damage. Most of them could be repaired, but a few were completely lost.

The good news for the Turners was that their house was still standing. Most of the crops were under water. There would be some heavy crop losses but, thankfully, there was also time for late planting that could make up for some of the loss.

If the late planting was unsuccessful in its yield, then the family could help in the harvesting of the new fields that Jesse had planted.

Ultimately, the flood had not destroyed the hopes and dreams of these men and their families who were so intricately bound together by blood and soil.

Mamie and Lena came out of the kitchen and announced that both dinner and supper were on the table.

"Come, and 'cide which one you wants. Well now, ya'll can have both, if ya likes."

"Is breakfast there, too?" teased Frank. "My stomach told me it had missed all three meals today."

"My stomach sed the same thing," echoed Samuel.

The sun, the earth and the river began to slowly reclaim the waters that had flooded the area. Each day the men went out to check the dampness of the fields. Jesse also captured their attention, demonstrating some of his creations in the barn. They were intrigued with his children's furniture and toys. Even his brother Frank had to concede that he was surprised at his brother's carving skills. He showed them a box of items he had made in memory of baby Jesse. Now he would use those things with little William. They especially liked the rocking horse with the real tail and padded seat.

Jesse also showed them a large metal hoop he had forged. It had several chains and was suspended from a large hook, but he would not tell them what it was.

"You will all find out soon enough. What it is, remains my secret."

Each day the sun began to fill the sky and its warm rays aided in the process of drying the soaked land. The Turner Family and Mr. and Mrs. Frank Ford made plans to return to their homes. Mamie asked Lena to help her prepare a feast of celebration and thanks for their home going.

When the food was finished, Mamie placed it in the warming oven of the big stove and proceeded to call everyone to the table. She knew she had a message to share but she didn't exactly know what it was going to be. She prayed for God to lay upon her heart just the right words.

"Dear loved ones," she began, as they gathered around the table.

"First of all, we gon' give God thanks and praise. He the one done brought us thru.' Next, we gon' love and praise each other. We done worked together to pull thru' this here crisis. And we done come thru' it all with some success. My church encourages families staying and praying together. We done all lived in peace these few days. We done worked together like a big happy family.

"They's always gonna be some problems in the family. But chil'ren, we got to hold on to one another. We each other's strength. We each other's backbone. We each other's freedom. We each other's power. We each other's prosperity.

"We gonna have our times of joy and happiness, but we gonna have times of misery, too. Remember, misery always out there waiting for us. So when we do get together, we gonna pray! We gonna sing! We gonna dance! But above all, we gonna praise God and we gonna keep on lovin' one another.

" We gotta understand that life for us follows that old rhythm of plantin,' weedin' and harvestin.' We gotta rise at the first light and we got to toil til the sunsets. We can't afford no attitudes. We can't afford no pullin' apart. Workin' and pullin' together help us to preserve important elements of our history. It helps us to move forward.

"We got to hand this down to our chil'ren. We got to give them the desire to know who they is and to know where they going. We got to work hard. We got to inspire one another. We got to do it! They ain't no other way! We got to do it!

"Um gonna pray that God takes any evil outta yo' hearts and that we all do these things I just talked about and that we's all blessed by God with good health and prosperity. Let's all say, Thank you, Jesus! Thank you, Jesus! Amen!"

Rose was so moved by Mamie's words that she went to the piano and played. Everyone moved from the table to the piano and sang.

This little light of mine, I'm gonna let it shine
Let it shine, let it shine, let it shine
Everywhere I go, I'm gonna let it shine
Let it shine, let it shine, let it shine
Jesus gave it to me, I 'm gonna let it shine
Let it shine, let it shine, let it shine

The singing and clapping kept up until all the food was on the table and everyone was seated. The table was filled with cowpeas, yams, rice, eggplants, red beans, corn pones and gumbo stew.

They were all surprised when Frank Ford asked if he could bless the food.

"God, Father of us all, keep us always together, loving and praising You and loving and praising one another. We thank You for this food which has been prepared for us by loving hands. We ask that You will bless it for the nourishment and strengthening of our bodies, for Christ's sake. Amen"

The summer of eighteen hundred eighty six was not too different than most of the summers of that decade. The Ford families and the Turner family were all depending on the promise of the soil as they had always done. But this year, they had entered a collaborative agreement to work as hard as they had ever worked before. Jesse Ford would keep the profits from his old farms, that is, after paying his sharecroppers. But the profits from the new crops would be divided between the three families. This would offset the losses of the two other families that had been caused by the flood.

There was still some tension between Rose and Lena but the two women remained cordial in the presence of their husbands. Rose and her family never visited Frank's home but Frank continued to drop by their place from time to time. The love and affection between the two brothers was obvious to Rose and she always tried to do little things that provided happiness and good times for the two of them. Whenever Frank visited, she would send home something fresh from her garden in addition to jams and jellies from her pantry. A few times, she sent breads and sweets.

Frank was quite diligent about sharing his wines with Jesse and Rose. He took particular pride in his production and in his varieties. He produced such flavors as blackberry, elderberry, wild plum, muscadine, and even dandelion. Sometimes, secretly, Rose would pass on a bottle to Ezekiel, who was always pleased to receive it despite Mamie's displeasure when she would find out about it.

Frank always said, "Special celebrations deserved to be toasted with a wonderful wine, and wine is good for the heart."

Every able-bodied person on both farms put in some time working the crops. Even Rose and Lena. Little William was only ten months old, but Rose insisted on going to the field when Molly came in for her dinner break. The new tenants had not seen how she could work and she wanted to make sure she set examples of efficiency in their production techniques. She also wanted to bolster their morale and attitude. Rose knew by doing this, production would rise. And this year especially, a good cash crop was needed. After this year, unless there was a catastrophe beyond their control, Mr. Ford had assured her their future was becoming pretty secure.

The month of August was exceedingly hot. The workers sweltered under the hot sun. The chiggers and fleas flourished in the heat, jumping and hopping everywhere and on everyone, stinging or biting them and causing intense itching. The workers had to cover themselves completely to ward off the bugs. Their over-abundance of clothing slowed down their work and made them miserably hot.

The bolls on the cotton stalks opened and the soft white fibers spilled out and hung down, waiting for skilled hands to pluck and stash them in long, heavy cotton sacks.

Chapter Nineteen

In September of the same year, after most of the cotton had been picked and sent to the gin to be processed, Jack, Thad and Tom, the sharecroppers, came to Jesse and asked for permission to have a fish-fry down on the pond. They told him they figured the fish population on the pond must have at least doubled or tripled. They concluded that the growth spurt of the fish and the expansion of the pond was the result of the combination of the spring flood followed by a very hot summer.

After Jesse gave his consent, the tenant families began making plans for a big celebration to be held at the end of September or the beginning of October, when the majority of the work would be almost completed.

Fish frys were planned for those who lived and worked on farms, and they could invite their friends and relatives to come together to celebrate, eat, socialize and catch up on any news or gossip that anyone knew. It was a time for those who had worked so hard to relax and let off some steam. Everyone would fish early in the morning. Some would set up facilities for cleaning and frying the fish. They would cook hush puppies in the same iron pots where the fish were fried. Fresh vegetables, potato salad and desserts would be prepared at home and brought to the pond. Games were planned for the men and children. The day would end with singing and praying.

Molly came to Rose and asked for her thoughts and suggestions for the fish fry. Rose's input was that they should not invite outsiders, just family members. She wanted Molly to clearly understand that she and Mr. Ford coveted their privacy. They didn't wish to promote any activity which would bring unwanted attention. She also reminded Molly of the times when the sheriff was looking for any reason at all to arrest her and throw her in jail. Rose told her about the state law which said it was illegal for a white person to live with a colored person, and especially, to marry one. She made it very clear to Molly that if she was ever arrested and put in jail, all of them would be out of work and out of a place to live. Rose asked her to pass that information on to the other tenants concerning the fish fry. She did not want the fish fry to draw a big crowd.

"Mr. Ford said he'd pack up his family an' move to some far-off place if anyone ever made a jail threat to us," were her parting words.

In the beginning, Jesse and Rose thought of participating in the fish fry. They wanted their tenant farmers, as they now called them, to have a feeling of closeness with them. But in the end, they both thought it best to follow their usual pattern of celebrating, only in the privacy of their own two houses.

They would continue to invite all the tenant farmers to their home each Christmas and distribute gifts and Christmas goodies as was their habit. It was a tradition which they looked forward to each year. But as their children grew bigger and older, they quite enjoyed their small celebrations with just Rose, Jesse and the children.

On the day of the fish fry, Rose made another surprising revelation to Jesse. She was going to have another child.

"Am I the first one to know the news this time, or am I again the last to know?"

"Why you talk like that, Mr. Ford? Of course, you the firs' to know besides me."

On the afternoon of the fish fry, Jesse put Rose and the three children in the buggy and took a ride to the top of the hill to the little graveyard that nestled there. There was a mystic stillness and a haunting silence on that spot. The sky was laced with bright sunlight. The wind blew forth a soft, gentle breeze. The hill country took on a celestial appearance from the top of the hill, which held only one small grave.

Jesse took a rake and cleaned off the tiny grave. He pulled some weeds and then made a few intricate patterns over his son's grave. The children broke the quiet with their happy, noisy, indescribable sounds as the girls ran around in circles and little William babbled and laughed. Tears silently fell from Rose's eyes and rolled down her cheeks. Jesse said a few words that no one clearly heard nor understood. Then he settled his family back in the buggy and headed for home.

The joyful noises of gleeful celebration at the fish fry could be heard for miles around. All four tenant families and their immediate family members, plus a few day workers, were present, including Mrs. Metoyer.

It was a dazzling day. The blue skies reigned and bestowed a clear, bright and warm autumn day. The sun-drenched cotton fields lay bare off in the distance. There was still sugar cane standing in the cane field and scattered stalks of corn in the cornfield. Eventually, all the fields would be stripped bare awaiting the onset of winter.

A fish fry had fast become a genuine southern tradition, especially among the Negroes. It was a safe bet that this group would find a way to have, at least, an annual fish fry. This was the first one at the Ford Farm, but for certain, it would not be the last.

Above the noise coming from the pond, the rollicking strumming of a banjo could be heard. Rose knew there would be a time for singing Spirituals and there would be a time for singing secular music as well. Some of the words would be known, but most of the words would be made up as the player strummed along. Finally, you would hear the familiar "call and respond' session. This would be more likely to happen as the day neared the end and everyone was full and tired.

Jesse had suspected that someone would bring along some corn liquor even though word had been sent out asking the men not to bring it. He wanted to make sure that no strangers were attracted to the gathering and that no one got out of control. He still did not trust the local sheriff. He was sure that if the slightest reason surfaced, the sheriff would take great pleasure in making another visit to the Ford Farm.

Although Rose was curious enough to want to check out the activities down on the pond, she would not ask Mr. Ford to take her there. She knew he was satisfied to spend the day with his family and she sincerely appreciated the deep love and devotion he had for his family. She knew there was nothing that made him more happy and content than simply passing time with her and the children.

As they returned from their visit to the cemetery, Kula ran out to meet them.

"I mus' find time to play mo' with Kula,"Rose muttered. "He such a good old dog but the babies keep me so busy. Yet, I promise I'll find the time."

After finishing supper and putting the children to bed for the night, Rose and Jesse sat in the swing, enjoying the cooling down of the evening along with the twinkling stars which lit up the sky like sparkling diamonds. It was a mellow, tranquil night. The joyous sounds of the celebration had long since ceased. The two lovers could hear the night animals still foraging for food. Kula lay snoozing near the swing.

"Rose, my love, in my wildest dreams, I would never have imagined I could love anyone as much as I love you, nor that I would be as happy as I am right now."

"I loves you too, Mr. Ford, you such a kind, gentle man. And you the best daddy in the whole world.'"

"Rose, you are my beloved, my perfect love. How fair and pleasant you are. Your kisses taste like sweet wine. I desire you. I will give you sweet love."

"There you go agin, with all yo' fancy words!"

"I have to confess. I borrowed those words from the book of Solomon. But every word of it comes from my own heart. I think he wrote them for me to say to you."

And right there, in the cool of the evening, in the swing, he filled her with his sweet love. She received it passionately and gave of her own precious love, again and again.

Early the next morning, as Rose gathered herbs and vegetables from her garden, Molly came over to talk with her and to tell her how well the fish fry had gone. She also had some chilling news for her.

"The sheriff and his deputy just happened to be passing by and they stopped to see what the celebration was all about."

"Well, I do declare," responded Rose. "Now how you reckon that happen'?"

"Rose, the fry was absolute' wonderful! It's the bes' fish-fry I ever been to. Nobody act up. Nobody drinkin' too much.

"Oh yeah, Rose, somebody did brang some corn likker. The sheriff never seen it, though. Afta' him and the deputy look around, they jus' all a' sudden like, took off. We jus' kept a' singin' an' praisin."

Rose brewed some tea and the two women sat in the sunroom sipping and talking for a long time. Molly wanted to know when the new baby was expected.

"It be here 'bout the firs' part of Jan'ary."

Is Miz Metoyer comin' fo' the birthin'?"

"I sho' hope she will."

"I be there too, if you wants me to."

A week after the fish fry, Jesse took Thad, Tom and Doc with him to the Turner Place to build the addition to Zeke and Mamie's house. It was a project that he had wanted to do for some time. They filled one wagon with building materials left over from his own building and from the tenant's house he built. Jesse and Doc went directly to the farm. Thad and Tom made a stop in town to purchase the rest of the items necessary to complete the job.

Jesse knew he was still scorned in town, so he avoided going there except when it was absolutely necessary. The talk of his keeping that Nigra woman in a house as fine as any around did not please the locals at all. A few of them, in fact, were always hatching plans to make them pay for their blatant flaunting of the law and their fornicatin.' They had heard that the two of them even had some babies! They knew that white men fathered many babies by colored women, but none of the men lived with those bastards.

It took three days for the men to complete their mission of adding two rooms to the house. They also shored up some of the foundation bricks which had been damaged in the flood. Mamie was overcome with joy and thanksgiving. She kept singing, praying and praising the Lord. Early in the day, she prepared her best dishes for the men to eat. She wanted them to know how happy and grateful she was.

Their sons were happy, too. It was the first time in their lives they had their very own room. And the girls had theirs. They promised Mr. Jesse that come next summer, they would work one day each week for him for as long as it took to pay off their debt. Jesse just smiled. He knew he owed his early farming success to the good advice and help he had gotten from Zeke. He figured he owed Zeke. Heck, he would even have given him a dowry for his beloved Rose. He had read about dowries but he knew this practice was not done in America, at least, not that he had heard of.

The room additions were completed. The men headed home to their own families.

` ` ` ` ` ` ` ` ` ` `

In late fall, Jesse Ford, accompanied by Frank, made his annual trip to Houston. By now, everyone who lived on or near the farm knew that Mr. Ford went to Houston in the fall to buy his seed, to look for new hardware and to purchase his Christmas presents as well as other miscellaneous supplies and equipment.

On this trip, he asked Thad's wife, Lucille, to stay at the house with Rose and the children. Their children were the oldest children on the farm and could be left alone. They could take care of themselves. He also knew that Thad would be there with Lucille, Rose and the children every night. Jack appeared to be a little jealous of that arrangement, but he knew he was still in charge of overseeing all the tenants. It was also Jack who took Mr. Ford to the train station and was always there to meet him when he returned from his trips.

Usually, Mr. Ford would bring back something special for Jack, something that he gave him in private, not at the Christmas gathering. This time, he gave him a twenty-two rifle. Jack could not believe it! This was too good to be true! Surely, his eyes were playing tricks on him. This was the best gift he'd ever received in his entire life! Now, he wouldn't have to just set traps for hunting. He could hunt with his rifle!

They placed all the packages in the wagon and began the journey home. Jack held his cheek to cheek grin so long, he figured it might never leave his face. He knew for sure it would last plumb into next year.

Early in December, Thad went to bring his mother to the farm because Jesse wanted her there in plenty of time in the event the baby decided on an early arrival. Cecilia Metoyer always came for Christmas anyway. This time, she would just be a few days early and that would provide Rose with a well-earned rest before delivery.

Jesse was spending long hours working in the barn. Rose worried about him because the weather had turned unusually cold and the barn was not a place to pass so much time. Several times during the day, she sent Mrs. Metoyer to the barn to request that he come in out of the cold or just to check on him.

"Tell Rose I'm almost finished, I'll be inside in a little while," he'd always respond.

"What on earth be keepin' him in that cold barn so long?" She questioned.

"Mr. Ford working wit those tools, Rose. He harrmerin' and nailin' and clangin. He got some kind of heat goin,' too. He even heatin' up the tools."

"Well, do tell. Wonder what he up to now?" mused Rose.

On the morning of Christmas Eve, it was dark, as if it was still night; the chilly winter winds blew hard and it started to rain. Rose hoped it was just a little squall because if it rained for any length of time, she knew Zeke, Mamie and the kids would not make the trip out to the farm. It was too hazardous for them to make that journey when the weather was so nasty.

But the sky opened up and it rained all day. Molly came to the house to help Mrs. Metoyer with the decoration and with some of the cooking. The other women would come early Christmas morning to set the tables and begin bringing some of the food they had prepared.

Cecilia's two sons dropped in with some squirrels they had trapped and some lovely holly trees they had cut down. They left the squirrels for their mother to prepare for the Christmas dinner, and a pine tree to be decorated.

Christmas day was just about the best day of the whole year. Jesse Ford always had the Christmas spirit. He was especially generous at that time to his family and to the tenants who worked his fields. He was pleased with the kind of relationship he had with them. He provided them with good living quarters and with food that was raised on the farm. They worked for him and he paid them decently for their hard work and their loyalty and dedication to him and his family.

Jesse gave gifts to all of the children who lived on the farm, even those who were just about grown. He gave toys to the small children, including some that he had made himself. Mr. Ford presented each of the wives, including Lena and Mrs. Metoyer, with a fancy mosquito net he had designed and made for their beds.

It was a round metal hoop with three small chains attached to a large hook which could be screwed overhead into a ceiling or in the wall. Yards and yards of fine gauze were attached to the hoop and it could swirl around in a circle and cover an entire bed. Everyone, including the children, were fascinated by Mr. Ford's invention. The women were extremely impressed and thrilled.

Now Rose knew why he had spent so much time in the barn. At that moment, she was so proud of her Mr. Ford, that she stood up and clapped her hands. Then everyone else stood and clapped and praised him for being such a wonderful and smart man.

As was his custom, Frank passed out fresh fruit and nuts to everyone. He also gave out some of his plum wine and bottles of homemade vinegar. These were prized possessions also, and as usual, fully anticipated and happily received.

There were faded blue overalls and a few tools for the men. Additionally, there were long stockings and sweet-smelling talcum for the ladies.

The last present of the evening was one reserved for Rose. It was a sewing machine! The women sent up a rousing round of applause and squeals of delight. Mrs. Metoyer and Lena were the only ones who knew how to operate a sewing machine. Cecilia had learned how to use one during slavery when she was assigned the job of making clothes for the house slaves. After the war, she managed to buy one of the sewing machines from a former plantation owner whose place had been pillaged.

Rose just sat there, too heavy with child to stand up again when the others did. On her face was a look of utter amazement as she looked at that marvelous machine that had been uncovered before her.

"My Mr. Ford thinks of ev'rythin. What he gon' do next?" She inquired demurely.

"It a' be my pleasure to teach ya'll how to use the sewin' machine," Cecilia Metoyer volunteered.

"I help, too, but um' not good as Mama." This was as much as Lena had said at one time all afternoon and evening.

` ` ` ` ` ` ` ` ` ` `

On January 11, 1887, Rose gave birth to James Joseph Ford. Now her family was all even at two girls and two boys. She finally was getting the boys she so dearly wanted. Only she had wanted the boys to come first. Gradually she had come to realize there was no real advantage to birth order. Just the sight of their little boys and girls made her heart skip faster. They are the products of our steadfast and jubilant love, she thought.

"Thank you, Rose, for another healthy child. I promise to continue to work hard and see to it their lives are comfortable and happy," said Jesse later that night as he slid into bed beside his precious Rose and their newest son.

"Mr. Ford," Rose said softly. "You know and I knows too, that I don't 'spress myself like you 'spress yo'self. But there is some things I needs to tell you.

"You been 'specially good and loving to me. You loves the children and you so kind and patient with them. I listen how you talk to me and to them and I try to learn to talk better. I try to be patient like you is. Sometime it work. Sometime it don't. Sometime I learn. Sometime I don't. Jus' the same, I keeps on tryin.'

"We gots these fine babies now. Two boys, two girls. Lord knows I wanted the boys to come firs,' jus' like my Ma and Pa. But the good Lord got His own plans. He don't take no orders from me.

"I wants you to know how happy I am. Our children are the prettiest and most handsome children ever anybody has laid eyes on. Justine is growing up so fast. She so beautiful! She looks like those dolls in them magazines what you brings home, even prettier. I been noticin' how people can't keep they eyes offa' her. She friendly, too. She smiles and talks to ev'ryone. She talks good too, just like her daddy.

"Mr. Ford! Are you 'sleep? Mr. Ford? You still listnin? Cause I wanna tell you how much I 'preciate how you even treats my Ma and Pa and they children. You so kind-hearted, givin' them so many things and helpin' them out in so many ways. I loves you, Mr. Ford.

"I loves you for the way you so thoughtful of the tenants. You always speak and act kindly towards them. And you do nice things for they children, too. I bet we have the biggest and best Christmas celebrations of anybody in the whole parish. All the tenants look forward to it ev'ry year. And so do I.

"Anyway, I think I done run out of words. But one thing I knows, God's done been good to us. He blessed us with each other and now, He done blessed us with four beautiful children. The land is harvestin' well. What mo' can we ask for?"

"Maybe four more children, just like these four."

"Now you just shush! We take what the good Lord see fit for us to have. Good night, Mr. Ford"

"Good night, Rose. I love you, too!" Jesse paused, squeezed Rose's hand, kissed her tenderly and said, "Rose, -- I don't speak perfect, I make mistakes, too."

Rose found herself completely occupied with the nurture and care of her four little children. However, she still found the time to grow her prized vegetables. She managed to rise each day before the sun peeked over the hills, to do her planting, hoeing and picking. Sometimes, when they were not working in the fields, the ladies on tenant's row would come over and help out in the garden because they were often the recipients of those marvelous vegetables.

When Rose went out to tend her garden in the late afternoon, the children were always somewhere under foot or in the wagon. Kula, more often than not, completed the scene. He was the ever-faithful little watchdog, keeping the children where Rose could always see them. And at the same time, amusing them with his antics.

Over the next few years, Jesse worked hard at fulfilling his dreams and visions. He had become a successful southern farmer. He had accumulated more than five hundred acres of land which was producing cotton, corn, peas, sugar cane, peanuts, alfalfa and a few other assorted crops.

There were seven families living on and working his land. They all knew they had a comfortable life working for Mr. Ford. They considered him to be a good man. A fair and honest man. They had cast their lot with him and Miz Rose and they were not disappointed. When they compared their living and working conditions with other tenant farmers in the area, they knew they were blessed there was a Mr. Ford and a Miz Rose.

During the next two years, everything on the Ford Farm moved along as anticipated. The farm was productive. The tenants gave the appearance of contentment. The weather was stable and cooperative. As Jesse took stock of what he owned, he was pleased and proud. Rose no longer went to the fields. She was busy in the house with their growing family. She soon presented Mr. Ford with their third son, Harry. He was followed by yet another son, Luther.

"The Lord is blessing us real good," said Jesse. "My treasure is here on earth."

` ` ` ` ` ` ` ` ` ` `

One balmy Sunday, towards the end of summer, Mamie Turner asked Ezekiel to drive her out to visit with Jesse and Rose. There was something quite important she wished to discuss with them.

It'a be my pleasure," Zeke answered, detecting a tone of eagerness in Mamie's request.

"I wonder what this 'oman is up to now?" he questioned under his breath.

The beautiful and serene countryside unfolded as the horses pulled the wagon up the sloping hills. To Mamie, it displayed itself as if someone was painting a picture of paradise. She loved this country; since the jubilee had come, she saw it as truly a magnificent and beautiful place. The wonder of it all teased at the senses. The fragrance of the honeysuckle that grew along the path provided just the right touch to complement the scenery. The journey was familiar, yet it was ever changing.

Even the horses seemed to know they were going to the Ford Farm. They required little guiding from Ezekiel who was enjoying the road he had traveled so many times.

The harvest was ripening in the field, and the brilliant summer sun, hot and glistening in the sky, was hastening it to its climax. There were a few more houses scattered along the roadside where none had been before. Although slow, there was a steady trickle of progress in the farm area.

As they continued on their ride, they encountered a few others traveling the road, and in genuine southern tradition, greeted each other. Some even stopped briefly in order to exchange pleasantries. The south was still mired in an economic depression but there was decency and goodness in its people. The hope of growth and prosperity remained the goal of every southerner, Negro or white.

And in a shorter time than usual, or so it seemed, they arrived at their destination.

Chapter Twenty

After the usual family greetings of kissing and hugging and the special time grandparents take to play and talk with their grandchildren, Mamie was anxious to come straight to the reason for her visit. She was more than a little nervous and wanted to get on with it.

"Rose, Justine needs to be attending school," she blurted.

Rose noticed something unusual in Mamie's pronouncement.

Ma sounds more like Mr. Ford, she thought.

Rose also heard the firmness in her voice. She knew immediately this was going to be something serious.

"Mr. Ford teaching her how to read."

"That's wonderful, but that's not all she needs. There's other things to be learned."

"They ain't no school close 'round here fo' no Negro children," Rose snapped. "Justine can read and she talks good, jus' like her daddy."

"Rose, that is not enough! The only way for our children to advance theyself is through education. Remember when I tell you what white folks say, 'if coloreds learn to read and write, then they be just as smart as we are.' That's the truth, Rose. We got to give our children an education so they can be just as smart."

"But Ma, they ain't no school nowheres 'round here."

"Rose, that's why I came here today to talk to you. Justine is almost eleven years old now and you have other children to keep you busy. Let Justine come and live with us during the school year."

A pain struck at Rose's heart and for a minute she was completely speechless. She just sat there staring off into space. The men were listening but they were not yet a part of the dialogue between the mother and daughter. Dialogue that concerned a first child and a first grandchild.

"Are you askin' me to let my baby come live with you?"

"Rose, Justine is not a baby. She's about the same age you was when you came to live with us.

"I made a big mistake when I didn't insist on you going to school. You was lucky. You came to us with a strong drive, probably 'cause of the hard life you was living. But Justine's life is sheltered. Does she know how to pick cotton? Does she know how to chop cotton, wash clothes or, heaven forbid, does she even know how to cook?

"Don't answer that! 'Cause I knows you still do ev'rythin. Which points up another fact. Your chil'ren needs schoolin' cause you thinks they too good to work. Justine is sho' nuff a pretty little girl, but without education, what's to become of her?

"Right now, she an innocent child. She don't know what life's all about. She don't even know what school is all about. It's up to her Mama and her Papa to see to it she gets an education. She needs to be able to define who she gonna be, not what some one else say she gonna be. Books will put visions in her head. She needs her own vision, not someone else's vision.

"Well, I just about done talked out. I said almost ev'rythin' I can think of for now. It's up to you, Rose, to make a decision to send that girl to school. I knows your Mr. Ford will go along with you. He knows how important it is to read and write. I done learnt me a lot in that school. I still got a long ways to go, but I can read and write now, and I speak a whole lot better than before. All our chil'ren, 'cept you, know how to read and write. Praise God! Halleluia!

"You think about what I said, Rose. And you think about what's good for Justine. When you and Mr. Ford makes up your minds, bring her on to the house before school begins this fall. It's only a few weeks from now and that gives you enough time to make up your mind to do the right thing."

All night long, Rose lay awake, turning and twisting, trying to put together a picture of the puzzle Mamie was talking about. Of course she knew schooling was important. Many times, she had wished she could read like Mr. Ford. More and more, he brought home papers, magazines and other things with writing all over them. Most of the time, she was too ashamed to ask him what those writings said. She had even stopped asking Mr. Ford to read the Bible to her, especially since he had taught Justine and Pinkie to read. She felt too ashamed to let them know she couldn't read.

Pinkie could read almost as well as Justine even though she was two and a half years younger. She was more attentive when their daddy sat at the table in the sunroom to read to them, and to teach them to read. Justine was always impatient and kept asking how long she had to sit or if it was time to go out and play. Like her mother, she loved the outdoors and was more content when she was horseback riding or playing games. Sometimes, Jesse took her fishing or hunting with him. She told him she loved it when just the two of them were out in the woods together. She enjoyed not having to share him with the others. Being together was their special time.

Rose clearly remembered when she was Justine's age, how she liked the wind in her hair and at her back. In her mind's eye, she saw herself running from one of her homes for the last time. She remembered the morning when the Turners found her asleep in the shed. She also saw herself sitting at the top of the big oak tree over in the meadow, talking to Papo. It had been her favorite place.

Finally, she recalled her days selling at the station and how much she had liked doing that. But Rose knew the long hours of hard work were the real reason why her selling venture became successful. She also knew Justine could never do anything even close to what she had done. She could never have survived the way Rose had. A mournful cry came from her mouth without her even being aware of it.

"What on earth is the matter?" asked Jesse, turning over.

"I'm sorry. I was just thinking," she murmured.

"Must be some sad thoughts," Jesse responded, pulling the cover over his head.

"How can she expect me give up my child?" asked Rose, sitting up in bed.

"Go back to sleep, dear, we'll talk about it tomorrow."

"I can't do it. I can't do it," she muttered, burrowing down under the sheets.

During the next few weeks, Rose went about her duties mechanically. She used most of her energy pushing any thoughts of Justine going to school out of her mind. It was as if the conversation with Mamie had never taken place. It was, in fact, as if Mamie had never made that trip to the farm at all to discuss school for Justine. Any such thoughts were discarded from Rose's head as soon as they surfaced. She simply refused to give birth to them.

Perhaps, Rose would have been successful in her refusal to give thought to Mamie's request if it weren't for the interesting journal Jesse Ford brought home one day. After supper, he took the journal out and silently began to read it. After a few minutes, he began reading aloud.

Jesse was reading, "Some New England lady school teachers were embarking on a mission to a few southern states for the purpose of providing schooling for the children of emancipated Negroes in areas that still were not providing any education for them. It is documented that a number of such genteel ladies have given up everything they had in order to become a part of this mission." He further read, "They were spinster ladies who were imbued with New England tradition and values and they were zealous in their attempt to increase the opportunities of Negro children to obtain education. Some of them had worked for years, with little success, to force the issue of public education in many southern states."

Rose was touched by what Mr. Ford had read. Momentarily, she considered opening her mind to the possibility of thinking about schooling for Justine. But just as quickly, she withheld any comment. She would wait and see if Mr. Ford would bring up the subject again. He did.

The next morning, at breakfast, he approached the subject cautiously.

"Rose," he said, "I think we need to discuss and plan some sort of future for our children, especially Justine"

"What you talkin' 'bout, Mr. Ford?"

"I suppose the only future around these parts is in the land. But it doesn't hold the same promise that it did when I chose to become a farmer. Maybe some of the children will want to farm but maybe some will want to consider other things."

"They ain't no other things!" Rose retorted.

"According to the newspapers and journals I read, many of the northern states are moving towards industrialization. The railroad system now goes from south to north and east to west; the whole country is changing. There are many factories in northern cities. All of these changes will call for workers and many opportunities will require special skills and education."

"Just what do that mean? What are you tryin' to say?"

"I'm saying that we need to think about what Mamie said. If our children don't get some kind of education, the world is going to move on and leave them behind. They can't even be good farmers without knowing how to read, write and compute."

"Can we have us a school in the hill country? Maybe one o' those teachers what you read about will come here," Rose said, hopefully.

"Maybe in time it can happen. But it won't happen soon enough and we can't waste that much time waiting. If and when a school comes to these parts, it'll be too late for both Justine and Pinkie. If we plan and work hard, maybe we can have a school by the time the other children grow up, but Justine can't wait for that. By then, she may feel the way you felt when Mamie wanted you to attend school."

"What you sayin,' Mr. Ford?"

"I'm saying we need to think about our children's future."

"You mean you wants us to send our baby to live away from our house?"

"For gosh sake, be reasonable, Rose. It's your own Ma and Pa and Justine is not a baby."

Rose felt chills go through her entire body and some of them stopped and clutched at her heart. She felt as if she had been stripped naked and left out in the cold wind. In desperation, she walked outside, surprised to find that it was, indeed, warm. Then she remembered, it wasn't even the end of summer, yet.

That evening, Justine curled up next to her mother as she sat in the swing watching the sun surrender to the night. The smell of hyacinth and honeysuckle lay heavy in the air. The crickets, frogs and katydids had already begun their night music. The lightning bugs were starting to send sparkles of light against a velvety night sky.

Justine gave her mother a kiss and hug and softly said, "Ma, I think Big Mama is right about me going to school but I don't have to live with her. I can rise early and ride Belle to school every day and get back home by dark."

"Have you been listenin' to grown folks talk? You knows I teach you better."

"Ma, Annie and Susie told me all about school and said it's wonderful and fun, too. Pa told me he went to school way out west in Kansas where he learned to read and write and he also learned about the history of the world. I want to learn to read and write just like Pa and Annie and Susie. They told me I can learn things I've never even imagined."

The second week in October, Rose took Justine to Mamie and Zeke's. She had been down this road many times before and the road had not changed, but today, she saw it through different eyes. It was not majestic and invigorating as she had always thought it to be. It was not singing with joy. It was empty and silent. This time the land did not reach out and embrace her. This time, the sun did not dapple through the trees interlacing the golden, red, brown and yellow leaves. Everything stood still. Instead of her looking at the landscape, the landscape was staring at her.

Her heart was drunk with sadness. There was a force much bigger than she was and it was stealing her beautiful, first-born child from her. Justine, so fair and enchanting, so lovely and full of life. Justine, so exquisitely pretty and filled with laughter. She wanted to hold on to her but she knew for the child's sake, she must let her go.

Jesse had made the decision to remain at home with the other children. He wanted mother and daughter to pass those parting moments together, alone. He also wanted to stay and give reassurance to the others, especially Pinkie, who would be without her best friend.

Parting with a child who was going away from home was not unique. It was something that occurred all over the south. Even all over the world. Sometimes, it was ephemeral, but occasionally, it was long-term. Jesse would see Justine more frequently than the rest of them because it was easier for him to get away, especially during the winter months when the fields lay dormant. But with so many children, and coupled with the short days and frequent inclement weather, seeing her would be less often for Rose. Yet she had the comfort of knowing they would see Justine at Christmas time, no matter what. In the meantime, Mr. Ford, from time to time, would take her little care packages from home.

Before Rose departed for home, Mamie had suggested that she talk often with everyone she could, in her area, about getting a school started in the hill country. She reminded her that the idea of school must always be kept in the minds of the people or complacency would set in and education would be pushed aside for years to come. The need for a school in the hill country was important because most of those children would never be able to leave home and attend school the way Justine could. Too many of them would remain illiterate and always at the mercy of white people.

"Getting a school open in the south won't be easy," she cautioned her.

"Thank you, Rose!"

"Thanks for what, Ma?

"For bein' smart 'nough to know what was good an' right for Justine and for havin' the stren'th to do it."

"See you soon, Ma," Rose said, tears welling up in her eyes.

"Go now, Mama, while I still feel happy," prompted Justine.

Rose gave Justine one last hug and squeeze, got in the buggy and disappeared beyond the gate.

Rose did not remember her return trip back home. Her only thoughts were of her beloved daughter, who was not beside her. Nor would she be there to greet her upon her arrival. That cool, bleak, October day would be one Rose would long remember.

` ` ` ` ` ` ` ` ` ` `

The next few years passed uneventfully in the Ford household. Rose, Jesse and the children saw their beautiful Justine during Christmas and spring vacations. And of course, she was home during the long summer months, which somehow seemed short to them. After Justine had spent two years at the elementary school, Pinkie went to live in the Turner household to attend school with her sister. This time there were no gut-wrenching decisions. This time, there was no chaos and pain. It seemed to be taken for granted this was the natural progression.

All of Mamie's children had finished the little country school which now had two rooms and two teachers, neither of whom were from New England. Samuel, the eldest son, was married and had his own small farm next to his parents' farm. Ephriam was still living at home, helping his parents with the crops which had increased in acreage and production. Aaron and the two girls, Annie and Susie, were twenty miles away, attending a boarding high school.

The cost of their schooling was more than the family could really afford but Mamie convinced them the sacrifice was worth it. Zeke, Mamie and Ephriam toiled hard six days every week during planting, growing and harvesting seasons, in order to pay for the schooling and to make ends meet. And when the children came home during the summers, they too, joined in working the fields. Even Samuel and his wife contributed to the cost of their schooling.

"It takes nearly every penny we make to keep them in school, but it's worth it," Mamie would say. "Education an' books put learnin' and dreams in your head. They gonna be somebody one day!"

When Justine was fifteen, she finished her schooling at the elementary school which went through the seventh grade. For most of the students, this would be the sum total of their education. Even at that level, less than half of the area's children were able to go to school at all and half of those never finished. They were needed to help with the farming in order to secure just the bare necessities and to keep food on the table. And there were always many mouths to feed.

Most families were having severe problems making ends meet. Many of the landowners saw to it that their sharecroppers never made enough money to have anything extra. At the end of harvesting season, when they were paid, many were always in debt to their unscrupulous landowners who cheated them out of whatever they could, and that was plenty. Any of the tenants who knew they were being cheated and wanted to move on, often had to steal away in the middle of the night, lest they be jailed and threatened within an inch of their lives. Consequently, school for their children was definitely out of the question.

Meanwhile, out in the hill country, Rose kept up her dialogue on the importance of building a school for the children. A few vague promises had been given but no solid commitments were ever made. There were some Negro politicians but they were uneducated themselves. And more often than not, they were controlled by whites who had no interest in Negroes obtaining schools. The Freedman's Bureau, which had earlier established a few schools, did not reach that corner of the state before their funds began to run low. The push to obtain legislated free schools gained no momentum during the last two decades of the century.

With so many children to care for and the hindrance of never learning to read or write, Rose became disillusioned about the prospect of getting a school any time soon for their area. She also was slowed down considerably by her pregnancy. She gained so much weight that getting from place to place had become a chore. Rose was now thankful to have her Ma and Pa. At least her children could go there and obtain an elementary education.

Three weeks after Justine's graduation, Rose gave birth to twin girls! Mrs. Metoyer did not deliver these babies. Rose had gone into labor much sooner than anyone had expected. There was no time to send for the midwife. Mercifully, it was not a long labor. Molly, assisted by Thad's wife, Lucille, attended to the birth of the twins. Mr. Ford was calm and assisted the two ladies with whatever they needed. He only became nervous after the two babies were cleaned and ready for viewing.

One twin was named Mildred after Jesse's mother.

"I will name the other one Mattie," said a tired and exhausted Rose.

"They must be identical," Jesse said, "Because they are exact carbon copies of each other. They even have the same wrinkle and the same birthmarks," he added.

"I sent Thad to pick up his mother. You'll be able to rest and recuperate better when Mrs. Metoyer arrives."

"Twins! Imagine that! The Lord's done outdid Hisself now!" said Rose.

` ` ` ` ` ` ` ` ` ` `

Now that Justine had graduated from the elementary school, Rose and Jesse would be faced with yet another decision. Should she be allowed to go to the boarding school, or was finishing the seventh grade all the education she needed?

Over the last few years, Justine had become a fully developed and ravishingly beautiful young lady. She had seductive, amber colored eyes under long, fluttery eyelashes. Her brown, wavy hair flowed half way down her back and she delighted in letting it hang loosely, much to Rose's displeasure. She was the color of caramel that had too much vanilla. Her bosom was full and her hips were rounded. Justine was medium height with shapely legs that stayed hidden under her long skirts. She was like a magnet, always attracting a crowd, even the girls. She had a sparkling personality, an infectious laugh and a good sense of humor. Somehow, she seemed to spread joy and laughter wherever she went.

By contrast, her sister Pinkie was quiet, retiring and shy. She was a reddish pink color with freckles, she was tall and quite skinny. She wore her hair braided and coiled around her head, or sometimes just one long braid falling down her back. Pinkie carried books with her wherever she went and often she could be found around the school grounds in a quiet place, sitting and reading. She adored her big sister and accepted the fact that Justine was the center of attention.

Pinkie knew she would miss Justine terribly come next year when she would no longer be at the elementary school. As yet, there had been no talk of her going on to the high school like Annie, Susie and Aaron had done. Pinkie secretly hoped Justine would be permitted to go to the High School because she definitely wanted to continue her education. She knew her chances of going would be better if Justine was there. Even if Justine did not go, however, Pinkie would do whatever she had to do in order to attend the high school. She loved school so much and knew she would be a lost soul if she weren't allowed to continue her education.

It was Jesse Ford who made the decision that Justine would indeed, matriculate at the board and care high school which was twenty miles by train from the local town. Justine was pleased but Pinkie was euphoric. If she worked hard the next school year, she could be accelerated and join her sister the following year instead of waiting the two years it was supposed to take. She had no doubt that she could do it because she always made perfect grades.

At summer's end and with everyone's cooperation and hard work, the crops had all been harvested on time. Jesse Ford made an unexpected announcement. There would be a big "going away to school" celebration at the Ford Farm. He wanted everyone to celebrate the educational successes and achievements of the three Turner children and of Justine and Pinkie Ford. He wanted to impress upon all the young people who would gather there, the value and importance of education.

Aaron had finished his first year of college and Annie and Susie had both graduated from the high school. Annie would attend the normal college in the fall but Susie would have to remain at home for a year or two before attending. There just wasn't enough money to have three children in college at the same time.

The south was still being squeezed economically. The price of farm products was down and taxes were continuing to go up. There was no free ride for anyone, Negro or white. The weather, too, was always a big factor in the rise and fall of what monies were brought in. If it was a 'good weather' year, they stood some chance of making a little money. If the weather was bad, the farmers might not break even.

The party at Ford Farm was the first one they had ever had. The Christmas celebrations did not count because they were planned for the tenants as much as they were planned for the family. It was a private time of celebration and worship. It also served as a vehicle for saying "thanks" to the tenants for their loyalty and their long, hard hours of work.

All of the Turners were present at the party as were some of their friends who had attended the little country school. Reverend Pennywell and his family came as did Mr. Bowen and the new teacher, Mr. Carter, who had been sent from Philadelphia.

Mr. Carter made friends quickly and easily because when he came, he brought along with him boxes of Bibles to give out to people who learned to read. A Bible Society in Philadelphia had donated them. Mamie was the proud owner of one of those Bibles. She was so happy she had learned to read and write. Her speaking skills also showed great improvement, and often she served as spokesperson for the farm community.

The party was a huge success! Everyone who came brought heaping dishes of food. Rose made her often sought-after molasses candy, teacakes and peach cobbler. Instead of fried chicken, Mamie brought fried meat pies. There were peas, greens, tomatoes, okra, corn, potato salad, ham and just about anything else that grows on a farm.

Mr. Carter, the new teacher, played tunes on his guitar that were unfamiliar to this country crowd of southern folks. But he easily joined in when they began to sing their familiar Spirituals. The festivities lasted until after sunset. Jesse, Jack and Ezekiel had set out coal oil lamps for those who would be staying over and wished to continue their partying.

A few people, like Reverend Pennywell and his family, left before dark. It was still the policy of the Negroes not to travel after dark unless it was absolutely necessary. There were too many incidents of Negroes being beaten or even killed when they were out at night. There were also some unsolved disappearances.

There was adequate room in the two houses, the screened-in porches, the breezeway and even the barn to spread pallets for exhausted and sleepy guests to sleep on.

"My! My! My! What a time! What a time!" said Mamie the next morning as she watched the guests departing without breakfast because most of them would be attending church later that day, since it was Sunday.

The kitchen was flooded with the morning sun as Annie, Susie, Justine and Pinkie giggled and talked about the party while making hot tea and putting leftovers on the table for anyone who wanted a bite to eat. Jesse, Ezekiel and the young men were out on the lawn making sure that it had been left in good shape.

The young ladies agreed that it was the finest party they had ever seen and hoped that some day they could give that kind of party.

"At least, I would like to be invited to one like it," commented Annie.

"You can say that again!" chorused the others.

When Justine went to the boarding high school, it was Rose who went with her on the train. She did not want to go. She wanted Mr. Ford to take her because he knew all about riding on trains. Even though Rose had sold her goods at the train station, she had never taken a train ride in her life. Jesse insisted it would be better if Rose went with Justine to help her get settled at the school. There would be distractions and questions if he took Justine. He wanted her to have a smooth beginning.

He also knew he would visit Justine at the school at some appointed time. He was aware there were a number of children who had white fathers and that a few of those fathers paid for their children's education. Even in rare instances, they made visits and donations to the schools. He most certainly would visit his daughter. It was important that she knew he loved her and was proud of her. And he wanted it known that he was her father.

When Jack took Rose and Justine to the train station, Rose was more than surprised to see Mamie standing on the platform. Rose surmised that she must be seeing Annie and Aaron off to college. Mamie told her they had left a few days before.

"I 'preciate your comin' to see us off. It's mighty kind of you."

"Oh, didn't Mr. Ford tell you? I'm going over to Benton with you. He 'spect you be more comfortable if I go with you."

"God bless my Mr. Ford! He thinks of ev'rythin. Ma, there is some good news. Word is goin' 'round they gonna open a school in the hill country. It 'spose to be ready when the new century come in."

"Thas' almost three years! Can't they do it sooner?

"The gover'ment works slow. Well, at least, my young'uns be able to stay home and go to school"

The train took off from the station, steam hissing and whistle blowing. Rose was scared, perplexed. Justine excited, apprehensive. Mamie, happy and proud!

The trip on the train lasted less than an hour but the reverberations from that journey in search of education would profoundly affect the lives of the three women who nervously, yet happily, sat looking out the window, watching the landscape disappear before their eyes.

Chapter Twenty-One

During the following year, Rose and Jesse managed their assets as best they could. Prices on all farm products, especially cotton, had continued in a downward spiral. Rose knew how to handle money and how to save money. Jesse knew how to run the farm. He knew how to plan on paper. Rose knew how to plan in her head. Between them, they kept the farm on an even keel. They were also able to keep all of their tenants on the farm. This was a big advantage for their operation.

Because of the low economic downturn in the area, the local women gathered, at Rose's invitation, and made clothing that the families would need during the coming year. They made warm coats, caps and jackets for the winter season. They made dresses and pants by hand and on Rose's sewing machine. The plan was to work together to make sure everyone's basic needs were met.

Some of the women canned foods that would feed them through the winter months. Others pieced intricate patterns of cloth that were made into beautiful quilts for their beds. The women salted down a variety of meats the men brought home and then hung them in their smokehouses.

Rose showed the women how to make moccasins. Mr. Ford, of course, still bought shoes for his family on his yearly trip to Houston. But even in the Ford household, they had to tighten their belt.

Rose used this time of working with the women to talk about the need for a school in the hill country. By now, she would talk to anybody who would lend an ear.

"You can sen' your chil'ren to school if they start us one out here."

"We needs the chil'ren workin' in the fields," stated Molly.

"They can go to school after the crops is harvested," responded Rose. "You needs to know how important it is for your chil'ren to learn to read n' write, less'en you wants them to be tenant farmers or sharecroppers all they life."

"What you tryin' tell us, Rose?"

"That we gonna have to work together to get us a school so our chil'ren won't have to leave home to get schoolin.'

"You kin count me in."

"I'm wit'cha."

"Wha' ever you say, I'ma do!"

Justine ended her first year at the boarding high school and came home about the same time as Aaron and Annie. Aaron graduated from the Normal College, receiving his diploma and a teaching certificate. Mamie and Ezekiel concluded there just wasn't enough money to travel to his graduation. They picked up the three young people at the train station when they arrived and took them home where they served a special dinner to celebrate Aaron's blessing and good fortune.

The next day, before taking Justine home, Mamie wanted to have a talk with her and Annie about any future plans they had. Aaron had already made it known that he wished to teach school. Unless the parish would hire him, and he had his doubts, he needed to find a sponsor. If these plans didn't materialize, he planned to use his knowledge of agriculture and hire himself out to aid farmers in improving their skills. At school he had learned that too much of the land had been left to deteriorate under poor cultivation habits. If he could find work helping to restore the land, then he could open up a private school.

Aaron knew he could never open a private school without some additional income because the farmers were simply too destitute to pay more than a pittance to send their children to school. Without some kind of assistance, there would be no funds for books and supplies. There was still a good deal of opposition to Negro schools by many white southerners; consequently, the Negroes had to depend upon self-help and philanthropy. Aaron had only a few short months to launch his hopes and dreams.

Annie wished to return to the Normal College in the fall. She wanted to earn a teaching certificate also. Perhaps, one day she could join her brother in the teaching profession. She saw little or no opportunity to do anything else.

In the meantime, Justine was proud to announce she had completed two years of study in her first year at the high school. She was looking at returning and completing her schooling there. Beyond that, she had not given much thought.

The following year began on a high note. The cotton prices had stopped their downward spiral and were holding. Rose persuaded Jesse and Frank to make plans to build a one-room schoolhouse on land next to the Baptist Church. Then she enlisted Jack to round up all the Negro men he could, to come and volunteer their time and help in building the school. The men came every Saturday and they each put in whatever time they could spare, clearing the land and then constructing the building. By the end of the first week in September, the one room school, complete with a cloakroom and an outhouse, was finished. The parish government never gave a helping hand, not to mention monies. Aaron Turner would be the new teacher when school began in October.

` ` ` ` ` ` ` ` ` ` `

It was the last year of the nineteenth century. Cotton production in the south had risen tremendously. The prices were still low but the increase in production made the financial picture a little brighter for the cotton growers. The Negro-white relationships were probably worse than at any time since the Civil War. Both groups enjoyed a small economic gain, but the social and political climate remained horrendous.

Both groups looked forward to the promise of the new century in ushering in better economic times. Politically, the whites wanted more domination over the Negroes. The Negroes were disfranchised. The whites wanted, and indeed they had, white supremacy. The Negroes just wanted a fair share, which they did not receive. Violence, for the white Southerners, was the other means to keeping the Negro down. Intimidation, brutality, robbery and murder were not uncommon. Even the right to vote had been taken away.

` ` ` ` ` ` ` ` ` ` `

At the end of the school year, Mamie went to the train station to pick up the three girls, Annie, Susie and Justine. There was excitement over Annie having received her teaching certificate and Susie having completed her first year at the Normal School. It was odd that the usual jovial and talkative Justine was strangely quiet.

"Justine, why you so quiet, sugar, is somethin' the matter?" asked Mamie.

"Nome."

Both Annie and Susie continued to be excited and animated as they shared experiences of the past school year. Just before they arrived at the gate, Mamie noticed that Justine was crying. She brought the wagon to a stop.

"Justine, there is somethin' wrong. We won't move without you tellin' us what's wrong."

Justine began to cry uncontrollably. Her sobs shook her whole body and she was quickly in the midst of undeniable wretchedness. She trembled. She shook. She made indistinguishable sounds. Neither Mamie nor her daughters had ever witnessed such strange behavior before.

As Mamie gathered Justine in her arms, she felt the fullness of her belly and immediately knew what the problem was. Before freedom came, she had witnessed similar circumstances of girls much younger than Justine's seventeen years who were pregnant, not by their own free actions.

Mamie wanted to cry out but she controlled herself. She only murmured and despaired in her heart.

"Dear Lord, help this child. Help us all!"

They rode home in silence.

Early the next morning, Mamie left the house. Although she knew how to go, she had never gone to Rose's without Zeke taking her. Now, she had to, wanted to, make this trip alone. She arrived at mid-morning. When Rose saw her at the gate alone, she instantly thought something was terribly wrong. She ran to the gate as fast as she had run when she was escaping from a cruel family. She reached the gate in a total state of discomfiture, her heart beating so loud and fast she thought it would jump out of her chest.

"Ma! Ma! What happened to Pa?" she shouted.

"Now calm down Rose, let me in the gate, then give me time to get in the house."

They left the horse hitched to the wagon, went inside and sat down to talk.

"On second thought, Rose, let's take a walk on the trail that leads to the meadow."

For a few minutes, the two women, mother and daughter, walked in silence along a path where Rose had frocks and buttercups planted. They could smell the sweet fragrance of the morning glory that wrapped itself around the fence.

"Please, Ma, what's the matter? Tell me 'fore I plain bust open."

"Something done happen' to Justine."

"My sweet Jesus! Is she dead, Ma?"

"Nothing like that. But I expect she wishes she was. Justine gonna have a baby, Rose."

A guttural noise came from Rose that sounded like nothing Mamie had ever heard before. She had heard many women moaning and groaning in labor and in giving birth, but the sound Rose made was more haunting and mournful than even grieving over the dead. Rose grabbed the neck of her dress and tore it open, then stretched her hands to the heavens and dropped to her knees. Her joy, her life, both disintegrated. Gone!

"It's all my fault. It's my fault! My fault! I sent my baby away from her home and family. She was out'in the big world without her Mama and Papa who could'a loved and protected her. We let her down! It's my fault. My fault," she cried. Ow-o-oo. Ow-o-oo! Ma! It hurts like nothing I ever felt before. Ma! Ma! Ma!"

"Rose, child, I know you hurtin,' but we got work to do. This ain't the first time this happen' and it won't be the last time. Justine hurtin,' too. Do you think for one minute it's going to be easy for her to face her Mama and Papa? She's gonna need your love more than ever before."

"What we gon' do? Lord, Lord! What we gon' do? Never mind, Ma. You don't have to answer. I know what we gon' do. Um going to the field to get Mr. Ford. We gon' brang our little girl home!"

Jesse Ford looked down at Rose's tear stained face as she spoke to him. Then he looked deep into her glassy, amber eyes and coolly asked her to repeat what she had just told him.

Within half an hour, they were on their way to the Turner Place. Jesse prepared the buggy for Rose while she was giving instructions to William on how to care for the rest of the children until they returned. She only told him they would be returning before dark. As was the custom, William asked no questions.

Rose was somewhat pleased Jesse decided to ride his horse. She knew they needed to talk things over. On the other hand, riding in silence gavé her the opportunity to think about this whole predicament.

"Who was the boy?"

"Did he intend to marry her?"

"Could he take care of her?"

"Had she been raped?"

"Where were the teachers who were supposed to watch over the students?"

"How did something like this happen at school?"

"Am I dreaming or is this real?"

"How could her precious Justine do such a thing?"

"Had she talked enough to Justine about the man-woman thing?'

"Where had they gone wrong in their teaching?"

"Did Justine become loose and wild at school?"

"What was Mr. Ford thinking?"

"Would he threaten, or worse, do the boy some bodily harm?"

All these and even more questions just wouldn't let go of her mind.

Rose decided she had cried her tears. Even her heart had cried its own blood red tears. There would be no more time to show signs of weakness. She had to summon forth all of the strength and courage she could in order to lead them all through the unreality of their child having a child. One of the first things she needed to admit to herself was that Justine was no longer a child. She would be eighteen years old on her next birthday.

She rode along the country road, sorted out her myriad thoughts, searched her soul, and wondered again what Mr. Ford was thinking and if he were silently asking himself some of the same questions. At times, he went ahead of her, at other times, he intentionally fell behind. She instinctively knew he was always surveying the road. Rose felt completely safe when Mr. Ford was anywhere around.

They arrived at the farm shortly after Mamie's arrival. She had had just enough time to let the children know that Rose and Mr. Ford would be arriving directly. She suggested to her own children to give them some space.

Jesse solemnly watched as Rose extended to their daughter small gestures of serene and silent tenderness. Memories of her birth and growing up suddenly danced before his eyes and in that moment his love for her transcended any hate he had for the person who had spoiled her. He gazed upon the awkward innocence of Justine's face. His love and his compassion for her flooded his whole being.

Jesse Ford gave his daughter a hug and a kiss which quelled some of the tension built up inside her. He could feel her nervousness and her sense of despair and sorrow. Her despair became his despair. Her sorrow, his sorrow. Her burden became his burden.

He turned and said, "Rose, let's take our daughter home."

As the days passed, Justine slowly and cautiously gave them bits of information about the young man who was the other half of this puzzle. Jesse decided the time had come for him to look up this fellow. He was oveflowing with curiosity about his position on his responsibility to Justine and to the unborn child.

According to the details provided by Justine, the young man's family lived between fifteen and twenty miles away. Jesse told Rose it might take him a day or two to complete his mission. She did not agree with his decision to go looking for him, but he convinced her it was an undertaking that a father had to do.

When Jesse arrived at Joe McCoy's house, a young woman answered his call at the gate. She went to the back yard and informed Joe that a white man was looking for him.

"What kind o' trouble you in this time?" she asked.

"None. I ain't done nothin'."

"Do you know my daughter, Justine Ford?" Jesse asked when he came around to the front.

"Yessah, I do."

"Do you know that she's going to have a baby?"

"Nosah, I don't."

"She said you're the father."

"Well, sah, I 'spect she means my brother. People gets us mixed up all'a time."

"I'd like to speak to your brother."

"Yessah. I take you to'is house."

The house was less than a quarter mile away. When the two men arrived, Joe told Jesse to wait out front while he went around back to find his brother. Jesse could hear the brothers shouting and yelling at each other. After a long time, they appeared at the front door. They do look alike, thought Jesse, when he saw them standing together.

Joe walked away while the two men talked. But he was never out of hearing range. After a prolonged conversation between the two men, Moses agreed that he would accept responsibility for what had happened to Justine. Yes, he would marry her if that is what her family wished. He promised to come to the Ford Farm as soon as the cotton chopping was finished. Jesse, who remained calm, gave him directions and said they would be expecting him.

"Joe, wha'have you did to me this time?" Moe bellowed at his brother as soon as Jesse disappeared around the curve.

"Moe, did'ya see'at white man's shot gun? I thought he was gonna kill me."

"Maybe he should'a. I'm tired o' takin' blame fo' yo' rotten ass."

"Well, Moe, I'ma give you Justine. You lucky. She sweet an' she bee-yu-te-ful!"

"You can't give no person. You done doneit this time! You done gone an' reach rock bottom. I can't marry that girl. I don't even know that girl!"

"You want that white man kill yo' brother? You gotsto save my butt! You can marry with her, but nothin' says you gotta stay married."

"But tha's yo' child. How we gon' handle that?"

"Jus' gimme some time. I thinks o' somethin'."

"Joe, you sho' nuff done messed up big this time."

"I know, Moe. I swear, one day I gonna make it all upto'ya."

"You better pray real good tonight, brother."

As soon as he finished the cotton chopping, Moe knew it was time to make his call on the Ford Family. He knew Justine would not fall for Joe's scheme. He had to tell her the truth. Surely, then she would call off his promise of marriage.

When he walked with Justine down the lane towards the edge of the woods, he apologized for the behavior of his no good brother.

"Justine," Moe said, "Joe already gots a wife an' three kids, he can't marry you. I'm sorry you had to find out like this. If you willin', we kin marry an' no one'll know any difference. You a beautiful girl, Justine. Any fella be glad to have you fo' his wife."

"I don't know," she stammered. "You do look just like Joe. You fooled me."

"I knows I ain't the same as Joe. He got a way wit' the ladies. But he pure rotten. When I come up here, I had no 'tention to marry wit' you, but now I meet yo' family an' see you, I think it jus' might work. I knows it'll make yo' family happy, so let's do it, okay?"

"I guess we might as well," responded Justine.

They were married the third of October. Because of her condition, Rose remained with her family. The baby girl arrived two weeks before Thanksgiving. Rose insisted on Justine staying home with them until she was strong enough to go to Moses' home and take care of herself and the new baby girl. He agreed to this arrangement saying that he also needed some more time to prepare his little house for a family.

"I'm the only one who ever live' there. It ain't yet fit fo' no wife an' baby."

Moses came to his in-laws' house for Thanksgiving and he returned for their annual Christmas celebration. He said his house was almost ready. He wanted to take his wife home after the Christmas visit, but Mamie insisted that Justine needed more time to gain enough strength to travel so far in the cold weather and then have to care for a baby and a husband so soon after the ordeal of childbirth.

"Give us a little more time," she pleaded.

On a clear, cool and crisp Sunday in mid-January, Rose packed her daughter and her granddaughter, Cora, into the buggy and headed off for what would be their new home. The weather was still cold but Rose knew she could not hold on to Justine any longer. Jesse Ford would be accompanying them. But, of course, he would be riding Major.

Rose had spent hours planning and preparing how to make the long ride as comfortable as possible. She also packed a number of items she figured Justine would be needing to set up proper housekeeping. She gave her some of the quilts Mamie had given to her. Rose took out the baby clothing she had saved for- she didn't exactly remember what. She put in as many of her canned food items as they were able to pack. Finally, she had Mr. Ford attach some linen and a few cooking utensils to the buggy.

As they were about to leave, Jesse added one more item for Justine. It was a filly which he had been training and preparing for the twins, Mildred and Mattie.

"I guess they really need two of them, anyway," he reasoned.

At that moment, Justine tried hard to hold back the tears that were filling her eyes and her heart. Her parents had been more loving and understanding than she had ever imagined they would be.

"Mama, Papa, I love you both. I can't even begin to tell you just how much. I know you love me and my baby. I also know how deeply I disappointed you. But I'll make up for it, I promise. I can't hold a candle to you, Mama, but I'm going to try to be as good a mother as you are."

Rose had decided that being a mother and a wife must have been Justine's destiny. Maybe it was even God's will. And even though her heart was weeping silently, her stomach churning, she was not going to cry. Her emotions would remain locked up inside of her. She had known that one-day her precious, beautiful daughter would grow up and leave home, but she had imagined different circumstances.

The chilling winds and sleets of winter laid bare the fields. The cold frost took hold of the stubby growths extruding from the ground. As the sun rose higher in the sky, the frost would loosen its hold until the penetrating cold of another night made its call.

They rode past marshy thickets and forests so dense that it was doubtful if the sun ever worked its way in to give even a little light for the smallest trees. Moss clung to some of the trees like giant hanging spider webs. It hung limp under its own wet weight. The floor of the forest was thickly carpeted with soft, lush pine needles. Many of the trees had no leaves; still the denseness remained.

When they reached the destination of the elementary school Justine had attended, Jesse signaled to them they should take a break. It was a brief one. A little more than half their journey still lay ahead of them. Jesse wanted to return home before dark. Or at least, be able to reach Mamie and Zeke's by nightfall.

They would never meet their time line. When Rose got her first glimpse of the house, she was upset. It was badly in need of repairs. And when she saw how dirty and unkempt the inside was, she immediately started cleaning. She wasted no time in telling Moe she would never leave her daughter and grandchild in such a filthy place. She gave him a number of assignments which he took care of with haste.

They emptied the buggy of all its contents. When Jesse told Moe the filly was for Justine and the baby, Moe was thrilled. They would have their own horse because the horse he had ridden on to visit them, was one he shared with his brothers.

When Jesse noticed the cracks and holes in the house, he asked for a saw, hammer and nails to patch whatever he could. He hadn't paid much attention to the house when he had called on Moe. After all, he had another matter on his mind. It was also summer time when such things wouldn't be noticed as much. Now, he remembered that Joe's house was in much better shape than this one, so he went there looking for materials and lumber he could use. He knew he didn't like the man; he had seemed so sneaky. But that didn't matter to him now, so long as he had something he could use.

Jesse sent Moe out to begin cutting a larger supply of firewood. He didn't trust the stack he saw in the yard to provide adequate warmth for any length of time.

"Make sure the wood is dry when you use it," he commanded.

Dark was setting in rapidly and they still had not finished all the repairs that needed to be done. Both Rose and Jesse knew they would have to stay the night. They both disliked the idea but figured they could finish their work in the morning and then head for home in daylight.

The chilling winds put a nip in the night air. It would be a long, drafty night but Jesse would have some time to talk with Moe. He planned to tell him that if adequate provisions weren't made for the family, he would take Justine and Cora back home.

"My children deserve and must have a safe, clean and warm place."

Rose and Jesse sized Moe up to be a reasonable and perhaps, responsible man. He probably had neglected the house because he lived alone, so it wasn't important to him. They did learn there were five brothers in his family. Two of the brothers had families of their own, now he made the third brother with a family. Their parents were both dead and the brothers lived on the five acres of land they had left behind.

Later that night, Jesse said to Rose, "Maybe we ought to invite them to come live on our place. Five acres of land cannot support that many people."

"We best wait awhile. I don't think now's the time. Lord knows I like that idea, but He's telling me to wait. Sometime we got to pray about it and wait on the Lord."

The next morning, they finished patching up the house as best they could. Joe came over to give a hand. His help was welcome but there was something about him that told Jesse he was not a person you could trust. Rose went out to meet him but Justine and the baby stayed inside, with the door closed.

By dinnertime, Rose and Jesse were on the road headed for home. Jesse could hear her singing.

> Ezekiel saw the wheel way up in the middle of the air
> Ezekiel saw the wheel way up in the middleof the air

Chapter Twenty-Two

On a biting cold night when the icy stillness of winter was gripping the hill country, Rose and Jesse sat in front of their fireplace recounting the turn of events that had changed their lives, quite possibly, forever.

"Rose, you are now a grandmother but you're still the most beautiful woman I have ever seen. Solomon was right when he said, 'a good wife is worth more than precious jewels'."

"Mr. Ford, you still talk the prettiest words I ever heard. An' I'm thankful I know more words than I ever did before. Thank you for helping me learn to 'spress myself better."

"You are wise, my dear, beyond your years. You have made this place my idyll."

"I want to ax you somthin' Mr. Ford, have we been too lax in raising our chil'ren? You never raise your voice at any of them. And, why you never, ever whips them? Even when they bad, you don't whip them."

"Rose, I've told you this before and my thinking about it hasn't changed. When I learned about the beatings of the slaves and other mistreatment of Negroes at the hand of whites, I knew I would never raise my hand to strike my children. I couldn't stand it if I was looked upon as a white man beating his Negro children. And, as you well know, I have other methods of punishing them. I think my methods work well."

"I just wonder if we made some mistakes and didn't punish them enough?"

"You're the best mother anywhere. I don't want you to ever forget that and never believe anything else, you hear, Mama Rose?"

"I just want the children to have a good life and I don't never want them to have to work as hard as I had to work. And, I don't want them to get in trouble like Justine did."

"They're all doing well in school and the twins are now learning to read."

"I still worries about them."

"What you mean is, you are worried about Justine."

"That girl never did learn how to cook."

"I hardly think they're going to starve. It's time to go to bed, Rose."

He kissed her all over with soft kisses. He whispered sweet, delightful words in her ear. He reassured her that things were fine. Justine was fine. Cora, the baby, was fine. Their other children were fine. He was the one who could use a little attention. And no one could give him the attention he needed quite as well as she could.

Passion warmed up the cold bed and the sounds of lovers indulging could faintly be heard, mingling with the rhythmic calls and sound effects of the swirling wintry winds beyond their door.

A new way of life had been established for the children in the hill country. Many of them were spending from five to seven months of the year in their new school. Aaron Turner had pleased everyone in the area with his energy, dedication and skills. His biggest fan was Rose Turner. She dropped by the school to visit almost every day.

Rose never took time to learn to read and write. On her frequent visits to the school she always brought food with her for the children who showed up with nothing at all to eat. Her familiar, diminutive figure could be seen carrying her basket which at various times contained molasses candy, ginger-bread, tea cakes, fried meat pies and fried black-eyed pea patties.

Once the children had something to eat, they settled down and eagerly did their assignments. The children's demeanor always became more upbeat and pleasant when they saw their beloved Mama Rose.

In the springtime, Mama Rose helped the children plant vegetables, herbs and flowers. She spent time teaching them how to prepare and use the vegetables and herbs. She taught them that the flowers represented beauty through nature and they should constantly strive to have beauty in their lives.

"Beauty is always around us," she would say, "But the best beauty is within us."

Rose and Aaron often took the children for walks through the woods, pointing out useful, friendly plants and trees. They told the children about the animals which inhabited the woods, their habits and their value. Aaron taught them about soil and about weather phenomenon and how weather affected plant and soil conditions.

Best of all, the children liked it when Rose told one of her stories. She told stories about animals, stories about the wind, sun, rain, moon and stars. She could hold them in the palm of her hand. Aaron was pleased with the storytelling sessions also. They gave him time to do some paper work or to write out plans for future lessons. Sometimes, he'd go out and sit under a tree and do some serious thought searching.

The students loved and respected Mama Rose and of course, she loved them back. Even her twins, Mildred and Mattie, were now calling her Mama Rose.

She was busy doing some thinking and planning of her own. It had been a long time since she'd had some time alone with Mamie. She dearly loved to sit and talk with her Ma and listen to the wisdom she dispensed.

On a warm spring day after the crops had been planted, it was agreed that Rose could take a few days for a visit down home with her parents. Rose was filled with joy and excitement as she guided her horse and buggy over the familiar terrain. Little had changed about the path over the years. A few more farmhouses had been built on land that had prior been just meadow or woods.

The sun-laced sky added to the splendor of the rural landscape and Rose took it all in as if she had never seen the place before. The sun was beginning to drench the newly planted fields with its warm, nurturing rays. At first glance, the fields seemed bare. But then, a closer look revealed the pale green of plants emerging from their seeds burrowed in the dark, rich earth.

Rose heard from a distance the call of the golden throated meadowlarks whose singing always sounded better and more delightful in the spring. She passed a clump of trees and heard the chattering of the mockingbirds. A smile lit up her face when she saw a passel of rabbits at play. Descending this hill was nostalgic for Rose. It was peaceful and celestial and she felt relaxed and comfortable. Rose decided to stop for a moment, just long enough to take it all in without the hurry she was usually in.

When she started up again, she soon came to a spot in the road where it dipped between hills on either side. She had been interested in those clay hills for years but never seemed to have the time to stop and explore them.

"Now is the time," she said as she brought the horse and buggy to a stop.

Rose looked curiously at the clay with its thin streaks of grayish white running through it. She took her hunting knife from the buggy and painstakingly filled one of the buckets with the clay. She smelled the stuff and she tasted it as she'd seen some people do. Not liking the taste, she quickly spat it out. The residue of the clay stuck to her tongue and she noticed how it clung to itself. She liked the feel and texture of the clay. She put a rag over her bucketful and continued her journey. She would play around with it later.

When she arrived at the spring beneath the trees, she stopped again. The spring was often used as a rest station as well as a place for watering the animals. Today, she took the time to notice how the stream, which flowed with regularity from the hill country, filled the spring and then continued on its journey. To where, she never knew. As her horse satiated its thirst, so did two deer, who knew Rose and the horse were there, but pretended not to and proceeded to nibble the tender leaves from a sapling which grew near the spring.

It was at the sight of the house off in the distance that she grew impatient and put the switch to Belle. She was filled with exuberance to be going home again. She would be spending some time with her Ma and Pa. Some precious, sweet time. Some private time. Some reflective time.

She wondered if some day any of her children would ever feel the warm and wonderful sensations she felt to be returning home after a long absence, to visit with their Mama and Papa. She sincerely hoped they would.

"What a beautiful spring day!" she thought. "Um going to make the most of these few days. These visits are few and far between."

She entered the lane and thought how wonderful the new addition looked.

As she climbed from the buggy, she was immediately greeted by Mamie with a kiss and a long embrace. The love and affection between the mother and daughter hung in the air like a lovely bouquet of spring flowers. Smiles lighted up their faces.

Rose was a little surprised and somewhat disturbed to see Zeke sitting at the table when she entered the house. This time of year, he usually would be out in the fields the entire day checking on every plant even before it fought its way to the surface of the earth.

"Is anything wrong, Pa?" She looked around, but saw nothing unusual.

"How you feelin'?"

"I 'spect I do all right, daught.' I jus' don't have energy like I useta. Ephriam outin' the field. He do a good job takin' care ev'rythin. Aaron is helped him to know all they is about farmin'. He doin' jus' fine."

Instead of soothing her, his answers left her with questions which she didn't ask.

What a glorious time Rose had with Mamie, Zeke and Ephriam! He was the only child still living at home with his parents. He knew that his Pa needed him to run the farm. He also knew that his father's health was declining, even though he never complained. He fully understood that productive days of working the farm were at an end for both his Ma and Pa. They had worked the farms of slaveholders from their earliest remembrances. Life had been real tough and difficult for them. Yet, they had managed their lives and their work well. But slavery, post slavery days and up until now, all the hard work had taken a heavy toll on their bodies. Therefore, Ephriam had made a decision not to leave them. He would remain at home, even if he married. His wife would have to agree to live on the Turner Place.

There were times during those few days when their conversations were lighthearted and bordered on the whimsical. At other times, they were serious, reverent and reflective.

Rose re-told what she remembered of her life with Papo. She still thought of the old man with fondness. She recounted his kindness, gentleness and his knowledge about the earth. One of the most cherished lessons she had learned from Papo was to respect living things and how to use them.

Mamie and Zeke recalled the day they found Rose asleep in the shed where the animals were kept.

"Wasn't you skeered?" asked Zeke.

"Papo told me, don't have no fear."

"You was sich a pretty lit'l thing."

"My name Rose, you said. That melted my heart right then n' there."

Rose refreshed their memory about her desire to sell at the station. "It was just an idea that popped into my head when I saw people buying snacks in town and then running to catch the train. I knew I could make something to sell to them."

"Your meeting up with and marryin' Mr. Ford was about the biggest thing that ever happened 'round here," said Mamie.

"I sho' did dis'prova that marriage," chimed in Zeke.

"I shonuff did, but now I think it was put together by God, Hisself," added Mamie.

On into each night those conversations went. Nights that were clear and sparkling.

Nights that were heavy with the scent from the blossoms of the fruit trees and the flowers that Mamie had so meticulously cultivated. Magic nights for the three of them to sit and talk and talk. Magic nights that only come on rare occasions. Each of them were aware of how valuable these moments were. This time was rich in nostalgia and early recollections. This time was resplendent with love and fondness and occured too infrequently in one's lifetime. They would make the most of it.

Rose would sit and finger her clay during these conversations. She confided in Mamie and Zeke that she had long had a curiosity and interest in the usefulness of the clay. She knew that everything on earth had some kind of use.

"One thing I know is, I don't want to eat it like some people do."

As she worked the pliable substance in her hands, Rose was utterly convinced that something useful could be made from this clay. By the end of the evening, she had worked it into the shape of a crock. Ephriam wrapped the form in a damp croker sack and said that Aaron had told him clay should be kept moist or it would dry up and become brittle.

Rose would recapture the joy of those three nights and days at some future time. But now, she knew she must get back home to her own family. She also realized she was worried about her Pa.

As she turned right out the gate, she had a yearning to turn left and take the long ride to visit Justine and her granddaughter. It had been four months since she had seen them. Instead, she goaded the horse into a trot and was on her way back home.

On her ride home, she made only one stop. That was where the road sloped between the two hills. She stopped just long enough to dig more clay.

Although Rose had learned to accept Justine's motherhood and marriage, the thought of it still caused her spirits to sag and her heart to ache. For that reason, she quickly pushed thoughts of Justine out of her head and replaced them with pleasant thoughts of Pinkie. Steady, reliable, dependable Pinkie. She was doing extremely well in school and was the top student in her class. She did not have Justine's looks nor her personality, but she had a natural, quiet beauty that made her seem at peace with the world. Rose knew she would do well and make them proud.

Pinkie soared with excitement when she gleaned new knowledge or information from her books or when she read the poetry or literature books her daddy ordered for her. She was always elated when Jesse read to her or when she read to him. Jesse began to secretly entertain ideas and plans to send Pinkie up north to college when she was ready.

He and the children welcomed Rose's return from visiting her parents as if she had been gone for weeks. They had supper prepared and the table in the sun room was set with a fresh bouquet of flowers. During supper, the children asked many questions about their grandparents. The conversation was in full swing when William abruptly interrupted everyone and announced that when he graduated from the seventh grade at the end of the month, he did not wish to attend high school. He also stated that his plan after graduation was to become a farmer like his daddy.

This announcement came as a complete surprise to Rose and Jesse. Jesse remained composed, and said they should discuss William's plans at another time. Rose seemed to ignore the pronouncement. James, who was only a year behind William, sat quietly without commenting. Rose and Jesse had already talked about the possibility of the two boys going off to school together.

"Your Grandpapa is not very well," Rose interjected.

"What seems to be his problem?"

"I don't rightly know, but he too tired to go to the fields."

"Did he go to see a doctor?"

"Um sho' he didn't."

"Rose, I'll take some time off and make plans to take Ezekiel to the doctor. I owe him that much."

The report from the doctor was not encouraging nor was it a surprise. Ezekiel's heart was not very strong. It was not able to pump a sufficient supply of oxygen to the lungs. His lungs were filled with fluid. His eyesight was also beginning to fail.

"In this condition," the doctor said, "Ezekial won't be able to work in the fields.

The summer rains fell and christened the earth with their clear, sparkling waters. Afterwards, the blue sky hung over the fields like a painted coverlet and from it came the warm sun that filled the land. Together, they nourished the earth and the crops began to flourish. The workers were in the fields before the sun touched the ground. They took their long dinner breaks, returned to work and toiled until long after the sun disappeared behind the hills.

There were days when the thunder rolled, the lightening flashed, and the rains came. There were also days when the heat was stifling and miserable. The workers sweltered, but they toiled on. The crops proliferated; so did the mosquitoes, fleas, chiggers and worms. The workers' bodies ached with tiredness and pain. Again, life followed its usual rhythm. Only this time, Ezekiel Turner was not part of it. He had been put on complete rest.

Eventually, the harvest season came to an end. Autumn, the most beautiful season of all in the hill country, was at its fullness. The pace was slow again and life was a wee bit more gentle.

Soon winter would stand at the threshold.

` ` ` ` ` ` ` ` ` `

"I finally have some time," said Rose, "to find out what shaping and molding clay is all about."

The clay she had left in the barn had turned brick hard. She knew she had neglected to keep it moist as Aaron had advised her. She was glad she had forgotten about it because seeing it in this brick-like form gave her a variety of ideas to begin her task. As she thought of the possibilities, she was anxious to commence.

Jesse set up a work area for her near where he did his wood crafting. He supplied her with a table and some tools he thought she'd be able to use. Aaron gave her a little booklet that was filled with illustrations for making Indian artifacts and pottery, and it included some simple instructions.

Once again, Rose regretted never having learned to read. Jesse, full of patience, carefully read the instructions to her. He repeated them several times until she was sure she remembered the steps.

Her enthusiasm was impressive and her intuition was amazing. She went about this new endeavor with the same fervor and energy that she had gone about her gardening and selling. She molded and dried her creations. And she baked them in the oven.

` ` ` ` ` ` ` ` ` ` `

Another Christmas arrived. Not just any Christmas. It was the first Christmas of the twentieth century! Once again, family, workers and friends gathered at the Ford home. Everyone knew the celebration this year would be spectacular.

The chilling winter winds had already descended upon the hill country. On Christmas Eve, the moon rose high in the heavens and the stars were amazingly bright. Justine, Moe and Cora arrived in the afternoon after a long, cold ride. Mrs. Metoyer had arrived the preceding day. She was considered a member of the family.

Both of the Ford houses were bustling with activity. The younger women were chattering and gossiping as they went from room to room placing fresh pine branches, holly berries, paper angels and popcorn garlands. The young men were making sure there were great fires and enough wood to keep them going. They went to the forest to find a suitable Christmas tree. If they were lucky, they might even find some game waiting to be bagged.

The pungent smells of Christmas sweets and goodies filled both houses. There was an abundance of unpretentious love and happiness flowing through the houses, filling everyone with the joy of the season.

It was a splendid evening. Even majestic! The earth sparkled beneath the moonlight. The air and the sky were crisp and cool. The silence of the shining stars wove a peaceful and charming quality to the night. The fireplace lent warmth, glow and crackling sounds.

Rose took her place at the piano and the playing and singing of Christmas carols and Spirituals was in high gear, sending harmony and music streaming across the hill country on this night of nights. There was a closeness among those gathered on this Christmas Eve that cemented their kindred spirits.

Jesse stood as proud as a peacock strutting his plumage when he saw the love and happiness that flowed through the house. He was especially proud of how Frank and Lena had worked their way back into the good graces of the family. They now had two children, a son, Lucas and a daughter, Mary.

At the stroke of midnight, Jesse suggested that everyone retire for the evening in order to wake up refreshed and ready for the big day ahead.

When the Turner clan arrived the next morning without Mamie and Zeke, Rose knew that this Christmas would not be a good one for her. She would hold her head high and go through the motions in order not to dampen anyone's spirit, but deep down inside, she was concerned about her Pa.

"Pa's too weak and the weather's too cold to take a chance on the long ride," explained Samuel, who came with his wife, Lily, and their son, Sammy, Jr. "Ma said for ev'ryone to have a Merry Christmas. She 'cided to stay home wit' Pa."

"Tell me the truth, Samuel. How is Pa?" pleaded Rose.

"He's slowed down a lot. His breathing is labored and he don't see too well, but he never complains. Ma's worried 'bout him, a whole lot."

"I 'spect I better prepare to go back with ya'll."

After having morning tea and sweetcakes together, everyone began to set up for the big Christmas Dinner. The children kept busy playing games, reading books and putting together jig-saw puzzles and toys that Mr. Ford had brought back from his trip to Houston.

When the families gathered in the dining room for the blessing of the food, Jesse Ford read the Bible account of the birth of the Christ Child as found in Luke 2: 1-20.

> And it came to pass in those days that there went out a decree from Caesar Augustus, that all the world should be taxed.
> And all went to be taxed, every one into his own city.
> And Joseph also went up from Galilee, out of the city of Nazareth, into Judea, unto the city of David, which is called Bethlehem.

To be taxed with Mary his espoused wife, being great with child. And so it was, that, while they were there, the days were accomplished that she should be delivered. And she brought forth her first born son, wrapped him in swaddling clothes, and laid him in a manger; because there was no room for them in the inn. And there were in the same country shepherds abiding in the field, keeping watch over their flock by night. And lo, the angel of the Lord came upon them, and the glory of the Lord shone round about them: and they were sore afraid. And the angel said unto them, Fear not: for, behold, I bring you good tidings of great joy, which shall be to all people.

For unto you is born this day in the city of David a Savior, which is Christ the Lord.

And this shall be a sign unto you; Ye shall find the babe wrapped in swaddling clothes, lying in a manger.

And suddenly there was with the angel a multitude of the heavenly host praising God and saying,

Glory to God in the highest, and on earth peace, good will toward men.

And it came to pass, as the angels were gone away from them into heaven, the shepherds said to one another, Let us now go even unto Bethlehem, and see this thing which is come to pass, which the Lord hath made known unto us.

And they came with haste, and found Mary and Joseph and the babe lying in a manger.

And when they had seen it, they made known abroad the saying which was told them concerning this child.

And all they that heard it wondered at those things which were told them by the shepherds.

But Mary kept all these things, and pondered them in her heart.

And the shepherds returned, glorifying and praising God for all the things that they had heard and seen, as it was told unto them.

The reading was followed by Cecilia Metoyer leading everyone in singing the Spiritual, "Amen."

> See the baby, A-amen
> Lying in a manger, A-amen
> A-a-Amen, A-men, Amen
> Born on Christmas
> A-a-Amen, A-men, Amen
> They named Him Jesus
> A-Amen, A-Amen, Amen

Two hours later, the dinner ended and all the gifts were distributed to everyone present. They all appeared to be enjoying the day but the laughter and gaiety of the past Christmases were diminished because Mamie and Zeke were not present. As was his custom, Jesse was generous to his family, friends and tenants. This year, his benevolence was well matched by the presents given by Frank and Lena Ford. The two of them were very pleased with themselves when they passed around their gifts. And the receivers were delighted with their special presents. They gave out pocket watches to the men, boots to the boys; shawls and stockings to the women and girls and of course, some of Frank's homemade wines for the grown ups.

This Christmas celebration at the Fords' ended with the singing of "Go Tell It On The Mountain."

> Go tell it on the mountain
> Over the hills and ev'rywhere
> Go, tell it on the mountain
> That Jesus Christ is born

Chapter 22

Swing Low, Sweet chariot
Swing low, Sweet chariot
Coming for to carry me home
If you get there before I do
Tell all my friends I'm comin' too
Coming for to carry me home

The next time the whole family gathered together again was for the wake and funeral of Ezekiel Turner, who quietly passed away in his sleep the first week of May in the year, 1901. They gathered in the Turner kitchen-parlor for the wake on the night before the church service. The family greeted each other in love and in sorrow. In grief and in mourning. But in solidarity and strength for Mamie, the family's matriarch. They knew they had lost someone whose shoes no one could fill. Someone whose strength, love and devotion to family was immeasurable. Someone whose work ethics were beyond comparison. They sat through the night consoling each other and recalling all the wonderful things about their departed husband, father, grandfather, great-grandfather and friend.

At the funeral the next day, Cecilia Metoyer and her daughter, Lena, sang "Swing Low Sweet Chariot." Both Jesse and Samuel read two of Ezekiel's favorite passages of scripture from the Bible. Aaron followed with a moving obit of his father's life:

"My father, Ezekiel Turner, lived a good life. In one month, he would have celebrated his sixty-sixth birthday. Yes sir, the Lord was real good to him. And how he loved the Lord!

He was born on the plantation of one, Mr. Isaac Turner in the year 1835. He didn't remember anything about his father but his mother told him his father was a good and proud man who was sold away from that plantation. His mother died before freedom came. That was one of his biggest regrets in life, that his mother was not alive for the jubilee.

My sisters and brothers! What a jubilee it must have been for all who were there! Our father surely celebrated it with his parents on his mind.

Today my father goes to the biggest of all jubilees! Heaven! He goes home owing no one anything. His debts are paid. He gave everyone he knew, respect and goodwill. He gave honest work for honest pay. And there was a long time when he gave honest work for no pay.

He set good examples for his children. He struggled and worked beyond expectation to provide us with a good home and with an education. He sacrificed himself for his family. He taught his sons how to be men! His daughters to be virtuous.

He leaves his dear wife, our mother. He leaves three sons and two daughters, eleven grandchildren and one great-grand child. His legacy is strong. His offspring have been brought up knowing the way of the Lord. Our father tilled the soil. His fields are flourishing. His family bears his fruit and will continue to do so. May he rest in peace until that great gettin' up day!"

Jesse Ford stood and said a few words about how Ezekiel was a family man and a man of the soil. Told about how well Zeke knew how to get a virgin farm planted and producing. He told about Ezekiel's patience, his quiet, loving and nurturing life style.

Rev. Pennywell preached a powerful eulogy that everyone agreed could have lasted half as long as it did. The weeping was loud. The sorrow was deep and the hurt was painful. The mourning was sad and lamenting. The grieving would last long beyond this day. The memories would live on.

The congregation sang another hymn and it was time to proceed to the grave to say a final farewell.

Steal away, steal away
Steal away home
I ain't got long
to stay here
My Lord, he calls me
He calls me by the thunder
The trumpet calls within my soul
I ain't got long to stay here

` ` ` ` ` ` ` ` ` ` `

In the summer of that same year, Justine gave birth to another little girl whom they named Precious. Jesse Ford had taken Mrs. Metoyer to serve as midwife for his daughter after Moe made it quite plain he wanted this baby to be born at his house. Rose had wanted to be with Justine for the baby's birth but the response she received from Moe told her it was best for her to remain home.

During the nearly three weeks that Mrs. Metoyer was in the home with Moses McCoy and his family, she noticed the silent treatment he maintained towards his family. At first, she assumed Moe was simply a quiet man who was brooding over the impending birth. But soon after Precious' birth, she came to believe his treatment of silence was some kind of isolation and punishment for Justine and little Cora. His demeanor with the new baby, by contrast, seemed warm and loving.

Mrs. Metoyer noted another strange behavior pattern. It was the frequent visits of his brother, Joe. His only purpose for visiting, seemingly, was just to laugh and play with little Cora. But his lecherous eyes would soon settle on Justine, who made no secret of the fact that she hated his uncouth guts. Moe remained silent. So did Mrs. Metoyer. When her time was up, Jesse picked her up and took her home.

As the months passed, Justine became more and more convinced that she should remove Cora from the house. Although Joe had never mentioned in her presence he was Cora's father, Justine resented his coming to the house. And increasingly, she also resented Moe's treatment of Cora.

When Precious was eight months old, Justine made the decision to take Cora to Mamie's for a while, or at least until she could convince Moe he must accept Cora as his child or she would no longer keep her in their household.

Justine decided to go to Mamie instead of Rose for several reasons. Mamie was located closer to her home than Rose. It took about three hours to reach Mamie's. It took almost twice as long to get to her Mama and Papa's. Also, on the day of the funeral, Mamie had asked if Cora could come and stay with her sometime.

"She'll keep me fully occupied. I need someone to do that," Mamie said.

"That time has come!" thought Justine, as she packed the wagon for the long trip.

She confided in her grandmother but she did not want her Mama and Papa to know that Moe was not Cora's father. She could not bear to have them suffer still another disappointment that she had caused.

She reaffirmed the fact that Moe was a diligent worker and provided them with most of what they needed. He was a good and honest man but he was overshadowed by his brother's good looks and charm. It seemed he was turning his dislike for his brother into dislike for the innocent child.

"Gramama, Moe is a good man. He needs some time. I think I can help him come to understand and cope with our unfortunate situation."

"You and Moe just take whatever time you need. Cora and me, we gonna be happy as two peas in a pod."

` ` ` ` ` ` ` ` ` ` `

Rose was now dividing her time between the Rosenwald-funded school next to the New Hope Baptist Church in the hill country and her new interest in working with clay. She had become fascinated with all the different shapes and objects she could mold. More and more, there was an irresistible pull for her to sit for hours molding and shaping the pliable substance beneath her fingers.

The soft, squishy clay and the interesting little objects she made seemed to satisfy Rose's need to keep busy. At the same time, she was mesmerized by her creations. She especially loved the cows and pigs she sculpted and thought the rabbits were so life like. She made bowls, crocks, pitchers and a variety of other containers.

On one of his trips to Houston, Jesse picked up some paint and glaze for Rose so she could take her art up to another level. She was fascinated and enthralled with the end results. This meant that she would be spending more time in the barn. She now had brown and white cows and black pot bellied pigs and hogs with white patches. Her bunnies were gray, brown, white and black and sometimes a mixture of those colors.

Aaron constructed a clay oven near the barn for Rose. This was one way he could repay her for all the time she worked at his school. She used the oven for baking her clay objects. She was now making big-bellied pots because Mamie had told her they were considered to be a symbol of good health and prosperity. She knew that everyone could benefit from anything with that meaning. Rose used a knife and an awl to make designs and swirls in her creations. Her favorite color was blue, so the majority of her bowls were blue on blue with white. She made some with roses on them.

Rose soon found out that her clay oven was also wonderful for making bread. She began to bake incredible breads for her family, for the tenants and for the children at school. And for one shining moment, Rose indulged herself with the fantasy that she could sell her bread as she had sold her vegetables and jams so long ago. It was a clever idea but she never let it leave her imagination.

By the time summer arrived for its annual visit, the shelves in the barn were filled with her beautiful creations. She kept them carefully under wrap. When asked when they could be seen, her answer was always, "pretty soon."

\` \` \` \` \` \` \` \` \` \` \`

This summer would be Pinkie's last one at home with her family for some time to come. After graduation from the high school, she would be leaving the hill country for some college in a city with the name, Philadelphia. Mr. Carter had arranged for her to have a sponsor in Philadelphia, who would assist her in continuing her education. Pinkie had graduated at the top of her class. She wanted to study science but it was strongly suggested that she should study to become a nurse because no one thought she would be able to gain entrance into the field of science.

Pinkie had become an attractive young lady. Attractive, but not beautiful and stunning, like Justine. She was tall, lithe, walnut brown with well cut-features. Her slenderness, her freckles and her red hair were her defining features. Visually, she gave the impression of high intellect and dignity. She was charming but in a soft and distinguished manner.

When it was time for Pinkie to depart, Jesse decided he would accompany her on the train as far as St. Louis. He wanted to give her the opportunity to see a big city and to acquire some idea of its life and movement. And he wanted to be the one to explain it to her. He also wanted to purchase her a wardrobe for the northern climate and he knew they needed some private talking and discovery time together.

Pinkie was awed by the big city. She was amazed by her father's knowledge and by his ability to answer her inquiring questions. Jesse understood her awkward innocence and he graciously enlightened her in every way he could. How he wished he had made this journey long before. This quality time with Pinkie reinforced how smart she was and that she possessed wisdom far beyond her years. Jesse realized how important it was for her to have this opportunity to seek higher learning. He wished that Rose could have shared this journey with them.

After he put his daughter on the train to continue on to Philadelphia, Jesse Ford decided to do his annual shopping for Christmas presents right there in St. Louis. He figured the big city would be a place to find some exciting new things to take home. He spent the better part of the day buying objects for his family and for the tenants. When he finished shopping, he needed, and indeed bought, a fine trunk to ship his items back home.

It was only when he settled down on the train for his return to the hill country, that he suffered the gut wrenching experience of having lost the presence of both his first and second born, his lovely daughters, Justine and Pinkie. It would be a long, long ride home.

William and James met their father at the station upon his return. Both were teen-agers and both were tall and rangy like their father. William was fair, almost as fair as his father, with the same blue eyes and sandy hair. James was the color of red oak with amber eyes and brown hair. Although Jesse would have been thrilled to send both sons to college, they had made decisions to become farmers like their father. He vowed to work hard to make sure they'd become the best farmers possible.

But Rose, in her feisty way, did not hesitate to show her displeasure in the boys' choices. In the end, she joined Mr. Ford in accepting their decision.

"Farming is hard, demanding work. The hours are long and the work can be back breaking," she had admonished. "Don't even mention the heat!"

"But, Mama, we know all that and farming is still our choice, we love it!"

"Just make sho' you love it when the excitement is gone and the weather is wicked."

"Someone has to carry on papa's life work and his dreams, Mama."

"Um touched by yo' mm, mm . . .I don't know what you call it."

During the harvesting and ingathering that fall, Jess had the two boys accompany him in all of the facets of overseeing and running each aspect of farm life. Together, they read the almanacs and reports sent out by the Cotton Exchange from Savannah.

"This newsletter is official," said Jesse. "The prices affixed by the Exchange are what we always go by. Never let anyone buy your cotton for less."

"Always read the farming literature and almanacs yourselves. That way, you will know what is new and developing and what is already common practice."

Both boys listened attentively to what their father said. They were eager to prove to him they could become successful farmers.

William and James knew their father had acquired additional acres across the river and they were aware that more hired hands were needed to develop and farm those acres. Their father's conversation had let them know that finding workers would be difficult because a large number of Negroes were journeying to the north to join other Negroes in urban centers. Many of them were simply fed up with the less than poor existence they had on the farms. They had heard there were other kinds of jobs, too. A good number of them were eager to try something else since farming was practically the only thing they had ever been allowed to do.

During the next few months, Jesse would use the knowledge of farming that Aaron had acquired at the Normal College. Jesse asked him to hold meetings with his sons and with the farm hands already in his employ. Even with a short supply of workers, Jesse still wanted to maintain the level of production they currently yielded.

Aaron began his sessions with the workers by asking Rose to talk to them about how to effectively use herbs for healing and to aid in keeping diseases and sickness at bay. He knew that keeping the workers healthy and able-bodied would be one route to successful production. He knew that Rose had already helped the tenants with healthy eating habits but now would be a good time to reinforce the importance of preparation and cleanliness, along with the daily use of appropriate herbs. Keeping the workers well and productive was top priority.

Aaron recommended work hours be altered to a schedule that would insure that each worker would have peak performance for most of the day. They would begin work sooner, take a two to three hour break at midday, depending on the intensity of the heat, and finish up later. This practice would not only be efficient but would keep the tenants in a pleasant and happy frame of mind. Aaron had learned that these two conditions promoted proficiency in farming.

Before the end of harvest season, Rose was back at school on an almost daily basis. She insisted on James attending this last year, although he had wanted to stay home and go through the business side of farming with his father and William. Rose did not give in on this. Reluctantly, James showed up at school each day.

At home, Jesse and William were busy reading and charting information from all the Farmer's Digests, farm periodicals and anything else they could get their hands on. They also read the accounts about Negroes leaving farms in large numbers. In the same journal, there was an article which stated there were more than three thousand Negroes in colleges throughout the country. They thought about Pinkie being one of them and felt proud of her being away in a college up north.

They read an account about a Negro named Booker T. Washington, who was an educator who had founded a college called Tuskegee. They were most interested in one story which said he was encouraging Negroes to remain on farms. But the same article went on to state there were other Negro educators who were upset about what Booker T. was urging young Negroes to do. It sounded as if he was encouraging subservient roles for them. Mr. Washington said Negroes were moving too fast in their demands and they should be pleased to perform farming duties. William and James were left confused about what they read, concerning Mr. Washington.

Pinkie had been gone almost three months when they received their second letter from her. The first letter had merely stated she had arrived safely and without undue stress. She was housed with a nice family. She had enrolled at the University and after she settled in, she would write them a more detailed letter.

15 November, 1901

My Dear Mama and Papa:

I am grateful that you permitted me to have this opportunity to travel north to continue my education. Even though I miss you so much, being here is an experience that will impact the rest of my life. I know that sending me here was a sacrifice for you and I love you for it.

I pray that everyone is well and getting along nicely. I especially pray for Justine and her family and I ask God to bless them. They are okay, aren't they? It will be a long time before I see you all again but the vision of each of you is ever present in my mind.

Philadelphia is a magnificent, wonderful, old city. It is like nothing I've ever seen nor even dreamed of. I am thankful that Papa took me as far as St. Louis and showed me life in a city. I will forever be grateful for the books I was provided. Else, I surely would have suffered shock upon my arrival here.

Although this city is expansive and exciting, I doubt that I could be happy living permanently in a place so huge. I miss the quiet serenity of the farm and its pastoral setting; however, I could never have the educational opportunity in the south that I am now experiencing.

Most of the people here are hospitable and kind to me. Occasionally, I run into someone who treats me in a hostile manner. But I know why I am here; consequently, I'll let nothing deter me from my dream. I want to make you both proud of me. It is also important to me to make my brothers and sisters feel proud of me, too. I love each of them so much!

You should all be here to see the fall colors; they are so brilliant and beautiful! Mama would have been bowled over by how the colors change. They go from green to every hue in the red family of colors, yellow, gold, red, brown, even violet to dark brown and purple. The colors change every autumn and then all the leaves fall off.

It feels like winter already. The first snow has fallen and the ground looks as if it was covered by a giant white blanket. The snow sticks to everything. I made my first snowball and threw it up into the sky and then ran under it. It splattered all over my face. I licked it but it only tasted like cold water. I played in the snow like a little child. Then the wind began to blow hard making the snow go in a swirling pattern. You can't imagine how cold it gets here! Even the water freezes!

I am still overwhelmed by the opportunity to attend college here. The people in this city stress education and its limitless possibilities. There must be more books in the library than there are in the whole rest of the country. It is astounding what you can find there. In just one day, Papa, I read some of both Shakespeare and Homer. What unspeakable joy!

The college campus is larger than our whole town! I can think of no other place on earth I'd rather be right now. It's like I died and went to heaven, only the streets here are not paved with gold; they're made of cobblestones and bricks. And most of the buildings and houses are made of bricks, too! There are even streetlights at night. Imagine that!

Miss Anna, my benefactor, found a wonderful family for me to live with, Mr. and Mrs. Dancy, they have four grown children and a big house. Mr. Dancy is a handy man at the college. Mrs. Dancy teaches at a neighborhood school. Their youngest daughter, who still lives at home, is studying music at the college. Like you, Mama, she plays the piano. I have my own room on the third floor and I walk to campus each day. It's a long walk but I enjoy it except when it's raining or snowing, then Mrs. Dancy insists that I ride the streetcar.

Mrs. Dancy prepares most of the meals. On the weekends, Mavis, their daughter, and I do the cooking. She does most of it. I'm not that good. We have to use recipe books but we end up with wonderful dishes. You would like the results.

On Sundays, we all attend the A.M.E. Church which is similar to our own church except the congregation is so well educated and very well dressed. Also, they don't hold worship service as long as the church at home but they do have another service on Sunday evening. So far, I have not attended an evening service.

I truly appreciate the clothes Papa bought for me in St. Louis. I'm sorry Mama didn't get to see them, they're so pretty! They have met most of my needs. Miss Anna bought me some fur-lined boots, a heavier coat and some warm underwear. She said the weather is going to get even colder. Everything else I have is just right! Thanks, Papa. I love you!

I have tried to cover most everything that has happened for the time being. I will try to keep you informed of the important events as well as any changes that take place. Please give my love and best regards to Gramama Mamie, to Rev. Pennywell and to Mr. Carter. One day, I will write to them.

I promise to study hard and learn all that I can!

I remain your loving daughter,

Pinkie

Jesse read the letter to the family. Afterwards, the children fought over who would get the first opportunity to read it alone. Jesse said it should go down the age line, although he knew the twins would have no interest in having a turn. Rose retreated to her chair in the sunroom to give extra thought to what the letter had said. This was another occasion when Rose deeply regretted she had not learned to read. She would love to be able to read that letter again and again. Perhaps later, she would ask Mr. Ford to read it to her.

Rose knew if she asked, he would be quite willing to teach her how to read. But for some unknown reason, she could never quite bring herself to ask him. A few times she sat down with the Bible and tried to read it. Each time, she simply could not do it. Once or twice, the twins caught her trying to read their primers and she pretended she was reading and enjoying the pictures. Mattie took the primer, read a few lines aloud and they all laughed at the funny sounding words.

` ` ` ` ` ` ` ` ` ` `

Once more it was Christmas time. This meant that family and friends would be gathering at the Ford Farm. Some relatives began arriving a few days early. Everyone would be there except, of course, Ezekiel and Pinkie. They would be missed but the celebration would go forth with praise, good cheer, lots of eating and the blessings of the season.

On Christmas Day, with everyone gathered, the praise celebration began when Rose played, "Mary Had A Baby" and they all joined in singing. William Ford read selected passages from the Bible, and Samuel, Mamie's eldest son, offered prayer. Mamie valiantly restrained her tears as she affectionately hung on to little Cora. Rose requested they all think about and pray for Pinkie, who was far away and without the comfort of her family this Christmas Season. They ended the praise part singing, "He's Got the Whole World In His Hand."

After dinner, Jesse Ford did his usual presentation of gifts to everyone in the house. For the first time ever, it was not his presents that garnered all of the attention. The crowning delight of this Christmas Day was the presentation of a set of beautiful blue bowls that Rose gave to each family. Once again, Rose was able to delight the people who surrounded her with her amazing abilities. The blue on blue bowls had lacy white patterns running around them. A few bowls were festooned with pale roses.

"These the prettiest things I ever saw," said Molly.

"How'd you do this?" Asked Mrs. Metoyer.

"The story too long to tell right now," responded Rose with a big smile.

"Mama, I love these. Thank you!" Sang Justine.

The beautiful blue and white bowls with roses on them took each family by surprise.

All the women present admired Rose. She had a splendid manner of demonstrating there was always something you could do to surpass anything you had already done. They thought she was an amazing woman!

And as usual, the Ford Brothers always made the celebration a wonderful occasion with all the gifts they presented to everyone. This year was no exception. Frank and his family arrived late in the afternoon with their wagon laden with Christmas presents and goodies. Their appearance made the celebration complete. Everyone who was expected, was present and they all agreed, it was a very Merry Christmas!

Rose went to bed that night with a feeling of sheer satisfaction and delight. It was awesome to know that just by using your hands, you could do so many things to please people. Long after Mr. Ford was sleeping soundly, she lay awake late into the night reflecting on some of the ways in which she had used her hands to bring joy to herself and others.

She had been able to pick more cotton than anyone she knew except her Pa, Ezekiel. Her expertise at growing vegetables had been widely praised along with her cooking and canning skills. She knew how to tan animal hides and use them to design and make slippers and other leather items. Also, her prowess as a hunter was borne out by all the gáme she provided for their dinner table as well as the tables of their tenants.

When Jesse gave her the piano, she had learned how to play tunes in no time at all and she provided family and friends with hours of great entertainment. Now, she had pleased them again, all because she got curious about the clay that was naturally a part of the country's landscape. The clay, after all, was part of God's creation. It simply gave her pleasure to work with it and then to create whatever she could.

Her joy continued as she peacefully and calmly slept through Christmas night with Jesse beside her.

Chapter Twenty-Four

The very next morning though, her joy evaporated! Was stolen from her! Snatched without warning! Devastated, withered, like a rose left beneath a burning sun. At first, she thought they were teasing her. Rose learned that Cora had been living with Mamie since early spring. And it was no joke!

"Why she not with her own Mama? Her own Daddy? Her own sister?"

"There are a few problems, Mama," said Justine, tearfully.

"No problem that big!"

"Moe's been acting mean to Cora. He don't treat her right."

"What you tryin' to tell me?"

"I never wanted to tell you, Mama. But, God help us all! You got to know."

In deep pain and anguish, she told Rose the whole chilling story. She told how Joe had swooned and mesmerized her and even persuaded her to agree to marry him. She was convinced that she was in love with him and that he loved her. She got caught up in his charm. He made love to her. A few days later, he disappeared. He never came back for her at the school as he had sworn he would.

"Moe just did what he thought was honorable." she told Rose.

"In desperation, I went along with the marriage when he swore no one would ever know and he vowed he would be the baby's daddy."

"What happened?" asked Rose.

"When I got pregnant again, Joe kept coming to the house, kept making eyes at me. He constantly laughed and played with Cora. Moe was very jealous. After Precious was born, Moe spent all his spare time with her. He had nothing to do with Cora, except mostly shout at her. He talked to me only when he had to."

"Why didn' you bring her to me?"

"Gramama was closer and I thought it would only last for a little while."

"Is you takin' her home now?"

"Moe wants her to stay with Gramama a little longer. Since she left, Joe has never been to the house. And now, I'm going to have another baby. Moe is a good man Mama, he's just a little confused right now. And Gramama, she's so happy to have Cora with her; says she gives her new life."

"You needs to know, Justine, that your child can't stay 'way too long. Right now, she innocent. But the day gonna come when she wonder why her own Mama and Daddy don't want her."

"Mama, we made some bad mistakes and then we made it worse by trying to fix them the wrong way. I learned that when you tell a big lie, you got to be ready to live with the consequences. Right now, we trapped in those lies."

When Rose repeated the conversation she'd had with Justine, Jesse concluded that maybe they'd acted too hastily in getting Justine married. He was upset but not angry. Somehow, he could never get angry with Justine.

"I guess we were trying to avoid some family shame, and at the same time, protect Justine the best way we knew how. I admit that since she was our first born, I wanted her to be a good example for the other children."

"We all learnt a hard lesson. I wonder how long we gonna have to pay for it?"

The revelation about who Cora's daddy was would not be discussed by them nor would they wish to have it mentioned again. This Christmas celebration had been very spiritual and immensely meaningful but Justine's disclosure deeply troubled both Rose and Jesse. Even though they felt considerable pain, they realized the situation was completely out of their hands. They would turn their attention to things over which they at least, had some control.

Jesse remarked that all the children were growing up so fast. Most were meeting family expectations and making everyone proud of their achievements. Rose was especially pleased with Aaron, Annie and Susie who had all finished college. She was proud of Pinkie who was way up in Philadelphia at a 'fine college.' Even the children of the tenants had made some good progress. By now, most of them had had some schooling because of Rose's tenacity and prodding. She often praised and rewarded their successes. And she was thankful for Aaron's help. He had become an outstanding teacher at their little school in the hill country. Both parents and students respected and adored him.

Just when the people of the hill country were thinking that winter would never end, the March winds began to blow down the rambling hills and usher spring time through the sparsely greening fields. The yellow sun seemed a little closer as it beamed its warming rays everywhere. Jesse announced to William and James that it was time to fully launch into their chosen line of work. Farming!

The coming of spring and the Easter break was the beacon Rose needed. She decided she would go and visit her Ma and her grandchild, Cora. Rose thought of leaving the twins home because she could enjoy some precious time alone with Mamie. But she knew they would make trouble for Luther and Harry, so she dutifully packed enough items for the three of them to go to Gramama's house.

All four brothers were delighted to see them go.

"Stay the whole year!" shouted Luther.

"Yeah! Stay the whole year" repeated Harry.

"You come home, Mama, but leave the twins with Gramama," added Harry.

"I want all of my pretty girls to come home, and real soon at that," said Jesse.

It was a splendid spring morning when Rose and the twins headed for Mamie's. The girls were all excited and anxious about their visit with Gramama Mamie and little Cora. It would be the twins' first stay away from home.

Rose had packed a lunch with plans to take advantage of the mild, lovely weather and the opportunity to take a few side ventures into the meadows. She would relish this infrequent time to be alone with her youngest children. She wanted to talk to them about farming and about developing a love and appreciation for school and learning. While they were at her Ma's, she would ask her to tell the girls about the history of Negroes.

"Ma has a good understandin' of things like that," she thought.

As the horse and buggy trudged their way downward over the winding path, Rose thought of the many times she had traveled this route. Times of unpretentious joy. Times of catastrophic sadness. Times of wonder about what lay ahead and that one time of sheer terror. The one Mr. Ford told her to forget had ever happened. Mostly, she did, but then there was the rare occasion, like today, when she remembered. Yes, she had traveled this road when life and death were on her mind.

But today was a day all its own, almost like no other. She wanted to take it at a slow pace; she wanted to savor it, to inhabit it. Today, there was no sadness, no urgency, no fear, no regrets. She was simply going to her Ma's home with her two youngest children. She would make this a pleasurable time, one that she hoped would provide a pleasant memory for her twins.

The land was awash in harmony with the season. The wind was soft and the sun was mellow as it made lacy patterns through the fresh green leaves. The spring air was invigorating, giving off aroma from buds not yet ready to yield their propagations. Birds were bobbing and soaring through the sky, some with a whistle or a song in their throats, some whose wings made staccato sounds. The majestic trees, and even the land itself, reached out to enfold them. The surrounding fields, though not yet planted, seemed poised with promises of growth.

The words and the tune of the Negro Spiritual, "Goin' Home," came into Rose's mind, but she knew it meant going to your Heavenly home. Since they were only going to her family home, she decided to pass on singing it and just enjoy her thoughts, her children and the beauty of the day.

When they arrived at the place on the side of the road, where the bubbling spring fed into a brook, Rose said it was a good time to stop and have their little picnic and enjoy the field animals who came to drink and congregate.

"Mama, this is such a pretty place, why haven't we been here before?" asked Mattie.

"Yes, Mama, why?" repeated Mildred.

"We always in a hurry when we pass. Today, we's takin' our time. I'm glad you like this little spot, I think it's lovely, too.

"You see, God made all these grand things, all these beautiful plants and animals. He wants you to love and enjoy ev'rythin' He made. He wants us to respect and to care for all His livin' things. There's a reason He put all these things on earth.

"Um glad Uncle Aaron is yo' teacher, 'cause he real good teachin' you 'bout nature. One day, um gonna teach you 'bout how to use herbs and barks for healin' and things like that. Today, Uma share the animal's secrets with you. When we finish our picnic, we gonna go thru' the meadow and Uma point out different plants and tell you how to use 'em. Um gonna show you how animals hide they selves."

"We sure had a good picnic and an exciting stop in the meadow. Thank you, Mama," commented Mildred when it was time to leave..

"Yes, Mama. Thanks a lot. This was a good way to begin our Easter time-out."

"You welcome. Um glad you enjoyed it."

When they finally arrived at Mamie's, they found her in the springhouse getting milk, butter and eggs to make a cake.

"I'm mighty glad to see ya'll! Something done told me we was going to have company. That's why I decided to bake a cake. You don't know how happy you done made me."

"We glad to be here, Ma. The twins are real excited about coming to stay with Gramama and I 'spect they also happy to have Cora to fuss over."

"How's Jesse and the boys? Any news from Pinkie?"

"Mr. Ford and the boys are jus' fine. They busy now, gettin' the spring plantin' done. Yes'm, we got a long letter from Pinkie. She happy as a lark, say that Philadelphy is one big city! She loves it, but most of all, she loves goin' to school there. Says it's plenty cold in the winter.

"Ma, have you seen or heard from Justine since Christmas?"

"Yes. As a matter of fact, Ephriam dropped in to see her on his way to the parish seat 'bout a month ago. He said she doing fine. It seems that he has agreed to take Cora to see her come Good Friday. He said it's too hard for Justine to travel down here with her young'un, her being pregnant and all, so he promised he'd take Cora up there to spend the day."

"Ma, I got a thought! Why don't we all ride out and surprise her? I sho' would like to see her and Precious. We could get a' early mornin' start."

"Not tomorrow, Rose. Maybe the day after. I have a few things that need tending."

The girls went outside to play. Mamie put the cake in the oven while Rose fried a chicken and prepared some vegetables. Then the two of them sat down to catch up on any news that each might have for the other.

"I think we gonna lose Rev. Pennywell. He's ailing now and it's becoming harder and harder for him to make it out here. He already gave up his other two churches. His rheumatiz' is real bad now. He gettin' old, too."

"Who you 'spect we gonna get?"

"I got no idea, but the Presiding Elder gonna be with us 'til they find a replacement."

"Tell me how Susie and her husban' doin."

"Susie and John live over on the lake, now. She still trying to find a teaching job. The only offer she had was out in Caddo Parish. Said she wasn't gonna leave her husband and go that far away for no job, she'll wait til one comes up in this parish. In the meantime, she's helping John with the farming. They making ends meet but just barely."

"Ephriam's been courting one of the Price girls. Maybe soon they be gettin' married. That means they gonna live here 'cause he not gonna leave home."

"How do you feel 'bout that?"

"It's fine with me. I got plenty room and I won't be left alone in this big house."

"Gotta give him credit, he's done a good job with the farm."

During the night, heavy clouds blew in from the west. When Mamie looked to the sky, she doubted they should plan a trip to visit Justine.

"I think those clouds gonna drop some rain on us."

"They sho' messin' with my plans. But maybe it's the Lord's will for us not to go. Last night, Ma, I dreamt about Justine. I dreamt we went to see her an' she had just birthed twin girls an' Moses was so upset, he told her to take them back an' bring home some boys. Justine starts to cry loud an' louder, then I woke up. Now, I gonna worry 'bout her."

"Worry don't bring no good to a body. What you need to do is pray!"

` ` ` ` ` ` ` ` ` ` `

At Easter Service there was a glorious reunion of the first generation of Turner children. Some of the brothers and sisters were caught by complete surprise. Aaron and Annie had come home on Good Friday to be with their mother. But when all of her children arrived, Mamie knew their presence was an answer to her prayers.

And to Rose's surprise, a late arrival at church was Mr. Ford and the boys. She was also surprised to see them all dressed in jackets and trousers. Jesse even wore a tie. It was only in recent years he'd refused to wear a tie, even though Rose told him he should wear one when they went to church. He insisted ties were restricting and uncomfortable. The boys naturally followed their father's habit. They had become the most informally dressed young men at church. Of course, like their father, they didn't attend as regularly as did Rose and the girls. Sometimes they attended the Baptist Church in the hill country. Rose suspected it was just to see the girls.

Rose smiled broadly and proudly as they filed in the pew behind her and the twins. Jesse and the boys had been seated only a few minutes when other late arrivals entered. Rose turned to look and gasped audibly. Among them were Justine, Moses and Precious.

Mamie was overcome with joy, with the Holy Spirit and with thankfulness that her family was all in church together and it wasn't at someone's funeral. There were four generations of Turners worshiping and praising God together!

"I feel the presence of the Lord, the presence of my mama and her mama before her, and my papa and his papa and all the others who have gone on to Glory. I feel the presence of Ezekiel and his Ma and Pa. I feel the spirits risin' up in this place. Glory Halleluia!" Mamie stood and testified.

The congregation shouted, "Halleluia!" "Halleluia!" They all began to hum and moan wave and clap their hands while patting their feet on the floor.

After the preaching, singing, praying and collection were finished, Rose went and whispered something to the Presiding Elder. A few minutes later he called Justine and Moses to the altar. They talked quietly for a few moments and then he announced that the children of Moses and Justine McCoy would be christened.

All the Turners and Jesse Ford and his children went to the front and gathered around Moses, who held Precious, and Justine, who held Cora, while the Presiding Elder christened, blessed and prayed for the two little girls and their family.

The events of that Easter Sunday in nineteen hundred two would linger for years to come in the memories of the members of the Turner family. They all knew it was not a planned event. In fact, most of them had made no plans to be in church on that Easter Sunday. Even Jesse said it was a last minute decision. Mamie was convinced it was a day ordained by God. Some figured it was plain destiny. Still others thought it was a simple coincidence. But they all agreed it was a divine and blessed day!

"I never felt so close to God and my family as I did on this Easter," remarked Rose.

"I never had a better day myself," said Jesse, "except the day you became my wife. But I did miss my Pinkie. I wish she had been here to share it with us."

"Will you write her a letter and tell her about it, please?"

"It will be my pleasure!"

` ` ` ` ` ` ` ` ` ` `

April, 1902

Dear Mama and Papa,

Your letter found me in good health and good spirits. At last, spring has come to this part of the world. I welcome it! The winter here was wet and cold. I admit I did enjoy the new experience of piles and drifts of snow. But after a while, I felt we'd had enough and it was time for it to stop.

Now, I feel like a bird let out of a cage. (The Dancys do have a parrot in a cage). I can walk to school everyday. And everyday I take pleasure in walking across campus. The grassy quadrangle is the prettiest place on campus. The grass stays green under all that snow! All the trees and plants have taken on a lovely springtime glow. Pale greens abound everywhere but the bright sun will change that.

I thank you for including little bits of news about everyone. And thank you for sharing the events of Easter Sunday. What a glorious day that must have been! While reading Papa's letter, I felt as if I were right there in church with you all. I am sure it was God's providence to have all of you together at that service. Justine and Moe surely must have cherished that day. What a wonderful christening for the girls!

My classes and my grades continue to be of prime interest to me. I made honor roll last term, and I aim to do the same this term. Please pray that I do.

Miss Anna is trying to find me a job for the summer months. I made some pocket change while filling in at the laundry at the end of the term. I can work there again, but it's very hard work and in the summer, it will be extremely hot. If I have to do it, I will, but I pray that Miss Anna is successful in her quest of finding something better than the laundry work.

So William and James will be working the farm full time! How marvelous that they have decided what it is they want to do! I am still undecided on whether to become a nurse or a Science Teacher. I have at least another year to make up my mind. What do you think?

Last Saturday, I took a walk down along the river front. That was an amazing experience. I have never seen so much water churning and roaring and running on an endless journey to an unknown destination. It was an awe-inspiring sight and exciting to watch.

My aim is still to study and work hard. I will not stray from my goal of obtaining my education.

I love you, Mama and Papa, for your loving me and standing with me on this journey. God knows I intend to fulfill your hopes and wishes for me!

I remain your loving daughter,
Pinkie

` ` ` ` ` ` ` ` ` ` `

William and James surprised Jesse and Rose with their dedication to their new roles as farmers. They were up doing their preparations even before their parents touched the floor. Rose always busied herself cooking a huge farm breakfast for the family. Hot biscuits were always on the table along with butter, mush, canned fruit, scrambled eggs, syrup, jelly and hot tea. Occasionally, there was salt pork bacon, ham or sausage, meats that had been cured, smoked and salted in the fall and stored in the smoke house until ready for use.

The boys would discuss their plans for the day with Jesse, listen to his advice and within minutes, the three of them would be on their way to the fields. Each had a definite assignment.

Rose continued to pursue her interest in pottery. She had given each of the younger children responsibilities, something she had not been as diligent about with Justine and Pinkie. Now, no one was excused from contributing to maintaining the upkeep of life on the farm. Consequently, the four younger children milked the cows, fed and watered the animals, cleaned the yards, churned, gathered eggs, swept floors, cleaned the barn and whatever else Rose or Jesse saw fit to assign to them. There was never a lack of chores to be done.

Early in July, Rose took the twins and left them at Gramama Mamie's. The very next morning, she continued on her journey to Justine's. The baby was due and Rose was determined that she would be the one who would assist in this birth. She didn't receive an invitation nor did she ask if she could be present.

She simply made up her mind she wanted and needed to spend some time with her daughter. Justine cried when she saw her mother; she admitted that she had prayed for her to come and be with her.

"Well now, the Lord done heard you and He done answered your prayer. Lordamighty! Look how this chile has growed!" Rose said, picking up Precious. Both of you is a sight for sore eyes."

"Mama, I want you to sit and tell me about everybody. I don't get any news way up here. I feel so left out."

"Everybody is right fine, Justine. I'm just so glad to see you and Precious. What time Moe be comin' home? Is supper ready?"

"Supper's ready, Mama. You just sit and rest and tell me about each one. One at a time. Start with Gramama and Cora, then Pinkie."

The mother and daughter talked until sunset. That's when Moe came in from the field.

"I seed yo' horse n' buggy, so I knowed you was here."

Two weeks after Rose's arrival, Justine gave birth to a son.

"Just like you, Mama. Two girls, and then a boy."

"Yes, Justine, like me, but not quite."

"Mama Rose! Mama Rose! I got me a boy! I got me my boy!" shouted Moe.

They named their first son, Arthur.

Rose stayed with Justine and Moe and the children for two more weeks, then decided it was time for her to return to her family. She left feeling satisfied that Moe would provide Justine with the help and support she needed. She could see how happy Moe was to have a son. The grin on his face was still there.

As Rose rode back to Mamie's, she thought about how Justine and Moe were having children at an even faster pace than she and her beloved Mr. Ford.

"They don't have enough land to feed that many mouths," she said. I better discuss with Mr. Ford how we gonna help them."

"Ma," Rose said that night to Mamie. "I'm worried 'bout Justine. She having too many chil'ren too fast! How they gonna feed and clothe them? And Ma, She didn't even say when they gonna come get Cora."

"Rose, Cora is fine just where she at."

Two days later, Rose and the twins were back at Ford Farm. Jesse Ford was more than pleased to have his girls home. He was more than happy to have Rose back in his arms and back in his bed. Jesse always had a way of letting Rose know she was dearly loved. He wanted her to know this every minute of her life, and everyday, he took the time to tell her so.

Chapter Twenty-Five

For the next two years, life on the farm for the Fords and the Turners followed the usual farming cycle. Workers rose at first light and toiled until sunset. Changes were slow and not easily noticed. Church also was always an important part of the cycle.

Generally, the seasons followed a predictable progression. The springs were soft, filled with gentle breezes and rainbow colors. Sunshine covered the land, followed by light rains giving life to the earth. Newborn animals struggled to find their balance, brought smiles to the faces of the people. As usual, spring brought hope and promise.

The summers provided proof that the harvest was proceeding on schedule. It also brought hot, humid and sometimes suffocating and long days of backbreaking work. The insects of summer added to the misery. But there was joy in knowing there would be provisions to take them safely through another year. And though the work was burdensome, you could often hear the workers singing their Jubilee Songs which kept everyone at a lively and productive pace.

The falls were times of triumph when the workers celebrated the results of their achievement. They prayed, sang and danced together. They encouraged each other because the white south was still promoting a reign of terror to torment and fragment their existence. The weather was cooling down and it was pleasant to gather at each other's homes as well as at the school and the local church, for prayer meetings and socials. At those meetings, they gave and received messages of faith and justice.

Rose and Jesse never attended those meetings but they gave their approval. Aaron, William and James were always in attendance and this was encouraging to the tenants, to their family and friends. These meetings offered hope for a brighter future.

Winters were quiet, reflective times on the farm. It was a time when the farmers gave themselves permission to partake of a little self-indulgence. They relaxed and rested their bodies more as if regenerating themselves for repetition in the next season. They spent more time with family members and friends. When the weather was gloomy and cold, the men went hunting and the women sewed and quilted. Many used the time teaching their young people to learn skills. Skills that had come all the way from parts of Africa, as well as more recently acquired ones. There were such trades as woodcraft and construction, needlework, weaving, machinery repair, masonry and black smithing. They also took time to pass on more oral history of their traditions to their children. Winter was a wonderful time of mystical communication between the generations whose cultures and traditions came from another continent.

When Cora was five and a half years old, Justine gave birth to another son. Two months following the birth of the baby, whom they named Garrett after Moe's father, Justine and Moe decided it was time for Cora to return home.

One morning, Moe simply said, "It's time fo' us to brang our eldest child home."

"Yes! Yes! It is time," answered Justine, anxiously.

Mamie did not want to give up her great-grandchild, but Justine convinced her that it would be better for Cora if she was home with her family. So Cora began another journey in her young life.

Although Mamie was saddened by Cora's sudden departure, she knew it was the right decision. She could only hope and pray that Cora would easily adjust to her change in surroundings. Cora was such a smart and sweet child.

"After all, Ephriam is still here and now, he got hisself a wife. Maybe soon they have a baby, too," Mamie pondered.

"Everything' gonna be all right!" she said with a tear in her eye.

But she had a smile on her face.

When word reached Rose that Justine and Moe had taken Cora home, she offered a prayer of thanksgiving that they had finally done what was right. She decided this was a good time to approach Mr. Ford again about the possibility of Justine and Moe coming to live at Ford Farm.

"There's surely enough land fo' us all and we could sell it to them real cheap. There jus' ain't enough space out there where they livin' to support that many people."

"You have made your point, Rose. It's well taken and I promise to look into the matter, real soon," responded Jesse.

By the time of the yearly Christmas celebration at Ford Farm, Jesse had completed a proposal for the acquisition of two ten-acre parcels of land for Justine and Moe. Justine was excited over the proposal but Moe said that he wanted to look it over and give it some thought.

"What's there to think about?" asked Justine. "Papa's offer is the answer to a prayer. At the pace we're going, we'll never have money enough for a place of our own anywhere else."

"I ain't sayin' no, Justine. I jus' needs to think about it. I ain't never been 'way from my brothers befo.'"

When it came planting time in the spring, Moe said to Justine, "I been thinkin' 'bout Mr. Ford's offer. He said he gonna give you ten acres o' land, but I want to pay fo' my ten acres cause I wants to pay for what I gits. After we finishes the plantin,' we ride out and tell them we 'cept they offer. It sounds like a good one to me."

Justine was filled with joy and relief. Joy to have their own land. Relief that she never pressured him. Accepting her Papa's offer was Moe's decision.

"Thank you, my dear husband. I know you are a good man and I trusted you would make a wise decision. I also knew one day, we would get through those awful times that were caused by my big mistake with Joe."

Justine caught herself when she realized that was the first time she had used Joe's name since their marriage. She glanced at Moe's face. Although it seemed to tighten a little, she did not see any trace of the old jealousy. Now, she was sure her patience with Moe had paid off and their future together loomed brighter.

"I knows I don't tell you, Justine, that I loves you, but girl, I sho' do. I loves you so much that I don't know what I do wit'out you. If I ever lost you, I go plumb crazy. The chil'ren, too, they my pride and joy. I loves you an' them with my whole heart! And, Justine, thanks for yo' patience and fo' puttin' up wit'me."

"Moe, this is the most glorious and wonderful day of my life. I love you, too!"

Soon after that convesation, Moe and his brothers finished their spring planting and were pleased with what they had done. They could relax a little now and wait for the elements to assist the growth. Half of the land was cotton. The other half had black-eyed peas, corn, potatoes and goobers. Most of the food they would consume themselves. They would sell the cotton and afterwards, they would hire themselves out in order to supplement their meager livelihood.

Moe was happy with the decision he had made. He knew this would give him and his family a better life. They would be able to improve their lot in the world. And he was pleased knowing that he was still his own man.

On a hot Saturday afternoon in early fall after the crops had been gathered, Moe and his brother, Joe, stopped in the local juke joint to relax and have a drink or two. It didn't take long for Joe to get into a physical confrontation with a couple of the men in the joint. The arguing escalated and soon, Joe was being beaten and kicked by two men and was held down by yet another man. When Moe went to his brother's rescue, he was jumped from behind and stabbed to death.

Joe's face froze in horror as he heard the man say, " Jesus Christ! We killed the wrong man!"

` ` ` ` ` ` ` ` ` ` `

Rose, Jesse, William and James came to help bury Moe and to pack up Justine and the children and what worthwhile belongings they possessed and took them home. Mamie asked if Cora could come live with her again, but Justine refused.

Day in and day out, Justine moved about like a person completely oblivious of everyone and everything. With Rose's help, she managed to take care of the children's needs, but neglected to do anything for herself. Everyone in the Ford household did everything they could think of to cheer her up, but to no avail.

Night and day she grieved. Her invisible tears filled her shrinking body. Her broken heart beat slower. Her movements were distant and strange. Her sleepless eyes, eyes that had once been so lively and lovely, sunk in her head. Her invigorating laughter and her animated conversations were now an empty silence.

"I want my beautiful Justine back," Rose said to Jesse one night.

"You've got to understand, Rose, that no matter what happens, you can never have the young Justine back. Time robs us all of the way we were. We grow up. We grow older. We change, whether we want to or not. It's simply the way "Father Time" works. None of us can turn the clock back.

"Our Justine is older, she's a mother, she's a widow at a time when she should be enjoying the pleasures and security of her husband. She is lost without her mate.

"We must be patient with her. We must continue to surround her with our love and understanding and maybe soon, she'll return to us."

` ` ` ` ` ` ` ` ` ` `

A letter came from Pinkie. It was addressed to Justine.

August 31, *1903*

My Beloved Sister, Justine,

I wish I were there with you at this very moment! You know that I love you and I grieve with you. I share in your loss. I cry when you cry. I ache when you ache. Your pain is my pain. Your sorrow is my sorrow. And your happiness is my happiness. We are bonded together for life. I pray for your healing and I look forward to the time when I can be at your side.

Next year, I will be graduating from college and I'll be coming home. I feel as if I'll be graduating for both of us because your spirit has been here with me for these three years. I have always felt your presence beside me. I have touched you and I have held conversations with you. At times, I think you answered me.

I will be getting my degree in Health Science. I can become a nurse or I can teach school. I've not made a decision yet. I will do nurse's training in a hospital this fall. Perhaps, that will help me to decide. However, Mrs. Dancy is encouraging me to go into teaching so I can have summers to travel back and forth to my home and family.

This year, I have been working part time in the infirmary at the college doing various and sundry odd jobs. Mrs. Dancy and I have been discussing job opportunities after graduation. She has told me there are far more opportunities here than in the south. But I must come home. I have to be with my family again. I will look around and check out possible available jobs when I return home next summer. I would not choose to live in Philadelphia, although over these three years I have come to like it here more and more. There is so much Negro culture to participate in in this city.

Papa tells me that Cora will be attending school this year. I can't imagine! Have you thought about this? Cora is the only one of your children I've ever seen. I desire ever so much to see the others. When one is away from family, one misses so much. I imagine the twins must be as tall as you by now. Papa writes me that they're doing well in school. I would love for them to have the privilege I am now enjoying, to come here and attend a great college or university. Only a few Negroes ever get a chance like this. Many more are qualified but the opportunity is so limited. I consider myself most blessed and lucky!

I can hardly wait until next summer when I will be able to be with you again. We can laugh and talk and share our innermost thoughts and secrets like we used to. Papa said that you are sad; I want to make you laugh again. I want to run and play with your children, my nieces and nephews, for whom I feel a special love and connection.

My Darling Sister, to grieve for a while is healthy. When you feel like crying, cry! When you feel like being alone, be alone! But never let grieving take over your life. If you do, it will consume you and you can't let that happen because your children need you. Your family needs you. I need you!

Please take the time to write me and tell me about all the things that a father never writes about. In addition to the big picture, I want to hear all about the little day-to-day things that bring a smile to your lips. I want to hear about the progress of the children and what they're saying and doing.

I end this letter by pleading with you to take care of yourself and remember how much you are loved by your children and your family. You will do honor to Moe's memory by fulfilling this request.

Your loving and devoted Sister,

Pinkie

Over the next few months, Rose did everything she could think of to get Justine out of her deep depression. They went to the lake to fish while Harry and the twins watched Justine's children. Rose tried to teach Justine how to use the rifle and to hunt for small game. She taught her her secrets for making chow chow, peach cobbler and fried pies, both the fruit and the meat types. They even planted a flower and an herb garden in Moe's memory, complete with a beautifully carved and stained marker made by Jesse.

"We can order one made of stone for his grave if you'd like," Jesse offered.

Justine smiled faintly but did not answer.

"But an even better memorial, one that I'm sure would please Moe, is to get your life back together, take care of the children and to find some happiness," he added. "I know Moe would love for you to do that."

At times, Justine perked up and seemed to put forth both interest and enthusiasm. Then she would suddenly relapse back into depression, sleeping and eating so little that it worried Rose.

It was Cora who provided a bright spot for the family. She had inherited Justine's infectious personality and her incredible sense of humor. She also made efforts of trying to cheer up her mother. She sang songs and recited little poems for her. She gathered flowers and fixed fresh, sweet-smelling bouquets for her. She became a great source of help to her sister and her two little brothers. Rose noticed how adept she was at anticipating and taking care of their needs. At times, she reminded Rose so much of what Justine was like as a little girl. With that thought, Rose walked alone down the path to the meadow and sat weeping as memories of happier days went rummaging through her mind. Jesse found her there and sat with her. After a time of unspoken words, he gathered her in his arms and carried her home.

In the world outside, Rose knew that time and events were moving on. But at the Ford house, it seemed as if time was frozen. Each day repeated the day before. It was like looking at a still painting in a mirror until the night darkened and you saw nothing. The next day the same reflection was repeated when daylight crept in. Justine simply hadn't yet acknowledged that being born and dying were part of the same life cycle.

Rose knew the children needed their mother, needed her smile, needed her energy, needed her old self, so she cleverly planned to direct the mood from one of mourning and sadness to one of happiness and praise. Praise for being alive. Praise for having each other. Praise for the blessings coming forth from the rich earth. Each day, when the men left the house for their daily trip to the fields, Rose woke up the rest of the household with her loud playing and singing.

Every time I feel the Spirit
Moving in my heart, I will pray
Every time I feel the Spirit
Moving in my heart, I will pray
Upon that mountain, my God spoke
I love that mountain, fire and smoke

After a few loud pass-throughs on the piano, the children started emerging and entering the parlor where Rose was singing and playing.

"Today is the day we gonna put Cora and Precious on the pony and show them how to trot that pony round and round the yard!" announced Rose. "First one dressed and in the sun room gonna get the hottest, fattest biscuit! I also got some fried eggs n' hominy.

"Justine, please put milk out for the chil'ren and make us some hot tea."

When Rose took the tray of warm food to the sunroom, the table was crowded with hungry, eager children. Justine was holding Garrett and talking to him. Rose's favorite room was flooded with bright yellow, morning sun. The satisfied smile on her face matched the brightness of the room.

In three more weeks, the school year would begin at the little country school. Until then, Rose used her amazing talents to plan activities that included all the children except Luther and Harry who said they were too old to play children's games. Rose assigned them to weed the garden and take care of the animals.

By the opening of school, Rose had seen a definite change in Justine. She was now initiating some of the children's activities and she helped out in the kitchen. Soon Jesse began to notice a slight glow and a faint smile on her face. It was a defining moment for them. Perhaps, she's finally adjusting, they thought.

Luther and Harry were going away to the boarding high school. Rose was pleased they had made this decision. She was also happy that Mr. Ford would be taking them to enroll. She remembered when she had taken Justine to the high school with such high hopes, only to have her return expecting a child.

This time there was an air of excitement because the boys were eager to continue with their schooling. And it was a decision they arrived at without any pressure from their parents. Jesse took over all the preparations for getting the boys ready for their new adventure. Rose, therefore, happily went about getting the others ready for the Rosenwald Elementary School.

Even though the school was within walking distance from Ford Farm, taking them each morning was an irresistible chore that Rose relished, especially now, since her granddaughter was in the first grade. Cora loved going to school. She was feisty and radiant, the way Justine had been. Mattie and Mildred were in the seventh grade and feeling grown up. But Rose made sure they knew their place, by her definition.

The whole community was pleased that Aaron and Annie continued teaching there. He had recently married but since the local school board frowned on women teachers being married, Annie had not entertained the idea. Rose thought it a foolish and cruel rule, like the one which legally prevented her from living with her children's father. But of course, no one in recent years had challenged their living arrangement.

Rose was still captivated by what education could do for you. She had been well drilled by Mamie. Although she still could not read or write, she continuously told the children how thrilling it was to know how. She used some of the same words Mamie had used with her.

"An education will make you as good and as smart as white people," she often told them. "Books tells you things you never even dreamed about. Get yo'self a education so you won't have to pick cotton all yo' life."

Rose remained fervent in her desire for children not to grow up being ignorant and, especially, not knowing how to read or write. The students, however, were not aware that she herself couldn't. They thought their Mama Rose knew most everything.

After a few hours at school each day, Rose would return to the house. Justine assumed this was her routine but, in fact, she came just to make sure that Justine didn't have any down time. Now that she was finally learning to cope, Rose wanted to keep her spirits up and her mind and hands busy.

Harvesting season at Ford Farm was going well and cotton prices were holding steady. They sold all the corn, peas, potatoes and beans they had available. Even the small amount of sugar cane they had had sold well. William and James knew how to prepare their products for market. Rose and Jesse were well satisfied with what their sons were accomplishing as farmers. They had certainly proven they were worthy to carry on their father's dreams. Jesse and Rose had been good and patient teachers and the young men had been excellent and willing learners.

"They have succeeded beyond my expectations," Jesse confided in Rose.

"Um sho' nuff pleased with how serious they were 'bout farming. I thought they'd give up most any time. But they made up they mind and they stuck to it. Praise God!"

One day Jesse said, "Rose, I think it's time for us to give some thought to dividing up the land. It's too soon to know what Luther and Harry will want to do. But all the children are entitled to their share of the land even if they don't decide to farm."

"What 'bout the girls?" Rose asked.

"They all share equally. If they wish to give up or sell their share, that's up to them. I'm going to make a trip soon to the parish seat and have them legally divide it up."

"Why you be in such a hurry to do that? Some other time be just fine."

"Now may be as good a time as any. When I look around and see how fast we're losing some people, I think it should be sooner rather than later."

"If you say so."

"I do say so. The white people in this parish are crazy, no telling what they'll try to do with this land in case I depart this world before my time."

"Don't be thinking like that, Mr. Ford. We's both got a lots'a time left."

Before leaving on his next trip to Houston, Jesse went to Bossier Parish's Courthouse. He was totally unprepared for the unprofessional and downright stupid answers he was given. He asked for an Affidavit of Heirship. He was told that since he was not married, he had no legal heirs.

Jesse was so infuriated with that information, he could neither see nor think straight. He quickly rushed outside, grateful for the brisk fall breeze. He walked a few miles gathering his thoughts for his course of action. After walking and organizing his plans for more than an hour, he returned to the Courthouse and asked to speak with the Clerk and Ex Officio. He requested an Official State of Louisiana, Parish of Bossier, Property Conveyance Form. Using a crude map from the Assessor's Block Book, Jesse Ford filled out land conveyance forms and had them recorded right then and there, eight of them in his children's names, with the Clerk and Ex Officio Recorder.

Jesse Ford strode from the Courthouse, walking tall in his boots and cowboy hat, sighed a big sigh of relief and said out loud.

"There! I've taken care of my children and my grandchildren's future!"

Two days later, Jesse and his sons, William and James, were on the train headed for Houston, Texas.

"I need to show you what it is that I do in Houston. You need to be aware of how merchandise is sold and bought. I will teach you how to make good deals and how to command respect. Although you are considered Negroes, you will gain entrance in the trading halls if you present yourselves in a certain manner. You must dress well, look dignified and behave as if you belong wherever it is that you go.

"You've got money and you want to buy. They want your money. It's that simple."

After purchasing their farm supplies, it was time to go Christmas shopping. This was a world the boys had never seen. Watching their father maneuver and buy so many lovely things was a grand adventure. One they were sure to repeat in the future.

Jack and Thad had picked them up at the train station. There were two wagonloads of supplies along with a multitude of Christmas packages.

"How did you get them in the hotel over night?" Justine asked upon their return.

"Oh, I rented two rooms at the rear of the hotel, opened the back door and they walked in." Jesse responded with a satisfied grin.

This year, the annual Christmas celebration planning at Ford Farms was in high gear. Rose, in her wisdom, asked Justine and William to be in charge of the festivities. Cecilia Metoyer was requested to come a full week ahead of time to get food planning and preparation under way.

Justine and William made plans for two separate celebrations. On Christmas Eve, all of the tenants and their children would come for cookies, candies and warm cider. Their presents would be given out at that time. Christmas Day would be their time to be with their own family and friends as they chose.

"Even though we have two houses to use, our families have grown so large it is difficult to plan and enjoy Christmas the way we did when our families were smaller," William explained, and Justine agreed.

"I knew that time had come a few years ago, son," said Jesse. "But I guess I just hated to see the tradition die. I got used to it and wanted it to go on forever"

"But William is right," added Rose. "This way, each family can plan they own Christmas and stay home with they own family."

"Like Uncle Frank," said Justine. "He hasn't come in three years cause his farm got bigger and he has more tenants, so he celebrates with them, like we always did. I think it's a wonderful idea. I wonder who thought of celebrating it like that?"

"Zeke gave the idea to me. He told me stories about how the plantation owner always gave gifts to the slaves and let them celebrate on

Christmas Day. He told me they were given the best foods on Christmas, even gave them liquor.

"He said Christmas Day was the only day in the whole year the slaves were given to celebrate anything, and everyone tried to make it a festive occasion.

"Zeke was a wise man, helped me tremendously. I still miss him," said Jesse.

Chapter Twenty-Six

On New Year's Eve, a deep winter freeze lashed into the hill country. The wind and freezing rain was so hazardous, schools remained closed. Many roads and paths were inundated with mud and ice. Nearly everyone had to remain indoors. The fierce storms gripped the area for almost two weeks. Sleet and hailstorms came blowing in almost daily, adding to the dangerous conditions. Dark and overcast days lasted so long, most folks couldn't remember when it was they last saw the sun.

During those two dreary weeks, only Jesse and the boys went outside. And only then, to do what was absolutely necessary. Trips to the barn to look after and feed the animals. Trips to the outhouse. A few trips to the woodshed to replenish wood for the fires. Jesse was determined to keep the two houses as snug and cozy as possible.

Even when the worst of the winter storms had blown over, the families still were not out of harm's reach. Jesse was keeping a watchful eye on his family but he was the one who came down with a bad cold, fever and coughing.

Rose ordered Justine, the twins and Justine's children to remain solely in the other house during this time in order to try and prevent the whole household from coming down with any serious ailment.

A few days passed and Mr. Ford's fever showed no signs of cooling down. Rose had used all the herbs she thought would ease the fever. She used hyssop, yarrow, chamomile and elderberry teas. She used roots and barks to loosen the congestion.

"Maybe I use too many herbs. Maybe those don't mix up too good," said Rose. Today, maybe I just make a herb poultice and put it on his chest and back."

She laid the warm towel on his chest; and then she prayed. At first, a long, silent prayer which impulsively became a loud, pleading prayer, along with testimony touting Mr. Ford's virtues. At the close of her prayer, while still on her knees, she rested her head on the bed next to her beloved Mr. Ford and drifted into sleep.

Rose didn't know how long she was on her knees sleeping when she felt Mr. Ford's hand stroking her forehead. She jumped up when she realized that his fingers were not so warm to the touch.

"Mr. Ford," she whispered with delight, "yo' fever done broke! Praise the Lord!"

Rose softly wiped away the dampness and helped him into a warm, dry nightshirt. She recognized that he had been weakened by this ordeal and she could see that he had lost some weight.

"I thank You, Lord," she prayed again, "for bringing my Mr. Ford back. Um gonna start fattening him up just soon as he can eat some solid food again."

A few days later, Rose herself came down with croup. Jesse insisted that she remain in bed until he was sure she was better. This was the first time she had been bedded down since having babies. Rose felt like she was being spoiled. She loved it! But she could only take so much of it. Her bodily senses told her she should be in the kitchen, told her she should be taking care of her family and her house.

Eventually, the cold rainy weather moved slowly to the east. The winds helped to dry the dampness a little, but everyone was praying for sunshine. The sunless days and the fog-shrouded nights had dampened their spirits long enough.

In the natural weather pattern, the winds soon increased. The clouds moved and the sun fought its way closer to the earth, in its usual place above the hill country. Soon the sky was blue again. Life began to manifest itself once more in the two houses and wonderful sounds could be heard anew. The pace began to quicken, reassuring everyone that all was well.

The children were back in school, and of course, Rose was there with them. Justine was talking and laughing and playing with her children. Jesse Ford and his sons, William and James, were making plans to commence their planting season. Spring would be here before you knew it.

May 16, 1904

My Dear Family,

Graduation was absolutely marvelous! I wish you could have been here. But we all understand how near impossible that would have been. Nevertheless, I felt the presence of each of you beside me. The whole Dancy Family was there. Even Miss Anna, my benefactor, came. Bless her heart! She has been very kind to me over these four years. She always saw to it that I had whatever I needed.

I could never have lasted this long in Philadelphia, if it had not been for her and the Dancys. They were truly my family away from home. Mrs. Dancy took me shopping for my graduation gown. Miss Anna offered to pay for it but Mrs. Dancy wanted it to be my gift from her family. I didn't know such kindness existed in this world.

It is a beautiful off-white dress! It is made of lace and satin. It has a lace yoke with a high collar. The lace sleeves have a pouf and satin-covered buttons. It has layered lace ruffles over a satin bodice and little satin rosettes going down the front. I felt so proud and beautiful walking down the aisle when my name was called. The Dancys stood up and clapped. So did Miss Anna.

Miss Anna is buying me a ticket to return home. I think I would just die if I had to wait any longer to see my dear, dear family. This process of securing a higher education has been a captivating and a fascinating experience. I have stories to tell you that you won't believe! For now, I most look forward to seeing each of you.

My nursing experience in the hospital was exceedingly incredible and I received an award for high achievement from the School of Nursing. But for the present, I have chosen to become a teacher. I want to impart my knowledge and quest for learning to young Negro students.

Mrs. Dancy has suggested that I apply at a Negro College. But what I want to do first is visit my family. After that, I can think about my next move. Miss Anna has encouraged me to go south where the need is greatest, but Mrs. Dancy thinks my best opportunities are here in the north. My decision will come after I have had some time with you all.

During my nurse training, I met a Doctor Edward Galloway who has become interested in me. The Dancys gave their approval for him to call on me at their home. Over this past year, we saw each other a number of times. Our schedules were too busy for us to see each other more often. I have a very good opinion of him and so do the Dancys. He has asked me to remain in Philadelphia to explore our friendship and whether or not we might consider the possibility of marriage.

I told him I was certain that I would go home before I considered anything. Of course, he's afraid that if I go home, I'll never return.

"That may be true," I told him. "But going is something I have to do."

Dr. Galloway's family is from South Carolina, and his grandparents came to Philadelphia on the Underground Railroad. You should hear the stories about how the Underground Railroad helped slaves to escape. He shared with me that he is afraid to ever visit the southern states. He has said that it is difficult enough to be a Negro in the north, but that it is downright oppressive for Negroes in the south. Now that I've been here these four years, I understand what he is saying. If only I could do something to help to change things. That is now my biggest dream.

I am fond of Dr. Galloway, but I hold fast to my wish that my decision must come after I have visited back home for a while. The Dancys have offered me the opportunity to continue living in their home should I decide to return to Philadelphia.

I have not shared with anyone here that my father is a white man. I simply never think of him that way. His color is unimportant. I know him only as Papa, the most wonderful, loving and caring husband and father in the world. That's the picture of him I'll always treasure and remember.

Miss Anna said if I change my mind about teaching and wish to pursue a nursing career, she would make contacts with some influential men she knows through her father, men who could get me a job in a hospital. Most of them are business associates or friends of her father, whom I have learned, is a very wealthy businessman in Pennsylvania.

I always thought I could do something important because the books Papa bought me fired up my imagination, my desire and my senses. But this college experience even surpassed my wild dreams. It was such a great achievement for me to obtain both a B. S. in Science and my Nursing Certificate from the college. I share this glory and honor with my family. You made it all possible. I love you!

By Mr. Dancy's calculations, if I make all of my train connections, I will be arriving on the morning train, May 28. When I leave Philadelphia, I will be riding in cars open to Negro and white until I reach Washington, then Negroes have to ride in a separate car just for them. Miss Anna tells me that I can eat in the dining room but it will be behind a green curtain and I will be served by Negro waiters who will make me feel comfortable.

I hope all my plans go well between now and then and that someone will be at the train station on May 28, to meet me.

I remain, your loving daughter and sister,

Pinkie

That summer, every member of Jesse Ford's immediate family was home. The two houses were filled to capacity. Every day, the men in the family worked from early morning til early evening. Occasionally, the Ford women joined the men. Rose made it clear that she now wanted her girls to know as much as possible about farming.

"You never know which way yo' future gon' go," she said. "Always be prepared, just in case. Justine and Pinkie know little something, but Mattie and Mildred know practically nothing at all about farm work. I guess it my fault, though. I always kept my girls away from the fields. I know now, that was a mistake. Uma take care of that this summer, for sho.' "

The twins balked but in the end, they knew Rose would have it her way. She always did! Even though it was late, there was still time to learn something about working in the field.

"Mama, I don't think I'll ever have to work in the fields," related Pinkie.

"You knows 'bout today, but you don't know what tomorrow brings. You rest easy when you knows you can return to yo' roots if you hafta."

In spite of Rose's plans, that summer became everyone's favorite summer. Perhaps, everyone suspected it was a summer that could never be repeated no matter how they would like to see it come again. Even though the family bonds were multilayered and strong, there was the realization that each of them was getting older and would someday soon have families of their own and some, no doubt, would not be living on a farm.

Luther and Harry were engrossed by the stories Pinkie told them. It was hard to believe what she told them about how awesome opportunities were for Negroes in the north. She told them about Negroes working in factories and on railroads. They had jobs laying bricks, doing delicate iron work and other building trades. She informed them about all the possibilities a good education promises. She had met doctors, nurses, lawyers, writers, teachers, scientists and other professional men and women.

So far, Pinkie had had no luck in finding a job in that rural Louisiana Parish, and this was casting a chilling blow to family hopes that she would remain at home or at least somewhere near by. No one liked her being as far away as Philadelphia.

The family was spending as much time together as was possible. Those summer nights were canopied with blue skies which darkened at twilight and became filled with twinkling stars and glimmering, glittering fireflies. The beguiling moon regaled them. Smiled at them. Winked at them. Bedazzled them. And shone on them with its pearly, luminous light. The owls, the crickets and the frogs sang their night songs. The farm seemed a lovely, peaceful place to be.

Rose played and sang jubilee songs and Spirituals. Jesse and the children all joined in singing, clapping, stomping and having a wickedly hilarious time until Rose would suddenly stop playing and remind them what time they had to rise the next morning. Their children kissed them goodnight and hurried off to bed.

"We must paint these wonderful pictures of this spring and summer in our memories so when we're old and gray and sitting in the swing, we can summon them forth and relive this marvelous time with our grown and our almost grown, children. The days of their youth are already imprinted. Still, it seems just like yesterday."

"I declare, Mr. Ford, you still got a distinct way with words. It seems like Um already forgetting some of the words I learned, but Mr. Ford, you forgot about the grandkids!"

"No, Rose, I didn't forget, they're included. I was so enthralled seeing them all in the same room. They are such handsome and beautiful children. Look at them! They look like an artist just molded and painted them and placed them here for us to enjoy."

"You right 'bout that, Mr. Ford. The Master Artist did just that 'fore He give 'em to us."

> Give me yo' hand, give me yo' hand
> All I want is the love of God
> Give me yo' hand, give me yo' hand
> You must be loving at God's command

Chapter Twenty-Seven

And it came to pass. . . . .

Pinkie remained with her family for five months before giving up on her search for a job. She had more than one offer but they were all miles away from areas that were close to her family. Even if she could work and live near Gramma Mamie, she would have been pleased. But after having lived for four years in Philadelphia, with all its activities and possibilities, she was not ready to settle for the isolated one-room schools in the backwoods that she was offered.

The Parish Board thought they were doing her a favor by offering her a job, even with her impressive credentials. When she turned down their offer, she overheard a comment as she left the room.

"Good riddance, she's an uppity Nigra anyway. We don't need that around here."

"How you reckon she got them credentials?"

"Probably she's the bastard daughter of some southern gentleman. I hear some of the gentlemen even founded schools to send their half breeds to."

As the days and weeks and even months passed, Pinkie became more and more disappointed at what her future would be like living in Bossier Parish. More and more, her thoughts turned to Dr. Edward Galloway and she began to fantasize what life would be like if she returned to Philadelphia and eventually became his wife.

The thought of leaving her family and living so far away was painful to her. On the other hand, if she had accepted one of those job offers, she would only be able to travel home twice a year. Once for the summer break and once for the Christmas break, if the weather allowed.

"Probably," she began to think, "I could still come home from Philadelphia during my summer vacation."

Pinkie decided to immerse herself in farm life in order to have that experience to relate to any children she might have. She also wanted to experience the work ethic of her mother, should she ever have to live and work on a farm, although she knew that was not what she ever dreamed or thought of doing. But her Mama and Papa had taught their children to be ready for whatever come their way.

"If I do have children," Pinkie said, "I would want them to grow up in a city like Philadelphia and have all the advantages a cultured city like that has to offer."

"There is definitely a Negro presence and heritage in that city," she added.

Pinkie had never experienced the cotton chopping time; she was so positive she'd never have to entertain the thought of working on a farm. But after her fruitless job search, she slowly began to understand that almost anything was possible in the south. And she meant to always be prepared for any eventuality. Still, she would hope and pray that that reality would never come to pass. She knew if she became Dr. Galloway's wife, the odds were in her favor. For the present, though, she decided not to take anything for granted.

Rose accompanied Pinkie on this big adventure. She showed her how to hang the heavy burlap sack with the long strap over her head and shoulder. It was a child's sack, because Rose knew it would take some time before she could handle an adult sack or even pick enough cotton to fill one.

They both had on overalls and had covered themselves all over to avoid the insects that would be hovering overhead in the relentless heat. Rose had instructed the twins to bring them fresh well water at least every hour or so.

Early in the morning, the two of them headed to the cotton field. Before the first hour passed, Pinkie was feeling tired and sore. Her back was uncomfortable from the bending and her fingers had been pricked several times despite Rose's warning on how to get the cotton out of the boll. It was not as easy as it had looked to Pinkie, who could barely wait for the dinner break. Mercifully, Rose declared it was time to leave a full hour ahead of schedule.

That evening at the supper table, Pinkie's day in the cotton field was the topic of conversation. William and James had already decided Pinkie was a scholar and would not be able to take farm work. Jesse advised her that one day was probably all she needed to do. To everyone's surprise, Pinkie announced she would make the entire week.

Before the end of the week, Rose was making a poultice of rosinwood and nettle to place on Pinkie's back. She also gave her tea to drink and directed her to relax on a firm surface.

After five days of picking cotton under a grueling sun, Pinkie knew what she wanted to do.

She made her decision to return to Philadelphia at the end of summer.

However, there was at least one other matter that needed to be resolved. Pinkie did not really know how to cook. In fact, the kitchen was never one of her favorite places and eating was not one of her favorite things to do. Rose always talked about 'fattening' her up. Pinkie fully understood that Negro women were expected to be great cooks. If she was going to get married, she needed to know how to cook. That's how she became her mother's apprentice in the kitchen for the rest of her stay.

"Perhaps, I won't become a great cook, but I will positively learn my way around in a kitchen."

Rose certainly had the necessary experience and skills and she loved sharing her secrets with Pinkie, who said she would order by mail some cookbooks, to be sent to her address in Philadelphia.

Cooking was a challenge Pinkie knew she must pursue and succeed in. She always took seriously anything she had to do and cooking was something that had to be done. Somehow, she would learn. She vowed to duplicate some of her mother's favorite dishes and share them with ladies in Philadelphia. Also, it was now her intention to try them out on Dr. Galloway.

The thought of him sent little shivers up and down her spine. She knew then she was anxious to see him again.

Working in the kitchen with Pinkie brought back fond memories for Rose, of the long hours Mamie had spent with her over a hot stove. Rose soaked up all that Mamie taught her and now she was sharing the same knowledge with Pinkie.

"Memories do have a way of repeating theyself," offered Rose.

"I surely hope so, Mama. This is the best summer I've ever had."

"With all that hard work you done done? You kiddin' me?"

"It's been hard, Mama, but no power on earth could have stopped me from knowing that I could do farm work if I had to. I shall cherish every moment! Thank you for insisting and for being so patient with me."

It was a sad farewell that Pinkie bade her family when it was time to board the train to return to Philadelphia. Sad because a family member would be so far away. Sad because neither of them knew when they would see each other again.

"I'll return each summer," she promised. "That's one of the reasons I chose to teach, so I'd have the long summers off to spend with my family."

They all cried when the train pulled out of the station.

` ` ` ` ` ` ` ` ` ` `

On Christmas Eve of that same year, Pinkie Naomi Ford and Dr. Edward Galloway were married in the A.M.E. Church in Philadelphia. It was a simple but beautiful ceremony. The entire Dancy and Galloway families were present. So was Miss Anna, some of Pinkie's classmates and a number of workers from the hospital.

Pinkie was employed as the Health-Science Teacher and the School Nurse in the same school where Mrs. Dancy taught. She was more than pleased with her new life. She wrote a long letter to her family giving them all the details. She even sent some photographs.

` ` ` ` ` ` ` ` ` ` `

In the winter of 1904-05, a terrible influenza epidemic swept through the hill country. The flu ran its course through the Ford household. There was still no doctor in the local town. Rose put her knowledge of home remedies and herbs to use again, making teas and poultices for everyone, and everyone except Justine recovered within two to three weeks of being ill.

William and James began to make their daily rounds to check on repair and various other odd jobs assigned to the tenants. They knew the tenants had their share of illnesses, too. They checked the fields and fences for weather damages and deterioration. They took care of all the outside jobs and made sure that needed supplies and staples were on hand.

Jesse stayed home to help Rose with the children and the household chores since much of her time was spent waiting on and caring for Justine. Her recovery was not showing any progress. Her cough had become increasingly worse and she was again plunged into depression. She was extremely thin, her appetite was poor. Rose prepared hazel roots for her, still there were far too many days when she was in bed all day. Rose worried. And worried some more.

Because the weather was damp and icy cold, Jesse took the twins and Cora to school each day. In the afternoons, he picked them up and helped with their homework. Just as he was a wonderful father, Jesse Ford was now showing his enthusiastic capabilities as a doting grandfather. When he finished helping the girls with their homework, he played with the boys on the floor in front of the roaring fire. He put sweet potatoes in the hot ashes to bake and when they were done, he peeled and spread butter on them and served them to the children.

Rose, it seemed, was always busy with Justine. At first, they thought Justine had just relapsed into her old state of depression. It wasn't long before Jesse and Rose realized there was something far more serious going on.

It was the cough that worried Jesse. But Rose noticed that Justine's thoughts wandered. Several times, Rose heard her carry on conversations with Moe as if he were there in the room.

"Moe, I'm so happy Cora is back with us. It seems like she was gone forever."

"Moe, did you think about the fact that we had two girls, then two boys, just like Mama and Papa?"

"Moe, isn't it wonderful how sweet life is for us, now? I'm so glad you're happy!"

"I think it's time to tell Papa we ready to buy that land from him."

"Look at them playing, Moe. They are the prettiest children God ever made."

"When you think is a good time to have Arthur and Garrett christened? I was thinking about Easter, 'cause it was Easter when the girls were christened."

One morning, after a sleepless night of worry about Justine's condition, Rose was tired and sleepy and remained in bed longer than usual. When she finally went to the kitchen, she was startled and shocked to find Justine preparing breakfast. On the stove was a platter of hoecakes, bacon, syrup and hot water for tea. Justine's movements were slow and deliberate and she was humming a Spiritual.

Rock a my soul in the bosom of Abraham
Rock a my soul in the bosom of Abraham
Rock a my soul in the bosom of Abraham
O ' rock-a-my soul!

Rose stood and looked at her eldest child. Her heart quivered. Although Justine had dwindled down to such a tiny wisp of her old self, there was something hauntingly beautiful about her. Something hauntingly tranquil.

Rose's vanishing hopes began to rise and take shape again. Suddenly, she saw some sunlight ahead in this dark cloud. She had suffered such desperation and agony. No one could know how bleak her world had been, not knowing if her darling Justine would live or die.

and it came to pass. . . . .

"Come on in, Mama. Let's sit and talk before the children wake up."

"Justine, you look so lovely and so much better this morning. I praise God for your renewed strength and healing.

"Thank you, Jesus! Thank you, Lord!" she shouted.

"Mama, I know you have a lot of faith in God. You shared that faith with your children. Right now, we need to be surrounded and embraced by love and faith. We need to be enfolded by the arms of God and all of His angels.

"Last night, Mama, while I was sleeping, an angel visited me. It was such a beautiful, peaceful, celestial being. I could hear other angels singing, Mama, and one angel touched me and I immediately felt better. Their singing was the sweetest music I ever heard. I sat up and talked with the angel and it told me it was going to take me to heaven.

"Jes. . .

"No, Mama. Let me talk.

"We all have a destiny, Mama. Moe had a destiny. Some destinies come early in one's life, some come late. Mama, I think my destiny is like Moe's. The Holy Ghost sent the angel to reveal to me that my destiny is near. Everybody in this family got the flu, but I'm the only one who didn't get well. I want you to know that I truly tried to escape from an early destiny. I called on the Lord. I prayed and I prayed. But I guess all the time, Moe and I belonged together. I tried to help heal myself. How I longed to get well. My body just gave out on me. And it can't go on much longer 'cause there's not enough strength left."

"Justine! What on earth you tellin' me, child? What angel you talkin' 'bout? You feelin' okay? "

"Mama, I know how much you and Papa love me, but loving someone can't always keep them living. I loved Grampa and Moe with all my heart, but they died anyway."

Rose sat and looked at her beloved daughter with hollow eyes. She put her hand to Justine's body and her forehead, thinking she must be out of her head. But at that moment, Justine looked exquisitely beautiful and not at all ravished by the illness which, Rose thought, surely must have taken away her senses.

The two of them sat there for some time looking at each other. Then they touched each other with obscure, tiny gestures. They embraced. They cried. They sat silently. Memories danced before their eyes and they somehow knew these specious moments held an eternity.

It was cold and still outside. The early morning was gray. Soon the sun began to fill the land with a soft, yellow glow, achieving an unexpected moment of calm and quiescence. It was warm and shadowy inside. Love and affection bound the mother and daughter together and then Justine spoke again, breaking the silence.

"Mama, the hardest thing in the world for me to do is leave my little children. They are just babies. Cora for sure, maybe Precious, will remember their parents. Arthur and Garrett will not. Please promise that you will tell them about their mother and father. Tell them that we both loved them very much and wanted to see them grow up but that it wasn't possible.

"After I'm gone, Mama, will you send Cora up north to live with Pinkie? She will have a good life with her. I want you and Papa to take care of the others. I know that William and James will help you raise them. And if my boys decide to become farmers like their father and their grandfather, see to it that they get my share of the land. Please send Precious to school for as long as she will go.

"Mama, I can go easy if I know you and Papa will bring my children up the way you brought us up. With plenty of love, kindness and discipline. With fear of the Lord. I can go easy if I know you understand that going is not my choice. It's my destiny.

"I don't choose to go and I don't go willingly, but I know my body won't last long. My heart never healed when I lost Moe and the rest of me is too weak to last for any length of time. When my heart started going, there simply was not enough left to fight the epidemic which took over my body. It just sucked the life right out of me.

"I'm so sorry, Mama. If I could go on, I would. I would, If I could. You did everything you possibly could. But predestination is bigger than all of us.

"Put your trust in God and always remember that I love you and daddy, my children and all my brothers and sisters.´ Please tell them so. Now, be strong!"

I want to die easy, when I die
I want to die easy, when I die
Shout salvation as I fly
Shout salvation as I fly

Justine was buried in the family cemetery at the top of the hill overlooking the farm. She was buried in an oak coffin that was lovingly crafted by her father. She was laid to rest next to her little brother, Jesse Jr.

The spring winds blow and the blossoms bud
Beautiful Justine lies sleeping on the hill
The sun shines brightly on the fields below
Beautiful Justine is silent, cold and still

The gentle rains fall softly to the earth
Ruby-throated birds sing their melody
Meadows ripple and the flowers bloom
But beautiful Justine cannot hear or see

Chapter Twenty-Eight

And it came to pass. . . . .

The years were coming and going faster than Rose and Jesse could believe. The seasons, too, were passing through so rapidly they often had to stop and think about the cycle they were in. The months, weeks and even the days flowed together.

Springs still came with their offers of hope and renewal. Often they were splendid, breathtaking, with gentle winds and soft rains to nourish the rich soil. Some spring seasons were dazzling and enchanting. The melodies of the birds of the air echoed throughout the countryside. Exquisite butterflies, hummingbirds and bees tended the flowering blossoms that abounded everywhere. Rivers, streams, brooks and springs flowed majestically inside banks and crevices that were sometimes hard-pressed to contain their fullness. Clear, sparkling waters. Muddy, red waters. Deep, dark waters. Only on rare occasions did the waters tumble over their boundaries and flow through the fields, impeding their growth and challenging the farmers.

The farmers worked in harmony. Up at the same time. Reporting to the fields at the same time, taking dinner breaks at the same time. Planting cotton. Planting corn. Planting peas. Planting sugar cane. Planting goobers. Planting. Planting. And ceasing their work at the close of day. Then watching and waiting and waiting and watching. Like a barren woman waiting for her womanhood. Waiting for conception. Waiting for the birth. Waiting for the growth.

Springs turned into summers. Sun filled the land. Hot, stifling sun. Baking the earth with its incessant heat. Oppressive, dry, then wet heat, covering the land. Thunder rolled and lightening flashed and the summer cycles continued. The farmers followed their established rhythm.

Soon the landscape glistened with a full harvest that would peak at summer's end. The summer sun hastened and swelled the growth. The cotton, the corn and the sugar cane soared towards the sky. The goobers and peas testily hovered close to the ground, their lush green convincing the farmers they had multiplied and prospered. The long, hot summer days slowly began to wane, their tenúre completed. Falls arrived at the appointed time for their yearly visits.

Philandering falls, flaunting the possessions that were produced by summer's toil and heat. The colors of setting suns erupted and settled over the land. There was blissful rapport in praise of resplendent harvests. Cotton was baled and ginned. Corn was milled. The cane was turned into crystal and syrup. The folk of the countryside readied themselves to give praise and to enjoy the simple pleasures of living. They enjoyed knowing that another year had come and gone. Most felt they could survive at least until the next spring.

The beauty and magnificence of the land belied an undercurrent of turbulence and misery in the lives of people scattered throughout the region. There were so many who were kept in economic depression and in social dislocation. There were also too many beatings, threats and acts of intimidation, and even hangings, for anyone to feel secure or comfortable in that tri-state corner.

` ` ` ` ` ` ` ` ` ` `

Mamie, now in the winter of her years, was keenly aware of the activities of the oppressors. In her late age, she desperately wanted to do something worthwhile for people outside her own family. She had a strong desire to do something about the widespread illiteracy in her surrounding area.

A shipment of books and other assorted learning materials had been sent to her by Pinkie and Mrs. Dancy plus a few other members at the A. M. E. Church they attended. Some of the old folks, who lived near Mamie, began dropping by her house to learn such simple basics as how to read and write their names and numbers. Once this was accomplished, she would move them on to simple reading and addition and subtraction.

Some of the old folks were bewildered by the symbols but most were determined to learn what they could. A few even learned to recognize and write the names of their children. But for some, the attempt to memorize and unlock the symbols proved too frustrating. Mamie commended them for trying and invited them to return at any time.

On Saturdays, Mamie became a fixture in the town. She had the idea to try and promote decency and goodwill among whatever persons who received her. She had always believed there was some good in everyone, even though meanness ran deep among most of the whites living in the area. As Mamie nosed about, she found a good number of them living in abject poverty. Her own livelihood was meager but her mission was to share whatever she had. Sometimes she would offer them such items as eggs, vegetables, milk and nuts.

Once she was chased away by one of the white men. His wife later trailed Mamie along her route and begged to be given some of her food. Mamie gave her milk, beans and eggs.

"My husban' full o' the devil. He hate ev'rybody. Even now blame colored fo'ks fer us bein' so po'."

"You come by the train station nex' Saturday. I'll have more food for you."

"Thank-ya, thank-ya, thank-ya!" the barefoot woman said as she walked back towards her home.

"Some of them worse off than us," said Mamie.

One mother told Mamie her children had a bad problem with worms and asked if she knew what to do. Mamie brought some red clay and alfalfa tea. Instructed them to eat some of the clay while drinking the tea.

"Rub some clay over they bodies. It will absorb and draw the poison from them."

Word went through the little town about Mamie and how she went about helping people. Soon, Mamie had a small following of townsfolk who walked with her as she made her Saturday rounds. She kept a supply of herbs that Rose had suggested always keeping handy for certain ailments. Rose also told her that the best place to gather herbs was near the marshes.

Even the storekeepers began to pay attention to Mamie's popularity in the town. She smiled politely at them and they began to smile back at her. They had their way of keeping her in her place, though. They called her, "Auntie."

"Auntie, what's good for constipation?" one asked.

"Try dandelion. Cook it or use it in salads. Good for rheumatiz, too."

"How best to treat diarrhea, Auntie?"

"Use tea made with boneset roots."

Mamie continued to make her journeys in the interest of "what the 'good book' tells me to do." She often reminded the Negroes to remember there were some good and decent white people who would come to their rescue when they needed and asked for help. They needed no reminder of the other kind. They would obliterate the Negroes, if they could.

"But life is too short," said Mamie, "to think that every white person in this town is a low down, rotten dirty rascal."

As her energy ebbed, Mamie began to turn her attention to her children and grandchildren. She began taking trips in her buggy to visit with them. Once she stayed six days with Aaron and his wife, Marie. They were the parents of two little girls. While she was in the area, she stopped a full week with her eldest daughter, Annie. Annie remained single because of the parish's view and practice of not hiring married women. Mamie thoroughly enjoyed her visits with Annie. She felt that Annie needed more of her time than the other children because she had no family and no hopes of having one.

"Annie," Mamie suggested, "if you want a husband, you can marry and keep it a secret."

"Mama, I have never met anyone I thought would make me a good husband, like Susie did. If someone came along that I loved, believe me, I'd do what Susie did, give up teaching. But Mama, I want you to know I'm very happy doing what I do. Next summer, I'm returning to college to try and earn a full degree and a full certificate."

Mamie returned home where her son Ephriam, his wife Nora, and their two children lived. A few weeks later, she went to visit Susie and her family. They lived on their farm, a good distance away. Since Susie hadn't gotten a teaching assignment, she helped work the farm, along with their daughter and two sons.

When she to Samuel and Lily's house, she had her shortest stay because they lived just across the farm and she saw them often. But she did not want to be accused of playing favorites, so she stayed two nights with them.

Rose had her turn in these visits also. In fact, Mamie felt like Rose's house was her house. Maybe it was because she had her very own room at the Ford House and everyone preened and fawned over her, including Jesse and her great-grandchildren. Mamie thought they were the most gorgeous children in the world, and smart, too! Her heart longed for Cora though, whom she thought was the mirror image of Justine.

Justine! Justine! The prettiest of them all. Gone too soon. Much too soon!

Rose and Mamie would talk late into the night. Talk of Ezekiel Turner. Talk of Justine. Talk of birthday celebrations. Talk of selling at the railroad station. Talk of the horse named Spirit. They talked of the handsome white man falling in love with the shy and pretty Negro girl and how she, Mamie had resented and resisted it.

"Rose, you chose what you knew was best. Your Mr. Ford has been the best thing that could have happened to you. There is no better father nor a better human being in all these parts! God smiled on you!"

"Well, I 'spect He smiled on Mr. Ford, too!" Rose said with a smile.

Mamie repeated her yearly cycle of visits with her family until her age and health slowed her down and the children insisted that she could not make those trips alone.

One night when she was about seventy-five years of age, she closed her eyes and smiled. Mamie was content in knowing that with the few precious gifts God had given her, she would leave a small legacy in her children and in her work of helping others. She demonstrated to more than a few people, the capacity to care. Her smiling face slept peacefully. The angels came and escorted her home.

and it came to pass. . . . .

William and James had pleased their mother and father with their farming skills and abilities. They were growing into fine young men and their parents were proud of them and knew they had made correct choices in wanting to become farmers.

They worked hard and each year their crop production increased, which was a good measure of success. Aaron ably assisted the young men by sharing with them as much knowledge and information about agriculture as was available to him. He was now spending his summer vacations in Texas, attending an Agricultural and Industrial College.

During the school year, Aaron was still teaching in the hill country and was now the father of three children.

Jesse Ford felt fortunate that Aaron was part of his family as Ezekial had been and he was grateful to him for his years of loyal assistance. To show his appreciation, Jesse whose farms had prospered with Aaron's guidance, paid his summer tuition at the college.

Chapter Twenty-Nine

And it came to pass. . . . .

Jesse no longer did field work of any kind. Though he still handled the money management of Ford Farms. He knew that he was able to secure better prices for their products simply because he was a white man.

It's the same cotton. It's the same corn. It's the same sugar cane . . .

"Sons," he said one day, "The day will soon come when you'll have to sell the crops yourselves. But for now, I want to leave you as much money as I can. So if the crackers want it this way, we'll have to do it their way.

"But, damn it! After I'm gone, always remember to get your price for what you grow! Get every penny you can!"

Year in and year out, Jesse and his sons, William and James, made careful ledgers of every transaction that was made. During the winter months, they discussed acquiring more land and what the value of the land was. They charted their plans and proposals. They made projections of what a good year would yield. They made projections of what it would be if there was a drought or, heaven forbid! A flood!

One fine, indescribably splendid, spring day, there was a visitor at the gate. The resplendent plum trees that lined the path to the gate were adorned with dainty and delicate blossoms. The sweet, divine scent from the blossoms stood in the air like a thick cloud.

The billowing meadows framed the entry to the farm. The tiny buds on the wildflowers were frothing with delicate blooms under an azure sky and a glowing sun. There was a blissful rapport between the land, the sun and the clouds. Beautiful butterflies darted everywhere, stopping here and there distributing pollen. Busy bees droned overhead, oblivious to everything, seeking their mellifluous nectar.

Jesse, still energetic in mind and body, bounded down the path in excellent spirits. What he caught sight of, stopped him cold. It was the sheriff, alone.

"Good mornin,' Mr. Ford."

"I don't know if it's good or not. What displeasure is this visit about?"

"Well now, Mr. Ford, the Tax Collector tells me you failed to pay taxes on the acres you purchased across the river last year. We posted a foreclosure note on it two months ago, and I come to tell you, I paid the delinquent taxes and now I own it."

"Uh huh. Now what else you need to tell me?"

"That come next week, I'll be sending my 'croppers to start workin' that parcel."

"If anyone so much as set foot on my land, he's as good as dead."

"Sorry, Mr. Ford. It ain't yo' land no more."

"Sheriff, you're standing on private land right now. If you don't possess a signed warrant from a judge, it's better you leave now."

"Are you threatnin' me?"

"Call it what you wish, but it's not an invitation."

The next day, Jesse, William and James, mounted their stallions and took off early in the morning for the parish seat.

Jesse had explained to his sons that a tax notice for the new land had never been received when notices for all the other parcels came.

"I smelled a big old rat and knew it would soon raise its ugly head. When I paid my taxes, I paid extra money to cover the notice that never arrived. I've got the receipt I asked for and we're calling on the Parish Tax Collector for some answers. I want you to take note of how I handle this."

Upon arriving at the Parish Hall and going directly to the Tax Collector's Office, Jesse became aware that the present Tax Collector was the ex officio sheriff. Jesse requested to speak with him. The clerk offered to give him assistance. Jesse declined his offer.

"The tax Collector is busy now, it'll be a long wait before he can see you."

"I'll just take a seat and wait."

It was thirty minutes before the man presented himself at the counter.

"Some bastard in this office is trying to steal my land, Mr. Tax Collector. Can you help me straighten this matter out, Sir?" Jesse bellowed, and then knowingly, softened his voice, accompanied by a folksy smile.

"You boys waitin' for me?" the Tax Collector asked, looking at William and James.

"The young men are with me."

The Tax Collector looked from one to the other, then he looked again at Jesse Ford. He scratched his bald head, but he hadn't a clue.

When he retrieved the property tax folder for Jesse Ford, he totaled up his property tax assessments. Jesse produced his written and recorded receipts showing that he indeed, had paid far over the amount necessary. He then requested the tax notice for the parcel in question and asked for another recorded receipt.

"I'm curious to know how it came that a delinquent notice was filed and the property was put up for foreclosure. Can you tell me who filed that petition? Can you also tell me why I never received a notice of foreclosure?"

The Tax Collector disappeared behind the closed doors for a few minutes. Jesse whispered something to William and James.

"It was retired Sheriff Bogard. I'm sure something must have been overlooked or misposted. I apologize for the error, Mr. Ford."

"No, no! I'm sure it wasn't intentional and I thank you sir, for your service and your fairness. I feel sure this will never, ever happen again! By the way, may I see the Assessor's Block for Township number twenty-two?"

Jesse took the coarsely made books and went over how the acres were divided among his children so that his two older sons were aware of locations and also knowledgeable of how they were recorded in the parish records. This gave him the opportunity to make sure the descriptions and boundaries were still the same as when he had drawn them up. And that the names of his children were still listed on each of their parcels.

Jesse Ford was happy with what he called his "Days of Sweet Reward," meaning he was pleased with his life. He was even more satisfied with his having chosen to marry Rose, even if the State of Louisiana never sanctioned the union. Still thought it was the best decision he ever made in his life. He had become a successful farmer and businessman. They had the most wonderful children and grandchildren anyone could ask for. They loved and respected him and he adored each of them. And he was proud of them! He knew he owed most of what he had to his darling Rose, who stood beside him in everything he had done. Each day, he continued to give God thanks for her being the love and light of his life.

Ford Farm was now completely operated by William and James. They convinced their father he had worked long enough and it was time for him to retire while he could still actively enjoy life.

The grandchildren were the only children left at home and they had grown to an age of independence. Jesse began to feel unneeded and restless. Rose tried to comfort and reassure him that his knowledge and wisdom were needed and appreciated more than ever. The truth is, Jesse missed his children. Luther and Harry were in Texas at Prairie View College and the twins were in their last year of high school in the city. William was married with a family of his own and had built a house across the river. James had built a small house on the north section of the land but promised that after he married, he would come and live in the second house.

Jesse decided he'd like to visit his sons in Texas. He had never visited Pinkie when she was attending college and had always regretted it. Since he was paying the bills, he figured it was high time he made a visit to a college campus. He felt the need to see for himself what was being learned at college.

Luther and Harry received the shock of their lives when, without warning, their father arrived on campus. But Jesse was even more shocked when he learned that Harry had dropped out of school.

"I have a job offer beginning next month, as a porter working on the railroad," he told Jesse. "It's a good job and I figured I should take advantage of the opportunity."

"Don't you think you should have told us about this, son?"

"I was going to stay until Luther's graduation next month, then come home with him and tell you my decision. Papa, I'm just too restless to stay in one place too long."

"Tell you what, son. While we're waiting for Luther's graduation, why don't we take a train trip up to Kansas? My feet are restless, too, and it would give me the opportunity to look up the old homestead and see those wide open plains one more time."

Two days later, they rode the train to Kansas. Upon arrival, Jesse rented horses and the two men set out to explore the countryside. They spent a full week riding across the plains, exploring the land, sleeping under the stars and cooking outdoors.

Finally, Jesse was able to locate the land that his father and mother had homesteaded before the Civil War and before Kansas had become a state. No one was living anywhere on the land. There were signs of the house that had once been there. He found graves where his father and mother were buried. Jesse went to a courthouse in town and asked permission to look up whatever information was available. The young Ford boys had run away and joined the Union Army soon after their parents had settled on the land to raise horses. Jesse recalled how isolated and harsh life had been on that fledgling ranch.

The County Clerk found an original land grant deed in the names of Jesse E. and Mildred Ford. When he verified Jesse's identification from his army papers, the clerk seemed happy to hand the deeds over.

"There's still a lotta land in Kansas that need families to settle," the clerk stated. "Welcome back home, Mr. Ford!"

Within a few days, Jesse conveyed the land to Harry. And when Harry had worked on the Kansas City run for two years, he built a house on the land, married and started a family. With his wife, they opened and operated a country store.

After graduation from Prairie View, Luther was offered a teaching position at the High School in Shreveport. It pleased Jesse and Rose to see their children putting down strong roots.

When Jesse was seventy-one years old, he passed away while sitting on the porch in the swing talking to his beloved Rose. He was laid to rest in the first position of the family grave at the top of the hill, where the beautiful Justine lay next to her baby brother, Jesse Jr.

and it came to pass. . . . .

The twin girls, Mattie and Mildred married men who chose to become farmers. They lived on adjacent farms, land they were given by their father. They both raised large families and remained almost inseparable most of their lives. They were proud of their farming heritage and their rural lifestyles. They had close ties to their family.

Both their husbands were mainly cotton farmers and vegetable growers and they provided each other with enough incentive and competition to be referred to as highly successful cotton growers and farmers. Justine's daughter, Precious, later lived with her Aunt Mattie and visited often with her Aunt Mildred and her family.

and it came to pass. . . . .

Frank and Lena Ford acquired about the same number of acres of land as Jesse had. They had only the two children, Mary and Lucas. Because their land was so rich and productive, It was necessary for them to use hired hands in addition to their tenant farmers. Luckily, the Ford Brothers had a reputation for being good bossmen. This fact helped Frank with securing top workers. Unlike Rose, Lena never went to the fields to work. She was almost never seen by their field hands and only occasionally by some who worked around the house and barn. As the years passed, she became even more reclusive.

Like his father, Lucas also became a farmer. Frank aided him in learning how to succeed in the work he had chosen to do. His land was in the dark, fertile river valley. He married a fair-skinned Negro girl and settled into his role of farmer and husband.

Mary married a farmer but quickly tired of farm life. She persuaded her husband to move to Shreveport, where life seemed more exciting and promising. They lived there for more than twelve years and never fared well financially or socially. Finally, they were forced to give up city life and return to the farm.

When Frank's health declined, Mary's husband, Ezra, took over the running of his farm, and life for them quickly improved because farming was the only thing Ezra really loved and knew how to do. He was never happy living in the city, but did so to please his demanding wife.

Frank and Lena had three natural grandchildren and one adopted grandchild. After Mary had one child, she said she'd never go through all that discomfort again. Her mother and father spent more time with her children than she did.

Ezra became a successful farmer but Mary always seemed unhappy with her role as a farmer's wife.

Both families, however, prospered and lived well.

Chapter Thirty

On a Good Friday, Rose went to the top of the hill to the family cemetery to clean the grave sites. She went in a handsome new buggy that her sons had bought for her. She had protested when they brought it home.

"Mama, you deserve this and then some," William had said.

"You're the only mother we'll ever have, nothing's too good for you," added James.

"Please accept it with our love and appreciation," said Luther. "I speak for Harry, too."

She smiled broadly to herself when she thought of the goodness in the hearts of her sons. Then she directed the horse and buggy up to the gate.

"We done real good, Mr. Ford," she spoke to the grave. " They fine boys! And Mr. Ford, you should see that puppy William brot' me from

Houston, jus' like you did one time. I name' her Sugar 'cause she so cuddly and sweet. She go most ev'rywhere with me."

When Rose walked along the fence, she looked out over the fields below. They were plowed but not yet planted. She looked across to the meadow where she gathered most of her herbs. The gentle spring wind was blowing under a lively sun and the colors shone magnificently.

"I declare," said Rose, "I think God done took his paint brush again and painted the meadow. The wind and sun are weaving patterns all over those colors."

Rose raked and swept the graveyard. There was a holy hush present on that hill. She stood in silence for a moment then she knelt and planted flowers that would bloom in the spring and summer, adding beauty to a place that held heartbreak and grief. But she would no longer allow herself to be caught up in that grief.

"There are too many fond memories and still some good times for me to live with. My head and my heart remembers. My soul remembers. My flesh remembers. My senses remember. Remember the touches. Remember the sights and sounds. Remember the smells and tastes. Remember the love and the loving," she reminiscenced.

"Tho' our years together have ended, I still recall the time when our romance and love blossomed. Recollect it as if it was yesterday. The flow of years have been good to me. I thank God, they was good for Mr. Ford, too. I truly believe he had his season of peace and that at his death, he was more than satisfied with his life.

"He said a long time ago, 'Rose, If I die tomorrow, I die a happy man. I have done most everything in life that I ever dreamed of. I have the most extraordinary wife in the world, she gave me the most remarkable children I could hope for. My life has been complete. I could not ask for anything more.'

Rose finished her cleaning chores at the graveyard and headed home. The prescient fields unfolded down the fertile slopes of land. She caught sight of a blue jay whose bright color matched the cloudless blue sky which hung like a spread covering the whole land. Rose hurried home to plant her vegetable garden as she had done for years, on Good Friday. She worked to the rhythm of the song.

I got shoes, you got shoes

All God's children got shoes
When I get to Heaven gonna put on my shoes
I'm gonna walk all over God's Heaven
Heaven, Heaven
Everybody talkin' bout Heaven ain't goin' there
Heaven, Heaven
Gonna walk all over God's Heaven

"Why you so happy, Mama Rose?" questioned Precious, Justine's daughter, who was now a teenager and looked remarkably like her mother. She was biscuit brown, medium tall, brown eyes and brown hair. She had a tiny waist which flowed into flared hips that knew exactly when to stop flaring. Precious had an infectious and charming personality like her mother. Her brothers, Arthur and Garrett, declared Grandpapa Jesse had spoiled her.

"Um happy because the spirit is in me. Um happy because God done blessed me with love and riches I never thought possible.

"I might have been born into slavery. I don't know. But I do know when I was jus' a little girl, I found freedom and I found a family who cared for me. They taught me 'bout God. They taught me 'bout family and respect. I learnt' how to be a businesswoman and make my own money. I worked hard but I loved it. Child, I worked from sun up til sun down. But I was free and somebody loved me and teached me things I never knew.

"Even befo' yo' great grandparents, there was Papo, the old man I lived with when I was a little bitty girl. He tol' me stories and teached me songs.

"I sings 'cause Um happy and it keeps Ol' Man Sorrow away from my house. Music keeps me connected. It brings me joy, it soothes my soul. When I think 'bout painful things, music makes it all better. When I think about happy things, music makes it even happier. Music is deep down within me."

The red flame of the setting sun began to cast long shadows on that Good Friday and the grandmother and her granddaughter went inside to put supper on the table. Soon the pungent smells summoned the grandsons from their chores in the barn.

"Next week, Precious and the boys will be returning to the city to finish up the school year," Rose mused. "My family around me is gettin' smaller and smaller. I miss not seein' them so regularly. I'll have to think of somethin' to keep more busy or my loneliness will start grievin.'"

Rose decided she'd spent too little time with her pottery. After all, her gifts of bowls, crocks, vases and assorted items were treasured by family and friends. Over the years, she had discovered new veins of clay among the hills.

Once again Rose set up her potter's wheel in the barn and began to shape and mold a variety of pieces of different sizes and shapes. She discovered that working with the clay also connected her with the things and people she loved. She remembered how proud Mr. Ford was of her talented hands. She thought of that Christmas when she first gave gifts of her pottery to her family and to the wives of the farm workers who were also like family to her.

Before long, the brick ovens were fired up with blazing heat and filled with clay objects. After a few days, Rose was furiously applying glaze and pastel colors to the forms. Her favorite color was still blue with white lacy patterns running throughout.

She smiled to herself, held up one of her lovely creations and said, "I love these things. They give me pleasure and they make me feel and hear things. The spirit of Mr. Ford still moves in this barn. I can hear his footsteps and I can feel his love.

"He once promised me I would have his love even after he was gone!

"O precious Jesus, he was right!"

Rose worked in her garden every morning and then again in the late evening. During the middle of the day, she worked on her pottery. One day, she carefully placed some of her prized pieces in layers and layers of newspapers, wrapped old clothing around each piece and tied them with string. She put in straw and soft pine needles to pad the boxes she put them in.

Rose Turner got in her fancy buggy the boys had given her and took the long trip into town to the post office. She mailed one box to Philadelphia, one to Kansas and one to Shreveport. She prayed the packages would all arrive intact.

When she reached the house, she did not stop. She headed straight up the hill. The day began to give up the sun. The silent shadows fell on the earth, faintly tawny, making changing patterns as the fading light touched the leaves which were blown by an easy wind.

Rose placed a beautiful blue crock with white and pink flowers encircling it at the foot of Mr. Ford's grave so that it lay between his and Justine's resting place, next to Baby Jesse. The crock was filled with lovely blooms which had grown from seedlings. But it was the crock, not the flowers that Rose presented to her love.

"There," she whispered, "people and things I love.

` ` ` ` ` ` ` ` ` ` `

Arthur sat straight up in bed, screaming, "What's that loud noise? Sounded like a shot."

"Oh, that's just Mama Rose. She's out hunting again."

"Garrett, I think we should tell her she's too old to be hunting."

"Not me! You can tell her. But you know she ain't gonna like it."

"But, Garrett, she is old! For heaven sakes, think! She's not our Mama, she's our Grandmama."

"We all know that. But Mama Rose is Mama Rose. She still thinks she can do anything, and she might near can. Face it, she's still the best shot in the family."

"You forgot Uncle Frank."

"Don't count. He's so old, he practically never leaves his house anymore."

"You right. We don't even see him at Christmas."

"Beat ya' to the table!"

In late summer, on a pleasant Sunday afternoon, Rose's children and grandchildren who still lived nearby, came over for Sunday dinner. They all gathered on the screened-in porch, just to sit and talk about the morning worship service, followed by the weather, harvesting the crops, then any news about local farmers and family. There was nothing in the world that gave Rose more pleasure than being surrounded by her children and grandchildren.

On this beautiful sunny day, the lilacs were in full bloom, the bees hummed blithely along, performing their duties. The yellow-breasted meadowlarks sang their mellow tunes. The blossoming trees and the wildflowers spread bright colors, providing a spectacular background. And the family savored and enjoyed their time together.

Afterwards, the family gathered in the parlor, where Rose played the piano and everyone joined in singing. Soon dinner was put on the table and they all sat down to eat.

After dinner, the conversation turned to talk about Mama Rose.

"Next month, Mama, Justine's children will be gone off to school and you'll be home alone. Have you given any thought to what you will do with all your time?"

"Don't you worry none 'bout that. I gots plenty to keep me busy."

"Like what, Mama?"

"James be movin' right nex' door in a few weeks."

"Mama, James has got little children. You done raised enough children in your lifetime. You need to make some changes in your life."

"Changes, what changes? My family is my life."

"Mama, what we're saying is, do something for yourself. You're always doing something for your children and for everyone else. Just once, we want you to do something for Mama Rose."

"I 'spect you have something in mind?"

"Yes!" they chorused. "Go to Philadelphia to visit Pinkie and Cora. You know you dying to see them."

"Philadelphy? You children plumb outta yo' minds!"

"You been on the train before, Mama."

"Yeah, but that was a long time ago."

"Mama, you could do it again. You such a strong, courageous woman and it's time for a new challenge in your life."

"Yes, Mama, you have that pioneering spirit. You're aggressive and you're tough, too. Can you think of anything better and more daring right now, than traveling across country by train to see your daughter and grandchildren?"

"Yeah, Mama Rose, do it!"

"Uma think about it. Mind you, I said 'think about it!"

That night, Rose dreamed she hitched up Cappy, the young stallion, and his mother Lizzie, to her fancy buggy and started off on the long ride to Philadelphia. It began as a wonderful journey, but before long, they got lost. She was angry with the horses and blamed them, so the horses decided to fly up in the sky to look for their barn and return home. Rose was holding on tightly to Sugar, who was barking furiously and she couldn't quiet her. Heavy clouds began to cover the earth so they couldn't see anything down below. The buggy and the horses and Rose were soon falling down, down. Falling. Falling. Sugar fell from her arms. They both landed on a train which took them to the platform where Rose had sold her vegetables, fruits and goodies.

"What a strange and irritatin' dream that was," said Rose as she got out of bed the next morning.

and it came to pass. . . . .

On the first day of September, Rose's children put her on the train to Philadelphia. Her trunk was checked through. Still she was loaded down with packages. She carried with her some personal things for herself. She was hand-carrying two pieces of glazed pottery she had made and an assortment of food in her basket. Enough to last until her arrival, even though most of it would, no doubt, spoil before then.

Rose did not want to leave Sugar but James promised to take good care of her until she returned from her trip.

She sat cautiously and rigidly upright in the adequate seats of the colored section of the train. Her sharp eyes took in everything. Her ears warmed up to sounds emanating from the engine and the whistle. She closed her eyes for a brief moment and sent up a silent prayer petitioning God for a safe, harmless journey and the wisdom to understand the events in store for her.

There was the steady rolling and rumbling of the wheels, the chugging of the engine and the hissing of the steam. Rose soon discovered that the colored section of the train was located close to the engine. There were only a few passengers. Much of the space seemed to be filled with boxes and packages of one kind or another.

The train stopped at indistinguishable little whistle stops, towns, villages and cities. Sometimes, a few people boarded. Sometimes, no one came on. The train traversed the countryside at speeds that caused Rose's heart to thump. Caused her to doubt her judgment of good sense. Why in the world was she here? What would happen to her? The scenery outside the window, though, was breathtaking. Trees tall and stately, rivers winding. Colors were vivid and radiant. In the midst of

Rose's solemn thoughts, she finally became conscious that a Negro man was working in her car. The sight of him helped to soothe her heart and calm her frayed nerves.

A while later, the porter spoke to the few Negro passengers and informed them that if they needed something, just ask him. He would be pleased to assist them with whatever it was they needed. He could also answer questions, if they had any.

Rose knew she was in for a long ride, so she settled down. After going for some time in silence, she felt like it was time to say hello to the stranger who had boarded at the last stop and quietly sat across from her. After all, he had tipped his hat and smiled broadly when he sat down. She would somehow think of a way to engage him in conversation. She opened up her basket of food. The good smells were still fresh.

"Would you like some fried chicken and some tea-cakes . . .young man?"

"I got some chicken, Mam. But I sho' would like some tea-cakes."

"Hereyaare. How far you goin'?"

"Thank-ya-mam. Um goin' to Cincinnati, Mam. That's in Ohio, 'bout you, Mam?"

Hm-mm,' she thought. He so polite.

"Um goin' to Philadelphy to visit my daughter and granddaughters. My daughter married to a doctor. They have two little girls o' they own and they raisin' my oldest granddaughter. Her Mama and Papa dead."

"Um sorry, Mam. When's the last time you saw them?"

"It been nearly five years. I ain't seen the two little ones yet."

For two days and two nights the two of them talked as if they had known each other all of their lives. He heard all about Miz Rose's children, even the ones she had lost. She told him about the son living in Kansas. Harry worked on the railroad and with his family, ran a general store in a little country town that had been settled by Negroes after the end of the Civil War.

"I wish we could run into my Harry on this here train. Maybe for my nex' train trip, Um gonna visit Harry's family."

"You plan to do lots'a' train travel, Miz Rose?"

"My children at home says I should do different things now that all the chil'ren is growed up. That I should visit my chil'ren who live in far off cities. Philadelphy is a long way. I don't know how far it is."

"When I get off in Cincinnati, you still have to go another day and night."

"I be sorry when that comes. You been such good company. I 'spect I done talk you to death, though."

The next day, Rose asked him to tell her mo' 'bout his family.

"My family moved north to get away from the oppression of the south and the hopeless future of forever workin' on someone else's farm. They went in search of better opportunities, working in factories. Some did pretty well, others didn't fare much better than when they was farmin.' Just didn' know how to cope with the harsh winters and city livin.' We lost some members in both flu epidemics. It was lack of many things, most of all, proper diet, bad weather and no doctors to take care of them.

"My family from Louann, Arkansas. We just buried my grandmother. She was the last one left back there. My daddy and mama remained in Louann, to settle a few things. I got to get back to work at the iron factory."

The next morning, the train arrived at the young man's destination. It was also where Rose had to change for the last leg of her journey. Rose was somewhat bewildered about her directions for changing. The young man promised to stay with her until she was settled on the next train.

He helped her with all the packages she was carrying. When they finally found the right train, he helped her to find her seat. Rose thanked him. As he left the train, she waved and called after him.

"God be with you . . . Uh Oh! I forget your name."

"Paul, Mam. Paul Jackson."

"God be with you, Paul Jackson. And your family."

"God be wit' you, Mam."

Rose settled back in her seat, intent on resting for a while now that the friendly young man had left the train. Soon she heard the call of the conductor, the whistle of the train and the clackety-clack of the wheels. Steel and iron grinding and turning on steel. The slow movement of the train working up to a fast, steady, clicking crescendo.

As the train left the city behind, it churned and rambled more rapidly and the countryside unfurled again before Rose's eyes. She was fascinated by the view of wide-open spaces. For a long time, she didn't see a living creature out there. She saw lots of land, surrounded by mountains. There were questions and doubts roving around in her head that she could bring no closure to. She looked around at the other passengers. It was only then she realized all the other passengers in the train car were white.

She looked in vain for the Negro porter she had seen working on the train. Perhaps, there's another porter, she thought. There was no other Negro passenger in her car. Not one! Now, who could she talk to? Of whom could she ask a question? She thought about how nice and helpful Paul Jackson had been. And so polite, too.

Rose's eyes swept through the car once more. She noticed seated across from her, a young white woman with a sleeping child on the seat beside her. She saw lots of baggage surrounding her. Rose remembered seeing the young woman with the baby board the train in Pittsburgh. The woman had soft brown curls which framed her face. Bright, steel grey eyes that surveyed the car with one sweeping glance. She chose the seat across from the old Negro woman who was seated alone.

About an hour after they left the station, Rose was still sitting with her eyes fixated out the window. She heard the baby's cry and then she felt a gentle nudge.

"Mam. Could you please watch my baby for a minute?" the young woman asked, handing the baby to Rose without waiting for an answer.

"Yes'm."

The baby's cry grew louder and Rose began rocking it back and forth across her bosom, all the while singing a Spiritual.

> Train is a comin', oh yes.
> Train is a comin,' train is a comin,'
> Train is a comin,' oh yes

By the time the baby's mother returned to her seat, the baby was peacefully sleeping across Rose's bosom as she continued soulfully humming her song.

"He looks so content in your arms. Will you hold him just a little longer to make sure he's sleeping soundly? I'd appreciate it so much!"

Rose was already thinking that she had never held a white child before. But this happened so fast, she never had a chance to say anything. It didn't seem any different, though, than holding her own children or grandchildren but still she wondered how she had come to this. She kept humming.

"My name is Hilda, Hilda Wagner." The baby's mother said.

"My name Rose. Rose Turner."

"Please to meet you, Mrs. Turner. That's Stefan you're holding. I'll fix a place for him where he can finish his nap. I know how heavy he is. Just give me a minute to get his basket."

"He ain't all that heavy, Mam."

The two women talked while the baby slept. Rose was happy to once again have someone to talk with but it was an unimaginable experience to sit and talk lady to lady with a white woman.

"Strange," she thought. "It don't feel no different from talking to a Negro lady."

Mama Rose, as her grandchildren called her, was going to Philadelphia to visit her daughter and her granddaughters. The young white woman was going to Philadelphia to visit her parents and she was bringing their grandchild for them to see. So the two women established a common bond.

Hilda invited Rose to have dinner with her in the dining car. There was no other Negro eating in the dining car and although the diners were being served by Negro waiters, Rose made no secret of how uncomfortable she was. Hilda assured her it was just fine for her to be there. Hilda knew the others would assume Rose was her maid but she didn't mention this fact to her new friend. And if she wasn't a maid, which she surely was not, Hilda knew that it was still all right. Rose was eating her first freshly cooked food in several days. And she was enjoying Hilda's company. Even the antics of Stefan did not ruin her first experience in a dining car and her first experience eating with a room full of white folks.

"Why did I think eating with them would be so different?" she asked herself.

After all, she had eaten for years with Mr. Ford and countless times with his brother. All people eat, and from what I see, they mostly do all o' the same things, she mused.

The wizened, wrinkled Negro woman and the young white woman shared conversation and meals for the balance of the trip. Rose passed practical hints to her on how to care for and raise her child. She also gave her information on using herbs for certain sicknesses that were common among children.

Hilda told Rose some pertinent facts about the city of Philadelphia and she was amused at Rose's facial expressions when she told her how old the city was and how during slavery, it had an Underground Railroad station. She told her about Independence Hall, the Liberty Bell, and how the city was once the Capitol of the United States. Rose was startled by this history she never knew.

"My, my, my. I gots me a lotta things to see and a lotta things to learn!"

"Rose, I've been meaning to ask, do you know something that relieves morning sickness? I suspect I'm pregnant again."

"Try you some raspberry tea. You could also try some ginger tea with honey."

"Rose Turner, how would you like to come live in Johnstown, and take care of me and my babies? You're such a wonderful, wise and delightful person!"

"It's mighty kind of you to offer, but in my whole life, I never did want to work for nobody. I always cherished my freedom to move about as I saw fit. Thank you, Mam, but I thinks I'll just ride the trains every year visitin' my children and grandchildren.

"Yes, Mam. These here trains have introduced me to a whole new life! I'm gonna spend lots o' time visitin' my children and grandchildren. One day soon, maybe I even be a great-grandmama.

"I do believe my Mr. Ford would love that!

"Next year, I'm gonna take the train to Kansas. Did I tell you 'bout my children what live in Kansas?"

The train arrived at the station. Hilda gave Rose a long good-by embrace as she spotted her parents coming towards her.

"Have fun in Philadelphia, Rose, and enjoy your grandchildren. It was a pleasure to meet you!"

"I hope I see you on the train when I'm on my way to Kansas". . . . Rose was saying

Her words trailed off as she saw Pinkie, Cora and the granddaughters she'd never seen, rushing towards her with joyful shouts.

"Mama Rose! Mama Rose!"